ALSO BY GISH JEN

Thank You, Mr. Nixon

The Resisters

*The Girl at the Baggage Claim:
Explaining the East-West Culture Gap*

*Tiger Writing:
Art, Culture, and the Independent Self*

World and Town

The Love Wife

Who's Irish?

Mona in the Promised Land

Typical American

Bad Bad Girl

Bad Bad Girl

A Novel

GISH JEN

Alfred A. Knopf
NEW YORK   2025

A BORZOI BOOK
FIRST HARDCOVER EDITION
PUBLISHED BY ALFRED A. KNOPF 2025

Copyright © 2025 by Gish Jen

Penguin Random House values and supports copyright. Copyright fuels creativity, encourages diverse voices, promotes free speech, and creates a vibrant culture. Thank you for buying an authorized edition of this book and for complying with copyright laws by not reproducing, scanning, or distributing any part of it in any form without permission. You are supporting writers and allowing Penguin Random House to continue to publish books for every reader. Please note that no part of this book may be used or reproduced in any manner for the purpose of training artificial intelligence technologies or systems.

Published by Alfred A. Knopf, a division of
Penguin Random House LLC, 1745 Broadway, New York, NY 10019.

Knopf, Borzoi Books, and the colophon are registered trademarks of Penguin Random House LLC.

Library of Congress Cataloging-in-Publication Data
Names: Jen, Gish, author.
Title: Bad bad girl : a novel / Gish Jen.
Description: First edition. | New York : Alfred A. Knopf, 2025.
Identifiers: LCCN 2024047385 | ISBN 9780593803738 (hardcover) | ISBN 9780593803745 (ebook)
Subjects: LCSH: Chinese American families—Fiction. | Chinese Americans—Fiction. | Emigration and immigration—Fiction. | Chinese diaspora—Fiction. | Mothers and daughters—Fiction. | LCGFT: Autobiographical fiction. | Novels.
Classification: LCC PS3560.E474 B34 2024 | DDC 813/.54—dc23/eng/20241021
LC record available at https://lccn.loc.gov/2024047385

penguinrandomhouse.com | aaknopf.com

Printed in the United States of America
1st Printing

The authorized representative in the EU for product safety and compliance is Penguin Random House Ireland, Morrison Chambers, 32 Nassau Street, Dublin D02 YH68, Ireland, https://eu-contact.penguin.ie.

To the memory of my mother

Agnes Jen
née **Loo Shu-hsin**
1924–2020

How sad it is to be a woman!
Nothing on earth is held so cheap.
Boys stand leaning at the door
Like Gods fallen out of Heaven.
Their hearts brave the Four Oceans,
The wind and dust of a thousand miles.
No one is glad when a girl is born:
By *her* the family sets no store.

—FU XUAN, "Woman"
(C. THIRD CENTURY CE, TRANSLATED BY ARTHUR WALEY)

Contents

Author's Note xi

Part I

CHAPTER I
A Daughter 3

CHAPTER II
A Newcomer 47

CHAPTER III
A Wife and a Mother 103

Part II

CHAPTER IV
A Daughter 149

CHAPTER V
A Dance 215

CHAPTER VI
A Sutra and a Toast 277

A Note About the Romanization 325

Acknowledgments 327

Author's Note

"You never wrote about your mother." It could be a pat on the back—a way of saying that you wrote from your imagination and were not a navel-gazer. It could be a way of saying that you did not keep company with what Nathaniel Hawthorne called "the damned mob of scribbling women"—that you were not a writer of what V. S. Naipaul dubbed "feminine tosh" with a "narrow view of the world."

But "You never wrote about your mother" could also be an observation, followed by a pause and a tilt of the head, and then the question: Why is that? A question that could be asked of me now that I have written enough books that the word "never" might be used. Nine books, and you never wrote about your mother, someone might say—going on to prod, So is it perhaps time to think about it now, with your tenth? And: Do you really want to realize one day that you never did write about a relationship—perhaps *the* relationship—that stood at the center of your life?

The conventional wisdom is that mothers want their daughters to show interest in them—that they want their daughters to ask about their lives and listen to their stories. (Full disclosure: it's true of me.) But those mothers were not my mother. I asked my mother about her life many times, without success. I offered many times,

AUTHOR'S NOTE

too, to write down whatever she had to say and give it back to her to revise or discard. Don't you want your grandchildren and great-grandchildren to know that you came from China, and what that meant? I'd ask. They might not speak a word of Chinese. They might not eat Chinese food. They might not even really know where China is. Don't you want them to understand what a distance you crossed and appreciate all you did to establish the family here? She never took me up on my offer, though. Only once, when she was ninety-two, did she relent enough to let me interview her. And she did say a few things then. But she was not anxious to be known.

There were many reasons for this. One was that she'd lived through much trauma. Who wanted to revisit the Battle of Shanghai, or the Japanese occupation, or the privations of immigration? If she wanted to leave the past behind her, who could blame her? Another reason was that women of her background simply do not have the autobiographical impulse we in the West tend to assume is universal. Her story was not of paramount importance to her; and to her way of thinking, to be seen was to be judged. It was always better to say nothing.

And perhaps, I think today, there was a third reason—namely a concern that if I had anything to do with its telling, our relationship would enter the story. Ironically, had she told her story herself, she could have kept our relationship out of it. But since she didn't, here it is now, a book in which I figure, too, and whose writing she would have adamantly opposed. I can hear her berating me from the grave: "Bad bad girl!" As for the possibility that I would write a book that sought to understand her—that portrayed her honestly but compassionately, and that ultimately forgave her—she would never have conceived of such a thing. Still, I have sought to do just that, as I had to. I suppose I could not have faced the observation "You never wrote about your mother" knowing that I simply lacked the maturity and courage to do so. This was especially true after she died during Covid. I did not see how I could go on calling myself a writer had I not at least tried.

I began this book as a memoir, and it probably would have stayed a memoir had I had more access to my mother's life. But because she left so little record of herself—some letters, account books, logs, and day planners, but nothing more—I had to imagine a great deal; and as I am a novelist, many things happened as I did. Characters appeared; events shifted; an arc materialized; the narrative made demands. I have stayed as true as I could to the facts of my mother's life as I knew them, and my goal—to convey, as honestly as possible, our troubled relationship—remained the same throughout. Still, reader, do not be confused: this is reality transmuted. It tells a forged truth. Even from beyond the grave, my mother, as you will hear, objects to many of the liberties I take. At the same time, I like to think she would finally agree both that this book is a novel and that there might be some truth to it.

Part I

CHAPTER I

A Daughter

My mother had died, but still I heard her voice.

Your grandmother was a Suzhou beauty, she says. Do you know where is Suzhou?

Of course, I say. West of Shanghai.

For I do know: Suzhou is where the classic Chinese gardens are—the Humble Administrator's Garden. The Lingering Garden. The Garden of the Master of the Fishing Nets. West of Shanghai is the correct answer. But my mother does not say so. She is the same now as she was when she was alive—a master of the art of withholding.

Your grandmother was a Suzhou beauty, my mother says again. She spoke Suzhou dialect, Chinese people say it is like singing. And she was tall and thin. By the standards of 1920s Shanghai, of course.

Meaning thin but maybe not so tall, I think. As was my mother in her youth, too, although I mostly picture her in her late-life, big-bellied stage, when she had the bulbous shape of a snake that has swallowed a large animal. Her stomach was so perfectly spherical that had she not been in her nineties, you might have thought her pregnant, and indeed it was likely the result of her five children, the second of whom was me.

But, whatever.

Go on, I say.

All my life, after all, I have wanted to know how our relationship went wrong—how I became her nemesis, her bête noire, her lightning rod, a scapegoat.

You look like her, she says. Only not so tall, not so thin, not so beautiful.

Oh, I laugh. Now, this is the mother I remember, tactful as a sledgehammer. You are too kind.

When I see you, I see her, she says.

Oh, no. Your mother? I say. Because of all the possible misfortunes of birth, to remind your mother of a mother who had rejected her is surely one of the worst—as well as, it seems, a great unmentionable. For what does she immediately say but: Bad bad girl! You don't know how to talk!

Well, she wasn't exactly the mother of your heart, was she? I say. That was your nursemaid, the one you called "Năi-mā"—milk mother—right? The one who was sent away.

She neither agrees nor disagrees. But then she repeats, Nai-ma. And as dead as she is, she begins to cry.

My grandmother was twenty-two and my grandfather forty-eight when they married, and for all I know, he was a ringer for James Bond. But in the only picture I have of him, he is short and rotund. He is wearing a padded Chinese gown; his arms splay in a way that might put one in mind of a penguin. And then there are his porthole glasses, thick and black as Mr. Magoo's. Actually, he was a crack Chinese banker up to whose porte-cochere chauffeured cars would roll, their shiny doors opening to reveal the gigantic shoes of foreigners. At one point, he saved China's rural banks from collapse by convincing the Shanghai to back them—or so the family story goes, at least—holding the meeting at his house because his was the only driveway big enough to handle so many cars. My aunt remembers coming downstairs and asking what was going on. To which my grandmother answered, *Baba has just saved banking in China.* But in the photograph, he mostly looks earthquake-proof—as if, were there to be a big one, he would be the last to topple.

His first wife having died—"of natural causes," my mother always said, as if we might suspect foul play—my grandfather needed to replace her. He had had two children by that first wife, after all. Someone had to take charge of them. And so: enter a matchmaker with a photo of my grandmother the Suzhou beauty.

My father would boom, "Hello, hello!" to the foreigners as they filled up the garden, my mother says now. It was the only English he knew. And so it was always "Hello, hello!"
What about your mother? What did she say? I ask.
My mother was always sort of like in the background, she says. You do not see her too much; she does not have too much to say.
People said she never even laughed out loud. Is that true?
She was a real lady. Very proper.
She had self-control, you mean.
That's right! Not like you, always talking, she says. Too much to say.

Proper though she might have been, my grandmother did smoke opium. She was not an addict. She was a social smoker, as most society women were—a smoker of expensive Persian opium, beautifully prepared for her and her friends by an opium sous-chef. Never mind the price, opium was so good for cramps, they agreed, and oh! How bright the opium-smoker's world, how bright and sharp and glorious! It was all the world should be, a world in which a woman might make demands—demands! can you imagine?—and even laugh out loud, keeping a hand over her mouth as a giggle bubbled up through her fingers.

Another world, indeed.

My grandmother could not read, but she was hardly alone. Never mind most women, most people in China couldn't read, not even in modern Shanghai. What with its neon lights and dance clubs and exciting crossroads style—its *hǎipài,* as people called it—Shanghai was known as "the Paris of the East." But alongside its cars and trams and double-decker buses rolled ox-drawn carts and rickshaws and wheelbarrows. The British racecourse boasted the largest grandstand in the world; its clubhouse featured so much teak and marble, it could have been a land-bound *Titanic*. But cheek by jowl with its splendors sprawled the sort of shantytowns for which words like "destitute" and "squalid" were coined. Many of the shanties did not even boast bamboo-pole walls; many were straw-mat lean-tos. This "Paris" was no Paris.

Even rickshaw pullers mobbed the schools and libraries that had been opened for them, though. Everyone hungered for an education, and my grandmother was no exception. Having taught herself a few characters, she had a newspaper delivered, so that she could practice. Then it was two papers, and then three. She went to the storytelling theaters as well, listening raptly as scenes from *The Dream of the Red Chamber* were read and performed—how she loved them. The poetry! The romance! No middle-aged widowers in that story. Instead, there was true love, enduring love, in a garden outside society. Was this what novels were? They were like opium fantasies.

In real life, meanwhile, she dutifully produced five children, one every two and a half years, as if meeting the terms of a contract. My mother was the first and a disappointment.

I should have been a boy, she explains now. I should have been a number one son.

Because? I say.

Because that's how Chinese people think, she says. The number one son carries on the family line.

And only boys carry it on, so what use is a girl? Except to bear sons?

If my mother did not have a son, there would be a new wife soon, my mother says.

As for the good news: at least my mother lived to feel everyone's disappointment. In the China of her childhood, after all, families like my father's, with five boys and no girls, were hardly unknown.

Why didn't Dad have any sisters? I ask now. Do you think they were drowned?

Bad bad girl! You don't know how to talk! she says. But then she says, Families in Shanghai did not do such things.

***How about in Yixing? I ask**—Yixing having been my father's hometown, a prosperous lake town a bit west of both Shanghai and Suzhou.*
She does not answer.

In any event, everyone agreed: it was too bad she was a girl. And on top of it, when my grandmother threw my mother's placenta into the Huangpu River, it floated far away. *Shēng háizi bèi lǎo,* people said—to have a child is to prepare for old age—but the placenta was an augury. My mother was destined to be raised and fed, only to drift away. Not only would she help carry on some other family's line, she would be of no help to my grandmother as she aged, either. In short, she would be of no use at all.

And children were supposed to be of use, I say now.
Of course, says my mother.
They weren't ends in themselves as they are here, at least theoretically.
I don't know what you are talking, she says.

At least there would be other children to rely on, and at least my grandmother would not have to raise any of them. That was what nursemaids were for.

My mother loved her nursemaid. Nai-ma nursed her and slept with her; Nai-ma was always there to dress her and pick her up and carry her around on her back. Nai-ma laughed and teased; she tickled my mother and chased her. She was lively and naughty— what my mother would later call "mis-cheevous"—a girl herself, in truth, who had been fired from her last job, although no one knew that but my mother. For stealing, Nai-ma once said (talking to herself, really; my mother was just a baby), which she did not do anymore, she said. She had learned her lesson. And anyway, it was such a small thing she took, just a pin—a tiny phoenix made of kingfisher feathers. She took it out and showed it to my mother and pinned it on her. Its feathers were blue and iridescent, like a glimpse of bright sky in a rain puddle; it had a beady red eye. The mistress who had owned it never wore it because the tip of one of its wings was bent. But Nai-ma had felt sorry for it—an abandoned thing no one wanted until it was gone. Then suddenly it was important! Suddenly it was valuable! My mother laughed to hear the story, if only because of the face Nai-ma made—her eyes opened wide, and her mouth, too, with its chipped front tooth.

Nai-ma was soft and lopsided and good-natured. When my mother was very little, Nai-ma let her play with her mouth, opening it wide and putting her fingers inside to feel her chipped tooth, and whenever she wanted to nurse, Nai-ma would untie her tunic and let her nurse. Of course, that was her job. But when it was time to wean my mother, that was her job, too, yet somehow she could not do it.

"She is too big to nurse anymore," my grandmother told Nai-ma. Her voice was soft on the outside but hard on the inside, like a lychee nut.

And Nai-ma soberly agreed. *"She is not a baby,"* she said with her most pious look. *"Not a baby anymore, no. She is not a baby."* She shook her head in that funny way she had, half shake and half wag.

But soon my mother was four years old, then five, and still unweaned.

"This cannot go on," my grandmother said. *"You must stop."*

With company, my grandmother might hardly speak, but with the servants, her voice had grown less timorous all the time, especially with Nai-ma.

"Stop," she said. *"You must stop."*

And Nai-ma agreed and agreed—Nai-ma was the very picture of agreement. *"We will. We will stop. We will stop,"* she promised, my mother hiding behind her. My mother held quiet until my grandmother left. Then she echoed, laughing, *"We will! We will stop! We will stop!"*—tickling Nai-ma until she laughed, too, and opened her tunic and let my mother nurse anyway.

Of all the babies she'd ever taken care of, my mother was Nai-ma's favorite. So hungry all the time! And who cared about this girl who was going to drift away? My mother was nothing, like the kingfisher phoenix pin before people knew it was gone, and that was even before her brother was born. A boy, a boy, a boy! The new baby was everything to my grandmother—a little emperor from his first cry. His umbilical cord was cut with scissors made of solid gold; so obviously more important was he than my mother that she was summarily moved out of her south-facing room, into a room that faced east. And my grandmother's distress when he caught a cold! Was he breathing? Why was he snorting? Was there a way of clearing his nose? He had his own nursemaid, of course—an experienced nursemaid from Suzhou, who knew how to suck the mucus out with her mouth, and who spoke the same dialect as my grandmother besides.

"Look how cute he looks!" she said when he sneezed.

And so successful was she in getting my grandmother to enjoy his sneezes that my mother and Nai-ma were soon attending them, too, laughing delightedly as if at a show. They kept watch so as not to miss any, though really what Nai-ma was watching was how this nursemaid charmed my grandmother.

"Shrimp have their way, and crabs have theirs," she said sometimes, and shrugged.

Other times she complained, though, about how rich people hired as many nursemaids as they liked, gossiping with their friends about which they liked best, while all the nursemaids could do was express some extra milk, have it put into a cake for their own babies, and hope that when the time came, they would be recommended to another family. Nai-ma's husband said she should try to stay as long as she could in this job, in part because it was such a good one. New clothes every year!

And so much food, and a room in the main house, a house with toilets, my mother puts in now.
Meaning no "honeypots"? I say.
That's right.
At a time when pretty much every lane in Shanghai stank.
You cannot imagine the smell, she says.

But Nai-ma's husband also thought she should try to stay because my grandmother, it seemed, was not going to recommend Nai-ma to anyone.

And so even after her little brother had stopped nursing, my mother and Nai-ma would sneak away. Then it was the new baby, my mother's little sister, to whom my grandmother would point, saying, "Look! How can you still be nursing when even Little Sister has stopped?"

"Little Sister had to stop because she bit her nursemaid and her nursemaid left," Nai-ma whispered to my mother. Only Nai-ma could whisper and laugh at the same time. "Little Sister had no choice."

So when my grandmother said again, "Look! Even Little Sister has stopped," my mother said from behind Nai-ma, "Little Sister had to stop because she bit her nursemaid and her nursemaid left! She had no choice!"

"What did you say?" said my grandmother. "Who told you that?"

"No one."

"No one," my grandmother repeated. She was cold with anger. "You have to learn how to talk," she said finally.

"I already know how to talk!"

"You think you know everything. But do you know what I know?"

The crickets chirped loudly in the silence as if to say, *You don't know! You don't know!*

"It is no good for a girl to be too smart," my grandmother said. "That's what I know. Especially if she does not know how to talk."

Her words fell as simply as rain. And when my mother laughed, my grandmother just as simply "did not continue," as my mother would put it later.

Meaning that she expressed her disapproval with withdrawal, I say now.

Only Americans have to say everything out loud, like a bird, says my mother.

My mother turned seven.

"How can you still be nursing?" my grandmother chided. "Are you going to nurse and read at the same time?"

She said this because thanks to my grandfather, my mother was being taught to read.

"You're just jealous that you can't read," my mother said—not hiding behind Nai-ma's legs but poking her head out from behind her waist.

The other children and their nursemaids tiptoed by. No one said anything.

"*You are too smart for your own good,*" my grandmother said finally. "*Who is ever going to marry you? No one.*" And to Nai-ma she said, "*I was complaining about you to my friends, and do you know what one of them said? She said she heard you were fired from your last job. She said you are not from Shanghai. Of course, we knew that last part already. I myself had told them that you speak Ningbo dialect, and that it was just as ugly-sounding as people say, hard as stone and iron. But that you were fired? We didn't know that. What's more, she said that in Ningbo, after you lost your job, you were a sir.*"

A "sir"? I ask now. What does that mean?
That means a prostitute, my mother says.

"*Who said that?*" Nai-ma demanded.

My grandmother slapped her for her impertinence. That tone! Nai-ma began to cry, hoping that there would be no more slaps, as other maids scolded their charges, calling to them, "*Come! Come!*" as a distraction. But still another slap came, and then another, and another.

"*Stop!*" my mother said. "*Stop!*" Then she said again, "*You're just jealous that you can't read!*"

And as she'd hoped, my grandmother stopped hitting Nai-ma. Instead, she slapped my mother.

"*I don't know where you came from, either,*" she said.

My mother was so shocked, she could not even cry.

Later, Nai-ma, comforting her, said, "*People are grouchy when they try to smoke less. And the government is trying to get them all to stop. Do you know what the government is?*"

My mother did not know and did not care. "*She hit me!*" she cried. "*As if I were a servant! She hit me!*"

"*The smoke world is so beautiful,*" explained Nai-ma. "*It makes this world ugly.*"

Still my mother cried. But finally she asked, "*Why did she say* you were a sir? What does that mean? After you lost your job, she said."

"That was crazy talk. She is like a drunken crab today. Crazy."

"But you told me that you lost your job, too," my mother said. "That your last family let you go. You told me."

"You don't remember that." Nai-ma stiffened.

"I do, I do remember," said my mother. "You showed me that bird pin. The one with the red eye."

"You don't remember. You can't remember," said Nai-ma. "You were too little. I never showed you anything."

"But I do remember."

"Your mother is right. You are too smart for your own good." Nai-ma refastened her soft tunic, tied it tight, and said, "If you are so smart, you won't tell anyone."

My mother did not tell anyone.

"Don't act so smart, either," advised Nai-ma.

But one day, my grandmother was in a good mood. She was having another child; her hands rested confidently on her belly as if she knew from the way the baby kicked that it would be another boy. *"Come here,"* she told my mother. *"Read me a story."*

My mother read. It wasn't a long story.

"How about another?" my grandmother said. And then, "Another." And, "Another."

And, proud of what she had learned, my mother read.

Before my grandfather moved to Shanghai, he had worked as a school principal. This was in his hometown of Wuzhen, a bucolic, thirteen-hundred-year-old town that sat on the Grand Canal. Connecting as it did the capital in Beijing with the bountiful Yangtze River Delta ("the land of rice and fish," as it was known), the Grand Canal brought not only prosperity to "water towns" like Wuzhen but also a charming riverine culture. Grocers would row right up to people's steps, their sampans heavy with fish and vegetables, and people commuted by boat, including the students who rockingly arrived for class at the all-important academy: in a country where the imperial exams were everything, the aptly named Aspiration Academy was everything, too. Of course, since girls could not sit for the exams, the school did not admit them. Even after the exams were abolished in 1905, most people held that to educate a girl was like washing coal; it made no sense, they said. My grandfather agreed.

But now, long after he had left his academy position to become a Shanghai banker, my grandfather wondered if he'd missed something. After all, though women like his mother had had their feet bound, foot-binding was no longer legal. Perhaps it was time to unbind women's minds as well? He had his daughter by his first wife taught to read.

And now by his second wife, he had a daughter who was just like him; everyone could see it. Even at age three, my mother had sat on his lap reciting poetry. *"How about 'Ode to the Goose'?"* he would say. And she would immediately recite:

> *Goose, goose, goose!*
> *You lift your neck to the sky and sing—*
> *White down bobbing on the green water,*
> *Red feet pedaling the clear waves.*

Or, *"How about 'Sympathy for the Farmers'?"* he would suggest, prompting her with her favorite line, *Lì lì jiē xīnkǔ*—meaning, Every last grain comes of hardship. Then she would chirpingly recite:

> *Hoeing crops at noon,*
> *Their sweat drips to the soil.*
> *Who sees that there in the bowl,*
> *Every last grain comes of hardship?*

"Get down. You are too big to sit on Baba's lap," my grandmother told her, even as my grandfather found my mother a special tutor. The tutor was a *xiùcai*—a scholar who had passed the county-level exams back when there were still exams; he knew everything except how to smile. But never mind. He spoke French and English and was willing to take on even a very small girl—or willing, at least, after he heard how much my grandfather was offering to pay. And already he had taught my mother so many characters that by the time my grandmother said, *"Read me a story,"* my mother read

easily. And when my grandmother said, *"Another,"* and *"Another,"* my mother read those stories just as easily. Was she acting too smart? Anyway, she read until finally my grandmother had had enough.

"You are better than the storytelling theater," she said, smiling. *"You read so well, I think you are too big for Nai-ma."*

"No! I am not too big!" said my mother, then asked: *"What is that funny look on your face?"*

"What funny look?" My grandmother placed a cigarette in her ivory holder and lit it.

And when my mother went back to her room, Nai-ma was gone. She waited all day, but Nai-ma did not come and did not come. Even that night, when the garden grew gray and the katydids loud, she did not come. One of the other maids gave my mother a bag of hot yams to warm her bed. But though she cried and cried, the maid just looked down as if wishing for a new pair of shoes. If she knew what had happened to Nai-ma, she would not say.

In the morning, my mother went everywhere to look for Nai-ma. She began with the servants' dorm in the garden—a long low building with a warren of packed rooms, where she had never been before. Then she searched the kitchen, another place she had never been, where there were live fish in a basin and dried fish in a basket and fires in all six of the stove burners. The pots and steam made it seem like a factory; some of the male cooks were not wearing shirts; and everyone laughed to see her there. *Dà jiě!*—the oldest girl, an important miss, what was she doing here? Outside of the kitchen, the servants were afraid of her. My mother never left the house without a bodyguard, and she never went anywhere herself; there was always a driver for the car, an assistant to open the car door, and a maid to carry things. They wore uniforms and did whatever she bade them do. But here in the kitchen, things were different. Here in the kitchen, the servants did not listen to her; it was as if they were drunk on the steam. Or had they been smoking opium? Not the expensive opium my grandmother smoked but the lower-grade stuff Nai-ma once told her that common people liked? They laughed loudly at her.

"No, no, she isn't here. Do you see anyone hiding? Look around, look around," they said. *"Go ahead and search! Did you look in all*

the cupboards? Did you look in the rice barrel? Come on, look some more."

Only one old cook whose name my mother did not even know said brusquely, *"You will not find her here."* His eyes were bulging and red; he had four fingers on his right hand. But if he knew where Nai-ma was or whether she'd left the house, he would not say. *"Was she fired?"* my mother asked at last. *"Was she fired?"* And because no one answered or even seemed to hear her, she finally said the most dangerous thing she could say, the thing she was never supposed to say, namely, *"Was she fired again?"* She said it because she wanted to know that they could hear her.

But no one reacted even to that. No one cared that she'd said it; her words vanished into the steam as the servants chopped and sorted and stirred and shouted, ignoring her.

And that was all, my mother says now.
That was it? I say.
That was it. No one said anything.
Do you think they knew?
Of course they knew.
How do you know?
I just know, she says. They knew.

Her family's house was on the outskirts of the International Settlement—a largely British-run part of town, with British water, electric, and telephone lines as well as British fire protection and trash collection. Surrounded by a high wall, the house was European-style—a three-story stucco villa with a portico, a dark red tile roof, and dark red-trimmed windows, including floor-to-ceiling windows on the ground floor. Besides the well-furnished living room and wood-paneled dining room with their graceful arched entryways, there were eight bedrooms, a solarium, a library, two studies, several balconies, and several fireplaces. There was also a wisteria-draped veranda, an expansive lawn lined with trees and shrubs, and a two-bay garage; the dorm was large enough for the family's two twenty-servant teams. All in all, it was a big enough compound that if my grandparents wanted to keep my mother from Nai-ma, they could. My mother could only cry and cry until her nose was sore from wiping and even the maid who had given her the sack of hot yams looked through her. My grandfather and grandmother ignored her, too, as did her siblings; the red-turbaned Sikh guard who used to practice his Chinese with her turned away if she walked by, scratching his wiry black beard as if it had suddenly begun to itch.

The only person who still seemed to see her was her tutor. Teacher Wu's long face showed nothing, of course, as her lessons went on, his frog-like eyes keeping strictly to their two positions—up for the student and down for the page. He taught her Chinese and French, and though eventually there was another tutor for math and science, with whom my mother could have worked if she liked, she was not interested. Her brother found those subjects interesting, but she found them boring; and anyway, they were not the important subjects. They were not the hard subjects. Anyone could do math and science; you had to have talent to do literature.

She had the head for literature, but these days, she did not have the heart. Sometimes she lay her head right on her book, even though she knew her tears would pucker the page. Then, expressionless as ever, Teacher Wu would jiggle the volume until she lifted her head back up. Once he gave her his own crumpled handkerchief for her tears and, when she used it, nodded ever so slightly, as if to say, *That's better.* Once, too, he gave her a poem by Li Zhiyi called *"Song of Divination"* to learn:

> *As I live up and you downstream,*
> *Day after day of you I dream.*
> *There's the Yangtze, but I don't see you,*
> *Drink both from the same river though we do.*
> *When will the river cease to flow?*
> *When will my grief cease to grow?*
> *Oh, that I knew your heart were like mine*
> *And that it is not in vain that I pine.*

My mother dutifully memorized the poem. But as she waited week after week for Nai-ma to return, it did seem to be in vain that she pined.

She wrote an essay for Teacher Wu. It read:

If you are too big for a nursemaid, they should tell you that you are getting big but that your maid will still be there if you need her. That is the right way. It is not right to just send her away.

"*This is too short. And what is the conclusion?*" he said, so she added:

All your brothers and sisters will learn a lesson. If you are too close to your maid, she will be sent away.

At night, she dreamed that she had left off nursing and had told my grandmother, and that Nai-ma came back then and slept with her again. But in the morning, Nai-ma was still not there.

Eventually, my mother got a new maid. She sent her new maid out for candy and treats—for sour plums in the summer and ginkgo nuts in the fall. She gobbled down the preserved plums and pear syrup candy and watermelon seeds that the maid brought for her, and the foreign sweets as well—sugar cookies and thumbprint cookies and Florentines and, her favorite, fat slices of chestnut cake with whipped cream. All of these she washed down with bottle after bottle of Coca-Cola from the icebox on the second floor, near her parents' bedroom. She loved the dark, sweet fizz of the cola, and the way that it bubbled all the way down your throat; and she loved the curvy green fluted bottles it came in, with that exotic American lettering. She loved even the metal caps you had to get a servant to pry off for you with a special metal bottle opener; once a servant tried to do it with his teeth, only to pry his front tooth loose instead. (He jiggled the tooth at the kids in the house and laughed, as did they, and it never did fall out.) And she loved the big wooden icebox, too, with its heavy latched doors. Sometimes in the summer she would open them all and stand in the cloud of cold air that whooshed out like a dragon.

"*Close the doors! Now! Now! Before the ice melts! Now!*" everyone would yell.

And sometimes she would. Other times, though, she would cool her hands on a watermelon before she did or, better yet, if there was an already-sliced melon in there, steal a few pieces for herself and her siblings. Watermelon was everyone's favorite. My grandmother used to eat it cooled in the wells of Suzhou, but it was even better cooled in an icebox.

Often my mother played in the garden with her baby sisters and their ivory dolls. She had two sisters now, whom she liked. But she had another brother, too, thanks to whom she had been displaced altogether from the second floor. Hers was the best room on the third floor—the south-facing room—to which, as the oldest girl living in the house, she was entitled. (Her half sister, like her half brother, lived in Qingdao.) And there was a lovely, shady balcony on the third floor, it was true, complete with a retractable awning. Still, it grated that a north-facing bedroom on the second floor was given to the boys' maids. Why couldn't she have had that one? But my grandmother had assigned the bedrooms, and there was nothing to be done.

It was hardly the only way in which my mother's place in the family was made clear. When she raced the older of her brothers around the dining room in their pedal cars, she always won; she was bigger, after all. But because he was a boy, he got a red car—a beautiful red Buick—while she got a brown Ford. And at mealtimes, he got the best pieces of meat, too, because it was important for a boy to be strong. As for why he got the brains of the fish, that was because eating fish brains made you smart. And he needed to be made smart, she told him. Or at least smarter than he was—a lot smarter.

When he cried, his whole face crumpled up, as if it were made of cloth.

"*Bad bad girl! You don't know how to talk,*" my grandmother scolded her. "*With a tongue like yours, no one will ever marry you.*"

My mother laughed.

"*Bad bad girl! Bad bad girl! Bad bad girl!*"

Still, my mother told her brother things like, "*It's a good thing you are a boy because otherwise you would be nothing.*" And, "*When they say it's too bad I'm not a boy, they mean it's too bad that you are. They mean it's too bad you're not a girl."

"Is it true it's too bad I'm a boy?" her brother asked my grandmother. "Because I am not smart? That's what Older Sister says." He tugged on her dress.

My grandmother unfastened his hand. "She has too much to say."

"Is it true girls at least know who loves them and who doesn't?" He grasped her skirt again—with both hands now, imploring her.

"Ignore her." My grandmother once more removed one hand, then the other from the fine fabric. His hands were sweaty; she was dressed for company. "When she talks to you, ignore her. Act like you do not hear her."

"But I do hear her."

"Well, stop."

"But I can't! I can't stop!" he wailed, lunging toward her again. "I hear her! I can't stop!"

My grandmother called for his maid.

People said it was probably something I inherited, that I talked that way, my mother says now. They said they tried to stop me but finally gave up. There was nothing anyone could do. Of course, no matter what, I was not as bad as you.

What do you mean?

Write down everything people say.

Ma, it's just a novel.

What about the parts that are true? she demands.

Okay, then, would you rather I call it a memoir?

Bad bad girl! she says. How can this be a memoir? I am dead. You never even met Nai-ma. You know what you should write?

What?

Nothing. You should write nothing.

Well, I'm not going to write nothing, Ma.

Bad bad girl! Bad bad girl! she says. You should not write anything!

When her brother was little, he would cry and hit my mother

in response to the things she said; and now that he was bigger, he hit her with a stick.

"*Whose fault is it?*" my grandmother would say if my mother showed her the bruises on her leg. "*Since you know everything, tell me. Whose fault is it?*"

And if my mother tried to argue that the hitter should be blamed, not the person being hit, my grandmother would stiffen.

"*You have nothing to say,*" she would say, meaning that my mother was not entitled to an opinion; and with that, she would discontinue the conversation.

My mother the terror was now a nonstop reader and fixated on, of all things, the leather-bound English-language books that packed my grandfather's shelves. Precocious as she was, she could not really read them yet. It would be years before she understood them cover to cover. But already she was beginning her project with her rudimentary English and a Chinese-English dictionary her tutor had given her. Her older half brother could read them, after all, as could many of the students in my grandfather's school, from whose library the books had come. And so, though my grandmother tried to have her barred from the library, my mother spirited the books into her room, where, eating candy, she read them under her covers by flashlight—*Great Expectations, Robinson Crusoe, Gulliver's Travels. Little Women, The Count of Monte Cristo, The Story of Dr. Doolittle. The Picture of Dorian Gray. The Adventures of Tom Sawyer, The Adventures of Huckleberry Finn. David Copperfield, Pride and Prejudice, Jane Eyre.* What sort of an influence were they? Though my grandmother could not read even their titles, she had a hunch: these books were not about filial piety. They were not about children who sat by their parents' beds shirtless, so that mosquitoes would bite them instead of their parents. They were not about children who hauled bags of rice over long distances for their parents to eat while they themselves ate wild vegetables. They were trouble. As for whether more education stood to make my mother even worse, my grandmother was sure that it did. Her own desire to read notwithstanding, she quoted Confucius to my grandfather.

"*An educated woman is a worthless woman,*" she said.

My grandfather scoffed. He was not so radical as to suggest it was time for Mr. Science and Mr. Democracy to replace Mr. Confucius; that was reckless student talk. But there were a number of girls' schools now, with more and more opening all the time—including a Catholic school not far from them, in the French Concession—and he was intrigued by this last enterprise, especially. This was a new school, a special school, an expensive, modern school where many good Shanghai families were sending their daughters—not that they were necessarily Catholic. Most families did not "eat," as they said, the foreign religion. And those who were Catholic were often Buddhist and Daoist and Confucian as well—religion to their mind being a thing about which one ought to be reasonable. But instruction in the new school would be both up-to-date and in English. And while people hated the Brits for the Opium Wars and the whole last century of humiliation—the condescension of these barbarians! the hypocrisy! the ruthlessness!—who knew but that the girls might emerge fluent? Especially a smart girl like my mother.

"*Too bad,*" my grandfather would say sometimes. "*If you were a boy, you could accomplish a lot.*"

And if his friends were there, they would nod their heads in agreement. "*What a shame, what a shame! If she were a boy, she would be the head of a bank at least.*" They thought it lucky that she had a brother. When the time came, they would invite him to meetings and conferences. They would show him how things worked, introduce him to the world. In the meantime, *What a shame!*

The sexism! I say now. Didn't anybody object?

Of course, there were grumblings, she says. But never a tidal wave.

Even with all the other protesting going on? I say. I am thinking of the May Fourth protests in 1919, for example—of the outrage over the Versailles treaty that gave Qingdao to the Japanese. Wasn't that a tidal wave?

You can say that way, but actually, most people believe woman should obey man. They think that is natural.

And you?

The norm was the norm. You don't buckle the norm, she says.

Still, my grandfather sent her to the special school. He would nod with his friends. And after they left, he would prepare his ink the way he always had—using an ink stick made of extra-fine pine soot and tung oil, and gently circling it around and around the shallow well of his inkstone. Like generations of scholars before him, he used no pressure; around and around went his hand, around and around. But as it did, he thought, Who knows but that this daughter will surpass me in learning? It is time for change.

The kingfisher phoenix pin appeared in my mother's room. It was pinned to her quilt but hidden under a fold so that she found it with her knee in the dark—something strange scratching her, something sharp, which she somehow recognized immediately. What was it doing there? Who did the pinning, and why? Where was Nai-ma?

This time she knew better than to cry and cry. She was a big girl now. She knew that she could wail all she wanted but that it would bring no one. And so at night she cried a little, but by day she just waited. Did the pin mean Nai-ma was still in the house? Or was it some sort of goodbye? Whatever it meant, it was up to my mother to keep it safe, and she did, hiding it behind a loose slat in the headboard of her bed. She could not lay it flat but had to stand it up, so that when she checked—as she did every now and then, to be sure it was still there—it looked straight back at her with its beady red eye, as if to remind her, *Say nothing*. Because maybe if she said nothing, Nai-ma would come back. Because maybe if she said nothing, Nai-ma would forgive her for having said that she remembered Nai-ma's telling her where the pin came from. Because maybe if she said nothing, she would be forgiven for asking the servants in the kitchen, *"Was she fired again?"*

She had not said it, she told herself sometimes. She hadn't said that terrible word, *"again."* She hadn't.

Sometimes she became confused herself.

In any case, she kept quiet for days, weeks, months.

Nothing happened.

What did it mean?

Years later, she thought that maybe Nai-ma had left the pin, not as a way of saying goodbye, or I am leaving something for you to remember me by, but something else.

Like maybe it was a way of saying, It was your fault that I was sent away? I say now.
Maybe, she says.
I think she meant to tell you she loved you, I say.
Chinese people don't say love this, love that, she says. Chinese people say you did something wrong.
Was that all Chinese people or just you? I ask. Because I've always wondered.
Chinese people are like that, she insists. They like to criticize.
So the pin must have meant you did something wrong? The red eye must have been telling you, You did something wrong?
It was to say I did something wrong, and now I should not do it again. It was to say, I should learn my lesson.
Nai-ma could have sold that pin, you know, I say. Think how much it would have been worth to her family! I bet her husband would have wanted her to sell it.
She thinks about that.
Maybe she gave it to me because she didn't want him to have it, she says finally. Or because she was afraid he would do something with it and get caught.
Or maybe she meant, Your mother sent me away, but someone loved you. Maybe she meant, Remember that. Someone loved you.
Maybe.

Whatever the pin meant, when my mother became a Catholic, the first thing she confessed was that she had it.

What fun to have landed among teachers from so many countries! English was the lingua franca, but it wasn't just English that the nuns spoke. They spoke French, Korean, Dutch, Swahili, Tagalog, Spanish, Finnish, Swedish, Portuguese, Hindi, Russian, German,

Latvian, Italian, Japanese, Arabic, Greek, and more. Some were short, and some were tall; some were skinny and some round, with bosoms big and soft as peony blooms. Most of them were Caucasian, though a few were Asian and a few my mother didn't-know-what. She had seen foreigners before. People from all over the world lived in the International Settlement; they blew in and out of downtown like clouds. But the women she'd seen up close were a type—well-dressed, well-mannered, and well-kept. They were not so varied as these nuns, several of whom had blue eyes, one with eyelashes like a cow's. One had a mole as big as a beetle; one had a dimple on her chin. They all had coarse skin and astonishing noses.

They carried mini-dictionaries in their big hidden pockets—some carried two—and when they struggled with street signs, they prayed as if praying would help them, as if they would look up from their hands and know where they were. When they struggled with chopsticks, they prayed for help, too, though God did not seem to know much about chopsticks. And they searched your sleeves for candy, but when they found it, they as often as not let you keep it, so long as you promised you wouldn't eat it in class. Was that what God told them to do? Did He know you would eat it anyway and trade it with your friends as well? He had to, knowing everything. Did that make it okay? The nuns sang songs with lyrics they tried in vain to get others to learn—every language, it seemed, having sounds that no one else could produce. Thank heavens they did better with treats—with pizzelles and profiteroles and baklava and halvah and pfeffernuesse. They were all on quests for hard-to-find ingredients, for molds and substitutes and special equipment, and they kept everyone abreast of their progress. But for my mother, the very most interesting thing about them was that none of them had married.

They hadn't, and why should anyone? she thought. Maybe she should join them. And so she might have, had a nun not begun taking her out for lunch and snacks, talking all the while about what a privilege it was to serve God.

"But I'll have to listen to the mother superior, won't I?" said my mother finally, one day.

"Of course," said the sister. "The mother superior is the representative of Christ." Her skin was thin as the skin of a fine restaurant dumpling—so see-through that my mother could see her bright blue branching veins.

"I can't listen to anyone," my mother told her. "I have too much to say."

And that was that.

Still, she was baptized. Her name remained Loo Shu-hsin—Shu-hsin meaning "cultivate trust"—but she was given an English name, too. Now she was Mary Agnes Loo—Aggie for short—named for Saint Agnes, who, having taken Christ for a spouse, had chosen to die at age twelve rather than marry an official's son. "Unstained" was the word the nuns used for her—meaning, my mother's classmates said, giggling, that she was a virgin. My mother was not entirely clear what that meant in either language, although she did gather that whether that was really so remarkable at age twelve was open to question. Anyway, my mother was going to church every Sunday and preparing to take Communion, which entailed first going to confession.

And it was there, kneeling in the dark, damp confessional, speaking to the dark green curtain, that she remembered all about the kingfisher phoenix pin—that she remembered where the pin came from (though Nai-ma had said she couldn't remember, she couldn't possibly), and also how she had said things about Nai-ma that she shouldn't have, and later found the pin and kept it, and never told her parents. The word "guilt" was new to her. She'd been brought up attuned to right and wrong, but Chinese wrongdoing was a different thing—more a failure to do one's duty than a capitulation to Satan—and she was expecting from her admission something she could hardly pronounce, "absolution." But the priest surprised her.

"You told no one because there is no one you can really trust," said the priest. "Is there?"

"No," she said, after a moment. "There isn't."

"You can trust in the Lord Jesus Christ," said the priest. He had a voice like an old laundry paddle, almost furry, it had been used so much.

And she found that she almost believed him; all sorts of things seemed possible in English that didn't in Chinese. But she didn't believe him enough to tell him what she wanted to tell him, namely: *I still have the pin, even now. I still have it. I have kept it.*

If there was a person she could trust, it was the head of the school, Mother Greenough. Mother Greenough did not have green anything. She had blond eyebrows you could hardly see, they were so pale; her eyelashes were almost white. And her eyes were not just blue, they were a blue my mother had never seen besides on a temple devil—a blazing blue, like the sky on a day so hot not even the clouds would come out. People said she could see right through you.

As perhaps she could, but Mother Greenough liked my mother—number one in everything, and half shy, half bold. My mother's family had always said that she was like my grandfather, but Mother Greenough thought, She's like me.

"You like English," she said. "You're good at it."

"It's my favorite subject," said my mother.

"That's excellent," said Mother Greenough thoughtfully. Adding, "It is more than a skill. It shows an interest in the world. No one learns anything but for a reason, you know. A reason that can be a secret even from yourself."

My mother considered this. "My family has always welcomed foreigners," she volunteered. "They come to our house. My father has always been very open."

"Interesting," said Mother Greenough. "Perhaps you mean 'open-minded.'"

"Open-minded."

Mother Greenough nodded. "You know, I am the only teacher here who speaks Mandarin."

"I know," said my mother.

"That makes us the only two bilinguists here. Or rather, the only two Chinese-English bilinguists."

"Yes," said my mother, though she was only guessing what "bilinguists" meant.

"You must be of exceptional intelligence to be a bilinguist," said Mother Greenough and, with a flash of her white eyelashes, winked.

Not sure what else to do, my mother winked back. She had never seen anyone wink before, much less winked at anyone herself, as Mother Greenough seemed to know.

"Like this," she said. "You don't have to squinch up your whole eye. It's just a quick down and up."

A quick down and up. Clutching the arms of her chair and sitting up straight, my mother tried again.

"Excellent. Now you are an expert. But be careful at whom you wink. No men, especially."

"But why not?"

"Because a wink is like a little note you are sending," said Mother Greenough, "except that you already know the other person's answer. And if you wink, it's preapproved."

My mother thought about that during lunch, the chatter of the other girls swirling around her. A note with an answer. If you wink, it's preapproved. What could that mean? And a reason secret even from yourself. What could that be?

Mother Greenough had started this mission school in the French Concession with a handful of other Sisters of the Sacred Heart. They were all eager to do something for girls in China, the plight of girls being, they said, just too dreadful. Poor girls could be drowned, sold, or enslaved, and even rich girls were second-class citizens. The majority were left uneducated, and many were beaten, if not as daughters then as wives—as if that were how children of the Lord ought to be treated! But all that was going to change now; that's why the sisters had come here. They were going to convert the rich girls and teach them to think, to think critically. To think for themselves. To insist on being treated with dignity. From there, progress would ripple outward. The sisters would see to it.

Never mind that the Jesuits running things in Shanghai had been downright discouraging—relegating them, for starters, to a building in a swamp. The invitation to tour this having arrived after a week of rain, the courtyard was flooded; the sisters had to remove their shoes and stockings to walk through it. They lifted their habits above their ankles. Sweat ran down their legs into the mud, and they left covered with mosquito bites, only to discover later that the men had none. Was it not ungodly, the nuns asked then, for the men to have failed to share their repellent? As one nun observed, "Some priests make it easy to keep your vows." Still, they immediately said yes to it all—to the mud, to the mosquitoes, to the mildew and mold. To the self-important Jesuits, and to the difficulties of navigating an alien, pagan culture where people spat on the ground. In their school, they agreed, the first rule would be "No spitting."

"But Christ gave us those hurdles," Mother Greenough said now. "We welcomed them." And: "It was our job to overcome them, and, as you can see, we have done so."

My mother had never heard anyone talk like that before. In her experience, foreign women talked about how exquisite the garden was, and how smashing the party. "Did you try this?" they said. "You must have at least a nibble. These people are so clever." Mother Greenough, meanwhile, had a little framed painting on the wall, of green grass with a white house surrounded by tall flowers; the flowers were pink and red and white and a burgundy so dark it looked almost black. "Hollyhocks," she said they were, and spelled it for my mother. H-o-l-l-y-h-o-c-k-s. "A species of self-sowing biennials," she continued, then explained what "self-sowing" meant and "biennials." And yes, the house was her home, she told my mother when she asked. As for how she could ever have left such a place, Mother Greenough replied, How could I have stayed?

"The world was not within those four walls," she said. "The world—the enormous world—lay outside of them. And God meant me for the world." My mother wanted to tell Mother Greenough about the kingfisher phoenix pin then, and how it was too bad she was a girl and how no one would ever marry her, but it all seemed so small—the concerns of someone who had never left her four walls.

"Were you afraid?" she asked instead.

"Never," Mother Greenough said.

Never, thought my mother, and vowed that she would never be afraid, either.

**And so I went to America, she says now.
Ma! Shhh! I say. You're giving away the plot!**

The most important day of the year was Christ's birthday. It was hard to believe that Mary, the mother of Christ, would really have had her baby in a stable full of animals and hay, but the nuns said she did, and no, there were no servants or family members to help, just her husband, that bearded carpenter Joseph. Poor Joseph! Poor Mary! Poor baby Jesus! Though at least kings came to visit, riding camels. They had to navigate by the stars but got there all right, and they brought Christmas presents, though of course they weren't called Christmas presents yet and weren't wrapped, and what odd presents they were. What was Mary going to do with frankincense and myrrh? Now Christmas was the day Santa Claus went everywhere in the world on a flying sleigh, landing on people's roofs and climbing down their chimneys. And if there was no chimney? "Then he *xiǎng bànfǎ*," one of my mother's classmates told her (using the Chinese phrase for "found a way," even though at school they were supposed to speak English and only English). "He *xiǎng bànfǎ*, just as a Chinese person would. He's not stupid."

"I didn't think he was stupid," my mother said. "I was just asking a question."

They were supposed to ask questions—that was the Western way of education—and my mother had a lot of them when speaking English. In Chinese, she could be shy, especially with her peers. Her confidence in Chinese was like a darting fish: the way a fish could be bright, then dark, then bright, then dark, she could be sharp-tongued, then tongue-tied, sharp-tongued, then tongue-tied. But in English, she was clear and bold and probing. Did Santa Claus know Jesus Christ? What did the North Pole have to do with the manger? And did the manger have something to do with gingerbread houses? She asked these things, one after another. And if the manger had nothing to do with gingerbread houses, why did the nuns all seem to know how to make them? And what did a Yule log have to do with the manger, the North Pole, or gingerbread houses, and could the Three Kings have come by reindeer, and did Christ have a nursemaid? My mother wanted to know all these things; the sisters patiently explained them. It was wonderful.

If only the Japanese had not come! But back in 1931, with no declaration of war, the Japanese had invaded Manchuria; and they had not stopped there. Their scourge had spread southward like an ink stain until, hard as it was to leave his German-style Qingdao mansion with its arch-lined walkways and sweeping view of the sea, my mother's half brother had felt it too dangerous to stay. He promised his family they would return. This was an illegal invasion, after all. Nations could not simply take over whole portions of other countries; order would be restored. In the meanwhile, he transported all seventy-five members of his household—his three wives, his seven or eight children, and his sixty-odd servants—to my grandfather's house. They were hardly the only ones fleeing. Tens of thousands of people were on the move, making even fitful progress a considerable operation. The buying and counting of tickets went on endlessly, as did the packing and negotiating and pleading and delegating, not to say the waiting—for trains, for cars, for buses, for carts. Everyone had to be fed all the while, and of course the children, understanding nothing, were cranky. And once the household had finally, miraculously reassembled in Shanghai, conditions were crowded. Some of the servants had to sleep, not on proper cots, but on straw mats.

Still, the refugees were relieved. There were Japanese people in Shanghai, too—a lot of them, especially in the "Little Tokyo" in the Hongkou district. But at least they were ordinary Japanese. They were not Japanese soldiers—those terrible, brutal soldiers, with short legs and no human feeling, who thought nothing of bayonetting a pregnant woman right in the belly. People said they would pull the baby out and brandish it like a melon on a stick, even as the woman screamed and the baby writhed. The idea that the Japanese should rule all of Asia! That it was their destiny! It was obscene.

Here in Shanghai there was blessed shelter from their arrogance, especially in the International Settlement, protected as it was by a coalition of foreign governments—or so the family thought. They had not even sorted out where to store their things, though, before there was trouble right around the corner. Apparently a newspaper article had appeared, lamenting the failure of an assassination attempt on Emperor Hirohito, in response to which the Japanese had sent a band of Buddhist priests to their neighborhood.

"Buddhist priests?" my grandfather laughed. *"I look forward to hearing their Lotus Sūtra."*

And indeed—what an aggressive way they had of promoting pacifism. There were five of them, one more goading than the next as they chanted pro-Japanese slogans. They offered pro-Japanese toasts. To the splendid success in Manchuria!

"Troublemakers in robes," my grandfather said. *"The question is, who sent them? And why?"*

As for the answer: a Japanese military attaché and his cross-dressing consort had, it seemed, sent the priests to stir up the local Japanese.

"Ah. So they are Buddhist agitators," said my grandfather.

The priests soon instigated a riot outside a towel factory, which wasn't hard. Five years earlier, after Japanese foremen started to carry pistols, a Chinese cotton mill worker was shot, precipitating strikes, arrests, riots, and more arrests until finally the police opened fire on a crowd. Boycotts followed; electricity to the Chinese mills was cut; and though the retaliations and counterretaliations did eventually subside, now it took nothing to rile people back up. The towel factory workers beat the Japanese priests, then lynched one.

"He hung in the air like a pig!" reported the servants. "They could have basted and roasted him!"

Everyone cheered. Only my grandfather shook his head.

"They should not have taken the bait," he said, even as word came that some Japanese had torched the towel factory in retaliation.

"Such a lot of trouble for such a small fire," my grandfather observed then.

As for his response when reports of two Chinese dying in the fire gave rise to anti-Japanese demonstrations, to counter which Japan sent thirty ships, several seaplanes, and two thousand troops to protect the Japanese population in Shanghai, all he could say was *"The Japanese had bigger flames in mind from the start."*

From their Manchurian base, the Japanese launched an invasion of the rest of China in 1937. Again, there was no formal declaration of war. They simply began pounding the Chinese coast, proceeding from north to south, and expecting to take Shanghai with ease. For weeks, though, they gained ground by day only to lose it by night—those mulish Chinese! On and on the fighting went, until finally the Japanese stood outside their goal. There Generalissimo Chiang Kai-shek prepared to take a dramatic stand. Surely, he thought, an attack on Shanghai would rouse international indignation—Shanghai being, after all, the fifth-largest city in the world. It was also, he believed, a Chinese city—perhaps the only Chinese city—whose reality Westerners grasped.

And of course he was right about that, my mother says now. The rest of China, you think they know where it is?
For Westerners, China was a blur and is still, I say.

The French sent troops to defend the French Concession; the Americans, British, and Italians sent troops to defend the International Settlement. Everywhere there were frightening sights—warships, troops, barbed wire, and sandbags—followed soon by tanks, howitzers, grenades, and machine guns. Then came stories of suicide bombers, and of house-to-house combat in which the Japanese would knife the men, lock the women up, rape them at night, and then kill them, too, in the morning.

Even in the International Settlement, my grandfather heard an explosion as he walked to work. Clouds of black smoke rained blood and body parts; the streets began streaming with screaming survivors. That "attack" was actually a nightmare error on the part of a Chinese bomber. But a nightmare it was, and right across Suzhou Creek from my mother's house, the Japanese were relentlessly firebombing entire neighborhoods. The flames were so intense that, watching from the third-floor balcony, my mother choked on the smoke; it was as if the pictures of hell she'd seen in her schoolbooks had come to life. Shutting the windows and jamming the cracks with tissue didn't help, and though my grandfather claimed that firemen were at work and the world was not ending, she could see that even he was not sure that was true.

Thousands of people were pouring out of the city now—their possessions and elderly and children heaped onto carts and backs, and jammed into baskets on shoulder poles—while thousands more stampeded the International Settlement. The streets were packed so tightly that no one could move; surrounding my mother's house, the mob attempted to break into the grounds. My mother watched, petrified, as shirtless men appeared at the top of the garden walls, then dropped down like body-bombs into the bushes. What would her family have done had not their enormous Sikh guards caught the intruders, beaten them mercilessly, and shoved them back out to the street? Mother Greenough would have disapproved. But when my grandfather simply paid the guards handsomely and expressed his deepest thanks, my mother could not help but share his gratitude.

So overwhelming was the situation that it was almost a relief when after three months of fighting, the city finally fell. How galling to see Japanese flags hoisted over the burnt-out buildings. And the brazenness of the Japanese troops! They swarmed through the city on foot and on horseback, shaking people down and looting shamelessly. But at least the bombing had ceased, and the crowds had shrunk.

With a death toll in the hundreds of thousands, the Battle of Shanghai was later known as the Stalingrad on the Yangtze. Bodies were thrown, one after the next after the next, into mass graves; they were heaved onto funeral pyres so enormous that when it rained, ashes rained down, too, in black globs. The servants complained about the extra cleaning, while my grandfather set about buying all the food he could, never mind what it was or what it cost: though inflation had made money all but worthless, enough of it thankfully still amounted to something, and many of the servants' families having sought shelter with them, he had hundreds of mouths to feed. Meanwhile, the Japanese guarded the food stores. They controlled the rice. There were shortages and food riots; everything had to be bought on the black market. My mother's family had often used the term *hòu mén*—back door—to mean an unofficial channel, but never before had food literally come into the house through a back door. Peasants risked their lives to sell rice to them this way, but what choice did they have? They had to sell it quickly, at night, before the Japanese took it.

We were lucky, my mother says now. We had money. We ate.
And that's what money means in China, isn't it? I say. Food. Survival.
Not just in China, she says.

"Nothing could be worse than what the Japanese have done here," people said. "Nothing."

My grandfather held his tongue, though, and later took no satisfaction in having predicted what was going to happen at the next city on which the Japanese called—an atrocity that would come to be known as the Rape of Nanjing.

During the occupation, there was an understanding: the Japanese soldiers might have their "comfort houses"—and people said they had dozens of them, all over the city—but they were not supposed to rape gentry women.

And if they did? I ask now.
If they did, there would be protests, my mother says.
I'm surprised that restrained them, I say.

My grandfather must have had his doubts, too, because with few exceptions, my mother and her sisters were kept strictly inside—"sort of like secluded," as my mother put it. The unoccupied *gūdǎo*—isolated island—that was the International Settlement and French Concession was in fact a ghetto, barricaded off from the rest of the city by barbed wire. But it was at least protected, while the lovely, leafy section of the International Settlement in which my mother's family lived, managed though it had been by the British for decades, was technically outside the Settlement line. The result was that the not-so-secret Japanese secret police—the notorious *Kempeitai*—established their headquarters right down the street from my mother's house.

"76 Jessfield Road?" my grandfather said. *"This cannot be happening."*

But it was. Just blocks away from them, the Japanese were torturing and executing people, sometimes hanging the victims' heads on the gateposts outside their villa.

My twelve-year-old mother continued boarding at school, often staying the weekend, and only occasionally braving the Japanese checkpoint with her bodyguard and maid and driver to go home. Talk of the Japanese police station was forbidden. Still, the servants argued quietly about whose head it was that they'd seen and how long it would be allowed to rot, as my mother could not help but overhear.

Traumatic? says my mother now. I always say it: you people do not know what means traumatic.

No wonder you and your family were always asking, Why do you go out? I say.

Best way is stay home, she agrees. Don't go out. Stay home.

Then in 1941, Japan bombed Pearl Harbor, joining the Axis powers, and even the International Settlement became "enemy territory."

"The Japanese say we can expect a visit anytime," my grandfather said.

And sure enough, though a British captain on the Huangpu River made a noble last stand, yelling, "Get off my bloody ship!" his boat was promptly sunk. Japanese trucks and tanks paraded up and down Settlement roads; they took a victory lap around the racecourse and raised their flag over the grand waterfront Wall Street that was the Bund. Notices appeared on the doors of banks and businesses, announcing that they were now under Japanese control as Japanese businessmen flooded in, each assigned to take over a particular job. Critical figures like my grandfather nominally kept their positions, but as the saying went, *Xīn kǒu bù yī*. His mouth said one thing and his heart another. He could quietly sabotage his captors. However, he had to do it carefully, the Japanese ethos being pithily captured in their Three Alls policy: Kill All, Burn All, Loot All. Those foreigners who had not managed to flee were forced to wear armbands coded A for America, B for Britain, and so on. First their assets were seized and their movements restricted; then they were rounded up into prison camps.

In the French Concession, Mother Greenough's convent became an internment camp for the religious. The Japanese having commandeered most of the building, nuns from ten different congregations crowded into the one floor of one wing allotted them. The halls overflowed with boxes and shelves; laundry hung everywhere. Of course, it was no longer possible for students to board at school. Girls who did not have cars to shuttle them back and forth from home had to drop out. Still, class was held, in a single room; my mother continued to study.

One day, Mother Greenough asked, "Can your mother read?" and when my mother said not really, Mother Greenough shook her head.

"This cannot go on, nor shall it," she said. "Your life shall be entirely different."

"It is already," my mother said.

"It is just beginning."

Mother Greenough could not only speak, read, and write Chinese, she had a PhD. "Do you know what that is?" she asked.

My mother did. But she had never heard of a woman with one.

"You could have such a degree, if you were so disposed," said Mother Greenough.

"I don't think so," said my mother.

"Indeed, I would go so far as to say that you should have a doctorate one day," said Mother Greenough. "But first, your studies here. This is a difficult time."

"It is."

Mother Greenough glanced out the open window to where Mass was being conducted in a downpour of sun. People were kneeling, some of them on bits of cloth they had laid down, some of them directly on the hot, wet ground. Beggars from the street, having found their way into the yard, were being forcibly removed; the recalcitrant were being beaten.

"I don't think Christ meant for anyone to be beaten so that we could hold Mass," Mother Greenough said, standing up abruptly. "Excuse me." She added, as she left the room, "Christ gave us these hurdles. We welcome our test." She was gripping her heavy silver cross hard.

My mother studied and studied, proving more outstanding every year. She was soon wearing glasses, like my grandfather; people said she read so much, she was wearing her eyes out. But he was proud.

"You see," he told my grandmother. *"Look at how well girls do, if you send them to school. Her English is outstanding."*

"You are right," answered my grandmother.

"Better than her older brother's, and much, much better than her younger brother's. He is good with numbers, but in other areas he is hopeless."

"It's too bad she is a girl."

"It's a shame. But you are too pessimistic," he went on. *"Someone will marry her. We'll find someone."*

"Of course."

"A family like ours, after all."

"Family matters," she agreed.

"The problem is the war. Everyone is preoccupied."

"Who can be interested in matchmaking, with the barbarian shrimp everywhere?"

"Anyway, she is still in school."

"She is."

"She probably would not accept a match anyway."

"No, she probably wouldn't."

"These so-called modern girls are so independent. Full of new ideas."

"They are."

"Only time will tell what will become of them. For now, all they know is what they don't want. She doesn't want to become like one of her older brother's wives, for example."

Or like me, my grandmother wanted to say but didn't. Instead, she said, *"His wives squabble too much."*

"They don't know what else to do. They don't know how else to be. They are limited in their opportunities but, even more, they are limited in their thinking," my grandfather said.

"I suppose perhaps they are," she said. "You would have to say so. Perhaps, a bit."

Peace came to Europe before it came to Asia. The Germans laid down their arms, but the Japanese never would have, people said, had it not been for the atomic bomb. Such an unimaginably devastating thing! Peace did come of it—peace, finally. Peace at last. But—

No but, my mother breaks in now. If you ask me, the Japanese deserved it.

Ma! How can you say that? I say. Civilians died. Women. Children. Babies.

You think the Japanese wouldn't drop that bomb if they had it? They dropped fleas infected with bubonic plague on Ningbo. Do you think they cared who the fleas bit? That's why Chinese people cheered when the Americans dropped the bomb. We cheered! You should write that the Americans should have dropped the bomb earlier. That was their mistake. They should have dropped it as soon as they had it.

Well, I'm not going to write that, first of all because they did drop it as soon as they had it, I say. I'm just going to say that peace arrived.

If you ask me, the Japanese deserved it! she says again.

Peace arrived. No more soldiers, no more arrests, no more interrogations. Offices were open, temples, markets, schools. People strolled through the streets; they window-shopped and cheered street performers; they got their hair cut and their ears cleaned. My mother's half brother and his entourage returned from Shanghai to Qingdao. Their house was damaged, they reported, but repairs were underway. Even the roof would be restored soon; it was just a matter of how long the new shingles would take to arrive. As for my mother's house, how much larger it seemed with so few people in it! Maybe even, my mother thought, a bit empty.

"Time to give this place a proper cleaning!" my grandmother said.

The maids got out their mops.

Normalcy was returning. Over the long years of the war, though, my mother had managed not only to earn a high school diploma but to enroll in the college affiliated with her school. Now she was in her senior year and hatching a plan for herself. She picked a warm day when everyone was in a good mood to broach the topic. My grandparents were drinking tea on the veranda in their white wicker armchairs while just beyond them, the peonies drove the gardeners crazy. First the blooms had needed staking. Then it rained and just like that, they dropped all their petals! The gardeners swept, grumbling. My mother stood in a patch of shade and smiled. Graduation was just a few weeks away.

"I want to go to America," she announced.

"America?" said my grandparents.

Hadn't her half brother done it before the war? Hadn't he gone to that hard-to-pronounce place—that "University of Penn-syl-va-nia"—and come home with a master's degree in architecture? Of course, she knew what they were going to ask.

"You're going to ask with whom I am going to go, and then you're going to ask who will arrange things for me," she said.

"Exactly," said my grandfather. *"With whom will you go? And who will arrange things for you?"*

"I intend to go by myself and to arrange things by myself," she said. She did not say that Christ gave us hurdles. But she did say that she expected many hurdles in an alien culture, and that she both welcomed them and thought it her job to overcome them.

"I am not afraid," she said, and then said again, *"I can arrange things by myself."*

"You have never needed anyone's help," observed my grandmother, after a pause. She did not like the phrase *"by myself"* and knew that my mother used it knowing full well she did not like it. *"And, of course, you know everything already,"* my grandmother said—meaning that now that she was educated, my mother *mù zhōng wú rén*—did not really consider others.

Still, my mother plowed ahead. *"I can do it. My English is excellent. In fact, I am on my way to becoming a* bilinguist.*"* She translated the word "bilinguist." No reaction. Then she added, *"I want to get a PhD."*

"A PhD!"

"In educational psychology," she said. *"No one learns anything except for a reason. A reason that can be a secret even from yourself. I'm interested in what that may be."*

My grandfather removed his glasses with one hand. With the other, he rubbed the deep red dents between his eyes.

"I think I really ought to have one," she said. *"A PhD, that is."*

He gazed across the lawn at an empty white bench as if hoping someone who knew what to say would come sit down on it. Then he reseated his glasses. *"Do you."*

"I do," she said, adding reasonably, *"First I will have to earn a master's."*

My grandmother smoked.

"She is your daughter," she said coolly.

And after another moment, my grandfather agreed. *"She is."*

"It's too bad she is a girl."

He considered the bench some more, then observed, *"People are jealous of students educated abroad, you know. It can be a problem."*

"Especially if it is a woman educated abroad," my mother said.

"Exactly."

"It's what they call 'double jeopardy,' *isn't it?"* She knew her older half brother had taught my grandfather that phrase.

My grandfather laughed. *"In the end, your position will be pretty high but not as high as if you were a man. Enough to have some influence but not enough to make things happen."*

"And no one will marry me, either, right?"

He did not laugh again. Instead, he removed the cover from his teacup. He had some tea. He replaced the lid.

Finally, he said, *"Well, as the saying goes, If your heart is in it, you can break metal and split rocks."*

"Luckily it is easier to get a PhD than to split rocks," my mother said.

"Ah! So you realize that you cannot split rocks," my grandmother said.

"I cannot break metal, either," my mother said cheerfully.

It turned out that for now she could apply for a master's degree but not a doctorate. Still, in the fall of 1947 she prepared to board the USS *General M. C. Meigs* for America, by herself, her kingfisher phoenix pin in her suitcase.

At the dock, she stared with disbelief at the matchstick gangplank. Did it really lead to that mousehole in the side of the gargantuan ship? Both seemed wildly out of scale, but really it was just the boat that was crazily outsized. How could something so big move? Though huge ropes secured it to the wharf, it was hard to see how the thing could need securing. As for those enormous blue smokestacks, had someone told her that the clouds in the sky were born of the smoke rising from them, she would have believed it.

My grandfather followed her gaze—registering her awe, it seemed. But then he said in an odd voice, *"You are the right age. You speak English. Go."*

What with the noise, and the number of people boarding, and their variety—had these people really all been in Shanghai?—she could only half hear what he was saying. *The right age ... speak English.* What?

"Your brother's English isn't good, and everyone else is too young," he said. "You are luckier than you know. Even though you are a girl, still—you are the luckiest of the children, the luckiest of us all."

Could he see that she was getting cold feet? For indeed, she was asking herself—had she really decided to do this?

"Go," my grandmother echoed.

Go, yes. Of course she was going. She had made up her mind to go.

"Can't wait to get rid of me, can you," she said finally. She was tearing up, if only because it seemed that my grandfather was ... was he really crying? It was the first time in her life she had ever seen him cry. But he had taken his glasses off, and my grandmother was dabbing at her eyes with an embroidered handkerchief as well.

"You are my daughter, after all," she said. *"Pain in the neck that you are."*

"I'll write," my mother promised. *"And I'll be home soon. Don't worry."*

"Remember us," said my grandfather.

"Baba," she said. *"It's only a year."*

"Remember us," he said, still. *"Remember us."*

She boarded then, so as not to worry them anymore, although ascending the gangplank was petrifying. She had never been so high up in the sky, and the railing was so flimsy. She had to will her feet to move; there was too much air. But the moment she reached the solid floor of the ship, my grandfather's words came back to her. *Remember us.* She found her way to her cabin, then quickly returned to the deck, squeezing into a spot by the railing as the ship blew its horn—how loud it was, louder even than an air raid siren! Everyone was waving and hooting as tugboats began to nudge the boat, and it astonishingly began—slowly but perceptibly—to move. Then she waved, too, although she was already confused as to which of the tiny heads in the throngs of people on the wharf belonged to Mama and Baba. Squint as she might, they had become a blur; they were melting into a far-off mass that was becoming a line on the horizon. Was she really at sea? It seemed that she was—that she really had left. It was time to turn away, yet somehow she could not turn away.

Your brother's English isn't good, and everyone else is too young. You are luckier than you know.

The luckiest of the children. The luckiest of us all.

Was Baba worried something was going to happen?

And, indeed, after she'd boarded and the ship began inching away, my grandfather said, *"Maybe we should all go with her."*

"When we do not speak English and cannot eat Western food?" said my grandmother.

"The Communists," he said. *"The fighting in the northeast. They won in the spring. They won in the summer. Now they are winning again."*

"They're not going to win."

"That Lin Biao," my grandfather said. *"He started with a hundred rifles. Now he has hundreds of thousands of them—machine guns, too. Artillery. How should we not worry when he managed to*

get the Japanese in Manchuria to surrender it all to him, while all Chiang knows is how to beg—and he is not even a successful beggar. You watch and see. The U.S. is going to stop their handouts."

"The U.S. is not going to stop anything. But anyway, you are over seventy years old. You cannot go anywhere."

He had to agree. *"Too old,"* he said.

"And with so many people dependent on you. Would you take them with you?"

"You mean, a monk may run away but a temple cannot."

"When she was born, her placenta floated down the river," said my grandmother. "Now she is going to join it. It is her fate, not yours, and anyway only for a year, right? Her visa is only for a year."

My grandfather tore his eyes from the ship.

"You're right about Western food," he said. "We could not stand it. Steak! Salad!" He shook his head. "Our stomachs are too Chinese. And you are right that we do not speak English. Probably I am too old even to go to Hong Kong, forget about America." But then, though my grandmother kept walking, a maid on either side, he turned back toward the ship one more time.

"My favorite daughter, so smart and so brave." He stood and stood. "She will figure out a way to stay. I have confidence. She will realize that she has to, and she will. She will find a way."

"Are you still here?" said my grandmother, behind him.

He did not reply. Instead, he recited:

> *Goose, goose, goose!*
> *You lift your neck to the sky and sing—*
> *White down bobbing on the green water,*
> *Red feet pedaling the clear waves.*

Then he bowed his head at the ever-shrinking ship. *"Yīlù píngān,"* he said. *"Safe travels, little goose."* And finally, he turned toward my grandmother.

Well, the part about my father made me cry, my mother says now.

Do you think he knew he would never see you again? I say.

I think he knew but didn't want to tell me.
Because you might not go.
Because if I knew, how could I?
But you did go, I say.
Yes, she says. I didn't know and so I did. I went.

CHAPTER II

A Newcomer

The ocean! My mother had always known that the Huangpu River led to the ocean, but she had not really understood what it was— the endlessness of it, the up-and-down and up-and-down of it. And had she really embarked on this adventure by herself? There were other Chinese girls on board, but they were classmates off to America together; and so, while they were friendly enough to my mother, and curious about her, their friendliness was like a corridor ending in a closed door. As for why she was alone, she didn't know what to tell them. She had supposed she would have God with her, like Mother Greenough, but she couldn't say that and so said nothing. How surprised her mother would be to know that she could be shy! But she was. My mother was shy. She had vowed to be fearless like Mother Greenough and was indeed fearless about some things. Making small talk, though, was not one of them.

She spent most of her days bundled up in a quilted coat, watching the water. How calming the endlessly repeating, endlessly changing patterns churned up by the boat—how peaceful. And the waves! The swelling of the seawater was like a Buddhist chant that went on and on, through bombs and gunfire and screams and nightmares, never stopping. What did it know of war or peace or invasions or refugees, much less settlements that were suddenly no longer settlements, or foreigners who forced their way into

China one day only to desert it the next? What did it know of the Japanese or the Communists—those Communists! How she wished Karl Marx had never been born. She stewed while before her, the water rose and sank and rose and sank. The water had no such wishes. It shone green, then gray. It glistened, then darkened, glistened, then darkened.

She loved to watch the sun on the water, to see the path it made every morning, as if readying itself to roll toward you. And she loved how even after it sank in the evening, it lit the sky as if to say, *Remember me, remember me.* She loved the moon, too—the waxing, waning moon, so delicately reflective of ache and yearning and all things complicated; the sun might give you life, but the moon read your heart. And both by day and by night, how perfectly matched the sky and ocean seemed, each a vast, incomprehensible thing, destined to meet in the perfect line that was the horizon—an expanse above, an expanse below. Yet how different they were, actually—the ocean full of mystery but a bounded thing, with a floor, while the sky opened and opened onto a whole unearthly realm. Where did it end? Did it have an end? Would humans ever know if it did? Was there a heaven? And how often did humans do this, pair things that were no pair at all? How rarely had she had time to wonder these things, she realized now—and maybe that was a mistake, too, not to make time?

She sent the same postcard to everyone in her family, as it was the only one for sale. It featured the USS *General M. C. Meigs* crossing under a bridge some other passengers thought must be the Golden Gate Bridge in San Francisco, America, although they weren't sure and she wasn't either. It was hard to tell in a black-and-white photo whether the bridge was golden. In any event, to the older of her sisters and her two brothers, she wrote:

> *I thought we were used to foreign food. But here it is served in compartments, with one food per compartment as if it could afford a private room. No roommates for the green beans! This is definitely not the Chinese way of eating.*

To her baby sister, she wrote:

The ocean is blue. Did you know that? It has many kinds of fish. Sometimes we can see fins sticking out from the water. And sometimes the fish jump! It looks like fun to be a fish.

To her parents, she wrote:

I study every day, and though the food is quite strange and I am sometimes a bit seasick, you don't have to worry. I am not losing weight. I hope you stay healthy and that all is peaceful. Out here on the ocean it is not clear why people have to fight and have wars. What is the matter with us? Or do fish fight, too? Maybe they fight underwater where we can't see them—the swordfish stabbing other fish like the Japanese.

And to Mother Greenough, she wrote (in English, of course):

Of course, everything is quite strange. And I am by myself, as you know. But how can I be afraid when I have God looking after me?

How confident she sounded. Yet even as she wrote the words, my mother wondered if God really was looking after her the way that He might. After all, unlike her namesake, Saint Agnes, who had died rather than marry a human, my mother had refused to marry God. So who knew what He had in mind for her now? Had she forgone His protection? And would He have been a help in any case when it came to the things that concerned her?

She was finding here on the ship that she was afraid of many more things than she'd ever imagined. It wasn't just small talk. She was also afraid of the sun. In China, she had spent little time outdoors; she was almost always in a building or a car. Now she had to maintain her vigilance, lest her skin darken like a peasant's. It was too windy on deck for an umbrella, but she kept a constant eye out for shade and plotted all her movements to stay in it. And how afraid she was of animals jumping on her! Though her family had kept dogs, Bao-bao and Zhen-zhen were trained, not only to go *xūxū* in the toilet but not to jump on people. They wore bows in their fur; they knew how to behave. Why did her fellow passengers bring their dogs on board, and why were they allowed to jump on people?

Those were not her only fears. There was also her age. She did not realize this until, after two weeks of sailing, the boat had finally reached America and she had packed her things back up—until she had bravely walked back down the matchstick gangplank, even scarier to descend than it had been to ascend. America! Its very ground felt different from China's—wobblier, although—wait—maybe this was *mal de débarquement*? Something Mother Greenough had warned her about. She was glad to have a name for this rubberiness in her legs.

What, though, to call the fear of being considered old that suddenly gripped her as she stood filling out forms in San Francisco? She had heard that you could change not only your first name but also your last if you became a U.S. citizen—such a strange idea. Did Americans not care about carrying on their family name? As for whether that gave people the idea that they could change their age on the forms, as she had heard people did—quite possibly, especially as all the East-West confusion about age made it easy.

Many Chinese people did not pay too much attention to birthdays to begin with, my mother says now. In many places, everyone just turned a year older at New Year's, all at the same time. And in China when they count, they include your year in the womb.

They weren't like Americans, who strangely start with birth, I say.

Also China was using three calendars at once, she says. We used the traditional Chinese lunar calendar but also the Western Gregorian calendar and the Republic of China calendar, too. The Republic of China calendar was solar like the Gregorian calendar, except that what Westerners called 1912 we called year one.

Because that was the year of the founding of the Republic of China, right? I say. And complicating things yet more,

most American officials could not read even one Chinese character.

Not even the character for "one," which was one stroke, or the character for "two," which was two strokes, she laughs. They were worse than you!

If you were entering the U.S. on a quota visa, the officials were tough. But if you were entering on a non-quota visa, they were lax. The trickiest part about changing her age was that my mother would have to change her Chinese zodiac sign as well. Though born a mouse, she would have to tell anyone who asked—and Chinese people would ask—that she was a cow, which would be lying. God would know. She would have to confess it in confession. Even as she filled out her form, her pen hovered midair, weirdly weighty; she could see its shadow on the page, wavering as if it, too, had *mal de débarquement*.

Then she heard her mother's voice—*No one will ever marry you*—and though my mother had always said she did not care, and though the nuns who had taught her weren't married and neither was Mother Greenough, she wrote neatly, in Arabic numerals, next to "year of birth" not 1924 but 1925. And just like that, she was a year younger. America! She was Agnes Shu-hsin Loo, age twenty-two, born in the year of the cow, 1925. As for how she was going to explain this when she went back to Shanghai, in a flash she decided: she wasn't. She wasn't going to have to explain it because she wasn't going back. She wasn't going back to her mother, she wasn't going back to *It's too bad she's a girl,* she wasn't going back to *You have to know how to talk.* She wasn't going to be trapped within four walls, with the whole world outside. No. She was going to apply for a PhD program and stay.

I was free, she says now. I was free!
I laugh with her.
I thought I was free.

First she had to make it to friends of her family in Chicago. Having never before pored over a train schedule, bought a ticket, located a track, or maneuvered a heavy suitcase onto a train, she felt accomplished when she had managed to do these things. And how marvelous the train!—a modern, golden "streamliner" called the *City of San Francisco*. She had a luxurious sleeper compartment and, by a stroke of luck, no bunkmate.

But she could not sleep. This was not like crossing the ocean. Fascinated as she had been by the water and the waves and the strangeness of that journey, the ocean scenery did not change every minute, while this—! The train did frustratingly bore through miles of dark tunnels. But the mountains, when they suddenly appeared—so bright, so tall, so massive and extensive! They were like nothing she could ever have imagined, not so much snowcapped as snowswept; pleats of snow were all that could cling to the sheer rock. And what a name the mountain range had—the "Sierra Nevadas." She had to ask the waiter in the dining car to repeat it twice to get it right. Then she wrote it down. Sierra Nevadas. It was helpful that "Nevada" was also the name of a state they were crossing; that left just "Utah," "Wyoming," "Nebraska," "Iowa," and "Illinois" to learn.

She would not have thought anything could be more impressive than these Sierra Nevadas. But then came a range Americans called the "Rockies"—short for the "Rocky Mountains"—which were even craggier and grander and more unimaginably huge, especially when the train snaked through canyons with cliffs rising on either side. How she would have loved to compare them to the Himalayas, which she had never seen or even thought to want to see before this but wanted to see now. And then, abruptly, the mountains ceased; the land was flat as a billiard table. Here and there the train stopped in a city or passed through a mining town. But mostly the land seemed like a kind of waterless ocean, vast and motionless and empty.

This journey did not take anywhere near as long as crossing the Pacific Ocean. It did go on for thirty-nine and a half hours, though—too long to go without sleep. By the time she arrived in Chicago, her most coherent thoughts centered on the dining car menu: Boiled Beef Tongue with Spinach. Poached Eggs on Buttered Rice. Fillet of Sole with Tartar Sauce. What was "Clam Nectar"? Were "Ripe Olives and Chilled Celery Hearts" enough for dinner? She was in a kind of stupor as she stepped off the train onto the platform and unprepared to be met immediately with wind. But the wind! It was an American wind, of course, yet somehow just what she'd always imagined the wind in north China to be—a cold, barbarian, slicing wind that froze her face and stiffened her knees. Someone helped her with her bag—a stranger with a mustache like water buffalo horns—but thank goodness, she made it down the train steps all right, and was reunited with her suitcase (the stranger not having walked off with it, as she'd feared). And here were the Pings!

Bundled up as they were, they were still easy to recognize, being the only Chinese people at the station. And of course, they recognized her just as easily. How strange it was to stick out the way they did, but how convenient, too. The Pings were wearing fur hats quite unlike the winter hats people wore in Shanghai—hats that always managed to look elegant and weightless. Uncle's she recognized from magazines as military in style, with an upturned fur visor and hanging earflaps—why did she think it made of muskrat?—while Auntie's looked as if a wild woodland animal had curled up for a nap on her head. How familiar the Pings sounded, though!—their voices immediately evoking a Shanghai garden party as they called, *"Loo Shu-hsin! Loo Shu-hsin! Welcome, welcome!"*

She was surprised at how happy she was to speak Shanghainese to the Pings, and to have them so easily understand every word—she had not even realized what a strain it had been, speaking English day in and day out, all that new vocabulary hurtling at her nonstop. What a relief, too, that they knew her parents, knew her family, knew their whole circle. It was a relief even to be chided first thing—*No hat? No boots?* How Shanghainese their fussing felt—their utter astonishment at her hatlessness and bootlessness (though they knew full well that she had come from California, where no one needed hats and boots). And the way they felt they had to introduce this place to her, to explain to her what was this "Chicago"—there was a bit of overkill in it, a bit of *shājī yòng niúdāo,* of bludgeoning a chicken, about it—but it was a warm bludgeoning. A familiar bludgeoning.

"This place is very cold!" Uncle told her. "Extremely cold! There is a lot of wind! A lot of snow!"

"Because of the lake!" Auntie said. "You will see. It is called 'Lake

Michigan.' *The biggest lake you ever saw, and very rough! Very, very rough!"*

"It is completely not like Chinese lakes. This lake is like the ocean, wild!"

"That is why there is so much wind and snow!"

"A lot of wind! A lot of snow!"

"The snow is not like Shanghai snow, either! Shanghai snow is gentle. This snow will bite your face if you let it!"

They were both shouting to be heard over the noise of the train and the crowds, and indeed the snow was everywhere, not pure and white as it had seemed from the train but granular and sooty up close—old snow, though it was only November, the start of winter. With Auntie's help, my mother navigated the icy path to the car in her high heels. Auntie held her arm tight under the elbow, as if Auntie were the younger person and my mother the elder one, in need of support. Her glasses slipped halfway down her nose; she could hardly see.

"Careful!" Auntie told her. *"Be careful!"*

My mother's heels were the best quality shoes, imported from Italy, the likes of which no one had seen in Shanghai all during the war. Handmade of supple leather, they had delicate straps and leather-covered buttons but soles so thin, she might as well have been walking barefoot. Auntie and Uncle, meanwhile, were wearing matching brown expedition boots. "Duck boots," she later learned they were called, and she could see then how they resembled a duck's body and neck. They were imported from Maine and apparently went with double-breasted coats and heavy woolen scarves, one of which Auntie immediately unwound from around her own neck and placed around my mother's. It was thick as an oxen yoke but still warm—heavenly. She was grateful to Uncle that he took her bag; such was his hurry to get her into the car that he did not take the time to flag down a porter but managed her suitcase himself, as if he did this all the time—which maybe he did? Not having any servants? My mother tried to imagine one of her brothers picking up a suitcase.

Impossible! she says now.
You were pretty privileged, I say.

Spoiled rotten, she agrees. And how we would have loved to stay that way!

The Pings' car was smaller than the cars she was used to and did not sparkle; its hubcaps especially, such a source of pride for the servants back home, were, like the snow, filigreed with dirt. As she settled in the back seat, my mother's glasses fogged up; she found a handkerchief in her purse and wiped them. Better. Could the first thing she spotted in Chicago really be a billboard reading "Drink Coca-Cola"? She smiled to see the familiar red-and-white logo with its scarf-like script—how she'd always loved those loop-de-loops—and thought she would, she absolutely would drink lots of Coca-Cola here. She would drink it every day! And was Uncle really driving the car himself? He chatted as he drove, something the chauffeurs in Shanghai never did. No pristine white cotton gloves for him, either. The gloves confidently spinning the wheel were well-creased leather.

And all this was typical of Americans, she soon came to understand. Not only did they do everything themselves—their own driving, their own cooking, their own repairing and sewing and gardening—they often did two things at once. Just as they chatted while they drove, they ate while riding the bus and cooked while talking on the telephone. And they did it fast! Even compared to rush-rush Shanghai, everything here was *fēngfēng huǒhuǒ*—wind wind fire fire! Uncle explained that in America, it wasn't enough to be diligent and hardworking. People had to be something called "productive."

"Productive." My mother repeated the new vocabulary word to herself. "Productive."

America was full of "skyscrapers" that really did scrape the very sky, but it was also full of something called "parking lots" that she thought should really be called "parking seas" because that's what they were—seas of cars.

"Careful!" said Auntie one more time as they headed up the walkway of the Pings' house. But it was too late. My mother had slipped on a patch of ice and scraped her cheek on a rosebush.

"Here. Let me help you." The Pings' son, George, ran out of the house without a coat. A warm, lively young man, not tall but not short, George was wearing a blue sweatshirt that read "Chicago Cubs" in red. He had bright eyes and dark bird-wing eyebrows, and was, she happened to already know (from his parents, who else?), getting a PhD in mechanical engineering. But even more striking was his accent. Since arriving in America, my mother had noticed that Americans spoke differently than did the nuns at her school—indeed, than did most English-speakers in Shanghai. But she had not met one who looked completely Chinese.

She put her hand up to her face and felt nothing. Her glove came away with blood, though—a shock. Back when her brother used to hit her, she had bruised; and of course she knew that if you scraped yourself, you could bleed. She had never in fact scraped herself before, however, and aside from her menstrual flow, had never seen her own blood.

"Here," George said again.

It wasn't all he said, over the next few days. But "here" was what she remembered best—that ringingly clear "r," which seemed to somehow go with the unabashed, uncomplicated, wholly American way he held out his hand, pulling her to her feet as if he did this all the time—as if he certainly did not expect a servant to help. Of course, she also remembered her mortification. To have worn the wrong shoes, to have fallen immediately, to have had a man touch her and, worst of all, to have reacted with such embarrassment that she could not even thank him . . . Had she really let him grasp her hand, pressing his palm to hers? Or was it her imagination that she had felt the warmth of his bare hands through her thin knit gloves? And, after a long moment, had she really let go as if his help were not even worth mentioning, only to have him wink at her?

Here she had barely arrived in America, and already someone had winked at her! How glad she was to have been prepared for this by Mother Greenough. What was it she had said? A wink is like a little note you are sending, except that you already know the other person's answer. And if you wink, it's preapproved.

As for whether he had indeed known her answer, he had. He had read her heart, and he had approved of its answer. Which was exactly why, just as she had said nothing to acknowledge his helping hand, she did nothing to acknowledge his wink, either—studiously ignoring it, although later, when Auntie and Uncle brought her to a store to buy winter boots, and George did not come—but why should he come?—she wondered if she had made a mistake. She particularly wondered this when he took the time to tell her all the things she should do in America. She had wanted to see the famous Chicago stockyards; people said live cows entered one end of the processing line and emerged from the other in cans. But he said, No! Forget the stockyards! The thing to do was to get out, as soon as it warmed up, to a baseball game. He told her all about Wrigley Field and the Chicago Cubs and the National League and the pennant and the Curse of the Billy Goat, but then just when she was getting it, or some of it, he suddenly had to go—what was a "burst pipe"?—and left without saying goodbye. Had he really just disappeared? And was that her fault? Every time she walked by his empty room, she wondered. Should she have winked back? Or smiled? Or done anything else besides freeze?

When Uncle and Auntie were out one day, she snuck into George's room and looked around. His room was very different than his sister Alicia's room, in which my mother was staying. Since the Pings had just two children, as it seemed many American families did, the kids not only had their own rooms, but in Alicia's case, an amazing amount of stuff. Her walls were full of pictures, her drawers were full of clothes, her bed was full of pillows. Her dresser was full of mementos. There was scarcely room for my mother's suitcase. George's room, though smaller, was more restrained. He had a few books; a violin; a baseball mitt. His sunlit desk was orderly. On it sat a brown leather blotter and a blue-and-red Chicago Cubs pencil cup, complete with a fountain pen, also blue with a red C. She would not have admitted to herself that she was looking for anything in particular. When she saw pictures of his family on his desk and bureau but no girlfriend, though, she vowed: if anyone ever winked at her again, she would wink back— and especially, of course, if it was George. And if someone ever again helped her up that way, with a bare, warm hand, she would heartily return his squeeze. She would be American!

She tried to impress Uncle and Auntie, hoping that they would think her a match for their son. Perhaps they would then arrange for him and her to meet again; certainly even Chinese parents who lived in America remained given to that sort of thing—if not out-and-out matchmaking, then a bit of discreet encouraging. Maybe in the spring? She and George would go to a baseball game at whatever that stadium was called. Wiggley? They would root for the Cubs. She would wear a blue dress and carry a red purse. They would eat hot dogs and hold hands.

In the meanwhile—could there really be a country wholly untouched by the war? America had slums. But where were the acres of rubble? Where were the forests of bamboo scaffolding? Where were the emaciated laborers with their quick short steps and bent brown backs, where were their baskets full of debris and their shoulder poles bowed to the breaking point? Where were the bite-pocked children and the dilapidated shanties? Chicagoans did not think theirs a rich city. But to my mother it was a fairy-tale city where bombs had never fallen and tanks had never rolled, and where even poor people had coats and shirts and shoes.

How many people could read in America! It wasn't a minority who could read; it was a minority who couldn't. And how few people there were overall, almost none of them Chinese. Instead, there were white people in some places, and in other places, Black people, as entirely separate as if one were land and the other sea. She was used to white people from her life in Shanghai. *Wàiguórén,* she still called them—foreigners—although they of course weren't foreigners here in their own country. It was only in her mind that they remained foreigners—foreigners who were continually asking her if she spoke English and who were surprised if she said yes, while foreigners back in Shanghai were not at all surprised. As for the Black people, they were to her more foreign than the foreigners. She tried not to stare, but how they stared at her. "Is she a child or a grown-up?" a child asked her mother. Another person asked her friend if my mother didn't look just like a doll. "A China doll!" the person's friend said, and laughed—to which my mother laughed, too, though she couldn't have said why and could see that it startled them; then they laughed back. It was American to smile and laugh with strangers, it seemed. Uncle and Auntie said she would get used to it, adding that George probably knew why; George knew everything. They didn't say they'd ask him to explain it to her, though. Graduate school in America was serious business. No one should trouble him.

She wrote to her family:

The roads are only for cars. There are no rickshaws here, and so of course no rickshaw pullers. There are carts and wheelbarrows, but they are not on the road, so the cars can go much faster than they do in Shanghai. Not even the poorest people pull carts, only animals do, and wheelbarrows are for loads, not people. There are no laborers with shoulder poles—no rice paddies, either. Instead, the countryside has fields of corn and wheat that the farmers plow with tractors. I did not see even one water buffalo—maybe it is too cold for them here. All they have are cows, which no one rides and which do not pull anything. They are for meat and for milk. People here drink milk the way we drink tea, especially children. I think that is why they are so tall. (They really are like skyscrapers!)

But in the city there are a lot of people living on the street, and that is a surprise. They do not have shanties, only blankets, and many of them do not have families, I don't know why. They huddle in the doorways of buildings because it is so cold. Auntie calls them "bums" and says they can't work because they drink, but Uncle says they drink to stay warm. America is a rich country in some ways. There is indoor plumbing everywhere, and electricity, too. And even small houses sometimes occupy large plots of land—you would be amazed. American lawns are so big, the lawn mowers have engines. And many, many people have cars! Yet not everybody in America is rich—far from it.

I hope you will not conclude from this description that I am gallivanting around. Quite the contrary, I have been working hard on my graduate school application. Meaning that yes, I am applying to stay on past a master's for the PhD program, as I told you I might. I've long set my sights on a PhD, as you know, and so am "throwing my hat into the ring," as they say here.

Did her family realize that a PhD program was a route to a so-called green card and that a green card meant you could stay and work in the U.S. indefinitely? She didn't go into it.

Let's see what happens. The application is no joke! It is long and hard, and I will have to type it, too.

Of course, this is nothing compared to the worry you must feel. I hope the Communists can be stopped. The newspaper here says that their winter offensive has been all too successful. I hope the reporters are exaggerating.

Here we have coffee every morning, as well as toast with butter and jam. Uncle and Auntie are very kind and make it for me every day. If you write to Older Brother, tell him that it always reminds me of the Western breakfasts he used to make for me when I was little, right after he came back from the States. He used to buy the bread from the French bakery, then "toast" it in a pan with imported butter, I remember. (Really it was "fried" but never mind. It was delicious.) Tell him that here Americans have a machine called a "toaster." Auntie says that they are very popular. When the toast is toasting, it smells so good, and when it is ready, it pops up automatically. You have to be careful taking it out because the toast is very hot, but it tastes wonderful. And yet I would rather have Older Brother's "fried" version all the same.

She looked at her words. If only they could all go back to that time! And sure as she had been that she wanted to leave Shanghai and never come back, now she just wished she hadn't written about Older Brother, or about the danger her family faced. How much easier it had been to forget it all before she wrote it—imagining it, ironically, having made it more real.

Is our family lucky to be rich, or unlucky? Here I can see that because Auntie and Uncle were far less rich, they did not have the protection of the International Settlement. But neither did they have a huge household to support. So they both had to and could move a long time ago. That wasn't easy. But now, though they miss Chinese food and Chinese people, they mostly think about their children and their old age, and that's all. How I wish you had that kind of peace.

Indeed. She heard her father's voice. *You are the right age. You speak English. You are luckier than you know.* And, *Go.* In all her life, she had never heard her father tell someone to leave, only to stay, and she had assumed he had only said that because he was trying to keep himself from telling her, *Stay.* But now it was dawning on her that he had meant it—that he really had meant, *Go*—and not just because no one was going to marry her in China.

No more letter-writing. She set to work on her school application instead, starting with the short-answer questions. Why was she applying? To earn a degree, she wanted to say.

Or really, to get away, she says now. Originally from my family but now from China, too. From everything.
But you couldn't say that, I say.
No. Not even to myself. I couldn't say it even to myself.

As for "What is your interest in education?" she was stuck at first. But then suddenly she knew her answer:

No one learns anything except for a reason, a reason that can be a secret even from yourself. I'm interested in discovering what that may be—in understanding what motivates students.

The next day, she expressed concern about the grammatical correctness of her answer, only to have the Pings offer to look at it for her. Though my mother had never shown even a short essay to anyone but a teacher, Auntie said she might be able to help with the English, and Uncle said parents in America often looked at their children's work. Reluctantly, my mother said okay.

"'A secret even from yourself'? *This makes no sense.*" Sitting at the kitchen table, Auntie was wearing a zip-up housecoat, matted slippers, and hair curlers as she squinted through her reading glasses. She marked the sentence with a red X. Then she marked another sentence, and another.

My mother nodded politely. She thanked Auntie for her help. Then she went to her room and cried. She hadn't cried when she left China; she hadn't cried on the long, lonely ship ride; she hadn't cried as she wrote to her family. She hadn't cried at the cruelty of the Japanese occupation, or at the abandonment of the International Settlement. She hadn't cried at the injustice of her brother being put ahead of her, all her life, at every turn. But now at this nothing, she cried as if she were a little girl and Nai-ma had been taken from her all over again. In the morning, she put Xs through Auntie's Xs. What would Mother Greenough have thought of her, crying like that? She composed some of her other answers and, though Auntie asked about them, declined to show them to her.

Instead, she borrowed the Pings' typewriter and a book called *Teach Yourself to Type.* Using the diagrams, she positioned her fingers over the keys and practiced:

> The quick brown fox jumps over the lazy dog.
> The quick brown fox jumps over the lazy dog.
> The quick brown fox jumps over the lazy dog.
> The quick brown fox jumps over the lazy dog.

Sometimes she changed the words, for fun.

> The brick brown fox tripped over the lazy hog.
> The thick black ox slipped in the saucy bog.
> The slick green otter flipped over the mossy log.

She made a lot of mistakes and wasted a lot of paper. But after practicing diligently for three days, she could type well enough to fill in the essay portion of the application form. The applicant information section of the form she filled in by hand, though her hand cramped; letters were so much harder to write than characters. And though it made her nervous, she used a fountain pen. But finally—there. She was happy when all was dry and done. Auntie Ping again offered to look her work over, but my mother again declined—which hurt Auntie's feelings, she could see. Still, she held firm. She brought her application to the post office and, checking the address on the manila envelope for misspellings one last time, mailed it.

She knew it would take months to hear back from the school but, all the same, found it hard to wait. What if she was rejected? She would not think about it, could not think about it, and yet thought about it all the time. Maybe it was just the bitter Chicago weather. (Auntie said that Chicago was called the Windy City, and though Uncle said it wasn't actually because of the wind, my mother thought, How could it not be?) Although maybe it was Auntie, with her endless stories of disaster, that made my mother dwell on bad possibilities? One day, it would be a Nationalist general's sick mistress, left behind enemy lines to fend for herself. *"She kept her jewelry in a belt around her waist. And piece by piece, she used it to pay peasants to take care of her until she had nothing left,"* said Auntie. Next, it would be an old woman in America, found frozen in her apartment. *"Later, they found out she had five children. She supported them all. But that's how American children are, you know. They stay if they need you. If they don't, they leave."* Auntie had not begun to live through what my mother's family had lived through, yet she seemed more morbid in her thinking than anyone my mother knew. Was it just her, or was it something about America? And was it infectious? By day, my mother was full of can-do. By night, though, the possibility of failure somehow stood facing her, while success presented its back.

She wished her family wrote more letters, especially her father. Instead, though she wrote dutifully, addressing them all, her mother seemed to have taken on the role of chief respondent—dictating, it seemed, through my mother's brother, and mostly reporting inconsequential things. The weather was very cold. The fashions were changing so fast, no one could keep up. And how indecent the side slits of some of these dresses! They had a new Chinese cook, also from Yangzhou, just like the old one. Her little sister's English and French were coming along so well, she could translate not only back and forth from Chinese but directly from English to French and back again, skipping Chinese altogether. But every now and then, her mother would add something like:

> *At least neighbor stood with neighbor against the Japanese. With the Communists, it is neighbor against neighbor. The fighting continues up north, but that is not the only battle. There are underground Communists all over the city, fighting invisibly. Maybe it is just crazy talk, you know how some people like to spread rumors. But a lot of people say the Communists are everywhere now, even in your own house. You have to worry about the workers, especially the servants—about the ideas they might be getting. You have to be careful what you say.*

Added her younger sisters at the bottom:

> *You are so lucky to be in America. You don't have to worry!*

And my mother was indeed lucky to be more worried about whether she should have winked back at George Ping than about what might be going on with the workers and servants. But perhaps she was just catching the worry habit from Auntie, for she did worry about the situation in China—about her father, especially. If only he had never become a banker! If only he had remained the principal of a school in Wuzhen, and never come to Shanghai! For what a target a banker was bound to be, and his whole family, too—especially, it turned out, because of certain servants.

Said the next letter, in between the reports about cousins and babies and everyone's health:

> *You know who became a Communist? Your old nursemaid.*

My mother read the lines over and over. Nai-ma? Nai-ma a Communist? It couldn't be. And how did they even know? Were they in touch with her? The letter went on:

> *She always had a terrible attitude, so we weren't surprised. Ours wasn't the first job she was fired from, as you know. She had been fired many times. Of course she would become a Communist. She is just the kind of person they are looking for, rotten to the core. Now we are trying to figure out who else might turn against us—who else among the servants she has recruited. They hold meetings in the kitchen, it seems. It is their clubhouse. Did you know her husband was working there as our cook?*

Suddenly my mother pictured the four-fingered cook with the red, bulging eyes. She wrote back helplessly:

> *Are you sure this is true? That the servants are against us? Against our family?*

She wanted to ask, *Are you sure it isn't just that you never liked Nai-ma?* But she didn't dare. She wrote instead:

> *Are you sure they are not just against landowners generally? And do you think the Communists might really take over the country? How can the Nationalists lose when they have so many more soldiers than the Communists?*

She wished she could hear the answer from her father, her clear-sighted father. Her mother, though, replied:

> *Yes, we are sure. Your nursemaid was the ringleader. What a troublemaker. Not only was she organizing our servants, it turns out that she was scraping our used opium pipes and selling the dregs—the "faucet dregs," as they call them. Her husband was also boiling these with water and selling the "faucet water." We were certainly right to fire her when we did. Good riddance.*

How could Nai-ma have recruited other servants if she had been fired? Was it through her husband? Or had she been hanging around the house? Was that how she had left the kingfisher phoenix pin in my mother's quilt? And could she have been in touch with my mother had she wanted to? Nai-ma couldn't be *rotten to the core*—my mother was sure of it. Or was she? What did she know? The girl who knew Nai-ma was a child.

Trying not to brood, she helped Auntie and Uncle around the house. They could of course afford a maid, Auntie said, but believed cleaning to be good exercise. Good exercise? In China, old people talked about taking it easy. *Mànmàn zǒu,* they said—go slowly. They believed in resting whenever possible. Uncle, meanwhile, thought snow shoveling good for his health. Moving your body and breathing fresh air made you fierce, he said. That wasn't for women, of course. But apparently, it was likewise good for Auntie's health to do housework—not to be waited upon but to be active. My mother gamely tried to help and did learn, not just to make toast but to make both coffee and tea. She learned how to clear the table as well and—her specialty—to wash and dry the dishes. She was amazed by the liquid dish soap. All those bubbles! And she would have helped cook had Auntie allowed her to. But Auntie preferred to cook alone.

"Cooking takes concentration," Auntie said. *"Americans grow up cooking, just as they grow up swimming and hitting baseballs and who knows what else. Also, their mothers teach them. So cooking is easy for them. But for us there's a lot to figure out."*

It didn't quite make sense, but my mother assumed the problem to be Auntie until she overheard Auntie on the phone one day. *"There's no point trying to teach her,"* Auntie complained—talking loudly, as she always did, as if not sure the person on the other end could hear her. *"It's more trouble than it's worth."* As for the problem, it wasn't even that my mother was a girl with too much to say, or a smart girl who should have been a boy. It was that she was a real *dà xiǎojiě*—a haughty rich girl completely unprepared for real life. *"All she knows is how to spend money,"* Auntie said. This last idea was reinforced, it seemed, every time my mother took the Pings out to eat. She had done this as often as she could to repay them for their hospitality, but perhaps she had only made them feel poor?

In short, it wasn't just the short essay answers she'd given on her application that received a red X from Auntie; it was she herself, Agnes Loo. She could feel it written on her. Left stroke, right stroke, red X, wrong. If my mother was hoping the Pings would think her a mate who could help George soar, they did not. What did it matter here who her family was in China? Here in America she was a useless Chinese girl who would need to be introduced to everything and everyone, not someone who could make introductions for George. Who did she know? No one.

She wasn't unwelcome in the Pings' house. With George and Alicia gone, Uncle and Auntie found the house too big—something no one ever complained about in China, but my mother could see the problem. It wasn't just the house. Old age in America was lonely; that was why people had pets. Yes, her family had had Bao-bao and Zhen-zhen, but they were for entertainment, not companionship. And the thought that her parents would have taken care of the animals themselves—! Mount Tai would fall into the sea before they put food in a dog dish. Yet that was how lonely Americans were, that they would not only feed their dogs but walk them every day, rain or shine. My mother could certainly understand how the Pings might feel unprepared to do that, even if it was "good exercise." Auntie said the dogs dislocated people's shoulders; they made people slip and fall. At the same time, she told endless loyal dog stories. Dogs who sat outside hospitals, waiting for their owners to reemerge. Dogs who got help for their owners when they were knocked unconscious. Dogs who would not leave their owners' graves after their owners died. Anyway, Uncle would interrupt, it was good that, at least for now, they had my mother to keep them company. And Auntie would agree.

So I was better than a dog, my mother says, if only because I did not have to be walked.
I laugh.

The Pings insisted that my mother could stay for as long as she liked. And when she at last heard that she'd been accepted to her program, and set a date to leave for school, they insisted that they were sorry. They said she could come back anytime. She promised she would keep in touch. But when she overheard them talking to George on the phone, she noticed that they told him to come home the day after she had said she would leave; and when she had to push her date back a week, they postponed his return date as well.

My mother did not think she would miss the Pings. New York, though, was even lonelier than Chicago. She joined some Chinese roommates with an extra room to rent, but like the girls she'd met on the ship, these girls were already friends. They were from Shandong province besides, meaning that they not only spoke a different dialect than she but liked different food, including lamb, which my mother thought had a funny smell and never ate. And yet ironically, the person in New York who made my mother feel the loneliest was Georgiana Huang, whose family had known her family back in Shanghai, and whom she had known in school.

Georgiana had been a year behind her and—talk about a *dà xiǎojiě*—had never seemed concerned about anything but enjoying herself. Her father was a Japanese stooge, people said, a collaborator, a turncoat—a traitor. In Shanghai, my mother had felt sorry for her. Was it right to snub Georgiana for her father's decisions, after all? Georgiana was unapologetic, it was true, but who knew how she really felt inside. Inside, she could not really have supported the Japanese; no Chinese could. That's what my mother believed. Plus, the Japanese had made it very hard for people to resist them. To avoid having to cooperate with them, her father had at one point been forced to check into a hospital, pretending to be sick. It was a dangerous strategy; had he been betrayed, he would have been killed. But he had had no other way of avoiding collaboration.

And so, my mother had shared her candy with Georgiana, the way she sometimes had with younger girls generally, especially the scholarship girls. Georgiana did not need treats. But my mother had offered her some anyway because though the nuns told the girls to be compassionate, most were not. Every weekend, Georgiana left with her head held high and fresh lipstick on her mouth, as if to flaunt her access to cosmetics; she slipped into a beautiful blue Buick with bulletproof glass. But she slunk in as quickly as she could, so the other girls could not see that her driver was Japanese.

Here in New York she had nothing to hide; here she was simply rich. When the Japanese were defeated, her family had promptly brought their wealth into exile. And that was not the only way in which they had prepared for a move: through connections, they had arranged for Georgiana to apply to a PhD program while still in China. Not that she was particularly interested in an advanced degree, but they had heard that she could get a green card this way; and, of course, her family knew all about green cards and more. Their situation having been clearer than my mother's, their course of action had been, too. And now, sitting pretty, Georgiana lived it up. The other Chinese students were mostly from other cities. Who knew what her father had done?

I was the only one, my mother says now.
Lucky you, I say.
In America, Georgiana was free.

My mother, in contrast, was beginning, for the first time in her life, to worry about money. Her parents were not sending funds; perhaps they did not realize that though my mother had gotten a tuition scholarship, she still had to cover her living expenses? That she reflexively told them not to worry was probably no help. And they were under pressure, as she understood. She did not know the details but guessed the pressure to be tremendous—hence her father's silence. As for whether Georgiana might understand my mother's situation and, remembering her kindness, now return it, quite the contrary. Georgiana hung out with the rich student set and, perhaps to keep her secrets hidden, snubbed my mother.

Those were not the only hard things, either. For all that my mother had always prided herself on her English and did think it improving "by leaps and bounds," as she'd learned to say, graduate school involved lists and lists of new vocabulary and, worse, lectures. In all her years of study in China, my mother had never attended a lecture in English. Now she found herself listening to thirty, forty, forty-five straight minutes of English, English, English. How did people do it? To her mortification, she sometimes found herself nodding off in a way that only terrible students did. Outstanding students never fell asleep. Yet there she was, unable to keep her eyes open, especially after lunch, and especially in Professor Gray's class.

Professor Gray. Professor Gray dressed in gray and spoke in gray. Moreover, he was gray. He had gray eyebrows that jutted out over his sunken eyes; his skin was gray. Even his subject matter was gray. His Theories and Methods class entailed so thorough an examination of failed educational approaches that the students could not agree whether to dub it "Failures" or just "Failure." For how brilliantly the course embodied its subject matter! Professor Gray was nothing like what my mother had imagined an American professor would be. Nor was he anything like the nuns she had had as teachers in Shanghai, every one of whom had crackled with adventure and mission. He appeared never to have left the classroom; rumor had it that he had been born in a supply closet.

Still, my mother gave her best to his class, and was shocked when her first report card came. One A, two Bs, and a C-. She stared hard at the C-. She had been a top student in both high school and college. She was practically a bilinguist. It could not be. Yet it was true. Professor Gray had given her a C-.

When Mother Greenough wrote, asking how her studies were going, she could not tell her what had happened. Instead, she wrote back:

> I have always loved school. Of course, graduate school
> here is no joke. But surely that is what the Lord intended,
> is it not?

It would take weeks for the letter to reach Mother Greenough. Maybe by the time it arrived, she would already have pulled her grades up. In fact, that was her vow: to pull her grades up, so that by the time her words reached Mother Greenough, they would not be misleading.

Meanwhile, was she misleading her parents, too? She was certainly not lying when she wrote:

It is very expensive here. I did receive a scholarship to cover my tuition, but living expenses are very high, and I don't have many ways of making money.

Should she have volunteered how she'd watched the small pile with which she'd arrived shrink shockingly fast? She had never handled money before or used the word "budget." Of course, her family had always been frugal on principle. Every one of her dresses, however fancy, had replacement collars. But frugality was not about necessity. It was about having consideration for others. It was about avoiding waste because one owed every last grain in one's bowl to someone's hardship—*Lì lì jiē xīnkǔ,* as she used to recite, sitting on her father's lap. It had nothing to do with making sure a certain amount of money lasted for a certain length of time, or matching inflow with outflow, much less with ensuring that one didn't run out of funds entirely.

Now she was confronted with this last possibility. She had spent nothing on extras. But having stayed with the Pings for months, she had felt obliged not only to treat them to dinners but to insist that they not hesitate to order the most expensive items on the menu, discovering only later how much dishes like filet mignon or that delicious lobster thermidor—her favorite—could cost. And how quickly appetizers and desserts and after-dinner drinks added up!

Then there was the cold weather gear she had needed. Auntie had urged her to buy top quality—as a way, my mother thought, of signaling that that was what Auntie herself did. My mother wasn't sure that was true. But as she knew her parents would have been embarrassed to hear her present herself as unused to the best, she went ahead and bought what the shopgirl called "classic pieces." They were not wildly extravagant. She was not like her older half brother, who back when he had gone to school in America had sent home pictures of himself dancing in the ballroom of the Plaza Hotel in New York City. In a picture he did not send to his parents but did send to a mutual friend—a friend who had also been educated in the States, and with whom he liked to talk on the phone in English—he had a boutonniere pinned to the lapel of his tux and a magnum of champagne in either hand; a white woman in a low-cut sequined dress clung to him. But the clothes my mother bought were made of soft materials, with bits of real fur here and there—around the hood of the red coat, for instance, and inside the matching muff. Auntie had called the coat a "good value" and had reassured her, too, that it would never go out of style. But in this way, my mother had found half her funds spent even before she left Chicago for New York.

And so, her letter. Shouldn't her parents be shocked at the implication that she was working and immediately wire money along with an order to focus on her studies? She could hear her father's voice, admonishing her not to worry about anything else. How horrified he would be if he knew that his daughter found herself suspended between two groups of students, the students who had to work and the students who didn't. But she did find herself in just that uncomfortable position. Students like Georgiana looked down on the students who had to work, while the students who had to work—mostly Americans—had no interest in adopting wealthy strays like my mother. Sometimes she wished she could buy yet more clothes—plainer clothes, like theirs—to fit in. Although maybe it would be more realistic to try to join Georgiana's group?

In any case, she waited and waited for an admonition that did not come. Why did her father not write her back? Had he even seen her letter? She wanted to write directly to him, or to bluntly say, *Tell Baba*. But that would be strange and pointed and rude.

How lucky that at just about this time, my mother became friendly with a girl who went to the same church she did, and always, as she did, to the eight o'clock Sunday Mass. She even liked to sit, as did my mother, not in the very front of the church but about a third of the way back, near the center aisle. Her name was Marnie Mulligan.

Marnie was in the working students' group and wore the same navy blue dress every day; her sensible shoes were so worn down at the heel that her ankles bowed out when she walked. Her face was plain and freckled, her brownish hair frizzy. When after church she and my mother went out for coffee, she asked many questions about China and my mother's family. Then she told my mother a little about herself—about how she'd grown up in Ohio, in a coal mining community where no one ever went to college, much less graduate school, and about how her father had died of black lung disease. Among coal miners it was as common as warts, she said, then explained what warts were. As for Marnie's direction, Marnie's mother had not approved of it; to begin with, she had not wanted her daughter to leave Ohio. Marnie left anyway.

"So you and I are more or less in the same boat," she said cheerfully. "Captains of our own canoes."

After a while, she asked if my mother could type. She didn't want to insult my mother by assuming she needed money. But Marnie had told ten people she would type their midterm papers and didn't know how she could possibly swing it. "I'm at my wit's end," she said. "Would you be interested in helping out?"

My mother was still far from an ace typist, but since coming to school had gotten better.

"Why don't you try it?" said Marnie.

My mother's first paper wasn't perfect, but Marnie showed her how to make it better, and suggested, too, that she might think about typing for the Chinese students, who would be less picky about mistakes.

"Your English might not be perfect, but it's a whole lot better than theirs," she said. "And their spelling! Talk about atrocious."

My mother's spelling was excellent, it was true. She didn't type as fast as Marnie, but she could translate Chinglish into English as she went along, and with Marnie to show her how to meet with clients, set expectations, and figure out what to charge, she was soon in business. Marnie sent more and more customers her way—so many that my mother was soon writing to her parents:

You will be surprised to hear that I am typing papers for other students now. It's not hard and only takes twenty-five hours a week. And you would not believe how beautiful my footnotes look! I can judge them perfectly.

She was still hoping her father would write back and say twenty-five hours a week was too much. She was still hoping he would tell her, *If you plant melons, you will harvest melons; if you plant beans, you will harvest beans*—meaning that to work when her purpose was to study was to plant beans when she wanted melons. Was she intending to become a secretary? Certainly there was some way to cut her hours back to fifteen at the most, she wanted him to say—or, better yet, insist that she should stop working altogether, save her twenty-five hours and, if she was done studying, maybe go have some fun the way her half brother used to do.

When finally a letter arrived, though, it was once again in her brother's handwriting and read:

You have always been so smart. So smart, you have ways of making money already! People say it is easier to make money in America than in China, but all the same, it is remarkable how you know everything and need no one. Every problem, you solve by yourself. Really it is too bad you are a girl.

Of course, her father would be consumed with the ongoing crisis. From the newspaper, my mother knew the Communist threat was growing every day. And he was bound to have much delicate negotiation underway. She well remembered how, in the middle of the Japanese occupation, he had somehow conjured up crates of individually wrapped Sunkist oranges, which he proceeded to present to various figures even as he refused to cooperate with them. But my mother could not shake the feeling that her mother was, if not keeping my mother's letters from her father outright, then quite deliberately taking the task of responding off his hands.

My mother met my father at a place called International House. This was for international students of every stripe, but the Chinese students liked to organize some events of their own, and the Shanghainese-speaking students especially liked to get together by themselves. It wasn't just that many of them did not speak Mandarin very well (although many of them did not speak Mandarin very well). It would simply not have had the same feeling had there been people speaking other dialects, as the non-Shanghainese speakers would have agreed. *The Shanghainese are so clannish, so snobby, and so Western,* they would have said. *Let them stick to themselves.*

The Shanghainese crowd, meanwhile, came not only from my mother's university but from schools as far away as Boston. So while Georgiana was often around, she did not preside over this world as she did over their school. Nor did my mother's changed circumstances much matter here. To be Shanghainese was to be one of the gang; she was always welcome in their favorite gathering spot, the dark-paneled Dodge Room. And how she loved that room, so reminiscent of her father's library, with its shelves full of leather-bound books and floor-to-ceiling drapes. Its red carpet and matching leather chairs, too, were just like her father's; the only difference was that these seats were cracked and cratered, while her father's were pristine and domed. And there was so much to talk about in the Dodge Room—from interesting restaurants, to strange sights, to the eternal mystery that were Americans. Were they really as friendly as they pretended? Then there were landlord issues, visa rules, and the art of calling a cab, and had anyone heard this new song, "On a Slow Boat to China"?

She learned, interestingly, as much about Shanghai as America—starting with all the dance halls and racetracks her parents would never have allowed her to visit. Had others really frequented the ultra-decadent Paramount, with its crystal dance floor? And the Canidrome in the French Concession?

Some of them had even seen not just the dog racing at the Canidrome but the dogs being raced with monkey jockeys on their backs! my mother says now.
Monkey jockeys? Really? I say.
Really! Monkey jockeys! Can you imagine that?

Never mind that as Chinese, they could never be full members of the British-run Shanghai Race Club; they had bet on the horses there anyway, and never missed a Champion's Day. They had seen for themselves, too, how the billiard table legs had been cut down for the Japanese officers during the occupation. (How shrimpy those Japanese really were!) And they very well knew not only how chummy Chiang Kai-shek had been with the Japanese but how chummy he now was with the ruthless Green Gang. They knew how, for all his public opposition to opium (including the quarterly bonfires with which he put pressure even on social smokers like my mother's mother), he was actually kept afloat by the drug trade—so much so that he had made the notorious leader of the Green Gang a general.

"*His crackdowns were really aimed at shutting down competitors,*" said someone. No one disagreed. "*It's almost enough to make you wish the Nationalists would lose, just not to the Communists,*" he went on.

And the speaker's father having been one of the thousands purged by Chiang Kai-shek over the years, no one disagreed with that statement, either.

Of course, American politics was a joke, too. Truman showed guts, people agreed, in dropping the atomic bomb. But how could he have sent that idiot George Marshall to China? The idea that such a naïve man could have brokered a peace between the Communists and the Nationalists! He was easier to trick than a child. And how on earth could he have failed so abysmally then be promoted to secretary of state?

"*You'd think America was China!*" my mother ventured. And though there was a moment's pause—women did not commonly interject in political discussions—how gratifying when she drew a laugh!

She had grown up thinking of crowds as mobs—as a force to be contained and avoided. Now she understood their appeal. There was nothing like the wholehearted agreement of a group. How alive she felt at International House, how full-throated and Shanghainese—and just as engaged as the men. For example, she was as worried as they about World War III, which was coming—everyone could see it—though like many people, she believed, too, that should the Communists threaten Shanghai, it would finally spark the international intervention that the Japanese invasion hadn't. Meanwhile, could the Nationalists' fallback plan really be to raze Shanghai to the ground if they lost, to be sure the Communists gained nothing?

"With absolutely no evacuation plans for the people?" said my mother.

If people were surprised to hear from her, they were less surprised than before.

"What an excellent way to alienate the common man," said someone.

"Don't worry—the Communists will alienate everyone, too, once people understand their agenda," said someone else.

"Still, they're going to win first," said a third person. "And that will be the end of everything we know. What is that American saying? It will all be 'gone with the wind.'"

Others thought that too pessimistic. They circled back to World War III. *"It's coming! It is!"*

"The Nationalists always think there will be international help," said someone. "But Truman is not interested in getting involved in a civil war."

"Even if the winner might be Communist? Even if it might help the Soviet Union?" asked my mother.

"American politicians are always chasing votes," said someone. "And the voters do not understand the big picture."

"Especially when it comes to Asia," said someone else.

And people heartily agreed. Although did even they understand Asia? Though they thought they had analyzed every angle of the situation, they were still taken off guard when in April 1949, the People's Liberation Army crossed the Yangtze River. Such a defensible barrier! How could it be? But a naval fleet had unexpectedly switched sides, and a fortress had flipped, too. The Communists took the Nationalist capital, Nanjing. Then they took Suzhou. And then in May, after just two weeks of fighting, as flowers bloomed everywhere in New York, they took Shanghai.

What was happening with their families? Were they alive? Were they hurt? Had they managed to keep clear of the fighting? That was all people wanted to hear. But there was no word.

"The Nationalists will rally and return!" predicted someone.

Few agreed now, though. The mood of this group had turned.

"If anyone says World War Three again, I'll scream," said my mother.

"That was nothing but 'grasping at straws,'" someone agreed.

In October, the Communists declared victory. The United States immediately broke off diplomatic ties with the new regime but Great Britain did not—meaning that there might be some way for people to stay in contact with their families, sending and receiving mail through Singapore and Hong Kong. How exactly was not clear, but people had friends and relatives there. Ways, they thought, could be found. In the meantime, there was no news.

The arrival of fresh blood was a welcome distraction. The impish new postdoc was named Jen Chao-pe and had just gotten his PhD in fluid mechanics from the University of Minnesota. His family was, like my mother's, in banking (although his family's dealings were local, not international); and he hailed from a town not unlike my mother's father's hometown. Yixing was a lake town, not a canal town like Wuzhen. But it was similarly linked to the Grand Canal and similarly consequently well-to-do. Chao-pe spoke Shanghainese, even if Yixing dialect was a little different from what my mother spoke, and he ate the same sweet, light food she did, with a lot of seafood. What's more, his name drew in an appropriately literary way from Mencius. The whole quote, *Xié Tàishān yǐ chāo Běihǎi*—meaning, Tuck Mount Tai under your arm and jump over the North Sea—artfully expressed the hope that Chao-pe would one day accomplish the impossible. Her father, my mother knew, would approve.

Chinese people say a bamboo door should match a bamboo door and a wood door should match a wood door, my mother says now.
And your doors matched, I say.
That's right.
It's like the opposite of Romeo and Juliet.
Romeo and Juliet is not real. The way Chinese people think, if they did not die, they will not get along anyway. Their backgrounds are too different.
And you and Dad got along?
In the beginning, we got along very well, she huffed.

Chao-pe's dimples were on frequent display, as were his large, excellent teeth. And though most of the men wore a dress shirt and slacks to events, he always wore a suit. My mother found herself carefully considering her dress before she headed to International House and, one day, adding Nai-ma's kingfisher phoenix pin.

"What is that?" he asked.

"It's a phoenix," she said.

"Made of kingfisher feathers."

"It is."

"That's a Chinese art. No one makes them here."

"Very true."

He said he had once found a kingfisher with its claws frozen to a railing. He put his hand around it and warmed it, he said, until its claws thawed. Then he opened his hand, and the bird flew away.

"You grasped it with your bare hand?" My mother was impressed.

"I'm a country boy." As if to make sure she didn't think him a peasant, though, he went on, *"My mother had a hairpin made of kingfisher feathers like that, but with many dangling bits. When she walked, it looked as if it might fall off her head."*

She giggled. She had never been much of a giggler, but talking to men made her silly. Who knew but that next she was going to be a winker.

And at that very moment, as if reading her mind, Chao-pe winked at her. It wasn't entirely clear to her why—maybe it was in response to her giggle? But never mind. She did not freeze as she had with George Ping in Chicago. Instead, she winked right back.

What would Mother Greenough say?

Chao-pe gave a thoughtful laugh—an appreciative laugh that came with a little nod. He liked her.

"Can I bring you some dumplings from the table?" he asked.

Yes, she said. Yes, he could.

"One? Two?"

"Three."

"Three." He smiled, nodding even more thoughtfully than before.

She smiled back. Where was her shyness? *"Yes. I'd like three,"* she said, amazed at herself.

And three dumplings it was.

Neither she nor he had heard any direct news, but rumor had it that the International Settlement was undamaged by the fighting; that was some reassurance to her, at least. What's more, superior as she could be, Georgiana did let my mother know that she had heard from her relatives in Hong Kong and that, like the rest of their circle, my mother's family was okay.

"Everyone is on edge," Georgiana said. *"But so far the soldiers have been polite and even helpful, and there have been no incidents. Also, you'd be surprised, but the soldiers all know a lot of songs. They like to sing. They are the complete opposite of the Japanese."*

Of course, she said "the Japanese" as if she had hated them as much as anyone, my mother says now.

How shameless, I say.

The Chinese have a saying—Like a cat weeping over a dead mouse.

She was that sincere, you mean.

That sincere, she says.

Disgusted as she was, my mother was too overwhelmed with relief and gratitude to do anything but let it go. "Thank you," she managed. "Thank you, thank you."

Chao-pe thought that his mother had moved with the Nationalist government to Taiwan. Back in August, when people could see that the government might fall, fifty or sixty planes a day had begun shuttling between Chongqing and Taipei. But though Chao-pe's second brother had a prominent position in the Nationalist government, nothing was sure. Had their mother made it out before the operation ended in December? Chao-pe hadn't heard. And what did it mean that the government was retreating to a small island lost to the Japanese by the Dowager Empress and only recently returned to China at Potsdam? At International House, someone had had to pull out a map to show others where Taiwan was.

"My older brother is very capable. He will manage the situation, I am sure," Chao-pe said.

But for all his professed confidence, Chao-pe worried, too, and to distract them both, began coming to visit my mother at her apartment. Having discovered that she liked grapefruit, he would section the fruit so it was all ready to eat, and wrap it up in waxed paper. Then, when she answered the door, he would draw the grapefruit out of his pocket. The first time he did this, she laughed with surprise. The next few times, she laughed, too, but with a kind of delight that made her gaze out the window. She lost even more focus in Professor Gray's class; she made mistakes in her typing. Did Chao-pe ever lose focus? He never seemed to be at a loss for anything. Indeed, he never stumbled or seemed the least bit self-conscious; he did not seem to know what hesitation was. Other Chinese men could be bashful. They used the word *"dare"* a lot, as in *"He did not dare do this"* and *"He did not dare do that."* But not Chao-pe. He joked with the doorman at International House; he would simply move a table if he thought it in an awkward place; and he smiled with all his teeth showing. Like a horse, she thought sometimes, but other times she thought it was just lucky he wasn't a woman.

No one would ever marry him—no, no matter how nicely he dressed, my mother says now, and laughs. Who would marry him?

She wished that she could write to her parents and tell them that despite all their warnings, a man seemed interested in her, potential PhD and all. How amazed they would be! And, of course, for her, what a vindication. But even if she could have told them, they had other things on their minds, she knew.

She never slipped and fell the way she had on the ice in Chicago, and so did not immediately have a chance to see whether Chao-pe had as firm a grip as George Ping. But on their first formal date, sitting in a movie theater, he took her hand. She did not much care for the film. This *Sunset Boulevard* was too weird and unsettling; the vocabulary word that came to mind was "creepy." (And how many sample sentences came to mind, too: "The movie was creepy." "I thought it was creepy." "It was all right, if a little creepy.") But never mind. She now did everything she had failed to do in Chicago. Her heart was pounding, but she returned his grip firmly, and at one point even squeezed his hand a little (though not so hard as to seem desperate like that Norma Desmond in the movie). She felt farther from home than ever, not just because things were so unfamiliar but because a whole new reality seemed to be coming into view. Did she really have a boyfriend? Was this man, this Jen Chao-pe, becoming part of her life? His name in English was Norman, a bit like Norma but not Norma, Norma*n*, with an "n" at the end; she learned it as if it were any other name, but she already knew it was not like other names. They held hands all the way back to her apartment, and though he did not kiss her—she was glad he did not try to kiss her—she found that after he left, she had many questions. Was he in love with her? Was she in love with him? Was she going to lose her head over him, only to have him disappear like George Ping? What did it all mean?

What a relief that there were no parents around to judge her worthy or unworthy of their son. Distraught as she was about what was happening to their families, there was that consolation. From the Pings, she might have earned a big red X—wrong!—as she had from her mother, and who knew but that she might have received the same from the Jens. From Chao-pe, though, she seemed to be earning an A. He was impressed that she had started a typing business—how practical and capable she was! Was it lying not to tell him that her parents had stopped sending her money and that she thought her mother was behind it? Was it wrong not to tell him that she feared her problem was her own fault, having spent too much money in Chicago? (Although she had had to, she really had; it wasn't as though she had spent money like water, it really wasn't.) Should she have told him that she would do anything not to have to make money—that she was not so much practical and capable as desperate, and lucky to have met Marnie Mulligan? And that she especially hated typing for Georgiana—should she have told him that?—that she hated the way Georgiana looked over the pages, judging them?

In fact, there was no one else who could correct Georgiana's

Chinglish the way my mother did. Georgiana was dependent upon my mother. Still, she would look over the pages with a critical air, making my mother stand there, awaiting her approval, like a servant. Once she made my mother type a page over. But usually she would finally say, *"Very good,"* open her purse, and take out some bills. And for her part, my mother would not count them as Georgiana handed them over, even though Georgiana had shorted her once. Indeed, she would not so much as take the bills in her hand.

"You can leave them on the table," she would say instead.

"If you would like more clients, I know some people at other schools," offered Georgiana one day.

"I don't need their business," my mother replied proudly. Actually, she could have used more business. But now she told Chao-pe that she was turning people away.

"There are interested people at other colleges," she said. *"I don't even want to talk to them, though."*

"Don't even want to talk to them?" Chao-pe was impressed. "Mister!" he said—"mister" being one of his favorite expressions, picked up from American engineers.

He told her all about himself—starting with the fact that he was, like her, well-heeled. Though his father had died young, his grandfather was like a local prince. He owned a great deal of land, thirteen small banks, and a string of stores that sold everyday necessities. He had built a family compound with hundreds of rooms and paved the town roads besides; the first electric light in the district was in his bedroom. Chao-pe remembered the day the light was switched on—how he and his brothers had heard the grown-ups saying over and over, *dî, dî*—but what was *"dî"*? At first he had thought that maybe it was a kind of fish, but his older brother said it was a kind of light. How could it be a kind of light? He saw a long string being strung up—a special string, not a regular string—and then suddenly there it was. He and his brothers were sitting on bamboo stools, playing with crickets, when a new star appeared, brighter and lower than any star they had ever seen before—a star that appeared caught in their grandfather's bedroom. How could it be? Their grandfather had captured a star from the sky! He had hung it from his ceiling!

Chao-pe remembered, too, the way his grandfather had brought up Chao-pe's uncles, exposing them to everything. He would bring them in a private train car to Shanghai, for example, where they would eat Western food using knives and forks, even as they brought along thermoses of Chinese tea with which to wash the strange food down. How primitive foreigners were, that they could eat such food, the uncles agreed. Were not raw vegetables more fit for pigs than people? And yet foreigners were responsible for that electric light and more. So even though Chao-pe's uncles laughed at foreign food, they practiced their English. They wore Western-style suits with felt fedoras, too, except when it was time to pay respects to Chao-pe's grandfather. Then they would all, quick, change into Chinese gowns.

Chao-pe's grandfather, meanwhile, quick, changed people's lives all the time. Chao-pe's most vivid memory was of how as a child he had been slated to be given away to a relative with no son, this being a common practice at the time: families needed males to carry on their line, after all, and why would someone like Chao-pe's mother need five boys? Five boys were a lot for a widow to handle. Did it not make sense for her to give one to the heirless relative? Maybe the fourth son? So the uncles figured, and off Chao-pe would have gone had his grandfather not asked for one last look at him.

Since his grandfather was in Shanghai at the time, Chao-pe's mother had to bring him into the city. He was four years old and had never seen anything as big as the train—so much, much bigger than a water buffalo, and so much louder and stronger, too! A train was like a metal dragon, belching fire clouds. And the city! In Yixing, his family compound was the grandest edifice in town. But nothing in the entire complex could compare with the buildings of Shanghai. These were mountain buildings, with cavernous rooms, one after the next; and what a shock to find that inside one of the caverns, in a big carved chair at a big carved desk, sat his grandfather. Servants waved a fly from his head as he looked down at Chao-pe; they fanned him. He smiled. Stern as he could be with grown-ups, he was gentle with children.

"You are very smart," he said, after a moment. *"I can see it."*

"I am!" said Chao-pe.

People laughed.

"He looks like his father," said someone—not his mother, someone else. (His mother did not dare say anything, it seemed.)

"I look just like him!" Chao-pe agreed.

Everyone laughed again as his grandfather nodded. A corner of his mouth pulled to the side in amusement.

"I've changed my mind. I am going to keep him," he said. *"Such a fine boy."*

And with that, Chao-pe's mother swept him back up into her arms. He wasn't going to live with the relative—he was staying home, to live with her and his brothers! It was the happiest moment of Chao-pe's life, and what could make more sense than for him and his mother to find, as they left the big stone building, that lights like the nine sons of the dragon king had been turned on. His mother, as amazed as he was, asked what they were called. *Níhóng dēng,* someone told her—neon lights.

"We saw neon lights!" Chao-pe told everyone when they got home. *"Neon lights! They are brighter than the sun!"*

He really was a country bumpkin, comments my mother now.

Above all, his grandfather taught the men in the family to fear nothing, which proved good preparation for the War Against the Japanese. Chao-pe by then was in college. While my mother's school struggled on in besieged Shanghai, his university moved inland to Chongqing with the government, to try to escape the bombing. It was the university president who had made the decision to relocate; Chao-pe admired him for it.

That journey through the Yangtze River gorges, though! The current was so strong that even with a motor, the boats were not moving and needed the help of the many towmen working the river. The long lines of harnessed men and their ancient system of ropes and rock-anchored fulcrums were something to see— mister!—the very sort of manpower that had built the Great Wall but that, if Chao-pe and his classmates could only get their training, was hopefully going to be obsolete one day. In the meanwhile, the towmen bent over, sweating and straining, pulling along the hot cliff paths while onboard, polemen pushed, their bamboo poles arced to the snapping point.

The boat did not move.

The men tried again, heaving with all their strength.

Nothing.

They tried again and again until finally the university president made another tough decision: to throw the lab equipment overboard. Chao-pe could not believe it even as he helped—they all helped—first to move things to the deck, then to heave them up over the railings into the water. What a splash! They started with the heaviest equipment, but in the end, it all went in the water—pumps, compressors, engines, heaters, coolers, tanks—no doubt making the river trip more hazardous for any boats that followed them, but they could not think of that now. They had no choice; it was hard enough to see such valuable machinery in the water, complete with all the gauges and dials over which they had once hovered, watching for even the slightest change. How were they going to do research without their measurements?

The towmen and polemen tried again. Again. Again. *Once more!* the president ordered. They tried yet again.

The books—they were going to have to dump the books. To load the boat in Nanjing, the students had organized a kind of brigade line, with each person handing a box of books to the next. Now they did it again, except that the last person in line did not carefully stack the box on top of the others but instead dumped it in the water. Over and over the railing they went, box after box after box of textbooks on math, physics, mechanical engineering, civil engineering, electrical engineering. The president watched, his face grim, but at least the towmen, their backs shining with sweat and their legs all but parallel to the ground, were finally able to gain some purchase. What a price—but they were, they were moving! Everyone rejoiced. There were hours of poling and towing ahead. Still, they were moving, first slowly, then faster, until they'd made it! They'd made it through the gorges! They were on their way to Chongqing!

If only they did not finally reach Chongqing only to discover that the Japanese were bombing there, too. Thank heavens for the mountain caves in which the school could set up classrooms and dorms. The caves were at least relatively safe and also blessedly cool, as everyone appreciated: there was a reason Chongqing was called one of the furnaces of China. Lighting the caves was not easy; many people would huddle around a single lightbulb to study. And water had to be ferried up from the river below—something boys immediately began doing for girls they liked. Sometimes the girls knew who their pail was from; sometimes they didn't. They excitedly discussed the possibilities even as bombs exploded outside.

"*Once I hid from a plane under the lotus leaves of a pond—a plane that went on to bomb a mountain cave in which classes were being held,*" Chao-pe said. "*That bomb set off a landslide, in which many people were killed—many, many people. There was a big funeral. Everyone was crying. But people were crying for me, too, not realizing that I was late to class because I had gotten stuck in the mud under the lotus leaves. So when I walked into the funeral, everyone stopped in shock. Then they all began clapping.*"

And, like them, listening now, my mother clapped, too. So many stories! Chao-pe knew how to take her mind off the revolution.

"*We will all go back one day,*" said Chao-pe. "*Maybe some people do not like the way things are. Maybe some people feel things are unfair. But no one wants the government to own everything. The way the Communists think is fundamentally wrong.*"

So he figured.

But the Communists soon passed an Agrarian Reform Law so radical that he and my mother would not have believed it had they not heard it read aloud in the Dodge Room.

"*Article 1. The land ownership system of feudal exploitation by the landlord class shall be abolished and a system of peasant land ownership shall be introduced in order to unleash rural productive forces, develop agricultural production, and pave the way for China's industrialization,*" their friend began. He held the paper with his fingertips as he read, his pinkies outstretched as if to distance themselves from the words. "*Article 2,*" he went on, and "*Article 3,*" then "*Article 4,*" until finally he ended with, "*Article 10. All land and other means of production thus confiscated and requisitioned... shall be taken over by the peasants' council for unified, equitable, and rational distribution to poverty-stricken peasants who have little or no land and who lack other means of production. Landlords shall be given an equal share so that they can make their living by their own labor and thus reform themselves."*

People stood, silent. In another room, a harp was being played. Arpeggios; a lingering last note; a pause. The faraway audience clapped.

"Why do they bother to call this a law?" said someone finally. "Why do they pretend there is something legal about it when it is theft, pure and simple?"

And what did it mean for families like Chao-pe's? Articles 2 and 4 suggested that the Jen compound was safe—their banks and shops, too.

But few people in the room were reassured.

"Safe for now, you mean," said someone.

As for families like the Jens making their living through labor, it was inconceivable. Labor? How could they do labor? With their government ties, Chao-pe thought that at least two of his brothers had gotten out, as well as, he fervently hoped, his mother. But what about his other two brothers and all his many relatives?

"You realize that the Communists have only just begun," said someone. "There is more to come."

"'Other shoes to drop,' as the Americans say."

"It's like what happened in Russia."

"They are worse than the Japanese."

"Our poor families."

"Our poor families."

"Our poor, poor families."

From somewhere came the clack of chairs being folded up and put back.

Did you know how bad it was? I ask now.

How could we know? my mother says.

Scholars today say a million people died in that reform alone. And it was just the start.

She is quiet.

Rumors were circulating wildly—about houses being requisitioned, with their owners given twenty-four hours to leave. About people being tried by their employees, even as others left town with diamond-stuffed hams.

"Hams!" said someone.

"House requisitions," said someone else. "They're just like the Japanese."

"The Communists may be peasants, but they don't want to live like peasants, it seems."

"Does anyone?"

People laughed choked laughs.

A friend with relatives in Taiwan had good and bad news for Chao-pe. The good news: not two but three of his brothers had indeed gotten out, along with their children and, yes, his mother! The bad news: one of his brothers had been left behind, as well as many relatives, and the family compound had been, predictably, requisitioned. As for what exactly that meant, who knew? Were people simply turned out? Were they given a chance to pack? Were the servants turned out, too? And did the servants help defend family members, or did they turn on them? Sometimes even irrepressible Chao-pe sat staring into space. Neither he nor my mother could sleep; neither he nor my mother could concentrate.

He focused on teaching my mother how to cook. She had learned to boil water and make coffee and tea from the Pings, but neither she nor her roommates knew much more. They all generally ate out; she complained it was making her fat. While living in the mountains in Chongqing, meanwhile, Chao-pe and his classmates had figured out not only how to cook but how to cook in their cave-classrooms, using stoves they had fashioned themselves out of scrap metal.

"One-to-one," he told her. "You can use a cup, a bowl, anything. Just one measure of water to one measure of rice. Then you bring it to a boil. When it's boiling, you turn it down and cover it."

Amazing! Upset as she was about everything, my mother could not help but wonder at him. How did he know such things? He brought her to the grocery store.

"The white meat is chicken," he said. "The pink meat is pork. And the red meat—that is beef. Someday we will be able to afford it. Right now we can only eat eggs, pork, and chicken. They should all be kept in the icebox."

Raw meat! How disgusting! It was weeks before she could bring herself to touch it. But having mastered both rice and hard-boiled eggs, she finally one day just did it. She bought a piece of pork and cut it up with a knife, slicing it against the grain, just as Chao-pe had shown her. Then she added cornstarch and sherry and soy sauce. (Chao-pe mixed the little mountain with his hands, but she used chopsticks.) She put it in the icebox and, as a surprise, presented the bowl of meat to him when he came to visit.

"Good work, Chef Loo!" he exclaimed. He showed her how to heat oil in a pan and stir-fry the meat until it was done. Then they had their first meal outside of a restaurant—stir-fried pork and rice.

"You know everything," she said.

"How can you say that? You don't know what I know."

"I know."

Still he insisted that she did not know and, what's more, that she did not even know what she did not know. Then he showed her some other things he knew she did not know, and he was right. She had not even known that she did not know them, though her body seemed to know them; it was as if he and her body were secretly in league. As for what else she did not know, she knew enough to know that she did not want to know whatever it was until they were married.

"Let's get married, then," he said.

"You know, my mother used to say no one would ever marry me," she said.

It was not something she had meant to tell him—or anyone, really. She had learned her lesson early, with Nai-ma—how she wished she had never asked, *Was she fired again?* And how many times had her father told her—told all the children—to watch their tongues? *"Westerners have a saying, 'Loose lips sink ships,'"* he said. *"It is a bit like our 'Just as illness comes in through a mouth, trouble comes out through a mouth.' The lesson is the same."* But she couldn't help herself. Maybe it was a kind of test—to see if it made

Chao-pe think twice about her. To see if some part of him could see why no one would ever marry her.

"Your mother said what?" he said.

And, taking a breath, she explained. She did not quote herself. The sharp things she could say, how she had said them—she left those out. But she did say that her mother had told her every day that no one would ever marry her. Then she waited.

Shouldn't he have said her mother was wrong?

Instead, he said, *"And my friends said I was going to lose my bet."*

"Bet?" she said. "What bet?"

"I bet them that I would be married in six months."

"How could you make a joke about something so serious?"

"Because I knew I would win."

"That's not a way to get married."

But he just pulled her to him and asked, *"Am I going to lose my bet?"*

Did George Ping ever pull a girl toward him that way? The nerve of this man!

"I want a ring," she said primly. "If that's what you're asking."

"And how do you like that? Look what I found in my pocket," he said.

That Chao-pe!

Should they write their parents to tell them their news? What with everything going on, they were not sure, especially since there was a new development: China had entered the Korean War. What did it mean that China was now at war with America?

"It means we are all stuck here, like it or not," said someone at International House.

"The U.S. government has declared a 'state of emergency' barring Chinese students from returning home," said someone else. *"Also, all scholars with technical skills capable of aiding China."*

"Old Wong tried to go back," reported a third person. *"He said he wanted to help the country regain its pride and reinvigorate itself! But he got taken off the boat in Hawaii."*

"How could that be legal?"
A good question.

It was outrageous! I say now.
We wanted to stay in America until we were told we had to, my mother says. Then we wanted to leave.
Of course you did, I say.

What did the Chinese *"Resist America, Aid Korea"* campaign mean for letter-writing? Writing to Chao-pe's mother in Taiwan was a challenge—who knew where she was?—but at least it was not a political issue. Writing to my mother's family could bring trouble.

"We don't want anyone accused of being a spy," my mother said.

Still, after much discussion, they decided each to write a letter, telling their family the happy news but avoiding any mention of politics. Through friends they found an accountant in Singapore who was discreetly forwarding letters to this "People's Republic of China"—such a strange name—and receiving them, too. The accountant didn't want to do too many. But as a favor to their mutual friend and given the enormity of their news, he agreed to do theirs, so long as they avoided saying anything that could get him in trouble, should the letter be checked by a censor. My mother wrote:

> *This will come as a surprise, I know, but here in America I have a boyfriend who would like to marry me. His family is from Yixing, on Lake Tai. Their family name is Jen. Theirs is a well-known family in that area, with many generations of scholar officials. His full name is Jen Chao-pe, and he is a graduate of National Central University who recently completed his PhD in fluid mechanics at the* University of Minnesota. *He now works as a civil engineer. I believe his future is bright. But more important, fate has joined us that we may hold hands and grow old together.*
>
> *Before we grow too old, I hope we can all reunite in Shanghai! May that day come soon. In the meanwhile,*

we think of you every day and hope that this one joy will scatter many griefs.

Was that last line too pointed? Chao-pe did not think such a common saying could be a problem, but to be on the safe side, she copied the letter over without it. She took out the references to America and the University of Minnesota as well, and to the hope that they could all reunite in Shanghai she added a wish to join the struggle to rebuild the motherland. How she hoped the letter would make it through to her family. And how she hoped, too, that there might be a reply, even if the reply was once again from her mother via her brother, and even if it included something along the lines of *Yes, it is quite a surprise. Someone wants to marry you!* No matter what, she wanted her family to know her news, especially her father. She wanted her father to know.

It was six weeks before she received an envelope from a foreign address. The letter was not from Singapore but from a plastics factory in Hong Kong. There it was, though! Her father's handwriting— or a version of it. It was not sloppy. But neither was it his supremely confident calligraphy, that precise march of small well-spaced characters with which he'd always written, from top to bottom, right to left, in the traditional way. The spacing was irregular, and some of the characters bore odd tails. Was something the matter? And then there were his words:

What a happy surprise! Of course, we wish you could get properly married with all your family in attendance and with great celebration, like your brother, who you may not have heard is also engaged. But given your health, that does not seem realistic. I hope you will be able to come back someday. We know your heart is not with the American imperialists. In the meanwhile, it warms us to know you have found someone to marry. I agree that it is best for you and Chao-pe to get officially married there. We will just postpone festivities until such time as your good health has returned.

It gives me peace of mind to know that you have found someone to take care of you. Your mother told me that you have been making some pocket money by doing a little typing. That is not the way to concentrate on your studies. You must take care not to tire yourself out. The freezing cold here makes it impossible to send money, but I hope you received the money I instructed her to send and, if you didn't need it, I hope you saved it. My guess is that you will find life brings many developments you cannot possibly anticipate. Do not worry—we are fine here. I only mean it is always good to be prepared.

How stirred she felt, reading this—so stirred, she could hardly say why. Was it because everyone was—or seemed, at least—okay? Was it because she was finally, finally, after so long a wait, hearing from her father? Was it because her brother was now engaged to someone she had never even met? Or was it because she could never have imagined a day when her father would have to pretend she was in ill health?

How strange to see the word *"imperialist"* in her father's handwriting. How worried he must be that his letter would be read; how concertedly he must be trying to keep out of trouble. And how ironic for them to be finally free of her mother's interference in their correspondence, only to have to worry about a new, far worse interference. It was upsetting, too, to learn that her mother had indeed told her father about the typing but had not wired the money he had intended to send. So it was true: her mother really had cut her off. And that reference to the *freezing cold*—yes, winters in Shanghai could be cold, but it was much more likely that her father was telling her his assets had been frozen. Was he hinting, too, that he hoped she had something put away, should the unimaginable come to pass and the family turn out to need those puny funds? Was she heartsick because that would indeed be unimaginable, or because there were no funds?

She could still hear him on the dock in Shanghai. *You are luckier than you know. The luckiest of the children, the luckiest of us all.* She recalled, too, the *"Song of Divination"* she had memorized for Teacher Wu:

> *As I live up and you downstream,*
> *Day after day of you I dream.*
> *There's the Yangtze, but I don't see you,*
> *Drink both from the same river though we do.*
> *When will the river cease to flow?*
> *When will my grief cease to grow?*

How long ago it was now that she'd learned the poem, and yet how the feeling lived on—as was impossible to explain. When Chao-pe asked her what the matter was, she could only answer with an aphorism. *"When a feather is sent a thousand miles, the gift is light but the feeling great,"* she said. Her father, she explained, just wished that they could get married in China.

There was more talk at International House. People were being jailed and executed, and not just a few. This was a full-blown campaign—a Campaign to Suppress Counterrevolutionaries, someone said. It was hard to know how many were targeted, but reports said it was in the hundreds of thousands, with mass public executions in places like that Canidrome my mother had never visited—the one with the dog racing and monkey jockeys.

"Does anything ever happen in China without people being mowed down?" said someone. "It's amazing there is anyone left."

"And the people are as bad as the leaders," said someone else. "They say blood was splattering on the onlookers, and people cheered all the same."

"That's like in Lu Xun," said my mother. "Remember the crowd cheering the death of Ah-Q?" Lu Xun was yet another author my mother knew her mother would not have approved of, but one of the nuns at her school had recommended his work and she was glad now she'd read it.

"That's right!" someone said. "What was that line? 'They're disappointed...'"

"'...that he did not choke out a single line of opera; they had followed him for nothing,'" said my mother.

"How nice that someone here is educated," said someone else. "But what is the matter with us? Where is our humanity?"

Other people joined in:

"There's nothing the matter with us. People cheer because they can't escape."

"And what is that advice from 'The Thirty-Six Stratagems'? 'Of the thirty-six stratagems, the best is to run away.'"

"Which is essentially what we've done, right? If you're going to run away, why not to New York?"

"Correction: we haven't run anywhere. We're just secretly relieved to have gotten stuck here, right or wrong?"

People laughed uneasily then, although in truth, even in New York things were complicated. The many anti-Communist parades apparently having made no impression, vandals attacked businesses in Chinatown. A Chinese, it seemed, was a Chinese—they were all suspect.

"But how we can be 'red' when we are Nationalists?" said someone.

"If you have black hair, you are 'red,'" explained another person.

"No, no. You need to have black hair and yellow skin," said a third.

"That's math in America. Black plus yellow equals 'red,'" said Chao-pe.

Everyone laughed again.

How astonishing to hear back from Chao-pe's mother! He had written to her care of his number two brother, care of the government, with no address—not even a city, much less a street name or building number. But somehow, she had received the letter. Though she was one of the rare women in her generation who had succeeded in teaching herself to read, she could read only printed materials and so had apparently had to hire a scribe both to read Chao-pe's letter and to write a return note. Why wasn't there a family member to help her? Was she somehow on her own? In any case, her note simply read:

> I send my blessings and heartfelt good wishes. Loo Shu-hsin sounds like a most suitable bride, of good family and good character. I hope that we will meet someday. In the

meanwhile, it seems that heaven has brought you together. May you fly like birds abreast in the sky and grow like trees entwined from the earth. And may you have a son early!

Chao-pe was quiet as he showed my mother the letter. Were they really starting lives their families could not begin to fathom, with people their families might never meet? Back home, people believed that husbands and wives were bound by their ankles from birth with a red string—that is, by fate. And so, it seemed, they were. But now they were afloat in a broad, rolling ocean, with nothing but that red string. Was it too slender? Would it be enough?

You should say how our fathers' names were so similar, says my mother now.

You mean, how both your fathers' names ended with the same Chinese character? I say.

It was such a coincidence that their official names were both Pǔ.

Your father's name being Lú Xuépǔ, meaning "study broadly."

"Study everything," really. "Pǔ" means vast. And on top of it, their common names were both Quán.

"Quán" meaning a spring or small stream, right?

It was as if they were brothers! This was not a normal red string. You should write that.

I don't know, Mom. American audiences don't understand that kind of thing.

You write whatever you want about me, but when the American audience won't understand it, then you leave it out.

You have too much to say, I say.

It's true! she says. Look how you cater to them! Bad bad girl!

My mother rented a gown; Chao-pe rented a tux. They rented a college gym for the reception. Someone brought a record player; people danced and ate lunch; she and her new husband had an official wedding portrait taken. Naturally, Chao-pe looked away as if enjoying a huge joke just as the camera snapped, but there was no money for a retake. (At least my mother was looking, as she was supposed to be, straight into the lens.) Later they went out, too, for smorgasbord, Chao-pe's favorite kind of meal—"All you can eat! Mister!" he liked to say. Then it was on to a honeymoon at Niagara Falls.

They could not visit the Canadian side of the falls because Chao-pe's official citizenship status was "no status." (What with it set to expire a month before his doctoral defense, he explained, he had had to overstay his visa to get his degree.) But never mind. The size of the falls! The roar of them! The force! The volume of the water fluctuated, depending on how much was drawn off by the hydroelectric dams upstream. But could an average of six hundred thousand gallons of water really go over Horseshoe Falls every second? Mister! Chao-pe was impressed. And in the morning, there was a rainbow over the water. It was the first rainbow either of them had ever seen, and at first they weren't sure what it was. Then they realized that it was, it really was, a rainbow! It was like seeing an angel.

In the museum, they read about daredevils who had gone over the falls strapped into barrels and lived.

"That is the word for them, 'daredevils,'" my mother said.

Chao-pe laughed at her. *"Always working on your vocabulary,"* he said.

How amazed they were to discover that the first person to go over the falls and survive was a sixty-three-year-old female schoolteacher!

For the Journey Behind the Falls tour, they donned special raincoats and rain boots, and took a long elevator ride down to a tunnel. This led to a portal that opened right onto the underside of the torrents. It was wet and slippery and loud and terrifying, but Chao-pe was unfazed. He laughed, and then she did, too, holding on to his arm, especially when the wind changed and the water began blowing straight into their eyes. It was like being blasted by a fire hose; her glasses were no protection.

"Sorry about the wind," the tour guide blithely said.

They both enjoyed the Maid of the Mist double-decker boat ride, a tamer experience. And how Chao-pe loved the dam museum! My mother was disappointed that the famous local shredded wheat factory had stopped giving tours; several friends had described the bowl of cereal with milk you got at the end. And now she enjoyed the view of the gorge from the dam museum far more than the documentary about the construction of the hydroelectric plant. Still, she sat patiently as Chao-pe watched the film twice. *"Someday China will have a dam like that,"* he said. *"Then instead of floods, there will be electricity."* He wished he could see the two-mile-long "ice boom" strung every December across the Niagara River to stop the "mini-icebergs" flowing down from frozen Lake Erie before they clogged the dam.

"Smart," he said, and she agreed.

But when later at a steak house, my mother said the falls were almost as terrifying as the Communists, he grew serious.

"These things are completely not the same," he said.

He told her then about how the Communists had ransacked his house when he was little. He must have been about five, he said, since his father had recently died—which had been terrible enough. His father had developed sores all over, and then gone blind and become paralyzed; Chao-pe didn't know why and learned only later that it was because of something called *"syphilis."* What he did know was that his mother had been left alone to handle many things, including facing the marauders. His grandfather was out of town, and as most of their relatives were at a wedding to which his mother would have gone had she not been feeling sick, she was on her own when the red-armbanded strangers came. The servants, terrified, hid; who knows what would have happened had his mother not simply taken him and his younger brother by the hand and, head up, calmly led them and her three older boys out of the compound. Such was her aplomb that the Communists let them go; by the time they realized their mistake, she had hidden the whole family in a cave in the summer garden.

"That is truly terrifying," my mother said. *"I never meant that the Communists are not terrifying. I am afraid of them, too."*

"You are afraid of the Communists, though you never saw them," said Chao-pe, slowly. *"Just as you were afraid of the Japanese, though you never saw them, either."*

"I saw them. They were all over so even though we were mostly secluded, we did see them," she said.

"Secluded."
"Sequestered. Sheltered."
"Sheltered."

Was it not all right to be sheltered? Had he not hidden under a lotus leaf from the Japanese bombers?

"*My father took care of us,*" she said. "*He protected us.*" She did not mean to imply that Chao-pe's philandering father had not taken care of him. But afraid he might think that, she added, "*The women and girls, especially.*"

"*My mother took care of us,*" he replied. "*I'm glad she's safely in Taiwan.*"

If only her parents were safe, too! My mother worried about them even as she wished that she had had a mother like his—and hoped, too, that Chao-pe was not having second thoughts about her. She hoped that he was not thinking, like the Pings, that she was a *dà xiǎojiě*. Or what was it that other Chinese said about Shanghai people? That they were *róu ruò*—soft and weak. Yes, that's what they said. Was it soft and weak, though, to be sheltered from the rape- and torture-happy Japanese? Sure, his mother had bravely and brilliantly marched right past the Communists. But wasn't that an act of protection, too? Wasn't protection love?

She sat forward and speared a piece of her prime rib with her fork. She did not like forks. She did not like the way that meat tasted, either, really; she liked seafood. But she was ready to face life, to face challenges. They would be like the falls, overwhelming. But she would be like Mother Greenough and Chao-pe's mother. Enterprising. Prepared. Unafraid. Tough chewing though she found the meat, she opened her mouth, chewed it, and swallowed it. Then she did it again.

"*Good appetite,*" said Chao-pe approvingly.

And later, she took her new husband's arm and let him lead her into the hotel room, where she learned many things about which neither her mother nor Mother Greenough had told her.

Bad bad girl! To write about such things, my mother says.
Trust me, Ma, that's nothing, I say.
You are not allowed to write it! Bad bad girl!

CHAPTER III

A Wife and a Mother

My mother and Chao-pe's new apartment in Washington Heights was more like a servant's quarters than proper housing and, though a bargain, was not clean. They gamely bought cleaning supplies—a bucket, a mop, a broom. Sponges, a feather duster, various sorts of soap. Rubber gloves, with which my mother was familiar thanks to the Pings. Everything was brightly colored. It wasn't so bad.

But when they opened the kitchen cabinets and found them full of cockroaches, they had to return to the hardware store for a can of insecticide. It emitted a fountain of noxious spray; they ran from the room so as not to be poisoned themselves, and the next day returned to so many carcasses that they could not walk in the door without crunching dozens of them underfoot—so many that in places they could hardly see the floor for the black cockroach sea. My mother almost threw up. They returned to the hardware store once more to rent a vacuum cleaner. What a weapon that was! And how satisfying to hear the dead insects rattle loudly as they were sucked up into the metal tube, filling the vacuum cleaner bag several times over.

Chao-pe, naturally, was less unnerved than she. She tried to emulate him. Next, though, came mopping. What would she have done without rubber gloves? The first time she had washed her own stockings, her skin had come off. Now she tried not to cry as she worked and was glad that Chao-pe at least did the mop wringing. She could not bear the dirty water with its clumps of who knew what—hair, splinters, Styrofoam—things that couldn't be washed down the drain but had to be picked out of the metal grate. And that was before they found the dead rat. She screamed and ran out of the apartment; Chao-pe laughed. By the time she returned, he had not only gotten rid of the thing but had finished the cleaning. He had even cleaned the windows using balled-up newspaper, not that the glass was now clear. Much brown grime remained on the outside. Still, it was good to know the windows were clean on the inside.

"*Time to paint,*" he said calmly.

How did he know what masking tape was? How did he know what spackle was, and primer, and a top coat? How did he know to have the paint cans shaken at the paint store, and that once home you opened them with a screwdriver, working your way around the lid? How did he know what to paint with a roller and what to paint with a brush, and that they could borrow a stepladder from the super? What a capable man, that Chao-pe!

Painting wasn't as bad as cleaning. She wore rubber gloves for this, too, and a shower cap to protect her hair, but found it almost fun to see the old green walls disappear, and—magic!—turn white. She was good at doing the window frames—neater and faster than Chao-pe. If only the smell of the turpentine they used for cleanup did not make her woozy. And how her arms ached at the end of the day, and if only there were somewhere to sit and rub her feet besides the ledge of the cold, brown-stained bathtub. At least she had brought her own clean towels with her; Chao-pe's appeared not to have been washed since he arrived from China. How far away this America from the America she had imagined as a child! How far, far away from the land of Sunkist oranges and Buicks and whipped cream. How could she ever have explained to her family that this, this was her American life? She understood that she was not going through anything like what they were. But what a long way she was, too, from the Plaza Hotel dances her half brother had enjoyed. And did she even want to know that Georgiana Huang had rented a quiet apartment with a view of a park, right near school? A "classic six," it was called, boasting as it did a living room, a dining room, a kitchen, two bedrooms, and even a maid's room, for which Georgiana was planning to hire a maid. You could find help cheap in Chinatown, she said. It cost practically nothing.

Yet was it still not something that my mother and Chao-pe had their own apartment—an apartment they had earned? That was a new word for her, "earned"—a new, American word. But now that she knew it, how many people could really say they had earned their place in the world? The last people she'd known who could have said it were Mother Greenough and her band of intrepid nuns. And her father, of course, her accomplished father. My mother was proud of herself and her new husband, even as she worried a bit. The look on Chao-pe's face when she asked for help balancing on the stepladder was not patience; and though, what with school now so far away, he was willing to show her how to use the subway, he had also asked her if she hadn't used it before and looked distinctly disappointed to hear that, though she had taken it with friends, she had never taken it alone. Because it was so noisy and dirty, she told him. Some of the people scared her. If the trolleys in their neighborhood ran south, rather than just north, she would take them, she went on. She had ridden the trolleys in Shanghai once or twice, after all, and probably would have ridden them more if not for the Japanese. But all in all, it was more comfortable to walk.

"More comfortable to walk," repeated Chao-pe. Was it her imagination, or was there an edge to his tone? *"More comfortable to walk."*

Better to discuss furniture. She saw a beautiful bedroom set in a showroom window—a light-colored, solid wood set with two twin beds, a nightstand, a bureau, and a chest of drawers. He hesitated over the price, but she told him that it was classic and would last forever. And it was on sale! They could pay it off in monthly installments in three years.

"That's assuming I continue to get jobs," Chao-pe said.

"Why wouldn't you get jobs?"

"Because Chinese people have to show we can do engineering," he said wryly. *"Our bosses need to see that our bridges don't fall down."*

"Why would they fall down?"

He laughed. *"Americans just like to worry."*

He agreed to the bedroom set, but did Americans really not believe that Chinese people could do engineering? The one chance she had had to visit him at his office, she was shocked to see that the Chinese engineers were not even given chairs. The white engineers sat on chairs. The Chinese engineers sat on backless stools. And unlike the white engineers, the Chinese engineers had no desk lamps, either.

"We are foreigners," said Chao-pe. "We would treat the Americans the same way if they came to work in China." Adding, "We don't have real jobs. That's why we don't have desks or chairs or lamps. We are just so-called temporary help. Contractors."

As she knew, of course. At the end of the job, the white engineers stayed, while the Chinese engineers were let go. Still, it was a shock.

"We'll make the payments on the bedroom set," she told him now. "I'll keep typing—maybe find some new clients." But no sooner had she offered than she was pregnant.

It did not seem possible. They had been careful. But maybe they had not been careful enough? Much was unclear; the rhythm method was tricky. She did not know whom to ask. All she knew was that morning sickness did not end in the morning.

Why do they call it that? my mother asks now.
Many a woman has asked, I say.

What was she going to do about clothes? And school. What was she going to do about school? *"I'll be fine,"* she told Chao-pe. But already she had slept through a week of class. She could not get herself out of bed; she was so tired she could not brush her teeth. The one morning she managed to wake and dress, she could not get herself on the subway. She made it down the dark, dirty stairs. But the turnstile defeated her—the jostling, the pushing, the pressure. In China, people would be making sure she ate right. They would be making sure she slept right. They would be making sure she wasn't doing too much. Probably their fussing would annoy her. But who here cared that she was pregnant? She was not even sure how much Chao-pe cared. Of course, he cared about the baby. But did he care about her?

"*How can we tell if it's a boy or a girl?*" he asked.

"*We can't.*"

"*There's really no way?*"

"*Are you worried?*"

"*No, no. A girl is great, too,*" he said.

In truth, though she knew she ought to be more modern in her thinking, even she hoped the baby would be a boy. A number one son! She would not be upset to have a girl the way her mother had been to have her. But she did not want to disappoint Chao-pe any more than she already had. Wasn't she proving herself tough and capable? she asked him sometimes.

She was, he agreed. She was.

Yet he talked more and more, she noticed, about the military men who had run his high school. They never carried umbrellas, he said admiringly. They did not brush their teeth. (Something he did not do, either, my mother noticed, somehow without ever developing cavities.) And they rarely changed their clothes (another way in which they had apparently inspired him). They spoke with awe of the soldiers of Genghis Khan.

"*Those horsemen could ride for days, biting the necks of their horses and drinking the blood so they wouldn't have to stop to eat,*" Chao-pe said.

"*Could they really?*" The nuns at my mother's school had never said anything like that. Even when they had described Roman gladiators and the Christian campaign to stop their pagan depravity, the Christians were consummately civilized—saints, really. "*The horses allowed the horsemen to do that?*" she pressed. "*They didn't rear up and throw them? And what did the horses eat? How could they run for days without eating?*"

He didn't know but insisted that what he was saying was true. "*The horsemen would bite their necks and suck their blood,*" he repeated. He did not care if they were barbarians, as my mother seemed to think. His teachers had admired their toughness, and he did, too.

Should they have a rented an apartment so far from school? The subway ride wasn't inconvenient once she'd gotten used to it—

as Chao-pe had pointed out from the start, the trip was a straight shot, with no transfers, and an express to boot. But the school community here was much more loosely knit than her community in Shanghai; it was hard to feel a part of things. She wondered if she should have given up her typing business. Of course, it was either that or give up her schoolwork; she had clearly seen she couldn't do both. And how she had enjoyed telling Georgiana that she was going to have to find a new typist. How she had relished the long pause that ensued, followed by Georgiana's panic.

"*I can't write these papers on my own,*" she had wailed. "*I can't! You can't make just one exception? Just one?*"

"*I'm so sorry,*" said my mother.

"*Maybe I can pay ten percent more?*" Georgiana, my mother could see, expected her to counterbid, naming a larger percentage so that Georgiana could propose a compromise figure.

"*No,*" my mother said instead. And what a satisfaction that was.

But she missed the little back-and-forth she had had with some of her other clients. They were not friends. Still, she had liked them. Even if they came from other parts of China and spoke dialects she did not understand, they at least knew where China was. They were at least concerned about China. Her neighborhood here was lively and full of children running and jumping and hiding, but what did her neighbors care about the new campaigns going on in China, one after the next?

The campaign targeting corruption and political opposition was alarming enough, I say now. And then came the Five-Antis Campaign, the express target of which was rich urban capitalists like your father.

It was terrifying, my mother says.

Though my mother was too babysick to go to International House anymore, Chao-pe sometimes went.

"What are people saying?" she wanted to know.

"They say that Mao needs money for the Korean War, but that all the foreigners are gone, and their assets already seized," he said. "So all that's left are Chinese enterprises. And of course, the Communists have always hated Shanghai anyway."

"'A parasitic city completely dependent on the imperialist economy for its existence' and so on," said my mother. "'A tool used by the West to dominate China.'"

"This is their chance to bring it to heel," Chao-pe said.

It was like a dress rehearsal for the Cultural Revolution, I say now. Parades of anti-capitalists complete with drums and banners. Comrades going door-to-door to get businessmen to confess their crimes and denounce each other. Employees exhorted to criticize and condemn their bosses.

My mother is quiet.

Companies issued thousands of confessions a day, trying to insulate themselves from attack, but even so, there were mass meetings, with loudspeakers blaring out the names of individuals who had yet to confess. In Shanghai there were three thousand of these meetings in one month alone, with 90 percent of the accused found guilty.

My poor father, she says.

Yes, your poor father. He did escape in the end, being very very lucky and very very connected and very very smart.

But still.

Yes, still. The pressure.

So many people jumped from the roofs of the buildings along the Bund that pedestrians had to walk in the gutter to avoid the corpses. The police put up netting, but people just took running jumps so they'd clear the nets, sometimes landing on rickshaw pullers and killing them.

My mother wrote to her family:

You will be happy to hear that Chao-pe and I are expecting a baby! It will be here in the fall. Naturally, I very much wish I were in China and not in capitalist America, where people are too concerned with making money to take care of pregnant women. But I shouldn't complain.

How is the weather? I wonder if it continues unseasonably cold, and also if something can't be done to warm you especially, Baba, now that you are getting old. After a lifetime of taking care of others, I think it is time for others to take care of you. People say almost all the big houses have been requisitioned by now. Is ours also being used to serve the people? Where are you living? People say, too, that the servants have been liberated. And of course life without servants is an adjustment, as I know myself, but I know that you will rejoice in their freedom. America is the home of slavery, and while our servants were not slaves, I'm sure you would not want to exploit others the way that Americans have. They are shameless.

We have a new apartment. It is a bit far from school, but we have cleaned and painted it all by ourselves! Even I proved a good painter by the end, you'd be surprised. Now Chao-pe is working harder than ever. He is the opposite of a parasite. I know you would all be proud of him.

It is odd to think of Littlest Sister growing older. She must be so big now! I have already been gone a long time— much longer than I'd planned. As you, Baba, used to warn us, life has brought many more developments than I ever anticipated.

She didn't know what else to say. This letter was, like her other letters, supposed to go through the plastics factory in Hong Kong, but she was less sure it would arrive as she had no new address for her family. She could only pray that the factory owner did.

If her father could survive the Communists, she could survive her pregnancy.

"I just have to get through the semester," she told Chao-pe. Or did she mean trimester? How confused she was already. She was fifteen points past her master's; that meant she had just fifteen points of coursework left to go for her PhD. She could do that. By the time the baby was born, she'd be working on her dissertation, which she could do at home.

Thank heavens, Marnie Mulligan came to visit every ten days or so. Marnie had a Lord & Taylor shopping bag she had picked up somewhere; if my mother missed class, Marnie would bring notes and assignments back and forth in it, reviewing chapters my mother found confusing. Marnie herself was so busy she did not have time, it seemed, even to part her hair straight: her part zigzagged as if somehow in sympathy with the way my mother felt. Still, she came. My mother could not thank her enough, especially since, entering her second trimester, she was growing worse instead of better. How could she still be throwing up? Was there something wrong?

There was nothing wrong. Dr. Leonard, her obstetrician, said this happened sometimes; some women threw up all through their entire pregnancies. His advice was to eat frequent small meals to keep the nausea at bay.

"Do you know what saltines are?" he asked.

"A kind of cracker," she answered. "They come in a long white box."

"Terrific!" he said. "You should also rest as much as possible. Do you know what a catnap is?"

"A short light sleep," she said. "Sort of like a doze."

"Terrific!" he said again. "You should try to take a couple a day. That's doctor's orders."

"Okay," she told him. "I will take some catnaps."

"Terrific!"

Did cats throw up between naps? And how did they study? It was a miracle she managed to finish the semester. Her grades would have shocked Mother Greenough. But still, despite her fog and exhaustion, she did at least pass everything. Thank you, Marnie! She was going to take Marnie out for lunch, though really she owed her friend much more than a sandwich. What should she do?

Before she could come up with an answer, dispiriting news arrived. Her thesis adviser had been assigned—Professor Gray.

She dragged herself in to school to meet with him.

"Just make sure you finish." Surprisingly, old and bloodless as he was, Professor Gray's rheumy eyes were lit with concern. "You are thirty points past your master's. You must write your dissertation. There's a world of difference between a PhD and an ABD."

An ABD. She did know more or less what that meant, but still she asked, "What is an ABD?"

"'All but dissertation,'" he said. "Some people call it the women's degree."

"Ah," she said. "I see."

"It's often part of a joint degree. The same way you can get an MD/PhD or a JD/PhD, you can get an Mrs/ABD."

"I see," she said again.

"I'm just trying to help you."

"Thank you."

How warm and sunny his office was—shouldn't it be gray? She could feel his interest. He was kinder than she realized. Still, he was not Mother Greenough. If Mother Greenough were her adviser, she would make it through somehow, if only to make Mother Greenough proud, if only to not disappoint her. That was not a good reason to get a PhD. Still, who cared what Professor Gray thought? Who cared whether or not he was proud of her?

The cockroaches were back. The apartment was not as infested as it had been, but the smell of bug spray so worsened her nausea, she could not use it. Instead, she whacked the insects with a shoe, two or three at a time, sweeping them into a corner for Chao-pe to get later. Never in her life had she thought to put her feet up, but she did it all the time now. Her ankles were swollen, and how her back hurt! She sat with her hands on her belly. Her skin, stretched tight as a balloon, was bisected by a strange black line; her belly button, popped out like a rubber cork, showed right through her clothes. How lucky that Marnie Mulligan had somehow found some hand-me-down maternity clothes for her! But how strange to wear someone else's clothes, and how strange the clothes were. A corduroy jumper with suspenders, a sailor-collared dress with smocking at the top of the belly. A flaring pink tent meant to be worn over slacks. She was glad that this phase was temporary, exciting as it was to feel the baby hiccupping and kicking and turning. Why did it turn? Was it trying to get comfortable? Did babies feel comfortable or uncomfortable, or was that something that came with life on the outside? And was that large round thing she felt a head?

"Such a big head!" Chao-pe was excited. "He is going to be smart."

"It could be a girl," my mother reminded him.

"Either way, very smart," he predicted. "A girl is also good."

"What if she's not smart?"

"The baby will be smart."

From time to time, he asked what was going on with her degree. Having himself had a great adviser in Minnesota, he wondered if she could switch to someone else—to anyone but Professor Gray. But to arrange appointments, to go in to school and speak to this one and that one—to argue and ask for an exception to the policy, as she might need to—impossible. She did not have the energy.

"You'll be busy after the baby is born," Chao-pe predicted. "Now is the time to look into it."

But, well, her brain, she wanted to say. It was as if every thought were hidden in a box. She could find it, but first she had to locate the box and open it. It took time.

"Don't push me," she said.

It was easier to tell him to leave her alone than to admit that she was worried, too. What if she never finished?

Chao-pe had stopped talking about the soldiers of Genghis Khan, but he did not carry an umbrella and scoffed at people who did, especially if it wasn't raining very hard. *Soft*, he called them. *Soft and weak.* Americans, for example. Americans were like Shanghai people, *soft and weak.*

Was she *soft and weak*? Sometimes she carried an umbrella when he was not around. When he was, she used a pleated clear plastic hair bonnet and let the rest of her get wet.

In wartime Shanghai, she had been grateful to be sequestered from the Japanese hell. Here, though, she felt shut in. Even with her beautiful bedroom set, she felt shut in, maybe because she liked walking on the streets, where there was so much going on. She missed the children, especially. Their energy! And their speed—everything they did, they did quick. There was one little girl she saw quite a lot, who did not seem to know how to walk, only to run, her ponytail coming loose behind her. One day, her hair elastic fell to the sidewalk; my mother rescued it and tried to return it but was too slow. Was her own child going to be quick like that? My mother was in motion as well, but in motion as the sun was in motion—momentously but imperceptibly. How would she keep up?

She was learning to cook more advanced dishes. She had found a Chinese cookbook in a used bookstore, and though at first she wasn't sure what a "tsp" was, or a "c," now she could make red-cooked pork, steamed pork with eggs, and stir-fried broccoli with oyster sauce. She could also steam a cod filet.

"Guess what I made?" she would ask Chao-pe when he came home. It would be dark. He would be taking off his shoes.

"What? What did you make?" he would ask, putting on his slippers.

Always, he would be enthusiastic. Chao-pe's nickname in college, after all, had been *Xiǎo Pàngzi*—Fatty. He loved to eat. There were never any leftovers, especially as she was eating more, too. Her dresses were as big as parachutes now, and so long that she bought a pack of needles and a spool of thread to hem them. Marnie showed her how, and sure enough, one evening she had results to model for Chao-pe. The dress was bright orange; she looked like a pumpkin. They laughed and laughed, and afterward, he felt the baby kick for a while.

Then he got out his slide rule. The apartment was a one-bedroom, but they had set up a desk and a blackboard for him in the foyer. Never mind that the chair blocked the doorway when he pulled it out; no one would be trying to get past him to the door while he was working anyway. It was like living on a ship, and the chair was a luxury compared to a backless stool. Plus, he had a nice bright desk lamp. He worked happily while she did the dishes.

Some nights she tried to write to Mother Greenough:

Since last I wrote, my grades have improved.

She could write that because her grades really had improved before they plummeted. But it was a half-truth. She started over:

I have finished all my coursework. So now I have thirty points past my master's. But I am worried about my dissertation. I know Christ has given me this hurdle, and I welcome it. However, I can't think of a topic. Maybe it is because I am pregnant. It is so hard to think, it is as if the baby is growing between my ears. But also I wonder if I am in the wrong field. I wonder if I am not actually interested in educational psychology, just my own educational psychology. How could I have been interested in so many things when I was young and now be interested in nothing?

That was the end of the letter, really. Still, she kept writing—as much to herself as to anyone else, she supposed:

I am afraid I only wanted you to respect me.
I am afraid I only wanted to be like you.
I am afraid I liked you because you liked me.
I am afraid that I am not actually like you.
I am afraid I only signed up for a PhD because I wanted to leave home.
I am afraid I didn't really know what America was.

She did not send this to Mother Greenough.

She would not have received it anyway, my mother says now. The school had to close.
And you had no forwarding address? I say.
Forwarding address? She laughs.

She started another letter:

I wonder if you are still in China. Many foreigners have left. I hope you have, too. Otherwise they will call you a Western imperialist agent wearing the cloak of religion. And how could you watch as your precious church and school are denounced? You would probably fight back. And then what? I know the Pope is not a regular leader, but in China we say leaders like to ask you to sacrifice your life but never sacrifice their own. I hope you have left and are safe in your little house with the beautiful biennial hollyhocks.

My mother looked at the sheet. She crumpled it up.
"*Maybe we should get a television,*" she told Chao-pe.
"*A television? So expensive!*" he said.

He was more intrigued by the idea than she would have thought, though. It was a newfangled thing, but he'd seen TV sets in store windows, and didn't more than half of all Americans have one? Television was the future. And so, to her shock, a week later, he brought one home. A Philco! It was a small set—maybe the smallest they made—but still.

"*Did you know there are now color televisions?*" Chao-pe said. "*Mister! They are expensive. But my boss's boss bought one and wanted to sell his black-and-white, so I bought it from him at a good price. The screen is just twelve and a half inches, but the picture is clear.*"

They plugged it in and turned it on, marveling as they switched the channels. It wasn't like having a movie projector in your house; it was like having many movie projectors. It was magic.

"*The TV will keep you company,*" Chao-pe said. "*It will talk to you. Your English is excellent, but the TV will improve it even more.*"

And the TV did keep her company, and it was indeed good for her English—her spirits, besides. Such an amazing box, with so many kinds of shows! She loved *The Price Is Right,* and *Truth or Consequences,* and *Texaco Star Theater*—really, she loved them all. *The Milton Berle Show! The Jackie Gleason Show! Toast of the Town,* with that Ed Sullivan! But most of all, she loved *I Love Lucy,* especially after Marnie told her that Ricky Ricardo really was married to Lucy.

"Ricky's not his real name. His real name is Desi Arnaz. But they are married in real life, just like on the show, and do you know what he is? He's an immigrant," she said. "His family fled to America after the Cuban Revolution. Before that, they were aristocrats and politicians."

"Really?" My mother couldn't believe it.

"Really. They were attacked by the revolutionaries and had all their property confiscated."

"That's just like what happened to my family!" my mother said.

"He came here with nothing but the clothes on his back. And now he is a TV star!"

My mother shook her head, amazed. "Dreams really do come true in America."

"Well, sometimes," said Marnie. "Not all the time, heaven knows. But sometimes."

It would have been worth buying the television just for *I Love Lucy*, but in addition this year there was the coronation of Queen Elizabeth to watch. My mother would never forgive the British for the Opium Wars, or for leaving the International Settlement to the mercy of the Japanese. And could the U.S. delegation to the coronation really be headed by that idiot George Marshall—the very general who had been sent to negotiate peace in China and ended up handing it to the Communists? The sight of his face made her want to turn the TV off. Still—the ceremony in Westminster Abbey! She had never seen anything so beautiful. And how could someone so young be so regal? Queen Elizabeth was twenty-seven!—about the same age as my mother.

"It makes you think about luck," she said to Chao-pe. "Here I am, and there she is. Of course, it could be worse. My father said I was the luckiest of the children in my family, and I am. But as lucky as she?"

"Not everyone can be the queen of England," he said.

"But imagine if we'd been born here. Imagine if we'd never seen a Japanese bomber. Imagine if the Communists had never taken over our homes."

He laughed. "Engineers don't ask those questions," he said. "But anyway, we will not have to imagine anything. Our baby will not know what a bomber looks like. He will not know what a bayonet is, or a Communist. Maybe he will not be able to tell a Japanese from a Chinese, just like the queen of England."

"That's not true. She can tell."

"Maybe."

"And what if he is a she?"

"She will not be able to tell, either."

"Will everyone say it's too bad she's a girl?"

"Only if it really is too bad," Chao-pe joked. He winked.

She half smiled. Was that like a note he was sending—a note whose answer was preapproved? Or was it a different kind of wink?

"The baby will be a U.S. citizen, you know," she said.

"Really? Even if we are not citizens?"

"Really. Because the baby will have been born here."

He shook his head. "America is not like other countries."

"It is not," she agreed. What's more, she informed him, she had read in the newspaper that under the terms of a new Refugee Relief Act, Chao-pe was now eligible for "an adjustment of status to permanent residence." If he applied, he would be on the same track as she. *"And you know what that means?"*

"What?"

"It means we both could eventually become so-called naturalized citizens *if we like."*

But he refused to apply.

"First of all, we're not refugees," he said. "Second of all, we are Chinese."

"A 'permanent resident' *is just a* 'permanent resident,'" she argued. "And if we do eventually 'naturalize,' we won't have to renounce our Chinese citizenship, you know. We can remain Chinese. We'll just have so-called dual citizenship."

"'Dual citizenship'? What a strange idea."

"I don't think it's so strange."

"That's because you grew up in the International Settlement and were really only half Chinese to begin with."

"What kind of way is that to talk," she said.

Still, he refused to apply for a green card. "We're being kept here against our will," he said. "We're not refugees. We're political prisoners."

He really was impossible, my mother says now.

Did he think you'd go back?

He did. He did not care what the government was. He said the government was changing all the time. Today China was

Communist, but yesterday it was Nationalist, and tomorrow it would be something else.

This Refugee Relief Act was kind of a big deal, I say. Usually there were all of 105 immigrant visas a year for Chinese people, but just this once, there were over 2,000. And Chinese people had only been allowed to naturalize at all as of 1943, you know.

Too bad you had not been born yet, otherwise you could tell him.

He didn't consider himself American, I guess.

He thought Americans were American, she says. We were Chinese.

Now every night, my mother had things to tell Chao-pe—things she had seen on the television. She repeated funny jokes she'd heard, and explained things she'd figured out, especially once she discovered the *Major League Baseball Game of the Week*.

"The point of the game looks simple—to hit the ball and run around the bases," she said. "But it's actually hard to do. There are different pitches, and different plays. For example, if a player hits the ball and runs to first base, he can try to steal second base when the next batter comes up to bat, before he has hit the ball. The pitcher has to keep an eye on the guy on base, especially since if the pitcher sees that he's trying to steal a base, the pitcher can, quick, throw and get him tagged out. Three outs, and it's the end of the inning for the team that's batting."

How proud George Ping would be of all she'd picked up! Chao-pe was too busy to be proud, or to root for the Yankees, either. But she was rooting for them. Yogi Berra! Mickey Mantle! Casey Stengel! Whitey Ford! She wished she could go watch a game. Was George Ping going to games in the warm evening air? Did he have a girl to take with him, and did they hold hands? She didn't want to wonder. She was a married woman! And yet she couldn't help it. She did.

That's not true! she says now.
Not even a little? I say.
She doesn't answer.

The Yankees! The Yankees! And yet just as the Yankees were about to go to the World Series to try for a fifth title, she was paying no attention whatsoever, having been put into a twilight sleep. She woke up with a large egg roll in her arms.

"Today is the biggest day of your life," said the nurse brightly. "Congratulations! Meet your son."

Could this little stranger have lived inside her not long ago? He had an improbably full head of downy black hair and, active as he had been in the womb, he now held very still, as if hoping to be put back. Chao-pe and she oohed and aahed, amazed and awed, though the baby was red and wrinkly and ugly. His legs were scrawny, and his arms were short. His tiny fingernails were perfect, it was true. And his eyelashes were like the finest of brushstrokes in a Chinese ink drawing. But it was his helplessness that touched her most—his helplessness and his eyes, which, when he opened them, shone as bright and disinterested as the moon.

"A boy!" said Chao-pe. *"A boy!"*

"He looks like you," she said.

"He does," Chao-pe agreed. *"Handsome and fat!"*

She laughed.

How lucky that she had grown up with younger brothers and sisters! Otherwise, she might have been afraid to touch the baby, like Chao-pe. But still, to take care of a baby yourself—with no nursemaid—there was nothing natural about it. The nurses showed her how to swaddle the baby. They showed her how to tell when he was hungry, and how to feed and burp him. They showed her how to pin on a new diaper so that it would stay on and not leak. And most important, they showed her how to support his head, explaining there was a spot on it that had not closed up.

"We should not be alarmed that it pulses," she told Chao-pe. *"It's just where the bones of the head are still growing so his brain can grow."*

But Chao-pe was not reassured. He was fascinated by the baby's entrancingly aimless motions—by the way he opened his mouth and puckered it; by the way he curled his tongue and stuck it out. And the way the baby could drop so suddenly into sleep he seemed to have left for another world—amazing! Chao-pe was too terrified, though, to hold the baby for more than a moment or two, even as he wrote to his mother:

We have great news. A son! Born during the Mid-Autumn Festival. He looks like a Jen. Someday you will meet him, and you will know right away, That is my grandson. We named him Qìngrú as we hope he will indeed prove a scholar. In English, his name is Reuben, *which not only sounds like rú but means "Behold, a son!"—an appropriate name, I think you will agree. Shu-hsin is in good health. She is recovering fast and learning fast, a real mother.*

We think of you often. Though we are far away on the other side of the world, when we look up, we know that we see the same moon you see. That is a comfort.

He needed some help with the saying about the moon, well-known as it was; luckily, even in her exhausted state, my mother still knew it went *Hǎi shàng shēng míng yuè, tiān yá gòng cǐ shí.*

"I hope we will be able to bring our son home soon," he said.

"We'll bring him," she told him. "Your mother will have a chance to see him. Don't worry."

My mother was afraid that her father would not get to meet his grandchild, either. But even more terrible was the fear that her mother would not much care one way or the other, especially since her brother had married and could soon have a child far more important than hers—a child who would, if it were a boy, carry on the Loo name.

In the meanwhile, what would they have done if Marnie Mulligan had not continued to visit, her hair messier than ever? Marnie herself had no desire for children. But she knew from her four sisters what new mothers needed, and produced all sorts of presents from her Lord & Taylor shopping bag: bibs and pacifiers, bags of candy, flowers she'd filched from the gardens at school, and, best of all, dinner. Tuna noodle casserole, macaroni and cheese, spaghetti with meatballs, meatloaf, and my mother's favorite: green beans with fried onion rings. What a magic ingredient, this cream of mushroom soup! And how happy my mother was to hear, as she ate, about Marnie's progress on her dissertation, though it seemed that Marnie might just head back to Ohio once she got her degree. Her mother, it seemed, was having more and more trouble walking. She couldn't manage without a daughter, and Marnie's sisters were all married and raising kids. Marnie wasn't complaining, but still my mother nodded sympathetically. What did this mean for Marnie's career? As for what my mother was going to do if Marnie really did leave, she couldn't begin to imagine.

She had begun taking short walks in the park and now recognized two or three other mothers. She thought, too, that she would start going to church again once she could leave Reuben with Chao-pe. But until then, she didn't like exposing such a little baby to germs and so mostly stayed home, where it was lonely, yes, but less lonely than it was before Reuben was born. She clapped when he smiled; she clapped when he rolled over. She clapped when he discovered his toes, and when he sat up, and when he started to pick things up, and when he drank from a cup. And of course, she clapped when he clapped. He liked her hair and, as soon as he could, pulled at it and put it in his mouth.

"Naughty boy!" she said, but it was always with a smile.

They watched baseball together and played; she fed him and played; she changed him and played.

"You know, your mommy can stay up all night, but your daddy needs to sleep," she would tell him. She blew on his face, making him laugh. *"Your mommy is busy with you, but your daddy has a job."*

She bought a secondhand stroller and started taking him for walks, showing him the city. "This is a swing. When you are older, you will swing in it," she told him, speaking in English, so he would learn English. "This is an ice cream store. When you are older, you will eat ice cream. This is a school. When you are older, you will study books and become illustrious. This is a high school. When you go there, your mommy will go back to school and study, too, if she is not too old."

Laundry, laundry, laundry. What she would have done for a washing machine! The diapers alone were a part-time job. She swished them in the toilet; then they had to be washed and bleached and hung up to dry. Reuben's clothes, too, were always dirty from when he leaked and spat up, as were her clothes. Everything smelled.

"In China, the servants do the wash," she told him. "Or at least they used to." She tried to imagine her mother doing her own wash. Probably her sisters were doing it. Did her sister-in-law help?

Reuben began to rock on all fours, and then to crawl using one foot and one knee, fast.

"*He is going to be an athlete,*" she told Chao-pe.

"*No, no, he is going to be a scholar,*" he said.

She researched nursery schools. Their cost shocked her.

"*We will find a way,*" Chao-pe promised. He was like a person with a concrete wall behind him; he never had to turn around and check what might be there. Neither did he ever waver. Every day, he was full of purpose; every day, he was on his way. She once asked him if he knew what desperation was.

"*What?*" he said.

She was embarrassed to have asked. And who had she become that she had thought to ask such a question?

Sometimes I did not recognize myself, she says now. Babies change everything, I say.

She hoped that Chao-pe's concrete wall would become hers, because if she had ever had one of her own, she didn't anymore. Though to raise little Reuben—wasn't that a worthy goal? To help Chao-pe build a family—weren't they a team?

When she became pregnant again, Reuben started throwing fits. Was it because she was pregnant? Or was it something else? Dr. Rock, the pediatrician—a white-haired white man in a white coat—gave her a book that said tantrums at a year and a half were to be expected. Still, it was a shock when Reuben hit her, and once even bit her. Was that normal?

"He needs a nursemaid," she told Chao-pe. "He needs grandparents, aunts, uncles, cousins. Brothers and sisters. Here he wants my attention all day long. If I turn away for even a moment, he gets upset."

Another day, she told Chao-pe, "Reuben is hard to control."

"His problem is that he is not afraid of anyone," he said.

"Mother Greenough used to say there is no fear in love. It's in the Bible."

"Mother Greenough never had a child. In Yixing, we say, If you do not beat and scold the child, this is not your child."

My mother laughed and admitted, "We said that in Shanghai, too."

"That is how Chinese people think, that's why. You have to teach your child. It is your duty."

Teach him or train him? I say now. Sometimes I wonder if for you and Dad, they were the same thing.

I don't know what you talking, she says.

So much of what you taught was not math or science but what we were and were not allowed to do. For example, leave the family.

Bad bad girl! You are not allowed to leave!

That's what I mean, I say.

Though she wasn't as sick as she had been during her first pregnancy, this time she was more depleted. If only she had some of the nourishing soups she would have had in China! Without them, her body felt so weak and heavy that, though it was right there in the same room, Reuben's crib sometimes seemed far away. *I'm coming!* she would say. *I'm coming!* But it was as if she had furniture to move before she could get anywhere—a bookcase, a bureau, a desk—and sometimes by the time she had gotten it all out of the way and picked him up, he was kicking so hard she worried for the baby inside her. Babies were well insulated, she knew. Still, they heard everything and sensed everything. It was important for the mother to be calm if they were to be calm, and how could she be calm? When she—they—were under attack.

Much of the day, she and Reuben watched television until he

napped. If she turned off the television, he threw a fit. Even if they were going outside, which he liked, he would throw a fit about having to put a jacket on first. She would try to make a game of it. "What does a dog need to go out? Fur!" she would tell him. "What does a turtle need to go out? A shell! What do little boys need to go out? A jacket!" And sometimes that would work. Other times, she had to scare him. "Do you know what happens to little boys who go out without a jacket?" she would say. "They freeze like an ice cube." Or, "Do you know what a snowman is? He is a little boy who went out without a jacket." Sometimes, too, she would hide his jacket. "Where's your jacket? Someone stole it! Now you have no more jacket! No more going to the playground!" It wasn't clear how much he understood, but one very cold day, having run out of patience, she brought him outside, let him feel how cold it was, and waited until he was sobbing before she allowed him back in. "Oh! There's your jacket!" she said. "The thief must have given it back."

Outside, thankfully, he would usually calm down. If only after the playground he did not beg to go see what was in the toy store window. Sometimes they would go in, but then he would want to play with the toys, and when all she could tell him was no, he couldn't have them, he would throw another fit. At home, she fashioned many entertaining things out of paper. She could make a turtle and a crane and a swan and a box and even a jumping frog—Nai-ma had taught her how. But he liked the plastic toys in the toy store.

"He needs more toys," she told Chao-pe.

Chao-pe did not believe in buying toys. *"You know what those things are? A lot of junk,"* he said.

My mother bought Reuben some toys anyway, only to witness herself how, yes, he would play with a car for a morning but lose interest in it by the afternoon. Then Chao-pe criticized her.

"We did not have such toys when we were growing up," he said. *"They are unnecessary."*

But he had had brothers and cousins, she pointed out. He had had a horse down the road to go visit. His family had had chickens and goats in the garden. And the servants! The servants knew all sorts of games and songs and tricks.

"Reuben spends all day in a city apartment with his mommy and a television," she said. *"He is bored."*

"The television is boring?"

"It's not boring." She did not want to say something so expensive was boring. *"But it's limited. It's not alive."*

"You should make some friends."

She agreed. What with no one to babysit they went less and less often to International House, and while there were family picnics with other Chinese engineers, those were held twice a year at the most. Faithful Marnie Mulligan still came to visit sometimes; when my mother learned the word "godsend," she thought, I know a godsend. Marnie is a godsend. But most days she and Reuben were all alone. Her main entertainment besides the television was the newspaper.

So, yes, she needed friends.

Sitting in the park, she tried to look friendly, not exhausted. And other mothers did stop sometimes, and once she got to talking with someone she thought could be a friend. A Spanish woman—or at least that was what my mother thought she was; she wasn't entirely sure where the woman was from. But she wore a bright coat and a bright smile, and her son was not only active like Reuben but had almost the same name.

"Reuben, Rubén!" the woman laughed. "Yours is Reuben! Mine is Rubén! Reuben, Rubén! Reuben, Rubén!"

The boys started playing together—the first time Reuben had ever played with another child. Rubén tried to teach him to play tag, which Reuben didn't seem to get, although he did understand that it meant that he should chase Rubén, and that Rubén would chase him. With the help of their mothers, they rode the seesaw up and down. The next day, my mother brought Reuben to the park with hope.

"Maybe we will see Rubén!" she said.

But Rubén and his mother were not there. My mother checked again the next day, and many days after that. No luck.

"I wish we could go back to China," she told Chao-pe.

Even if the U.S. government weren't blocking their return, though, the China they knew was gone. A letter arrived from my mother's family—once again in her brother's handwriting:

Do you remember that rental building we had? Thank heavens we had it. Otherwise, where would we have moved once we left our big house? Of course, we are happy that so many other families are now able to live in the rental building with us. Really, it was a shame that so many people had to live on the street while buildings like this were occupied by just a few families. Now there are twelve families here. We all share the downstairs kitchen. Your sisters do the cooking and bring water up in buckets for drinking and bathing. We have three rooms for the seven of us. Three rooms is more than anyone else has, and some people grouse about that. But others feel sorry for us since the whole building was originally ours. We tell them we don't need their sympathy.

The Communists have accomplished many good things. For example, they have gotten rid of all kinds of vice. Gambling and prostitution, drugs, and petty theft have been eliminated. There are no more gangs, no more mahjong, even. The fashion is for plain blue cotton clothes, which saves everyone a lot of time. Also, everyone is studying Russian. We are not surprised. Every war brings a new language. First it was English and then Japanese. Now Russian. We are too old to make such sounds, but we can hear young people practicing in the other apartments. "Tovarish!" they say. That means "comrade." Your sister says that from what she's seen, Russian grammar is even harder than English grammar, and a lot of the words are long. Still, the young people study diligently. So many of them signed up to join the People's Liberation Army that many had to be turned away. They seem to sincerely believe we are going to catch up to Britain and surpass Japan, and are working hard to accomplish that goal.

Of course, our family has had some adjustments to make. Don't worry too much, but if you have any spare Chinese funds, could you think about repatriating them? We also need needles for our phonograph, but I'm afraid no one can help us with that, not even an American relative. Luckily, we have radios, thanks to your brother who can build them himself. He is very talented.

Baba stays home every day now. It is good for him to rest. His work was always so much pressure, as you know, and teaching others to take over his job was not easy at his age. When we moved, we found a large trunk full of IOUs written to him by people to whom he had lent money. He always intended for us to burn the slips when he dies, and only accepted them to help the people save face. But now he worries. We tell him that the IOUs do not mean he exploited anyone but rather that he helped people. Everyone knows he is a good man. Did you know that not one of his employees ever wrote a letter to criticize him? Still, his health suffers.

Please send pictures of your son. We think he must be strong and eat very well. Is he lively and naughty? How is his Chinese? You should pay attention to his pronunciation so that when he comes back, people do not think he is a foreigner.

Her father no longer working. Her family forced out of their home. All seven of them squeezed into three rooms of a former rental building. My mother tried to picture the building but couldn't remember it. And what did that mean, that her father's health was suffering? Was that why he didn't write? What did he do all day? It was hard to imagine him cooped up with the rest of the family. Did he have a desk? She hoped he had a desk by a window—he'd always liked his desk near a window—even as she knew, of course, that he did not. How galling that he should have to worry that his good deeds would be used against him! And was her mother really asking for money?

How could she expect me to help her? After she left me to fend for myself in a strange country? she says now.
Something you could not write, I say.

Of course not.
Especially since the money wasn't just for her, but the whole family, I say.
I have no choice.

She dutifully researched how to send funds. It was illegal, but everyone was doing it; there were ways. Assuming, that is, that she could find some money to send—her family thought all Americans were rich, but she and Chao-pe were not.

Reuben was throwing a fit; inside her, the baby was kicking. She ignored them both.

She would talk to Chao-pe about what they could do.

Reuben seemed like he wanted to talk but couldn't. Was that his problem? He had babbled nonstop as a baby; how she and he had both loved the back-and-forth of pretend talk, with its tidal expressions of surprise and delight and mock scolding. If only they could go back to that wordlessness now! He could say "Mama" and "Dada," of course, and "uh-oh," and "bye-bye." He knew the word "cup," too, and could say "ap" for apple. And he understood some Shanghainese baby talk—*kuèn go* for "sleep," and *zēn zēn tâo yi* for "really annoying," and *viâo ko* for "don't cry." But he seemed frustrated. Would he be doing better if she spoke English baby talk? What was a binky? Was that the same as a blankie? It was so strange the way English speakers added the long "e" to everything. Goody, sweetie, teddy, doggy. And what was it she'd learned the other day? Itty-bitty.

"Do you speak to him in Chinese or in English?" Dr. Rock twirled a pen as they spoke.

"Both," my mother said.

It wasn't a plan; it was just what they did.

"Of course, my husband and I speak Chinese," she said—adding, when Dr. Rock looked blank, "because we are Chinese."

"Well, that could be confusing for Reuben," Dr. Rock said. "It could be confusing for anyone, really."

"It's not confusing for us," she said.

Still, she took his reaction to heart. *"Do you think Reuben is* confused that we speak to him in both English and Chinese?" she asked Chao-pe.

"Maybe."

"I wonder if we should teach him one language at a time."

"Reasonable enough. But which one?"

She hesitated. *"English,"* she said finally.

It was hard. Realistically, though, English was important not only for Reuben but Chao-pe, too. There were teaching jobs open at the universities, yes. To teach, though, it wasn't enough to know how to design. You had to be understood.

"I'll call you Norman, and you call me Agnes," my mother said.

"Okay, Agnes." His impish grin had not changed since the day they met at International House.

"Very good, Norman." She smiled back.

Yet even speaking just English, my mother could see frustration build in Reuben—frustration she was sure would subside like swells on the ocean if only he could express what he wanted. Instead, it crested and broke violently, as if hitting land. Dr. Rock said she shouldn't compare, but my mother couldn't help but notice that another child at the park had many more words than Reuben. The other child was around Reuben's age but said, "No dog!" to a teen who had brought a poodle to the playground. He said, "Mama, up!" when he wanted to be picked up. And he would not play with Reuben, my mother said, because Reuben could not talk the way he did. When Reuben chased him, he didn't chase back; he ran away. So sometimes when Reuben caught up to him, he hit him.

"Reuben is jealous," my mother told Dr. Rock. "He hits because the other child can talk and he can't."

"Possibly," said Dr. Rock. "But children have lots of feelings. Maybe he just likes chasing and wishes the other child did, too."

She considered that.

"You should try to teach him that he can't hit, no matter what his feelings. Because otherwise he will have trouble when he goes to school."

"Okay," she said.

But later, she said to Norman, "Reuben is jealous of the new baby, and that's why he hits."

"*How can he know you are pregnant?*" Norman was supposed to be speaking English but spoke in Chinese anyway.

"He knows," she insisted in English.

"*Shouldn't he be happy to have a playmate?*"

"He doesn't know the baby will be a playmate. How can he even know what a playmate is?"

"*How can he know what jealousy is? Does a baby bird feel jealous?*"

"You don't think they compete with other baby birds? You don't think they both want the same worm sometimes?"

"*You studied too much psychology.*"

"All you know is engineering."

Another day, she said, "Reuben needs more exercise. He needs room to run and play. He can't just sit home with his pregnant mommy watching television."

They found a new apartment in Queens. Norman didn't mind taking the subway to work, and it no longer mattered how long it took her to get to school; she had taken a leave of absence. Here they could afford a two-bedroom garden apartment with a shared yard. There was a playground down the street with two slides and even a fence, so parents did not have to worry about their children wandering away. The biggest problem was that the ice cream truck stopped there every day; she knew that Reuben was going to be pestering her for ice cream. But she could handle that.

"Is this better?" Norman said.

"Much better," she said.

The more Norman focused on the future, the more English he spoke.

"First, I am going to get a real job," he announced. "You watch and see. I will get a professor job. No more contract work. Then we will buy a house."

"A house? How can we buy a house?"

No one in their crowd had bought a house. It was true that Chinese people were allowed to own property in New York, unlike in some other states, but he was not even a permanent resident.

What's more, though he might want a professor's job, so far he did not have one.

"You watch," he said. "See how I do. You watch."

My mother couldn't imagine it. Still, brushing off her typing skills, she helped him prepare a résumé. Then she helped him find a three-piece suit for his interview. Though the vest was a little big, Marnie Mulligan expertly took it in.

"Where I come from, there's no one looking after us but ourselves," she explained. She was using a fold in her skirt for a pincushion.

Norman was impressed. If only my mother were more like Marnie!

As if Marnie Mulligan had to make the adjustment I did, my mother says now.

He did not appreciate how hard it was to take care of a baby, either, I say.

He thought children raised themselves.

But never mind. With their help, he got not one assistant professorship offer but two.

"Which chairman is easier to get along with?" he asked his fellow engineers. And that was the department he joined. He also applied for a green card, having no choice; he couldn't work without one. The school said it would sponsor him.

"Finally, the right decision," my mother said.

He wrote papers; she typed them. He taught classes and attended conferences. And slowly, my mother began to dream his dream. A house wasn't a PhD, but it was a heartening new goal; and the more she embraced it, the more other things receded. She would not forget Mother Greenough and how disappointed she would be in her. She would not forget being looked down on by Georgiana, or being betrayed by her mother. She would not forget her worry about her father, or her hatred of the Japanese—the Communists, too. But a kind of film lay over them all. Far brighter and clearer, now, shone this vision of the future. A house!

If only Marnie Mulligan had not returned to Ohio the day after she got her degree!

"Are you really leaving?" My mother almost couldn't speak.

"Both of my mom's legs are kaput now," said Marnie. "Someone's got to push her chair." As she had gotten her hair done for graduation, it fell in smooth shiny curls, and she was wearing new shoes. They were just like her old ones but less beat-up.

"What about your career?" said my mother. "Shouldn't you—"

"Life is long," Marnie said firmly. "You have to believe that, especially if you're a woman."

She opened her Lord & Taylor bag and produced two cantaloupes. "I brought you these. They aren't really a present. I just didn't want to them to go bad."

"We'll eat them," my mother said reassuringly. "Don't worry. They won't go to waste."

"I wish I weren't leaving, either," Marnie said. "But you'll be okay."

"You will, too," my mother said, and then blurted out, "Dr. Marnie Mulligan!"

Marnie laughed, but there were tears in her eyes. "You've got to finish. Promise me you'll finish."

"I promise."

"After all those meals I brought you, you owe me that."

"I promise," my mother said again and, as Marnie stood to leave, "Thank you."

"Ohio's not that far. When your kids are bigger, you can drive out and visit."

"We'll come someday."

"In the meanwhile, you pray for me and I'll pray for you," she said.

"I'll pray for you every day." My mother tried to mimic Marnie's no-nonsense style and closed the door matter-of-factly behind her friend. But after a moment, she quietly opened it again. She watched Marnie make her way down the block, empty Lord & Taylor bag under her arm, and did not close the door until well after her friend had disappeared.

Norman sat her down at the chalkboard. He laid out his plan.

"Even if we go back to China, this will be a good thing," he said.

Then he explained to her what appreciation was, ending with a confident, "And this kind of house, it will appreciate." He sat back. "This is America. Everything here is go up."

"Appreciate." My mother knew that word, and no doubt her father the banker knew it, too, but how did Norman know it? He seemed to find things on the sidewalk; he learned from the air.

"I will learn to drive so I can get to work," Norman went on. "We will get a car."

"Okay," she said.

"Of course, we will have to save up a lot of money."

"Okay."

She bought an accounting book. He would teach and she would save, and the next time they moved it would be into their own home.

And sure enough, there are your expenses, in a little red-and-black book, I say now. "Paper .40, laundry 2.00, extension cord 1.23, grocery 13.61, Reuben baseball hat .87."

Before I came to America, I did not know how to save money, she says. Now I was an expert.

Her body stretched out for the new baby as if her very bones knew how to be pregnant. Reuben continued to throw tantrums, but she was getting better and better at ignoring him. She remembered some of the servants acting this way sometimes, as if they did not see you; her aunts and uncles did it, too, just more delicately. When she lost Nai-ma, for example—she remembered.

American mothers seemed to think it important to react to everything the child did. In my mother's mind, though, it was good enough that she was there. As the saying went, *As long as the mountain does not move, the river will flow.* And heaven knows—at eight months, nine months, then ten months pregnant—she was a mountain. Strangely, too, she found that she liked ignoring Reuben sometimes. Norman, as well. There was a satisfaction in not feeling she was at their beck and call. It was the power of the powerless, perhaps, but still. It was power.

Reuben liked feeling the baby kick and move. "Pah-puh?" he

wanted to know, meaning, "Puppy?" And Norman was excited, too, although distracted. The teaching was easy, but conversing with Americans all day was hard. They talked about so many topics, switching from sports to the stock market to department politics back to sports. About the only thing they were not interested in was China. They were interested in his having come from there and vaguely realized that there had been a revolution. But mostly they wanted to know about Chinese food and Chinese women.

"I don't know anything about Chinese women," he would say.

"Ah, come on. You're holding out on us," they'd say.

That was when it was convenient to pretend he had no idea what they meant. "'Hold out on,'" he'd say. "What means, 'hold out on'?"

Then he would wink and laugh, though my mother knew he felt a lot of pressure to do well.

"It will work out," she would reassure him. She understood, however, why he needed to focus on his research as well as why, when he wasn't in the lab, he had to focus on his teaching.

"The students like me," he reported. "The professors like me, too."

"Of course," she said. "Who wouldn't like you?"

The other assistant professor, he said. The other assistant professor didn't like him.

"He tell everyone, how can this person teach, he do not even speak English. The students say they can understand me. They say they can understand everything, everything is clear."

"They stick up for you."

"But he does not think my teaching method is sound. Because I do not use notes. Because I lecture without notes."

"You don't use notes?"

"I learn that from my professor in Minnesota," he said. "Professor Johnson. Professor Johnson always used to say, every chapter has just one idea. If you understand that idea, you do not need notes."

"Interesting," she said.

"He was a great professor. Too bad you did not get an adviser like that."

"Yes," she agreed, although the world of advisers and degrees was far away now, like something in a book. "How did I get assigned Professor Gray? Of all people, Professor Gray!"

"Maybe you can still ask to change one. Ask for someone else."

"No, it's too late."

And, mountain of confidence though he was, not even Norman could disagree. "It's too bad," he said instead.

"Yes, it's a pity."

Her new hurdle was ironing Norman's shirts; a professor's shirts needed to look better than a contractor's. She bought a new iron, carefully studied the guide that came with it, and after a few tries she was producing perfect collars. She thought Norman would be pleased. But when he found out that she sat down to do the ironing, he was irritated.

"Soft," he said.

"I am not soft, I am pregnant."

Still, that's what he thought, she could tell, until number two was born and he saw how big she was. Eight and half pounds, and her head!

That was me! I say now.
A pain in the neck from the start, my mother says.

As she went into labor during a hurricane, Norman had to carry her through the flooded streets to the hospital. He managed it, only to have the doctor, worried about his family, leave immediately after the birth, before the placenta had emerged. Was he distracted the whole time? Was that why she first tore, and then hemorrhaged? Even after she was sent home, she had to sit on an inflatable ring. Oh, to have some family to help! Though she and Norman couldn't really afford it, they hired a sitter named Mrs. Tupper. Mrs. Tupper had a funny smell and hung her shoulder bag from her neck like a horse's feed bag. But she was available and cheap and could at least take Reuben to the park for a few hours. Reuben did not like her. When he realized that his choices were to go with her or stay home with the crying baby, though, he went.

They named the baby Bìlián in Chinese, Lillian in English. It was an elegant name. Both names had the lily flower for a root, and they rhymed. Bìlián, Lillian. In their minds, the baby should have been happy to receive such a name. She should have been happy, too, to have been born almost exactly on Norman's birthday, and in the same zodiac year: that made them both sheep and, as the zodiac cycle was twelve years, almost exactly thirty-six years apart. And her godmother was Marnie Mulligan, who couldn't leave her mother to attend the baptism but was allowed to be named the baby's godmother anyway. Wasn't that lucky?

The baby, though, was not happy. She cried when she was hungry, but she cried after she was fed, too. The only time she did not cry was when she was asleep.

At the two-week checkup, my mother told the doctor, "She has some kind of trouble."

Dr. Rock nodded understandingly but, putting his pen behind his ear, said, "Babies take time to get back to their birth weight."

"This baby cries all the time."

"Some babies are colicky."

"What is 'colicky'?"

"It means something is bothering them, so they cry. It means they are irritable, especially in the evening. Is she worse in the evening?"

My mother nodded. "How can we make her stop?"

"Let's try a different formula."

My mother tried the new formula—a formula for fussy babies. It did not help.

"She'll grow out of it," said Dr. Rock at the next visit.

"When?"

"Usually by three or four months," he said, adding, "You can call the office if you need help."

But my mother knew that if she called, the nurse would only say the same thing—that some babies are colicky and no one knows why. She tried patting the baby on the back, wrapping her up, rocking her.

The baby was still not gaining weight.

Dr. Rock's brows connected up like a fat white snake. "How is her stool?"

"Watery all the time."

"Let's put her on banana flakes," he said. "We don't want her to fail to thrive."

"What does that mean, 'fail to thrive'?"

"She isn't failing," said Dr. Rock. "We just want to make sure she doesn't." He paused. "Maybe you should keep a log."

"What is a 'log'?"

"A notebook," he said. "Write everything down."

It was August 28. The baby was sixteen days old and weighed eight pounds, seven ounces. At the top of the first page, my mother wrote on the left, "Lactum 17 oz, boiled water 13 oz," and on the right, "Banana flakes 1 tsp at 10 a.m. and 6 p.m." She wrote down, too, every feeding, and every stool, marking them "L" for loose or "S" for solid. Of course, solid was not really solid; it was more like toothpaste. But it was not as watery as some of the stools were.

It's so interesting, Ma, how you organized your entries, I say now. Like you didn't put one week on a page. You put six days, or eight days, or seven—whatever filled up the page, as if the most important thing was not to waste any space.

I don't want to waste paper, that's all, she says.

You didn't think in terms of the week. That wasn't your unit of organization. And you made columns, going from top to bottom, as if you were writing Chinese.

That's just how I wrote it, she says.

You were an English-speaking, Chinese-thinking person. You have too much to say.

"Are they getting better?" Norman was worried.

The stools stayed mostly L, she reported, but occasionally she was able to write S. And by the time the baby was two months, she was up to ten pounds, eight ounces—a gain of over two pounds! By three months, she was eleven pounds, seven ounces. That was a relief, even if she was still crying.

In December, my mother switched the baby to cow's milk, but if anything, that made her cry more. Sometimes my mother felt sorry for her, but other times she wanted to drop her out the window—though she would never, of course, "bathe the baby," as people did in China with unwanted girls.

Shanghai people did not do such things, she says now.
I remember you said that before, I say. You said people in Shanghai weren't like people in Yixing.
They are sort of like old China over there, she says.

She did, however, very much wish that she could hand the baby over to a nursemaid.

Of course I did, she says. You were a pain in the neck.

Why had she had a second child? And why, if she had a daughter, did she have to be so homely? A homely child who never stopped crying—no one would ever marry her.

"Do you have any help?" asked Dr. Rock one day. "Because sometimes—"

My mother waited.

"—sometimes a baby is struggling because the mother is struggling."

"I am not struggling."

"Your baby cries all the time," he said. "When do you rest?"

"I have a sitter."

In fact, Mrs. Tupper had quit. Reuben was too rambunctious, she complained. If she made him a nice sandwich for the park, he might eat two bites. Then he would throw the rest up in the air, laughing as it came down and birds flocked over.

"I don't need help," my mother insisted. "I can manage by myself."

Dr. Rock looked out the window.

"We should go back to China," Norman said.

It was something they could finally contemplate, China and America having at last agreed to allow Chinese citizens to return home if they liked. And, of course, though the world she and Norman had known was gone, their families were still there. But if they went back, where would they live? If before the children they couldn't have fit into the three-bedroom apartment my mother's family now occupied, how could they do it now? As for Taiwan, Beijing had bombed two of its islands. The U.S. had intervened, but the situation was unstable, and anyway, Norman did not consider himself from Taiwan.

"My family is from Yixing," he said.

They stayed in America. A year later, though, the baby was still crying.

"Crying will get you nowhere," my mother told her. "You know what you are? You are spoiled rotten." She let the baby cry herself to sleep, though it could take hours. Such a stubborn child.

"She cries all the time!" Reuben said.

"Babies are like that," my mother said. "And some babies are colicky besides."

"I don't like her."

"Don't say that," my mother said. "Babies are cute."

"She's not cute! She's . . . she's a bug!"

My mother sighed. "Wait until she can talk and play. Wouldn't you like a playmate?"

She watched more and more television. In her heart, she wanted a bigger set, a color set. But she didn't dare bring up the subject. Though he himself had bought the TV, Norman now called it an idiot box.

"It's good for Reuben's English," she countered.

And it could not be denied that Reuben talked more around the television than at any other time.

"Look! Look!" he would say. "Look at his hat. Why is he mad? Look, he fell down!"

Other times he asked questions. "What is a bunny? What is a tank? What is a gun?"

He and my mother loved to watch baseball together.

"The pitcher throws the ball," she told him. "The catcher catches the ball. The batter tries to hit the ball, but most of the time he misses. That is called a strike. But sometimes he hits it! And sometimes he hits it right out of the park!"

She taught him to root and cheer.

"Go, Yankees!" he shouted, bobbing up and down. "Go, Yankees!"

She held the baby in her lap while they watched. Often the baby would cry, though, especially after being fed.

"Stop!" Reuben would yell. "I can't hear! Stop! Stop!"

Then she would put the baby in her room and close the door, though Lillian was so strong now, and could pull so hard on the crib rails, that the whole crib banged against the wall and the neighbors complained.

"There is something the matter," she told Dr. Rock.

"Some children are easy and some are hard," he said, consolingly. "Many a young mother has felt overwhelmed, especially when they have too many children, as some groups are apt to do."

"I have two children," said my mother. She did not tell Dr. Rock she was having another. As for why, overwhelmed as she was, she had gone ahead and planned a third child two and half years after her last, it just seemed the right way. It was what her mother had done.

"I don't mean you." Dr. Rock straightened some papers on his desk. "But it's an awesome responsibility Nature has conferred on you ladies, and even more so when a baby has colic."

"When will it end, this colic?"

"Usually it's gone by now, but sometimes it goes on. It's hard to say, but take my word for it. She'll grow out of it."

"When? When will she grow out of it?"

"Let's just say I've yet to see a child go to college with colic," he said.

Sometimes she would give Lillian her bottle to drink by herself. She was strong; she could hold it. But often she would not drink the milk. Often she would leave the bottle upside down in the corner of the crib, dripping.

"She does it to spite me," my mother said.

"Are you sure?" Norman said. "She is a baby."

"She is too smart for her own good."

Dr. Rock retired. Another doctor took over his practice.

"Dr. Brock?" said Norman. "Are you sure you got his name right?"

"Yes," she said. "I'm sure."

"Dr. Brock" sounded like "Dr. Rock," but Dr. Brock was very different. Dr. Rock was old. Dr. Brock was young and short, with a serious air and a widow's peak.

"Tell me again," he said at the baby's two-year checkup. "She cries after you feed her? She rejects the bottle?"

"There is something the matter," my mother said.

"You're right." Dr. Brock frowned. "Have you ever tried goat's milk?"

Goat's milk was expensive—fifty cents a bottle. My mother tried just three bottles to start, but then she bought another four. Then another six.

"She stopped crying!" she told Dr. Brock at the next visit. "Finally, she stopped crying!"

"Maybe she has a milk allergy," he said. "Take good care of her; she's had a rough start in life."

"She can talk," my mother said. "She talks more than Reuben already."

"Is that so," said Dr. Brock.

"It frustrates him."

What she did not say was that when Reuben felt frustrated, he hit the baby.

"Well, what matters is that you give them each enough attention," he said. "If you love them enough, they will thrive."

She heard him and tried. But no sooner had she started Lillian on goat milk than she had her third child—another girl. My mother had to keep reminding herself how much harder her life would be if she were in China, especially with yet another campaign going on, the Anti-Rightist Campaign. This one targeted anyone who failed to condemn capitalism, challenged one-party rule, or questioned the giant collective farms.

Did you know what was happening? I say now. Mao called people like your father "poisonous weeds and noxious fumes."

They were supposed to be rooted out and dispelled. Hundreds of thousands of people were sent to hard labor camps.

I read that in the newspaper, she says. *But who could believe such things? Who could imagine that?*

Her family's situation was far worse than hers. Far, far worse. She understood that. There was no comparison. Still, it was all she could manage to write a short report about the new baby. *Another girl,* she wrote:

> *Her name is Lìshā. "Beautiful tiny grass" has a botanical root like the "lotus" in Bìlián, and Lìshā not only sounds like Lisa, her English name, but has a "li" sound like Lillian. So they pair well, I think. She is not like Bilian, though, big and strong. She is small and weak—a beautiful tiny grass, indeed. It seems that Bilian used up everything in the womb, but don't worry. I will be extra good to Lisha because she is the baby. Of course, it is not easy raising three children with no help, but we are managing.*

> *Qingru is in nursery school and really looks like a big boy now. He likes to wear a baseball cap and throw baseballs like an American. Also, he is very energetic. The other day, he pushed Bilian out of the car! She lost her front teeth when her mouth hit the curb, but she is okay. He likes the baby better because Lisha does not talk.*

> *I hope that this letter reaches you. You don't have to worry about me. Everything is fine here.*

Everything is fine here. In the beginning, number three was easier than number two, but when she switched to solid foods, she was even harder—such a fussy, fussy eater. Feeding her was so exhausting that sometimes my mother could not get out of bed in the morning. And when in the afternoon the baby napped, she herself slept so hard that when the baby woke up, number two had to come rouse her.

"The baby is crying!" she shouted. "You have to wake up! The baby needs her mommy! The baby needs her mommy! You have to wake up!"

The baby needs her mommy. The baby needs her mommy. Sometimes in her half sleep my mother thought, Three years old, and full sentences already. But sometimes she thought, Yes, yes, she needed Nai-ma. Where was she? Where did she go? When was she coming back? And many times then, though my mother was a grown woman with three children, she cried, too. Why did they take Nai-ma away? Who did that? Was she never coming back? My mother was angry—so angry that one day, when number two shook her and yelled louder, she slapped her.

"I don't know where you came from," she said.

And when number two cried, she slapped her again, and found that she herself stopped crying then. It was a kind of trick—a trick she wished she had not discovered but knew almost immediately would be hard to forget. Her mother had had opium; she did not have opium. Hitting made her feel much better, though—so much better, it was almost as if she had never cried at all.

Part II

CHAPTER IV

A Daughter

A letter arrived in my grandmother's voice and my uncle's handwriting:

> You do not have to worry about us. Yes, there are shortages and the lines are long. We have many family members to take turns queuing for winter cabbage, though, and we have enough to eat since portions are rationed and there are penalties for hoarding.
>
> Still, we have sad news. Baba has passed away. It was not really a surprise. In fact, his life force had been waning for a long time. Some days he was himself. For his eightieth birthday, we had a party for him—just five tables, but we managed to obtain some pork, and it was very lively. Everyone ate noodles and wished him long life, even though these days a long life is not so fashionable as it was before. One person even said, The times are killing us. But Baba said that the times are killing other people, we are still here. That was his mood that day.
>
> In the last few months, though, he would often say that he was an arrow at the end of its flight. Sometimes he would recite, "In Shenshi Garden, the willow is too old to bear

flowers" or even "Now I take leave from you, before the Spring ends / as I cannot bear to see the flowers fall." We do not know why he died, but we are all grieving deeply. At least he joined our ancestors peacefully, in his sleep. Little Brother said he could not bear to see all the flowers fall, but Little Sister said he could not bear any more winter cabbage.

Following Buddhist tradition, we will "do sevens" to help his spirit through the forty-nine days it needs to reincarnate. The weekly ceremonies will be held at Jing'an Temple, Jade Buddha Temple, and Fazangjiang Temple. It is convenient that there are seven of you children, so that each can be responsible for a ceremony. Since you are number five in responsibility, after the three boys and your elder half sister, your duty is to carry the Spirit Tablet and organize the feast on the night of the fifth "seven." It will be held at Jing'an Temple, with a 3 a.m.–5 a.m. watch at night and a Daoist priest chanting sutras. Of course, since you cannot come, we will arrange things on your behalf.

Regarding the burial, we would have liked to bury him in the countryside. But as there is no suitable location, we will bury him in a nearby cemetery in Shanghai instead. We will contact you again around Qingming Festival and let you know when the burial date has been decided. A proper burial is quite expensive, but maybe with each child covering as much as they can of the cost, we can manage.

My mother sobbed.

My father, she says even now. My father!
He knew when he said goodbye to you at the dock that he would never see you again, I say.
I wish I could see him one more time, she says. I wish I could say goodbye.
Or that you could have gotten him out, maybe.
I wish there was a way.

Did you know what was happening?

I knew that there was a so-called Great Leap Forward. I knew that the Communists took all the pots and pans and melted them down to try and make steel.

What about the food shortages mentioned in this letter? Which even your family may not have realized at the time were part of a Great Famine.

I didn't understand right away. But later on, I heard that in some places people were eating tree bark and grass and, what. Insects. Coal.

People ate clay and cotton and corn husks. They ate egret droppings. Entire villages were wiped out; there were thousands of cases of cannibalism. People argue about the numbers, but thirty million people died, maybe? Thirty-five? Something like that.

Terrible, she says. Terrible. To tell you the truth, though, even back then, I just wanted to forget everything. Even back then, I wanted to watch baseball and be American and not receive any more letters.

But.

She laughs a kind of laugh. I am Chinese. I have no choice.

The letter ended:

> *We think of you and your children every day. The night before he died, Baba said it was good to know that even if their name is not Lu, they have Lu blood. He was glad that one branch of the Lu family continues in America.*

And, of course, you did perpetuate your family in many ways, I say now. I guess even if you leave a family, you don't want to see it die.

She is quiet for a moment. That was my assignment, she says finally. Sort of like homework.

In many ways, you even reproduced it, only with a difference.

What difference?

With the difference that you were now the mother, not the daughter.

Too much psychological, she says.

But am I wrong? I say. Because people have been known to replay things. Victims will become perpetrators. The bullied will become bullies. Not always. But sometimes.

Actually, in my opinion, I am just a mother now, she says. I am act the way a mother acts.

You could have tried to do things differently, you know, I say. I myself, when I had kids, tried to do things differently.

But she just says, I had three children already, I work very hard, you don't know how hard.

You did work hard.

You don't know how hard, she says again. You like to blame me, but you don't know. You don't know.

In our garden apartment in Queens, she read aloud to Reuben but not me.

"He is the number one son," she said. "You are too smart already, and Lisa is the baby."

These were truths she held to be self-evident.

"You taught yourself to read," she went on, as if I had done something bad. "Too smart for your own good, that's what you are."

"Who cares?" I said.

"Bad bad girl!" she said. "You don't know how to talk!"

"Who cares? Who cares? Who cares?" I went on anyway—just more quietly so she wouldn't hit me. Usually she hit me on my back or arm—not so hard as to leave a bruise but hard enough that years later, when others in my Mandarin class were surprised to learn the word "*dǎ*," meaning "to beat," and to practice sentences like *Bié dǎ wǒ*—Don't beat me—I wasn't. It was a sentence I could have used. *Bié dǎ wǒ!* In the meanwhile, I relied on volume control for self-preservation.

"Who cares?" I whispered. "Who cares? Who cares?"

She never hit Reuben. When she wasn't reading to him, they were watching baseball on TV together. They sat on the sofa and cheered the Yankees while I watched Lisa sleep in her crib. My father had lowered her mattress, which foiled her escape attempts somewhat, but now it was on the lowest setting and still she could reach her foot up on top of the rail like an octopus. As soon as she woke up from her nap and did that, I was supposed to say, Stop! Wait for Mommy! because she could fall and because if there were no nursemaids, oldest daughters were the nursemaids.

"She needs a bed," my mother said sometimes. But other times, she said that maybe we should save money and just put Lisa's mattress on the floor because everything with my mother was "save money." It was her religion.

You try raising three children on a professor's salary, she objects now.
Okay, fair enough, I say.

Everything with my mother was "save money," understandably.

One day, between innings, my mother saw a girl in an ad on TV and said, "If she was pretty, she would not have to work so hard. People take care of pretty girls."

"What about ugly girls?" I asked.

"Ugly girls take care of everyone else."

"Am I an ugly girl?"

"You have too much to say," she said. But then she said, "It is too bad you are a girl and Reuben is a boy."

Meaning that yes, I was going to have to take care of everyone else.

"Who cares?" I said, though in fact I did care.

It was true that Reuben was good-looking, even strangers in the park said looks like that were wasted on a boy. But he was wild. He climbed the monkey bars and stood at the very top, waving his arms and yelling, "Look, Mom, no hands! Look, Mom! Look!" while the other mothers yelled, "Get down! That's dangerous! You're going to break your neck!"

"Get down!" my mother yelled, too. "That's dangerous! You're going to break your neck!"

But she was proud of him.

If your grandmother had met him, she would say, He is too handsome to be your son, my mother says now.

While I was just the daughter she would have expected you to have.

It was too bad, she agrees. Reuben should have been you, and you should have been Reuben.

As you so kindly told us both.

Because it was true.

Just as you should have been your brother and your brother should have been you.

You don't know how to talk! she says. You never learned how to talk!

My father hated the TV and loved his blackboard. He loved to draw on paper napkins, too, and to write in spiral-bound notebooks, but nothing beat the blackboard. He would start off with a squeaky new piece of chalk, using it until it was the size of a marble you could barely hold, and he could sit there for hours, working on problems with his pants full of chalk dust. I was his favorite, but when he sat at the blackboard teaching math, he sat with Reuben because fathers worked with number one sons—this truth as self-evident to him as it was to my mother. Number one sons were number one sons.

The corollary to this was "No good for a girl be too smart," as my mother would say over and over, like a record with a skip in it. That, and: "No one is ever going to marry you."

"Who cares? I don't want to get married," I would say, especially if my father was there for protection. Because if he was there, like he was today, I knew he would laugh.

"Don't encourage her," she said.

But my father said, "This is America. If she want, she can marry a dog. She can marry a fish."

"I can marry a car!" I said.

"She can marry a monkey."

"I can marry a tree!"

"You know what you are? You are crazy," my mother said. Adding, "Just wait until the little one learns from the bad example of the big one."

"Then they can marry each other." My father winked.

"You are crazy," she said again and told me to get off my father's lap. "You are too big to sit on Daddy."

"He's my moveable chair."

"He is not your moveable anything," she said. "Get down!"

I just stayed there, though, arranging my father's arms in different positions.

"You encourage her!" she yelled. "When she doesn't listen, you should stop her! You have abdicated your responsibility!"

But he just went on laughing and winking and letting me move his arms around.

Typical Dad, she says, mad even now.

But why couldn't I sit in his lap? Didn't you sit in your father's lap? I say.

Makes no difference.

And where did you get phrases like "abdicated your responsibility" anyway?

I thought you know everything, she sniffs. That's just how we say in Chinese.

After Queens we moved to Yonkers, though I didn't want to because I had a good friend in Queens and didn't want to leave her. Her name was Beth, and the day my family moved I left her a goodbye present, the plastic box from some bubble gum cigarettes someone once gave me. It was my most precious possession. I had already chewed the gum, but I had saved the cylindrical wrappers and put them back into their square snap-shut box; they still lined up perfectly, magically filled with nothing like bubbles, and I loved them. The day the moving van came, though, I left them outside Beth's apartment on the sisal doormat because I did not know if I would ever see her again.

Beth had a one-eyed stuffed dog with a pirate's patch and a necklace and a bracelet. Her mother had given the dog the patch and the jewelry and helped put them all on him, which was no simple matter; there's a reason dogs don't go in much for bracelets, she said. But she somehow got the bracelet to stay on. The necklace had a heart-shaped locket that Beth said would one day have my picture in it. But for now she put my name in it, with her mother's help. Her mother did the writing and helped her cut the paper small enough to fit inside the locket, and then asked me why I didn't have any stuffed animals. And when I said I didn't know, she gave me a teddy bear. I named her Beth, but if I had known Beth's mother's name, I probably would have named the teddy bear after her, because she was really nice.

I didn't want to move, but my mother and father had saved every dime, and every nickel, and every penny for years to buy a house. I was surprised when later I read in a book about half-pennies because if there were halfpennies, how come we didn't save them? It turned out, though, that halfpennies were only used in England, which was another country. My mother wrote down every single thing she bought in a column of her red account book, while in the other column were things like the quarter I found one day on the street. I thought the quarter should be mine because finders keepers but she took it, and in the end, I agreed to give it to the family because after paying for the house, my parents didn't even have enough money for a moving van. Of course, my mother didn't want to ask for help, she was proud that way.

What kind of people have to borrow money? she says now.

But they had no choice, they needed sixty dollars. And so my father asked their friend Mr. Koo from International House, who lent them the money immediately. *No problem,* he told them. *Your credit rating is A+. Could not be better.*

A truck pulled up to our Queens apartment. The driver had a crew cut and biceps as big as Popeye the Sailor Man's. "I'm strong to the finich, 'cause I eats me spinach," Reuben sang as the man hoisted furniture up onto his shoulder. He covered everything with moving blankets, and the next thing we knew, he was uncovering it all over again like a magician, abracadabra! And then there it was, the same old furniture in a brand-new house.

We made it! my mother says, excited even now by the memory. We made it!

You did! You made it! I say. You made it!

We had a living room with a picture window and a cathedral ceiling and a balcony with a wrought-iron railing, and there were three bedrooms—one for my parents, one for my brother, and one for my sister and me. We could make as much noise as we wanted because there were no neighbors to complain, and we didn't have to listen to them fighting and arguing, either. And there was a finished basement, with a wall for my father's blackboard and a big glass door that opened right onto a patio and our own backyard. There were no trees or grass yet, but we were going to plant some, and though we only had three neighbors so far, there were going to be more neighbors soon, and they were all going to plant trees and grass, too.

A split-level with attached garage! my mother says now. We got the corner lot because we were the first ones in the neighborhood to sign a contract. Also, we got the number one in our address. One Spring Road. Our house was exactly like the model house, except with a red roof. It was not made of real clay tile like the roof of my family's house in Shanghai, but it was the same red color, and we were so happy I didn't know if I should tell my family in China.

Why wouldn't you? I say.

Because if we told them, they would think we were rich and want more help.

Were they asking for help?

She laughs. Sometimes they just hint.

You mean when they wrote things like: "After the Loh family in Kowloon learned the news about Baba's death, they sent us a sum of money. It was quite a large sum, which was really so considerate of them. If you are in touch with them, please thank them on our behalf"?

Exactly.

The real message being, They sent some money, how about you?

Exactly.

When you didn't have enough money for a moving van. Which they didn't understand but you could not tell them, either.

How can I tell them? You tell me. Of course I cannot tell them.

We ran around so wild that first day that I slipped on the slippery new floor and split my head open on a wire bookcase, it was just lucky that the phone company had already dropped off a phone book so we could find a hospital in the yellow pages. Also, our phone was working, so my father could call them. Then he was speeding over there while I lay down on the back seat of the car, pressing a washcloth to my head. At the emergency room, the light was so bright there were no shadows, and the doctor was like an overgrown leprechaun, tall but spry. He crouched down and parted my hair with his spindly fingers, squinting and saying I was going to be just fine. However, he was going to have to shave off part of my hair.

"Stitches aren't pretty," he said cheerfully. "But they're a sight prettier than your innards leaking out."

I got twelve stitches, each of them as big and black as something you'd see on Halloween. The nurse said they were like Frankenstein's and, when I didn't know who Frankenstein was, explained that he was a monster.

"Oh," I said.

"Your mother is in for a surprise," she went on.

But my mother never said anything. In fact, no one said anything, it was as if I had turned into Frankenstein myself.

Why were you running around wild like that? my mother says now.

Didn't you use to race pedal cars around your dining room in Shanghai? I say.

I was never wild like you.

My father taped up the corners of the bookcase with black electrical tape, and after a while, my mother sent her family our new address, not as if it was special but just another place we had moved. She immediately got another letter from my grandmother:

These days your younger sister does not help queue because she has been sent to a labor camp in the far west for reeducation. What a shock when the police came—two of them together, as if one by himself would not be able to manage her. As for her crime, it seems to be simply that she is Catholic.

Now we do not hear from her, as communication in Qinghai is quite primitive. Our understanding is that her assignment involves digging for construction. Naturally, we are happy to know that she is serving the people in a place where the motherland needs help if it is ever to recover from the centuries of humiliation it has endured. However, you know how slight she is and how prone to coughs. Her lungs, as you will remember, have always been weak. (Neither she nor any of your younger siblings is as strong as you because you were the firstborn and used up the nutrients in the womb.) We were able to find her some cod-liver oil to take with her. But otherwise we can do nothing.

My mother could not even cry.

I was just feel nothing, she says now. More and more, nothing.
Your poor sister, I say.
She really suffered.
Those camps were death camps, really. And what happened to her could very well have happened to you, the other Catholic in the family, and to Mother Greenough as well.
I hope Mother Greenough got out. I hope.
I read somewhere that she did. She was one of the very last missionaries to leave, but she got out.
Thank God.
Still, it must have been hard to rejoice in a new house when your sister was in a labor camp.
It was very hard, she says. You don't know how hard.

Digging for us meant raking the rocks out of the dirt. It meant planting and watering and soaking the peat moss until it was like a sponge. We had never had so much dirt jammed under our fingernails and caked around our cuticles, we had never had so many broken nails and blisters, or used so many Band-Aids. My mother said we were becoming peasants, but we didn't care. We loved it.

The only problem was the Haggerty Road Gang, who seemed to have coordinated their schedule with the Welcome Wagon. No sooner had we sorted through our gift basket full of goodies and coupons and advertisements for local businesses than Reuben came home with a bloody nose and his whole face scraped so bad, we had to get out another washcloth. Then it was off to the hospital again.

"What happened?" my parents asked my brother on the way. "What kids? Who are they? What happened?"

Reuben said the boys had surrounded him and made slant eyes at him and chanted Ching Chong Polly Wolly Wing Wong and told him to go back to where he came from. And when he told them that he came from the city and couldn't go back because the landlord had already rented the apartment to someone else—hadn't they ever heard of a lease?—they beat him up so bad that sure enough, the leprechaun doctor at the hospital said Reuben would need stitches like mine.

"Now you match your sister," he said when he was done. "Are there more of you?"

"The first week, Lil got stitches, and the second week, Reuben got stitches," my parents said at home. Their faces were sunken, as if they had gotten punched, too. "What kind of a place is this?"

"Maybe we make some mistake," my father said.

But the next day, their faces were back to normal.

"Not so good, but not so bad," they decided. As for their advice to us kids, it was to ignore them.

It was still better than China, my mother says now.

You mean, at least we weren't eating tree bark or being sent to a labor camp, I say.

Also, we had a house to live in, don't forget.

And the Haggerty Road Gang might have had fists and rocks, but they did not have bayonets and guns.
That's right. They were nothing, she says.

We ignored them as directed. The attacks weren't every day, anyway, just some days, and the gang didn't beat up Lisa and me the way they did Reuben. With us girls, they mostly just threw rocks, except in the winter when they threw snowballs with the rocks buried in them. Those were scary at first but easy to duck because Jonny Creamer had terrible aim, and Billy Hall wasn't trying very hard to hit us—he just couldn't get up his animus. They weren't like Jed Dempsey, who was big and mean and a quarterback, meaning that he had a great arm for throwing rocks and unfortunately could throw a punch, too. Luckily, Lisa and I were low-value targets for him. Reuben, though, was another story. Jed lavished so much attention on Reuben that we all got used to him coming home bloody, sometimes he didn't even change out of his bloody clothes but just stayed in them until bedtime. My parents found a martial arts school where he could take karate lessons. Since it was right in the same shopping center as the grocery store, it was really convenient. While we shopped, he could learn to break boards with his bare hands.

"He has to teach those boys a lesson, otherwise they will never stop," my mother said.

"He has to teach them a lesson," Lisa and I echoed. First Reuben was going to break boards, and then he was going to make the Haggerty Road Gang stop. He was.

Meanwhile, my mother hit me the way Reuben was supposed to hit the Haggerty Road Gang. She was trying to teach me a lesson, too, but it was no use, I still didn't listen when she told me to clean the bathroom. "Why why why," she would say. "When are you going to stop why why why?" But I kept asking because I didn't see why I should have to clean when Reuben and Lisa didn't.

"I am not a servant," I said. But my mother said Reuben had to study because he was a boy, and that Lisa was the baby. Also Lisa was too weak to clean because I had used up everything in the womb before she got there.

So Mom, you realize that's not how it works, right? I say now. Babies don't use up the womb, dooming the children who come after them. And neither can peanut butter make up for it, by the way.

The doctor said peanut butter is very nutritious, she says.

Every night, she would give Lisa a spoonful of peanut butter, which Lisa would sit licking and licking, turning it over as if to see if one side tasted better than the other.

You know, some people say the oldest daughter thing is the biggest scam going, I say. There are support groups.

Still, my mother says that just as the mother is the mother, and the father is the father, the number one son is supposed to study, and the number one daughter is supposed to help.

It is like a baseball team, she says. The pitcher has a job, and the catcher has a job. Even the baby has a job.

What's the baby's job?

The baby's job is to make everyone smile. Everyone spoil her because she is so cute.

But Mom, why would an oldest daughter agree to this system? Maybe it made sense back when the oldest son really would support the whole family if he passed the Chinese imperial exams, and it took the whole family working together to see him through. But today? Here in America?

Too many questions.

Too many questions, but I notice that just as I was failing to fulfill my duty as an oldest daughter, you were failing to fulfill your duty as an overseas daughter. Wasn't there a kind of question in that?

Actually, I sent money, she says.

You did. But you had all but stopped writing to them. Look how many letters say things like "Have you received the letter and photos? Why do you not reply?" Or, "If in your busy schedule you could write a few letters, it would be nice to hear how your family is doing." Or, "Are you too busy raising your third child? Is that why you are too lazy to write?"

She is quiet.

And though you sent money, your mother did not seem to think you sent enough. Otherwise, why would she say things like, "With the remittance you sent this time, I was able to repay a portion of the loan I borrowed last year for your younger brother's wedding. You know I am not accustomed to asking others for money."

Bad bad girl! she says. You don't know how to talk!

But when I say, It sounds like you were a bit of a bad bad girl yourself, she doesn't say she wasn't.

Meanwhile, I made some new friends, Cindy Newman and Ellen Agostino. They were not related, but they both had red hair. Cindy's was short and Ellen's was long, and my mother didn't like them because I met them in the woods. You don't know where they come from, she said, but I said, Who cares? They were older than me, which meant that they wanted to be the parents when we played and assigned me to be the baby until I said I wanted to be the mommy! Then we took turns, even though they said mommies would never say things like "You are a bad bad girl," or "I found you in the garbage can," or "When you grow up, I hope you have a daughter just like you." They said mommies made cookies and sang songs and tried not to let themselves go, but I said my mommy didn't. And when they asked what she did, I said she read the newspaper and watched baseball and yelled and hit me.

"That is so weird. I mean, like, my father hits my brother with a belt," said Ellen. "But my mother doesn't hit anyone."

"Your mother sounds like a monster," Cindy said.

"I don't know, it's not like she's Frankenstein," I said.

"Who's Frankenstein?" said Ellen.

Also, I made friends with an old woman down in the dead end named Mrs. Cunningham. Mrs. Cunningham taught me to crochet and gave me little balls of extra yarn so I could practice by myself.

"Like this," she said. "Around, and catch it, then pull the yarn through. See? Around, and catch it, then pull the yarn through. You try it."

I couldn't do it and couldn't do it. But then suddenly it was as if I'd stepped through a door, and I could.

"You got it!" she exclaimed. "Now do it again."

I did it again and was surprised at how giddy I felt—so giddy it was as if there were something the matter with me.

"You can make things this way," she told me, showing me some pot holders she had made. She had also made blankets and pillows and even a rug, her house could have been called the House of Crochet. She said that she knit, too, but that in her view, knitting was mostly for sweaters and scarves. Stuff you wore—"apparel," she called them.

"I use crochet for household items. For example, this is a tea cozy," she said. "It keeps the teapot warm. Do you see? It's like a little house."

The cozy was like something from a fairy tale—an elf house, with a chimney and a door and windows with shutters. Each set of shutters was a different color, and the door was blue with a button for a doorknob.

"Does your family drink tea?" asked Mrs. Cunningham.

"My mother does," I said. "But she's the only one."

"Interesting," she said.

"She doesn't use a teapot. We got her one from the gift shop at Patricia Murphy's for Mother's Day, but she doesn't use it because it's too beautiful. She has a covered mug she uses instead, I guess she's more used to it."

"Does your family like Patricia Murphy's?"

"We've only gone once, for my brother's First Communion. But it was beautiful!"

"Did you like the little lake?"

"Yes!"

"And what about the swans? With those long necks? They're like teacup handles, aren't they?"

"They are! We had popovers there! Maybe we'll go again sometime."

"Well, if you do, you'll have to tell me what you order," said Mrs. Cunningham.

It was so easy to talk to her, it was like talking to a tree, or the sky, or God. Her skin was both wrinkly and not, like waxed paper that had been bunched up but then smoothed out, and she smelled like roses.

"My mother says no one is ever going to marry me," I said.

And she laughed a laugh then that was about the happiest sound I had ever heard.

"What an idea!" she said. "Why would she put an idea like that in your head?"

It had never occurred to me before that ideas got put in your head—that they came from somewhere and you didn't just think them.

"As the mother of six girls, all of whom got married and two of whom got married twice, I can tell you that many a man would like a wife and weddings are hardly a rarity," she went on. Then she got back to business. "What would you like to make?"

"A teddy bear," I said.

"A teddy bear is a little complicated for a first project, but you can do it," she said. "Come pick the color you want to use."

When I picked a brown the same color as my bear Beth, Mrs. Cunningham gave me not just the yarn but also a shiny blue crochet hook to keep.

I couldn't believe it. "Forever and ever?"

"Forever and ever."

"Thanks."

It was time to go home for supper. I could come back anytime. Still, even after I left, I stood and stood outside her house, stood and stood and stood.

Our new school was called St. Theresa's. As it was a Catholic school, we wore uniforms. For Lisa and me that meant a white shirt with a Peter Pan collar and a Wyatt Earp bow tie, and a navy blue jumper with a pleated skirt. We also wore oxfords and navy blue knee socks, and tights with their feet cut off, to protect our knees from the cold. (My mother was always worried about the cold, and especially about cold joints.) We were supposed to roll the tights down like awnings while we stood waiting in the morning for the bus. Then when we got to school, we were supposed to roll them back up under our skirts so that no one could see them. But one day at recess, Mary Pat Rossi lifted my skirt up from behind and yelled, "Look! Look! Look what she's wearing! Under her skirt!" and showed everyone. I tried to run and hide behind the Virgin Mary shrine at the end of the parking lot, but my tights rolled down as I ran, which made everyone laugh. Then Mary Pat Rossi started singing, "London Bridge is falling down, falling down, falling down, London Bridge is falling down," and everyone laughed some more.

Of course, one of the reasons they could see the tights was that to save money, my mother had bought our uniforms two sizes too big and rolled up the hems, which made them stick out all around like the hooped skirt the Queen of Hearts wore in *Alice in Wonderland*. Also, it was hard to run because my mother bought our shoes big, too. Even if we tied them tight, they gapped in the back and clopped, which probably did look funny, you couldn't completely blame people for laughing.

Though could you blame me for trying to stretch things out? she says now. I think I managed the household very well.

You did, Mom, I agree. You did. I just wonder if you ever thought about our feelings.

Feelings? she says.

Not everyone was mean, some people felt sorry for my sister and me. But no one had ever seen anyone who looked like us before.

"Like, where is China?" this one boy asked me. And when I told him I didn't know because I had never been there, he looked confused.

"I thought you were Chinese," he said.

Because St. Theresa's believed in corporal punishment for the boys but not the girls, the sexes were separated in sixth grade; Reuben knew all about the boys' class even before he got there. There were two rulers, Big Bertha and Little Bertha, one was eighteen inches long and the other twelve inches long, and if you flinched while your hands were being hit, Mr. Smote hit you another ten times. People said he took boys into the library and made them take their clothes off, too, but not if you were a tough boy. So there were a lot of reasons to be tough.

The library wasn't a real library, it was a donation library in a small, dark room. Its shelves were half full and included books on lawn care. So when I got to third grade, my teacher sent me to the fourth-grade classroom for books. I had to go by myself and was afraid I'd gone to the wrong class, the room seemed so big, and with everyone staring at me, the walk from the door to the teacher's desk seemed like miles. Then I had to explain who I was and what I was doing there, which was hard. Though I talked a lot at home and with Mrs. Cunningham, at school I sometimes couldn't talk at all, it was as though I'd dropped through a trapdoor to hell; everything—my face, my neck, my body, everything—burned. But it turned out that I had come to the right class, and in the end, the nun gave me so many books I almost couldn't carry them all. She stacked them against my body as if I were a wall, the pile came clear up to my chin. But I managed to carry it, straight-armed, back to my classroom, and then I had books about Helen Keller and Florence Nightingale to read for the rest of the year. My teacher set up a special place at the back of the room that was my shelf, and I was allowed to take a book and bring it home any day I liked.

And this was how it happened that I was reading about Anne Sullivan spelling "w-a-t-e-r" into Helen Keller's hand when my mother received not another letter from her family but a letter from the family she had stayed with when she first got to America, the Pings.

> *How is life in New York? Here it is very windy, as always. Uncle has back trouble from shoveling snow and I have so-called dishpan hands. I only washed the dishes once without rubber gloves, but that was enough. You should learn from my example and never make that mistake! It is quite uncomfortable.*
>
> *We write because we are just back from Hong Kong, where we heard some news about your sister. You probably know that she has been in Qinghai for a couple of years already, but maybe you do not know why. Of course, she is a Catholic, and all Catholics are considered*

counterrevolutionary. But her crime is that she refused to betray any other Catholics in her circle. When her interrogators read out names to her, she refused to nod her head. And for this refusal, she was sent to a hard labor camp.

Qinghai is so far away, it is hard to know exactly what the conditions are like. But recently one prisoner cracked. He gave the authorities all the names he could remember, which wasn't so terrible. Actually, the government already had all the names he gave them, so no one new was arrested. But now that he has been released, he has told his relatives everything about the camp, and from them we got a report. The prisoners are supposed to be digging ditches for construction but do not have enough tools and are often made to dig with their hands. They are awakened at four in the morning to start even if the ground is still frozen and sometimes they work for eighteen hours a day. He said your sister is definitely at this camp and that she is skin and bones. One day, she was carrying some rocks with a shoulder pole in the middle of a storm when her pole partner just ahead of her was struck by lightning and killed. She passed out from shock, and later said she wished it had been her.

Sorry for the bad news, but we thought you would want to hear the report all the same. Hope this finds you well. We hear you have three children now. You should bring them on a field trip to Chicago *so they can see a real* Great Lake.

Wishing you health and happiness,

Auntie and Uncle Ping

PS George sends greetings. He has had a hard time. His wife died in a car accident—maybe you heard about it— leaving him with four children to raise alone. However, there is good news. He has just announced an engagement

*to a second wife, who says she knows you. Her name is
Georgiana. Do you remember her? She says she went to
high school and college and graduate school with you. They
will marry as soon as her divorce comes through.*

"What's the matter?" I said. "Why do you look like that?"
"Like what?" said my mother.
"Why are you making such a funny face?"

My poor sister! my mother says now. I could not believe what was happening to her. Digging with her hands? Skin and bones? How much longer could she last? And how could I, in the middle of such news, feel almost as upset about George and Georgiana? How could I have been wondering if Auntie Ping might have helped me with George had I let her look at my application one more time—if I had not made many small mistakes with her?
Bad bad girl, I say. You are a bad bad girl.
I think I am, she says. My poor sister! I think I am.

My mother signed Lisa and me up for ballet lessons because, she said, "girls are supposed to be graceful," never mind that our teacher could not have been less ladylike. Carmen swore and smoked—because she was a Commie from Cuba, where everyone smoked cigars, people said. But she was also magic—a perfectly normal person until she lifted her arm and leaned her head back and smiled. Then she could have been someone from the movies, it was as if she had her own spotlight that she could just switch on. She could make her arms ripple like water and her hands fall like petals, and when she tilted her head to the side and looked up, you would swear she was seeing a spaceship.

So even though I hated being made to go to ballet, I loved going. We were learning to plain walk across the room, then dance walk across, and I loved that. I loved the way Carmen would stand in front of her giant gray tape recorder with its reels and buttons, fiddling and swearing until just like that, out came music different than any other music I'd ever heard, music that made me think of the word "beautiful." Because it was beautiful. And from Carmen's mouth came words I thought were French, although the way she said them, some kids thought they were Spanish. *Plié! Jeté! Tombé! Pirouette! Pas de chat! Rond de jambe!* We listened to everything she said, and when she held up a naked GI Joe doll and showed us how to turn our hips out, no one laughed because he was naked and couldn't point his toes.

"Head up! Shoulders down! Imagine that a string is coming up out of your head! Good! Smile!" she would say. "Good!" Every now and then, she would say to me, "Very nice, Miss Jen," and then I would jump even higher and spin even faster, to make her say it again—jumping so high and spinning so fast that she said she would give me a little solo in the recital.

I leapt with happiness.

"The difference between dancing and walking," she would say, "is the difference between driving on the road and bumper cars. There is a system. There is a method. A mentality. There are principles. And where does all this come from?" She would point to her temple and say, "Here. Only not just from here. From many people thinking for many years. What is the best way, what is the beautiful way? Should we hold our hands like this? No, no. Like this. People argued for a long time. And that is now what I teach you—the answer. The answer is: Like this." She would move her arm to show us, and when we moved ours the way she did, she would say, "Correct."

We listened to Carmen in a way we didn't listen to the nuns at school because they mostly just said, Do this, and Do that. They were like my mother. They didn't believe in explaining anything. For example, we kids were supposed to go to the bathroom when it was our class's turn, and since the grades went in order, the first graders went first and then didn't get to go again all day. They had to hold it until they got home because the rules were the rules, never mind that they then had accidents and cried.

After school, we loved to play in the woods, where there were no rules, just piles of leaves that tickled and rasped, and a big gray rock we called Elephant Rock. From the top, you could see everywhere, and at one end there were three holes that filled up with water that turned to ice in the winter. The ice was higher in the middle than around the edges, and one spring when I touched it, the finger of my glove froze and stuck to it. Once from up there, too, I saw a giant cat with a long body and a bushy tail like a tube, Cindy Newman said it was a fox! The woods were magic. But the woods were also where boys pulled Ellen Agostino's pants down.

"Why?" I said. I couldn't understand why they would do that.

"They turned me around!" she said. "They turned me around and looked at me and laughed!" Her face was red and pitted like a strawberry from crying, and her long hair was stringy.

"They laughed?"

"Because they are boys," explained Cindy. Then she asked Ellen, "Did they touch you?"

Ellen nodded. "It was gross!" she said. "And I couldn't get away! Because they held my arms! And they put mud on me!"

Somehow the mud seemed like the worst part.

"You should tell your mother what happened," Cindy said.

"Maybe she'll wash your clothes in the washing machine for you," I said. "Or else you can do it yourself. It's easy, you just have to push a button."

"She'll go yell at the boys' mothers and get them to stop," said Cindy. "Because that's her job."

But Ellen just cried some more.

"The mud's not so bad if you have a washing machine," I said again. I was trying to make her feel better.

"Shut up. You'll get it when you're older and get a bra," Cindy told me.

My brother, meanwhile, didn't just get beat up by Jed Dempsey and the Haggerty Road Gang. He also got hit by my father for things like climbing the water tower.

"Why you do that?" my father yelled. "Why? You could get so-called JD card for that!"

A JD card was a juvenile delinquent card and meant, among other things, that if you were arrested for some reason, you got tried in adult court.

"And then what? Then you go to jail!" my father yelled. "And do you know who goes to college after jail? No one! No one goes!"

Reuben became an altar boy. He was trying to be good, he was. But he was always wrecking his gown, and once got into a fist-fight right on the altar. He and the other altar boy knocked over a cross, making the nuns cry, a priest had to break it up, and Reuben almost got excommunicated. I don't know how many Hail Marys he had to say, but he was on his knees until they turned the church lights out. And I don't know if my father was right to hit him after that, but my mother hit me for a whole lot less.

For example, when I told her the president had been shot, she said I was crazy.

"You think you know everything," she said.

"But he was!" I said. "He was! You should turn on the TV!"

And when the TV said the same thing, she said, "You have too much to say." And, "You have to learn how to talk."

"You have to learn how to listen!" I shot back. "You do! You have to learn how to listen!"

But that just made her yell, "Since when does the mother listen to the daughter?" and hit me even as my father came in to watch the TV, too.

Which Mrs. Cunningham said later just meant that my mother didn't like her daughter knowing more than she did because in China, a mother was a mother, and children had to listen to her.

That's right! my mother says now.

"But we live in America," I said.

"Of course we do," said Mrs. Cunningham. "But some people are only half here." She said her mother was the same way. "Her body was in America, but her soul was in Ireland," she said. "I guess she forgot to pack it when she came."

We were working on the hardest parts of my teddy bear, which were its face and ears.

"So is your teddy going to be a girl or a boy?" asked Mrs. Cunningham.

"A girl."

"Okay. You're going to need some buttons for her eyes," she said. "What do you think, black or brown or blue?"

"Black," I said.

At home, I wasn't always sure I could finish my teddy bear, I kept having to do some parts over. I stuck with it for a week, though, then another week, and then another.

"And now you've done it." Mrs. Cunningham was beaming. She thought I should make a scarf next, and I said okay, but maybe I could make it for my teddy bear? Which she thought was a great idea. In fact, we could make her a whole outfit. And I said I'd like that, although wasn't that apparel, which should be knit with knitting needles? Anyway, I said, first I wanted to make a tent.

"A tent?"

"For my new teddy and her friend Beth," I said.

"Ah," said Mrs. Cunningham. "Have you ever stayed in a tent?"

"No."

"Then who put this idea in your head?"

"Florence Nightingale," I said. "Florence Nightingale worked in a tent."

"Ah," she said again. "And where did you learn about Florence Nightingale?"

"From a book," I said, and explained how I was sent to the fourth grade for books.

"Now I understand," said Mrs. Cunningham. "And what are the bears going to do in the tent?"

"They're going to play music. They're going to dance and put on plays and read books." I thought. "It's going to be a big tent."

"Like a hospital tent, you mean, only not for patients."

I nod.

"Are they going to read about Florence Nightingale?"

"Yes. And they're going to read *Heidi* and *Little Women*. They're going to read by a special light."

"Like Florence Nightingale's?"

How did Mrs. Cunningham know Florence Nightingale had a special light she used when she went to check on wounded soldiers?

"Yes," I said.

"Have you read *Heidi* and *Little Women*?"

I nodded. "My godmother, Marnie, sent them to me for Christmas."

"'Christmas won't be Christmas without any presents,'" she said.

I laughed with surprise. "'It's so dreadful to be poor!'" I said.

Then it was her turn to laugh. "So Beth and your new teddy will read in the tent by the special light," she went on.

"Yes."

"What's your new teddy's name?"

"Jo."

"I see. And they'll play music and put on plays and dance?"

"Yes."

"And what color should the tent be?" she asked. "And how are we going to make it stand up? It's an engineering problem, isn't it."

We set to working it out.

Though the plan had been for three kids, my mother had a surprise.

"A gift from God," she called him. "This one is a gift from God."

She even named the baby Sean, which means "gift from God." In Chinese, his name was *Qìngshàn* because *shàn* sounds like Sean, she said, and because it means "kind and virtuous," as a gift from God should be. And maybe he was a gift, but Lisa and I were so disappointed that he was a boy that my father had to buy us Tammy dolls before we would go see him. My father bought flowers for my mother, too—the only time I'd ever seen him do that.

"Oh!" she said, making a show of smelling them, though I had already sniffed them and knew they didn't have any scent.

My father liked the baby, but Lisa and I didn't think Sean anywhere near as cute as a baby doll. Dolls were plastic, we knew, and Sean was real. But he did not look new. He looked like a used baby, with so many bruises and red marks you might not have picked him to take home even at 50 percent off. When he opened his eyes, he immediately closed them again, as if to express how uninterested in us he was, and he slept all the time. He did not look like fun. And my mother looked even more tired than he was. Her glasses were smudged as if she hadn't cleaned them in a week, and her stomach hadn't shrunk at all. It was as if she didn't have the energy to pull it in.

We liked Sean better when he came home. His fingers and toes were so little, and he moved in such a cute jerky way, as if he did not know his arms from his legs and they were surprised, too, to find themselves attached to him. What's more, he burped real burps and smelled like real baby powder. And we could give him a real bottle and dress him in the striped baseball outfit my godmother, Marnie, sent, which even Reuben liked.

If only his diapers were not real diapers I had to swish out in the toilet and put in this white bucket for the diaper service. They weren't so bad in the beginning, but after a while they were, even though the bucket had a deodorizer cake in it, when you opened the lid, the stink could knock you over. And then my mother doubled the diapers by having another baby. The new baby was to keep Sean company, she said, she didn't want Sean to be lonely. And so there was Shane, the *xié* of whose Chinese name, Qìngxié, sounded like Shane and meant "accompany."

You didn't think Sean and Shane sounded too much alike? I say now.
Chinese people like to make the names go together, she says.
Like your name was Xīn and your sister was Xín.
They were two completely different characters!
And now you had five children, just like your mother.
Nothing the matter with that, she huffs.

We had become the kind of family everyone called beautiful when they really meant big. What a beautiful family! they would say, meaning, What a big family! Especially when we climbed out of our Volkswagen Beetle, they would say it, because my parents sat in the front seat and we three big kids sat in the back, with the two babies tucked into the luggage compartment behind us, which we called "the box." When we stopped and parked, the seven of us piled out and out like clowns in a circus act, which made people gape.

We just laughed.

We loved our Volkswagen Beetle. Before our Beetle, we had had an American car that couldn't make it up the hill to the town's miniature golf course. Its radiator overheated so often that my father kept a jug of water in the trunk, and in the winter, it spun its wheels in the snow. Our VW had no radiator and could motor up any hill, snow or no snow.

"Engine in the back, weight over the wheels," my father liked to say. "Smart."

"Engine in the back! Weight over the wheels!" we echoed.

Our VW was like us. We, too, could make it up anything. We just had to forget about China.

My mother filed a petition for naturalization, and a year later, my father did, too, because he had been asked to do some consulting for the U.S. Navy and Air Force. And to do that, he had to become a citizen, which he no longer minded the way he used to. In fact, now it was Chinese citizenship he objected to.

"What do we have to do with Taiwan?" he said. "Nothing. We have never even been there."

"If you don't want to be citizens of Nationalist China, we can renounce our Chinese citizenship, but it is a big job," said my mother.

"Why they make it so hard? I cannot understand it."

"They just want to say we are kind of like on their side," she said. "But anyway, we are Chinese. You always say it."

"We are Chinese," he agrees. "But if you ask me today, become American is the right choice. Forget about China."

"I never said forget about China," she said.

But he said it again anyway. "Forget about China."

And why not forget about China, when America meant the New York World's Fair? We were taking a convertible to the future, we were riding the monorail and the giant tire Ferris wheel, we were eating Belgian waffles! We were singing "It's a Small World After All" in a boat, and making dinosaurs at the Mold-a-Rama at Dinoland! Naturally, we had to go to the IBM exhibit, because the most interesting part of the whole future to my father was not push-button phones or the Ford Mustang but the fact that people were going to stop using slide rules. Machines were going to do math and change everything, he claimed, but we didn't really believe he was going to throw his slide rule away. He loved his slide rule. He was probably going to be buried with his slide rule. And how could machines doing math change anything? We took the Sky Streak elevator up to the deck of the New York State Pavilion. We took pictures of rockets and space capsules, and cheered the China pavilion that was really the Taiwan pavilion, and skipped the Japan pavilion because my parents hated the Japanese.

And then because we were Catholic, we went to the Vatican pavilion. There were long lines, which was a mystery. It was true you got to stand on a conveyor belt, but it wasn't a ride—you didn't have to strap in or anything—and instead of the future or the world or even a tunnel, there in a spotlight was a statue called the *Pietà*, whatever that meant. No one was singing anything. Instead, there was quiet. The conveyor belt curved around the statue so you could see from different angles how Christ was wearing a diaper and no clothes like Sean and Shane when it was hot, which wasn't a complete shock. We had seen Christ dressed like that before. There was a crucifix hanging in every classroom at school, after all. But instead of hanging on a cross, he was lying there like an overgrown baby in Mary's lap, and Mary was so young—the same age as Christ, it seemed, even though she was his mother. The statue had been carved by a famous artist, but I was not sure I liked it. This Mary was so much sadder than the Mary in the shrine behind the parking lot at school—too sad, I thought. She made you want to cry. When in the gift shop at the end of the day each of us kids was allowed to buy a souvenir, though, I still picked a little reproduction of the *Pietà* on a wooden base instead of a perpetual calendar or a Unisphere egg timer or a future anything. And when I looked at it later in my room, I thought it beautiful like my ballet teacher, Carmen, when she danced. It seemed to have some kind of "mentality." Mary looked a little like my friend Beth's mother in Queens, too, and I thought that when Mary got older, her skin probably looked crinkly smooth like Mrs. Cunningham's. I didn't know that for a fact. But still I found the statue a home by my bed.

Sean and Shane talked to each other in their own language. *Doot-do* was car, and *ho-ho* was windshield wipers, and *wuh-wuh* was dog. And they could slide down the stairs on their stomachs like seals! But they mostly toddled around putting things in their mouths they weren't supposed to and hitting each other and crying to be picked up. Then they had to be changed, only to hit each other again, then cry to be picked up again and need to be changed again, so I'm not sure why there was more fighting with them around. But supper was later every day, and my father was yelling more and more, especially when Reuben played hooky from school.

One day, the principal called. My father talked to him calmly on our blue Princess phone. Instead of just yelling when he hung up, though, he got out a stick and made Reuben kneel while he beat him.

"You don't want to go to school? You want to fool around, you want to hang around with those hoodlums?"

"Norman, you are being crazy!" my mother said.

"Stop, Daddy!" I said, too. "Stop, Daddy! Stop!"

But it was like trying to stop a train. He hit Reuben and hit Reuben, saying he was going to beat him until he learned his lesson. Reuben wasn't learning anything, though, because by then he was in sixth grade, where he'd learned to act tough while getting hit with Big Bertha and attacked by the Haggerty Road Gang. He did not flinch. All he said was "Fuck you" and "You can't hurt me." He didn't even try to stand up, which made my father so mad he looked like there was something the matter with him.

"Don't be crazy," my mother kept saying. "You're being crazy!"

"He isn't going to play hooky anymore," I said. "He isn't! He's going to go to school! Stop, Daddy! Stop! He's going to go to school every day and study and get As! Stop! You're going to kill him!"

But not even I could stop him. He beat Reuben until he was too tired to beat him anymore. Then my mother said, "You are being crazy," one last time, and told Reuben, "Go!"

"Fuck you. You can't hurt me," Reuben said once more. "Fuck you."

I thought he might punch my father, because he had gotten

good at fighting thanks to all the practice he got. Or maybe he would deploy his karate. But instead, he just went up to his room.

"You cannot force him to do this, force him to do that," my mother said the next day (never mind that she forced me to do this and forced me to do that all the time). "We are not in China. You do not understand the American system. Force does not work in this society."

But my father wasn't sorry.

"Chinese people say, If you do not beat and scold the child, this is not your child," he told me later, cracking open a peanut. (We kids were too lazy to eat unshelled peanuts, but he liked them.) And the next thing anyone knew, he was sitting with Reuben at the blackboard again and giving Reuben a problem, and Reuben was trying to solve it three ways, the way my father wanted him to. My father set Reuben up with a desk and a lamp, too, and sure enough, he sat at it just like my father sat at his desk, with his lamp on so he could study.

"No more hooky," my father said with satisfaction.

His fights with my mother didn't end like that. They were mostly in Chinese, so we couldn't understand what they were saying because back when my parents decided to just teach Reuben English, they decided for the rest of us, too. Lisa and I didn't matter because we were girls, and by the time Sean and Shane came, my parents had given up on Chinese. Now all we gleaned from their fights was an English phrase here and an English phrase there, like "Not just that" or "What do you mean?" or "You've abdicated your responsibility" or "All you know is spend money" or—my mother's favorite—"You know what you are? You are crazy." Sometimes my father threw chairs, and once, while we kids watched from between the rails of the balcony over the living room, he threw a brass vase through the big front picture window. There was a loud crash, and then there was a huge jagged hole in the window. The outside air was rushing in, and the snow, and the whole time my mother was yelling, "You are crazy!" And "Don't you dare touch me!"

That was the night she walked out of the house with Sean and Shane. Figuring that we older kids could take care of ourselves, she had one baby hoisted on each hip so they looked like a version of the Holy Trinity. But as it was dark and snowing, and there was nowhere to go, she didn't last long, and almost sadder than her leaving was watching her stop out in the street, just standing there under a streetlamp with the two boys crying and the snow turning into sleet. White mush was collecting on their heads and shoulders, and though Sean was crying calmly, Shane was throwing such a fit, she finally turned around.

So why didn't you leave him? I ask now.
Chinese people do not do such things, she says.
But didn't Auntie Georgiana divorce Uncle Whatshisname so she could marry Uncle George?
Auntie Georgiana always did whatever she feels like.
Why was that?
Because in China she was the baby in her family. And then her whole family got out and she became completely American.
Not like you, I say.
I am kind of like more Chinese, she agrees.

The only good thing was that the day after the incident with the picture window, she decided she was going to learn to drive and found a driving school that could start lessons right away. Also she could boast that in this fight, as in all their fights, "Dad never touched me," which was a big deal because, as my father was the first to admit, men in China were taught that you had to hit your wives in order to manage them. It was just one of those things. But the fact remained that she was stuck with my father and me, and Reuben was stuck with Jed Dempsey.

Jed Dempsey would have beaten Reuben senseless if it hadn't been for baseball. To get him away from the hoodlums, though, my father had signed Reuben up for the Boys' Club, which rotated the kids through various sports until they found one they "didn't suck at," as the boys put it. Was my brother good at baseball because he had grown up wearing a baseball hat and watching it on TV? Had something about it—what Carmen would have called its "mentality"—just sunk in? Anyway, the uniforms! The equipment!

The organization! And, best of all, the coach! His name was Coach Jack, and he made himself clear first thing. If you were late, you got cut from the team. If you mouthed off, you got cut from the team. If you caught a ball with your bare hand instead of your mitt, you got a ball pounded into that hand twenty times. And that made an impression because he used to play pro ball and could still throw eighty miles an hour.

"You know what he is like? He is like my teachers in China," my father said, approvingly. "The boys all afraid of him? You watch. His method works."

And what do you know, pretty soon Reuben was throwing balls at a can. Then he was throwing balls at a target my father set up for him. He was stretching his muscles and standing on one foot and kicking his leg up; he was doing push-ups and sit-ups, and running sprints around the yard, too, and he never took off his Yankees cap. The rest of us figured he'd gone crazy, but my mother the baseball nut was happy as can be about it, especially since she had gotten a letter from Georgiana:

Dear Aggie!

We hope you will come to the wedding! I know it's far to travel, and don't you have eight children or something like that? A horde, I heard. Still, George and I are so excited to discover that we both know you, and his parents are looking forward to seeing you again. Did you really live with them forever when you first came to the States? Auntie said you were like a daughter to them but that you needed a lot of help with your grad school application. She was so relieved when you got in! (I told her that you did perfectly well when you got there, and that the Chinese students all pitched in to help you by hiring you for typing work— also that even if you didn't get your PhD, *she shouldn't be surprised if one day you went back and did. We're all rooting for you!)*

And guess what? George and I will be moving to New York, if his transfer ever comes through and if we can find a house. We do need a huge one, having six children between us, and with my two girls each seeming to need not only their own bedroom but their own bathroom. Are yours this way? Totally American?

Anyway, maybe we will have a chance to all go to a ball game! George's number one is a Little League pitcher *and as much of a* Cubs fanatic *as his dad, so we have season box tickets at* Wrigley Field *and will probably get them for* Shea Stadium, *too, though that is the home of the enemy. Do you root for those terrible* Yankees? *Well, I guess we can put up with it in such an old friend.*

Hope to see you and Chao-pe! We have so much to catch up on. Is he tenured, I hope? I got tenure last year! It's such a relief, you can't imagine!

Tenure? Auntie Georgiana? I say now. How did Auntie Georgiana, who never studied and needed so much help with her papers, become a professor?
Her family gave an auditorium to the school, my mother says. They named it after her father.
You mean her father the Japanese collaborator?
All those Chinese names, you think anyone here cares who they are? my mother says. You think anyone knows?

At least my mother passed her driving test on the first try. She even aced parallel parking, and could now go watch not only Reuben's home games but his away games, too.

Besides playing in the league, Reuben played on the street with the neighborhood boys, sometimes in the dead end and sometimes on Jennifer Lane, neither of which was perfect. The dead end was round but not flat, and Jennifer Lane had so much traffic that Lisa and I were not allowed to go there. If we did, my father would hit us on the hands with a ruler just like Mr. Smote. Did he learn from Mr. Smote to hit us again if we flinched? Anyway, that was his instructional method, as even little Lisa found out. She cried herself to sleep and refused to eat her peanut butter for days.

Only Reuben was allowed on Jennifer Lane, and though some of his teammates were in the Haggerty Road Gang, they accepted him because he could strike everyone out. He wasn't as good at batting, and once hit a foul ball right through a second-floor window in the dead end. Mrs. Mancini came storming up to the house yelling about how the ball had sailed right into her bedroom and landed on the bed, she said there was so much broken glass, she couldn't get it all up even with a vacuum cleaner, no one could sit on the bed or walk on the floor or anything. She was a tiny woman, but she had a loud voice and she put her hands on her hips in an unladylike fashion as she told my mother that she wanted her to pay for a new window. But my mother said it couldn't have been Reuben who did it.

"It was!" Mrs. Mancini's face was red as my friend Ellen Agostino's after the boys pulled down her pants in the woods. "You lying shit, I saw him! It was!"

Still my mother said, "My son is a pitcher, he would have had a designated hitter," and shut the door right in her face. And when Mrs. Mancini finally went stomping back down the street, so mad that all of Spring Road knew about it, my mother started laughing.

"You can come downstairs now," she told Reuben.

Then they both laughed because that was how they were, a team.

A lot of days she could hardly get out of bed, yet still she made it to every one of his baseball games, and on time, too.

"How come she is always late picking us up from ballet?" Lisa wanted to know. We were sitting outside on Carmen's steps after class, waiting and waiting for such a long time that Carmen came out with a big red shirt over her leotard and asked us if she should call our mother.

We wanted to say yes. But we said, "She's coming!" instead. "She's coming any minute! She is!"

And Carmen went back inside then the way she always did, shaking her head. "If you want to come in and wait, you don't have to knock," she said. "Just open the door and make yourselves at home."

But even if it was raining or snowing out, we didn't take her up on her offer because that would mean our mother wasn't coming any minute. She was late driving us to our recital rehearsals, too. And at the recital, all she talked about was how cute Lisa was, and what a surprise it was that the baby could actually dance! Of course, by then the baby could actually do a lot of things, which was why she was put ahead a grade in school. As for my solo, I don't know if my mother ever even saw it.

Every Saturday night, meanwhile, there she was, sitting on the metal bleachers drinking Coca-Cola and cheering while Lisa and I did homework and watched Sean and Shane. "We want a pitcher, not a glass of water!" she would yell if someone besides Reuben was put on the mound. And as the teams were all sponsored by businesses, and Reuben played for Minnow's Appliance, when they won, my mother would stand up and chant, "Min-now's! Min-now's! Min-now's!" She really liked winning.

Oh, those games were fun, she says even now.

They weren't like the rest of life, were they? I say. They weren't about scrimping and saving and letters about labor camps. And they weren't like China, where all you could do was survive. Baseball was a game you could win.

Reuben won all the time, she agrees. He was like the Yankees! It was fun!

When Reuben was in the paper, she would cut out the article and tape it to a kitchen cabinet door, and she made us all go to his baseball banquet, where he was introduced to a famous pitcher. My father and us other kids didn't know who he was, but my mother and Reuben said he was Tom Seaver!

"We've got this Chinese pitcher," Coach Jack told Seaver. "You'd be surprised how good he can throw."

"You don't say." Seaver wasn't as big as Coach Jack, but he looked strong. It wasn't just his arms, even his neck looked strong. "Do you know how to throw a curve?" he asked Reuben. And when Reuben said no, Seaver showed him the grip for a curveball.

"Start with the four-seam," he said. "That's it. Not too tight. Don't choke the ball. You want to be able to flick your thumb up behind the ball when it leaves your hand."

Reuben was listening so hard, he looked like he had a hearing problem.

"If you're not so big, it's okay. You just need control," said Seaver.

My brother nodded. "Thanks." His voice was lower and more serious than I'd ever heard it before.

Then Seaver turned to my mother. "Are you the mom who produced this fine young man?"

"He's my son," she said.

And that was probably the proudest she had been in her whole life. As for whether she was planning to tell George Ping all about it one day, she was. Georgiana, too. She was going to tell Georgiana.

My father was also proud but he thought Reuben spent too much time watching TV. Baseball was bad enough. Even worse, though, were cartoons. And *The Three Stooges*! That Larry, that Moe, that Curly! What kind of influence were they? The day my brother's report card came, my father disconnected the antenna.

"You watch the idiot box, you become idiot yourself," he said.

"You are crazy!" my mother said.

My father threatened to throw the TV out, my mother threatened to leave him, my father threatened to move back to China. They threw some stuff.

Still things were mostly okay. My father claimed he could teach me to ride a bike in an afternoon. "You want me to teach her, I'll show you how," he said, but no one believed him until he chased me with a stick. And sure enough then, just like that, I learned! I pedaled all around and everyone laughed, and everything would have been great if Jed Dempsey hadn't gotten moved out of football at the Boys' Club.

But he got moved because he wasn't the starting quarterback anymore and his father complained until he was moved into baseball. Then his father complained some more until Jed was made a pitcher, even though he couldn't pitch.

"Throwing a football and throwing a baseball are completely different," Reuben told us at supper. "They take completely different muscles. They take completely different grips. They take completely different motions. Because the ball is completely different."

"They both use your arm," Lisa said helpfully.

Reuben looked disgusted.

"They're practically unrelated," he said.

"Anyway, you're trying to say Jed can't pitch," I said.

"He sucks raw eggs," agreed Reuben. "Honestly, he's a danger to batters."

"That's what Coach Jack said!" I said.

"Well, he is," Reuben said. "I just said what Coach said because it's true."

Apparently, everyone on the team agreed. But all the same, Jed got mad when Reuben got started instead of him.

"You mean, you're going to start that chink?" he said.

"Guess I am," said Coach Jack. "If you don't like it, you can take your white ass back to football."

Then he cut him from the team, which would have been great if Jed hadn't ambushed Reuben the next day. He got the whole Haggerty Road Gang to help him, including Jonny Creamer and Billy Hall and a lot of guys who'd been playing baseball with Reuben, and they beat him up worse than ever. It was so bad that for the first time in his life, Reuben cried.

"I told him, Just don't hurt my arm," he kept saying. "I told him, Just don't hurt my arm."

Of course, that made Jed get out this big rock. The other kids held Reuben down so Jed could slam it down the way he wanted, making sure he broke the arm in a couple of places. We had to go back to the hospital, and this time Reuben didn't just come out with stitches. This time he came out with a big fat cast from his shoulder to his wrist and a sling to hold it up. Jed got a JD card, and a whole bunch of the gang were kicked out of the Boys' Club.

"It serves them right!" my mother said.

Still it was sad. We didn't get to cheer for Minnow's Appliance anymore, and when George Ping and Georgiana finally set a date for their wedding, my mother said she wasn't coming, it was just too far.

. . .

Jed Dempsey wasn't the only reason we moved to Scarsdale. The other reason was Reuben's education. Unrealistic as it was, my parents had discussed and discussed private school for him, until one day in the paper, my mother spotted a list of the top ten public schools nationwide. Then before you could say "rhododendron," we were leaving Yonkers for a Dutch colonial at the edge of a town called Scarsdale.

In our old neighborhood, every tree was staked down as if it might get stolen. Here the whole town was like Patricia Murphy's. The bushes were like squirrel housing projects, and the forsythia was not trimmed into well-behaved can shapes the way it was in Yonkers, but was allowed to explode into twiggy yellow fireworks. Probably our new neighbors thought pine trees, too, should be allowed every inch of their natural majesty, but my father thought ours could fall on the house and so lopped them off at the waist. They looked like giant green corncobs that had been snapped in half.

Still, this was the sort of town my mother would be proud to show Georgiana and George Ping, if they ever did move to New York, and it was a town I knew she wished she could have told my grandfather about. It didn't have canals like their hometown of Wuzhen, but it was atmospheric and full of history and culture, including music and art and literature.

She just told her family, though, that we'd moved to an old house.

It must have been lonely to have no one to tell, I say now. My whole life was lonely, she says.

The house sat on a bend in the Bronx River Parkway, meaning that sometimes cars missed the curve and drove up onto our lawn, but we didn't mind. We figured we could always fix the fence. There was a lot of traffic noise, too, which we ignored, and though we had bugs because the windows had no screens, we just swatted them. It was the social rules that were discombobulating. You didn't wander outside to play with your friends on the street or in the woods here; people called you up for "dates." It was strange, but I actually got called pretty often, which you might think would have made my mother happy. Mrs. Cunningham would have been delighted that I was making friends. All my mother said, though, was "You are becoming a social butterfly."

I never understood why you said that, I say now. I mean, maybe that was something girls became in Shanghai, but here?
Too many friends, not enough study, she says.
I wonder if you thought better schools would mean more homework and more discipline, I say. And the town, too. I wonder if you thought it would be more orderly.
We feel, what kind of place is this, the kids just run around wild? she says. After we work so hard. We cannot understand it.

At recess here, you did not play hopscotch or jump rope in the parking lot. Instead, there was a big field with grass you could sit on. You could even just lie on it looking up at the sky if you wanted, although if you wanted to, you could also play on the playground. For example, you could play four square, which was played with a special kind of ball called a playground ball, or you could play basketball or swing on the swings. You always got to do what you felt like here, and it wasn't just during recess. In class, too, you could go to the bathroom whenever you wanted. You didn't even have to ask permission, which somehow seemed normal since the days were full of "activities" you did on your own anyway. The self-paced color-coded spelling program with workstations scattered around the classroom, for example, was half school, half scavenger hunt and meant you were already walking around, so the bathroom was just one more stop.

We were not required to wear uniforms, which was a good thing since these kids would never have worn a Wyatt Earp tie and a jumper. Just as they were used to doing whatever they wanted, they were used to wearing whatever they wanted, like matching Danskin shorts and tops in different colors. One of the first girls to ask me for a date told me that she wore them in the order of the rainbow.

"Monday is red, Tuesday is orange, Wednesday is yellow, Thursday is green, Friday is blue, and Saturday is violet," she told me.

"What do you wear on Sunday?" I asked.

"Guess."

"White?"

"Right!"

She told me she had gone to a kindergarten that taught the days of the week that way and had dressed to match them ever since.

"Cool," I said.

"Do you want some sherbet?" she said. And when I hesitated, she said, "It's kind of like ice cream."

"Okay."

"What kind do you want?" she asked. And when I didn't answer, she said, "Don't be shy."

"Lemon," I said then, because it was Wednesday, and she was wearing yellow.

"That's what I'm having!" she said, and just like that, we were friends.

Reuben and Lisa made friends, too, but Reuben didn't like the baseball because it wasn't real baseball. He said he showed up the first Saturday and found out it was like everything else here—you could come play if you wanted to but didn't have to if you didn't feel like it. No one ever got cut from the team because they were late, and nobody got told they sucked raw eggs or got called Dorothy and asked if they were checking for tornados out there in the outfield. Everyone was so laissez-faire and polite, he never went back. Who knew if they ever even realized he was this star pitcher and that his arm had healed up as good as new.

My mother was disappointed, though, especially when a new letter from Georgiana arrived:

Aggie!

I know I've said this before, but we really are moving soon! In fact, we even have a house picked out (which, yes, has the seven bedrooms we seem to require, our kids are truly completely spoiled). But we haven't moved yet, guess why? It's partly that George's position is mired in red tape. But partly we can't leave because his son's team is going to the baseball nationals*! And if there is anyone who cannot desert the team, it's their number one pitcher. I know it sounds silly, but do you remember what the sisters in Shanghai used to say about how seriously Americans take sports? It's true! His son is a star—you can't imagine. But it means we cannot leave until not just the* season *ends but the* postseason. *Because what kind of parents would mess up their son's* postseason*?*

What kind of parents, indeed.

I dreamed that Reuben would one day pitch against George Ping's son, my mother says now. I dreamed that he would win, and that George Ping would wish then that he hadn't married Georgiana and had asked me for a date instead. Of course, it was just a dream.
But if only you could have lived the life you'd hoped for when you came, I say. If only you could have lived a life like George and Georgiana's—a life where your family had gotten out, and where you had gotten your degree and become a professor.
A life where I was lucky, yes. Not just the luckiest one in an unlucky family, but lucky.
And now you just really missed Reuben's baseball games. Because what else did you have to distract you from those letters.
I did not want any more letters, she says.

She meant letters like:

As you know, your younger brother got married and so will be starting a family. That means finances are even tighter than before. My medical expenses are high, so though your brother and sisters try their best, I often cannot make ends meet and sometimes have to borrow money from relatives and friends. Therefore I want to discuss with you whether you can remit some living expenses to me every month from now on. After all, you are my own daughter, and many of our friends have remittances sent to them by relatives overseas. The state welcomes remittances from overseas Chinese family members so there is no inconvenience to us. They can be wired directly, and can also be sent from the United States using traveler's checks.

You had virtually stopped answering, but the letters kept coming anyway, I say.
They never stopped, my mother says.

There was a lot about Yonkers that we kids didn't miss. It was great that nobody beat anybody up here, and that nobody threw rocks at me and Lisa. And that creepy old St. Theresa's library! Who missed that? Greenacres Elementary School was full of tables, something we didn't have at St. Theresa's, and the library had more tables than anywhere else. And all around the library tables were shelf after shelf after shelf of books. I took armfuls of them out every day. I loved the Walter Farley books, like the Black Stallion books and *Misty of Chincoteague,* and I knew just where they were, lined up on a low shelf near the floor. I loved *The Phantom Tollbooth,* too, and *Pippi Longstocking,* and I loved seeing copies of *Heidi* and *Little Women,* it was like running into friends somewhere you never would have expected to see them. Clara! Marmee! Jo! What are you doing here? I wanted to say. And oh, Nancy Drew! *The Secret of the Old Clock*! *The Message in the Hollow Oak*! *The Mystery at the Moss-Covered Mansion*! *The Clue in the Jewel Box*! Mostly, though, I just read everything. If it was a book, I wanted to see what was in it. I couldn't go home without a pile like the one I was allowed to borrow when I was in third grade at St. Theresa's. I loved being loaded down, and I loved reading in bed, under my covers, with a flashlight.

Did you know I was doing this? I say now. Reading the way you did when you were young?

I didn't, my mother says.

It's too bad, I say. Because this library was even better than your father's library.

I never had a library like that.

I know, I say. If only you did.

When I had worked through all the different-colored spelling stations, my fifth-grade teacher, Mr. Baron, gave me *The New York Times* to read. He taught me how to fold it the way the commuters did and how to look up words I didn't know in this huge dictionary with thin pages; the first word I looked up was "purge." Was my mother reading the *Times* from cover to cover at home? It was strange to think that I was reading what she was reading, but I didn't tell her. And I didn't show her how commuters folded the paper, either, because I knew she wouldn't be interested.

Why would I be interested? I wasn't a commuter, she says now.

You read the paper the way your mother did, with the pages opened out on a table, I say.

I was a much better reader than my mother, she huffs.

Neither did I tell her when Mr. Baron started a class magazine. I had seen *Highlights* and *Life* and *Reader's Digest* at the dentist's office, but I'd never seen any other magazines, and even though in *Little Women* Jo March was a writer, I had somehow never thought of my teddy bears Beth and Jo writing anything in their tent. Once Mr. Baron explained what we were up to, though, I submitted enough jokes and articles to fill up the whole magazine myself, and knew that Beth and Jo were going to have a magazine, too. I even wrote a short story after Mr. Baron explained what a short story was. My story was about a maid who steals some gold and hides it inside a hat. But when the hat is picked up, the gold falls out! And so she gets fired.

Why did you write that? my mother says now. It's as if you know something about Nai-ma. But I never told you.

I don't know why I wrote it, I say. But you're right. It's as if I knew something you never told me. Fiction is funny that way.

My story was five pages long. I carefully copied it onto what Mr. Baron called mimeograph sheets, which were special pieces of paper that took what you wrote on one side and turned it into ink on the other. I had to print very clearly and in straight lines, and scrape off any mistakes with a razor blade; my fingers turned purple like the ink. But finally I finished. Mr. Baron put my story together with stuff other people wrote and ran it all off on this machine. Each turn of the barrel printed out a page; the pages smelled funny. Also, they had to be collated and stapled. But a bunch of kids and I helped, and then we read what everyone had written.

"Did you really write that whole thing?" Betsy Feinstein asked. "I can't believe you wrote that whole thing."

"And, like, did that really happen?" asked Barry Fingerstone.

"Of course, it didn't happen, you numbskull. She made it up," said Rhonda Hecht.

"I don't know, I just thought maybe it happened in China or something," said Barry.

"Like your head must have been made in Japan," said Betsy.

"You shouldn't talk like that, that's a mean thing to say," said Annie Dreyfus. "No one was made in Japan, and for that matter, no one was made in China, either."

"Actually, a lot of people are made in China," said Betsy, and turned to me. "Right?"

Everyone looked at me then, as if I were an expert and would know.

Still, in my opinion, Scarsdale was okay.

Our new house was a fixer-upper. Fixing it up was fun for Lisa and me, but my mother didn't like the building supply store, which she said was "so-called low-class." So she stayed home while my father let Lisa and me pick everything. Of course, being age ten and twelve, we picked yellow-and-green psychedelic Formica panels for the bottom halves of the walls of the guest bathroom, and a yellow-and-green plaid wallpaper for the top. And for the kitchen, we adopted the top half–bottom half approach again, with wood-look paneling on the bottom half of the walls, and a gold basketweave-patterned wallpaper on the top. The gold basketweave pattern tied in with the harvest gold stove and a matching harvest gold double-door icebox that reminded my mother of the icebox her family had had in Shanghai; its wood-tone handles tied in with the wood-look Black Forest cuckoo clock my father had brought home from a conference in Austria. The only thing that didn't coordinate was the suspended ceiling with fluorescent light panels my father installed. It was the easiest way to cover up the cracks in the original ceiling but looked like it belonged in an office, not a house.

"He just does whatever he wants," my mother said, and that was sort of true.

As for my father putting me and Lisa in charge of the decorating, all she said was "Typical Dad."

So why did you let him do that? I ask now. It was as if the house was his house and not yours.

Oh, I don't know, she says. I didn't care too much.

You didn't care about the wallpaper in your own house?

Not too much, no.

Were you still getting letters from China?

To tell you the truth, sometimes I did not even read them anymore.

And you had stopped writing back altogether. At one point, the person in Hong Kong who had been forwarding your family's letters to you and vice versa even wrote to you herself. Do you remember?

Oh, I don't know, she says.

The person at the Nan Sing Plastics factory in Hong Kong who had been forwarding my mother's family's letters from Shanghai took it upon herself not only to write a letter but to send it via registered airmail. In English, she wrote:

Dear Mrs. Jen,

I have been asked by your sister, whom I knew when I was in Shanghai, to forward you the enclosed letter in Chinese. Prior to this, I have always forwarded to you other letters received from your family. I understand that they have so far received no reply from you and am wondering whether this letter has been received by you.

Both your mother and sisters are very anxious to hear from you, and a word from you to them will greatly relieve them. If it is not convenient for you to write to your family, perhaps you will communicate with me. I can assure you that if there is anything I can do for you, I shall always be pleased to be of service.

Yours very truly,

Constant Y. C. Tse

All they wanted was money, my mother says now.
Are you sure? I say.
Also, I was very tired, she says.

Some days she slept all afternoon. First it was because of her toothaches. The pain, she said. Then it was because she had to have two root canals. The anesthesia, she said. And then when the root canals didn't work and she had to have the two teeth pulled, it was the stress of having a plate made with false teeth, and the discomfort of wearing it. And after that she slept, she said, because the afternoon was when the boys napped. But more and more when they got up, she was still asleep.

Lisa and I went on decorating. We picked the living room wallpaper and then the carpet, too, flipping through these enormous samples in a carpet salesroom; they were like the pages of a book in a giant's house. We laughed at the salesman, who wore paisley bell-bottoms and a psychedelic tie.

"Where's your mother?" he asked us. And then he said it again. "Where's your mother?"

We ignored him. But when he turned his back, I whispered to Lisa, "He doesn't think we are really in charge of picking a carpet."

"I wish Mom would pick," she said.

"Or how about Dad," I said.

"Mom."

We stood there awhile. The other customers were all grown-ups.

"What color do you think she'd pick?" I said finally.

"I don't know. She likes lobsters," Lisa said.

But there wasn't a lobster-red option, so finally we picked a beautiful thick French-blue carpet that went with the French provincial blue-and-white flocked wallpaper we'd found in the building supply store, and that meant we could keep a white French provincial hall table left by the previous owners. Later in the building supply store, we picked a blue-and-white French provincial double-sink vanity, too, for the bathroom upstairs, and two French provincial medicine cabinets. When we were done, I wondered what French provincial was anyway, and why everything was called that. But I didn't know who to ask.

My mother slept until it was time to fight with my father about supper. Then she woke up to defend herself. He couldn't understand why we ate at eight or eight thirty or even nine o'clock when he was the one teaching and writing papers and going to meetings and doing research in the lab. Wasn't she home all day doing nothing?

"Sleeping, sleeping, always sleeping!" he yelled. "Why are you sleeping? You should be wake up!"

He hated that she spent so much time reading the newspaper. "Forget about newspaper!" he yelled. "No more newspaper!"

But his biggest complaint was "Late, late, late! Never on time! Always have to late!"—something he yelled more and more, it seemed, the more consulting he took on. "Lotta pressure, mister!" he would say sometimes. "Lotta, lotta pressure." But no matter how much he yelled, she slept all afternoon as if she were on vacation, only getting up at six or seven to start supper.

That meant first cutting up the meat. "Across the grain," she told me, as I was the meat slicer, of course. Then she would marinate it in cornstarch and sherry and soy sauce—*jiàng yu*, as we called it in Shanghainese. We ate everything that could be eaten—the heart and neck and gizzards of a chicken, for example, as well as its *pìpì*—its behind. In fact, that was one of my father's favorite foods, along with fish brains and fish eyeballs.

When the chopping was done, my mother would turn the stove as hot as it would go, and then into the pan went the food, with a loud *whooch*! Then she was stirring really loud and banging the metal spoon on the side of the pan as the rice cooker went off with a click and I hollered, "Time for supper!"—throwing the bowls and chopsticks on the table in a clatter. Everyone would show up, eat, and leave. Then my parents would start fighting again.

"Soft! No drive! What do you do! Nothing!" my father would yell. "Sit there doing nothing!"

To this she sometimes yelled back, "Five children, you think they raise themselves?" But other times she ignored him, and got back at him by giving me the special treatment.

Now that he was a full professor, my father was consulting for the Navy and the Air Force in Washington, D.C., all summer. "Dad is eating with Uncle Sam again," we would joke at supper—a good thing in a way, as it turned out that my mother and father were like the birds on the cuckoo clock. When one went in, the other came out. My mother slept less with him gone. She went shopping at different malls and got excited about the July Fourth sales. Those magic words "40 percent off!" were like a fairy dust that brought her to life. She started talking about things like coat interlinings and "this year's color."

But I was still my father's representative she could pick on anytime, and the longer my father was gone, the worse things got. In school, everyone wanted me to talk more. "And what about you? What do you think?" the teachers were always asking. One liked to wink and say, "A penny for your thoughts?"—especially as the inferno that used to keep me from talking in class was cooling. I could not have said why, but I could see that I was delighting my teachers. "Now, what's going on in that head of yours?" they wanted to know.

My mother, in contrast, definitely didn't want to know. "Too much to say!" she said over and over. She did not want me asking why I couldn't wear pants or miniskirts or use tampons, or why I couldn't ask the doctor how much contact lenses cost now that I was babysitting and could maybe make enough money to pay for them. Everything was no. I was not allowed to wear eyeliner. I was not allowed to wear lip gloss. I was not allowed to wear blue jeans. I was not allowed to go on sleepovers.

"But why, Ma?"

"Forget about why!"

I wished my father would come home. Sometimes I would think I heard the garage door slam, and then even if I was asleep, I would wake and think, He's home! But it was always something else, never him.

Some of my new friends had charge accounts in the stores in Scarsdale Village. If they liked something, they just charged it to their parents.

"Like, I liked this sweater," my friend Annie Dreyfus explained. "Because it was really soft, and I like soft stuff, so I bought it." Then she asked me what I liked, and when I said I didn't know, she said, "What do you mean you don't know? How can you not know?"

"I don't know," I said.

All I had ever noticed about a sweater was whether it was on regular sale or final sale. But also, in my family, we were not allowed to say we liked or didn't like something, especially me, and especially at supper. Since we ate Chinese-style, serving ourselves from bowls of food in the middle of the table, we could generally avoid food we didn't like by not helping ourselves to any. But one day, my mother gave me a big helping of stir-fried chicken livers and, when I made a face, shoved the whole dish in front of me.

"You eat," she said.

"Ma," I said. I could see she really had it out for me, though, and so I ate some.

"Eat the rest," she said.

"Ma."

"You finish."

"Ma."

"Whole thing."

"I thought you're always telling us not to stuff ourselves."

She hated it when I used something she herself had said against her.

"Eat," she said.

Reuben started to stand up from the table. She glared at him. He sat back down.

"Eat," she told me again.

And as no one was allowed to leave the table until I had eaten the rest of the dish, I ate while they watched. The livers were rubbery and cold. It was like eating a dish of erasers.

"In this house, no American 'I don't eat this, I don't eat that'!" my mother said at the end. "Chinese people eat everything! You hear me?"

"Faintly," I said.

And so it was that even after eating all those chicken livers, I got hit anyway while everyone else skedaddled.

You didn't listen, that's why, she says now.
By "listen," you mean "obey," I say. You mean I didn't obey.
You were the most disobedient child there ever was.
The most difficult to control, you mean.
That's right. The most difficult to control.

With my father back home, the school year was not as bad as the summer. Scarsdale might have been terrible for baseball, but it did have school-sponsored ski trips, which Reuben loved and my father supported enthusiastically. Whenever a parent had to pick Reuben and his friends up in the middle of the night, my father always volunteered. And when the rest of us kids all wanted to learn to ski, too, he lined us up on the bench at the ski area and, kneeling at our feet and going down the line, helped us with our lace-up boots, one after another. He would tinker with any bindings that needed adjusting, using a bag of tools he brought from home, and then he would park himself in the lodge with a cup of tea and a pile of student papers. He was the only one in the ski lodge wearing a wool overcoat, but he didn't mind. He would sit grading papers by the window with his leather briefcase beside him and watch us come down. Sometimes he would take a break and stand at the bottom of the hill. "That's Lisa!" he would say, pointing. "That's Sean!" "That's Shane!" And as we braked in front of him, spraying up snow, he would clap and say, "Very good! Very good!"

Meanwhile, besides skiing, Scarsdale for me also meant learning to protest. Protesting wasn't the only thing I did with my new best friend, Allison; we designed plasma-powered space suits and wrote poems in color, too. (If the sound of a word and the shape of the poem mattered, after all, why not the color of a poem?) Allison also introduced me to classical guitar: I had made enough money babysitting to buy myself a record player, and had spent many hours listening to the Beatles and Joni Mitchell and Simon and Garfunkel. But Andrés Segovia! John Williams! Fernando Sor! These were musicians I never would have discovered on my own. Neither would I have discovered fantasy and science fiction writers like Robert A. Heinlein and Arthur C. Clarke and, my favorite, Ray Bradbury.

But we had started protesting back in sixth grade when we made posters to help save the Bronx River Parkway—should it not, we asked, be allowed to "keep its bumps and curves"?—and now that we were in seventh grade, we marched around the cafeteria with signs demanding that girls be allowed to take shop. We weren't the only ones protesting. It was 1967, after all. Civil rights! Vietnam! The whole country was protesting. It's true we weren't exactly resisting the draft or making sure all Americans could vote. But still—how come girls had to sew and cook while the boys got to use hammers and saws to make big things? Why did we not have a choice? Allison and I did not spark any kind of mass movement. We were, however, eventually granted permission to use the shop ourselves, after school.

Did I even really want to make something? With all those boys around? The first time I followed Allison into the shop, I was so nervous I tripped.

"Are you guys lost?" said Andy Bezos.

"Shut your trap, Bozo, or I'll shut it for you," said Jeff Green.

Mr. Gorman calmly showed us what to do. He wore a tie-dyed Grateful Dead T-shirt and a pencil behind his ear.

"First rule here is PUT IT BACK," he said. "Got that? We got a lot of tools here, and you can use any of them. But after you use it, you have to PUT IT BACK."

"I thought the first rule in this shop was SAFETY FIRST," said Andy.

"That's for you boys," said Mr. Gorman. "These young ladies already know that. Girls are way ahead of you on pretty much everything; try to hold on to that. Then when they ask you if you learned anything in shop, you can tell them."

"You mean we didn't just learn to PUT IT BACK?"

"What's a genius like you doing in seventh grade, eh?" said Mr. Gorman. "Yes. If you pay attention, you can leave this class having learned two things, unlike the thirty or forty these young ladies are going to take away, you watch."

Then he turned to us. "What's this?" he said.

"A hammer," said Allison.

"And this?"

I could barely get out the words. "A screwdriver."

"Brilliant," said Mr. Gorman. "What are they for?"

"They're for putting back," we said.

"Best students I'll ever have," said Mr. Gorman. "Beats me why girls can't take shop. A-plus."

We came back again, and then showed up and showed up, until we had managed to pick out hunks of wood, situate them in vise clamps, and hollow them out with a gouge. Then we sanded and sanded until our hunks had become bowls we could take home. We put them on our shelves like trophies.

Meanwhile, my mother received another letter from Auntie Ping:

> *Our relatives just came back from Hong Kong with some things to report. Do you know the phrase "struggled against"? These days in China it is used a lot thanks to something called the Cultural Revolution. Maybe you have*

heard about it. Society is now divided into red families and black families. The Nine Black Categories—the bad guys—are landlords, traitors, spies, counterrevolutionaries, capitalist roaders, intellectuals, and some other people. I forget them all, but you get the idea. People like your family and ours are particularly targeted because we represent the Four Olds: old customs, old culture, old habits, and old ideas. As for what happens when you are struggled against, you don't want to know. These students called Red Guards will stop at nothing. Thousands of teachers have been killed by their own students. You would not believe how many drownings and knifings and beheadings there have been.

I am sorry to give this report. I only write because your family is probably afraid to tell you themselves—too dangerous. It is terrible they did not get out of China. My relatives are planning to travel to Hong Kong again next year and might hear more then. I'll let you know.

Having briefly responded to Constant Y. C. Tse at the Hong Kong plastics factory, my mother was also now barraged by letters from her family. They said almost nothing about what was happening, however, but only things like:

How is your health? I hear you have arthritis. Is the cold weather difficult? It is always important with arthritis to keep warm.

And:

Your children are so hardworking, like you and Brother Chao-pe. They will certainly be successful.

And:

> *Are the boys naughty? Their cousins here are all very naughty.*

And:

> *You should take ginseng and also white fungus. Do you know how to prepare it?*

Apparently aware that she did not want to be pestered with requests for money, they refrained from asking. There was only one reference to their circumstances, in a letter from my grandmother:

> *We are all fine. The Red Guards have come through our apartment five times now, but they did such an excellent job cleaning out our jewelry and paintings and books— everything feudal—that all there is to do now is praise the thoroughness of the Red Guards who visited before.*
>
> *They always bring me out of the apartment into the open air when they come. I do not go out often, since my balance is not so steady, but they will work together to carry me downstairs to the courtyard. As for the things they say, I cannot always understand them because of my hearing. Still, I manage to learn some lessons I will not forget.*
>
> *We have received no news from your younger sister but trust that if she were no longer able to work, we would be notified.*

Of course, I feel very bad, my mother says now.
And yet still you refused to write back to your mother, I say. You wrote to your sisters and brothers, but not one line to your mother.
She is quiet.
Did you know what was happening? I ask. Did you know

that the Red Guards were rampaging through the country, beating, torturing, humiliating, and killing people? They even went after pets, calling them "symbols of bourgeois decadence." Thousands of cats were killed, and so many Pekinese dogs, the breed almost went extinct.

Poor Bao-bao and Zhen-zhen.

Yes. Your poor dogs were probably killed.

She is quiet once more.

They repeatedly dragged your mother into the courtyard, as she told you. They put a dunce cap on her, and cursed and harangued her, and spit on her.

I didn't know the details.

But did you have an idea what was happening?

An idea.

Then aren't you sorry today that through it all, you held on to your anger and refused to write to her? When it might have been some small comfort? Aren't you a little sorry?

She is silent.

School-sponsored skiing might be okay, but was I allowed to visit my friend Annie Dreyfus on Shelter Island for the weekend? No.

"Why?" I said. And, "Please, Ma, please? Gillian Cantor is going, and Lori Kahn, and Annie invited me to come, too."

"You are becoming a social butterfly," she said. "Tell them I say you are stay home, period."

"But why, Mom? Why?" And brimming with protest spirit, I packed my things in a pillowcase, then snuck out the next morning and walked over to Gillian's house, where Annie's mother picked us up. She said she could have picked me up at my house, but I told her this worked better because I had just slept over at Gillian's anyway.

Annie's mother raised an eyebrow but kept driving.

I'd never been on a car ferry before and was sorry the ride was so short—even the drive that came afterward seemed too short, what with all the beautiful rambling roses lining the way. It was that much sooner that we were on Annie's dock, though, dangling our bare feet in the water. Annie said it was her favorite thing, and I could see why. The water was so cold and splashy, and the bay so bright and wide open. Little fish nibbled at our toes, which I thought tickled but which made Lori shriek, "They're biting us!" until Annie convinced her they were taking off our dead skin. Then just when Lori relaxed, what should appear under the dock but a huge snapping turtle!

"I'll save us!" Annie said. She hoisted a blue-and-yellow sail up the mast of a Sunfish and helped us squish together with our feet in the cockpit. Then we set sail into the light. The water was so twinkly, and the clouds so wispy they didn't look real. And the sun pressed on our backs as if encouraging us to bend down and trail our hands in the water, so we did—even Lori, who wasn't going to but changed her mind when she saw that nothing was biting us—while Annie steered us around using the wind, just like in *Treasure Island*. She was wearing her mother's sunglasses and a visor, which made her look even more expert.

"It's easy," she said, explaining about upwind and downwind and coming about, all of which made sense but still somehow so confused me that she said she could see she would have to show me on a piece of paper later, especially since the wind was picking up. We bumped fast across the water, waving at the other people out on boats except when they were Mafia.

"Are they really Mafia? Are you sure?" I said.

Annie was sure. "What else do you think they do with their money?" She pulled her mother's sunglasses down her nose so she could look over them at me.

Gillian agreed. "They have to put it someplace. So they put it in houses and boats."

"I thought they put it in a bank," I said.

That made them laugh. "The Mafia don't use banks," they said. "They do their business in cash. So they have too much cash and have to buy things with it."

"Plus, they want to diversify, just like us," said Annie.

I had no idea what she was talking about but didn't want to ask any more questions because I had already asked too many. And so I just tried to duck when I was supposed to and not get hit by what Annie said was called the boom exactly because it could—*boom!*—smack you in the head.

Later on, Annie's mother was mad that we'd gone out without life jackets, especially when she realized I couldn't swim. Her frosted-pink lips stretched grimly from ear to ear.

"You ladies are lucky you didn't capsize," she said.

But it had never occurred to Annie that I might not be able to swim, just as it had never occurred to me that the boat could tip over. I did want to learn to swim now, though, especially when we all went swimming and Annie's mother ran to find me an inflatable ring.

"You look like a ballerina!" Annie said, twirling around on her toes.

I did not feel like a ballerina. But when I got a sunburn—my first sunburn ever, complete with a white bow on my back from my bikini top—I felt like one of the gang again because everyone was sunburnt and we all had white bows. Annie got out the Solarcaine so we could spray each other, shrieking at the cold. Then we had pineapple pizza and ice cream with Marshmallow Fluff and fudge sauce on the beach, and I came home so happy, why should my mother hit me?

But she said I was disobedient and wild and had no consideration for others.

"How could you sneak out? Make everyone worry sick!"

"If you were so worried, why didn't you call the police?" I said.

"Because we knew where you went. We knew you went with Annie even after we told you no!"

"Then why were you worried sick?"

"Bad bad girl," she said, hitting me. "If you lie and sneak out like that again, we will disown you!"

"I wish you would," I said, making her hit me even more. "I wish you would." And, "Why should I listen to you?"

"You think you know everything!"

"I know a lot more than you," I said. Because what did she know about Sunfish and coming about and where the Mafia put their money, much less pineapple pizza? "You don't want me to have fun because you don't have any fun, and you don't want me to have friends because you don't have any friends."

"You can go to hell!" my mother said then—surprising me, as she did sometimes, with her new vocabulary.

. . .

That was not the end of the hitting. In fact, it went on all week, until finally I took all the money I had—almost ten dollars—out of my small gray metal lockbox. I bundled it up in a pillowcase with my mini-*Pietà,* and then I left again.

I walked to the next town over, taking the path through the woods, by the stream and the skunk cabbage. Hartsdale was a commercial area, with a train station; I thought I could take the train to Yonkers and Mrs. Cunningham's house. That was wrong. There was no train to anywhere near our old neighborhood. There was a bus, though. I took that down Central Park Avenue and got off by the Adventurers Inn. Then I walked from there back to our old house. It was uphill forever, but I kept walking until finally I reached Jennifer Lane and Spring Road.

Our old house had a strange car in the driveway, and in the years since we moved, the saplings in the neighborhood had turned into trees. The stakes were gone, there was grass everywhere, and some of the bushes could even be called overgrown. But stranger yet was walking down to the dead end—a much shorter walk than I remembered—and finding nobody home at Mrs. Cunningham's house. Where was she? Why were her curtains closed? Her curtains were blue on the inside, but in the window facing the street, they looked white. I remembered reading somewhere that the sun could bleach things, and as I sat down on her step, I wondered if that was what had happened—if the curtains had gotten bleached out. It was like waiting to be picked up at Carmen my ballet teacher's house except that I wasn't waiting for my mother. Mrs. Cunningham was bound to come home soon from wherever she was, and then wouldn't she be surprised! I could see how we would sit at her kitchen table and discuss the teddy bear tent, although maybe it would be easier just to make a crochet house like hers—less engineering. Then who did I see instead but that Mrs. Mancini who had come yelling and complaining years ago after Reuben hit a baseball through her window. She wasn't any bigger, but she had a lot of gray hair now and was a lot less mad as she came up the walk to say hello.

"What are you doing sitting there?" she exclaimed. "All grown up like a weed! It's great to see you back in the neighborhood. How's the family?"

She smiled until I told her I was looking for Mrs. Cunningham. Then it was as if someone had unplugged a lamp.

"Oh," she said. "Did you come back special to find her?"

I said yes, and that's when she told me that Mrs. Cunningham had had a stroke just the week before and died. And when I started crying, she took me to her house and into her kitchen and poured me some lemonade.

"She had a big heart," she said. "I miss her, too. And damn, she would have loved to have seen you—to know you came back. If only you'd come a little earlier, you could have caught her, you know. She was walking around to the end—gardening and grocery shopping, everything. She was working on this giant afghan that meant she had all these little squares all over her living room, and I mean all over. You couldn't sit anywhere, there were so many."

Mrs. Mancini heated up some lasagna I couldn't eat because I was crying so hard, and when finally I had no more tears and couldn't cry anymore, she offered to call my parents so they could come get me.

"Please don't," I said. "I ran away."

She looked at my pillowcase then as if just noticing it. "Oh," she said, and gave me a hug that made me start crying again. "You poor thing. Mrs. Cunningham used to say you didn't get along with your mother, you know."

"Did she?"

"She thought your mother was too hard on you. And truth be told, your mother wasn't the fairest person around—in fact, I think I once called her a lying shit. But as Mrs. Cunningham used to say, your mother is your mother, like it or not. It's what you call a fact of life."

She wrapped the lasagna in some tinfoil and insisted on driving me home.

"You know, a lot of mothers fight with their daughters," she said when we got to my door. "I only had boys, thank the Lord. Because for some reason, mothers and daughters are like cats and dogs. But I'll tell you something that might make you feel better. You know what Mrs. Cunningham used to call you?"

"What?"

"She used to call you her Chinese daughter. She'd say, 'You know who came to visit me today? My Chinese daughter.'"

I didn't know what to say.

Mrs. Mancini handed me the lasagna as I opened the car door. "If you put it in the fridge, heat it up before you eat it," she said.

"Okay," I said.

"Cold lasagna is like rubber," she said, and gave me another hug. "Good luck."

No sooner had my father closed the front door than the screaming began.

"Who do you think you are, you can just run away? Last week, this week—do you think you can run away every week?" My mother was livid, and it wasn't just her; it was my father, too. I had thought he would shake his head when he heard I'd gone back to our old neighborhood, and maybe laugh. But for once, he and my mother agreed. In fact, he was the one who got out a metal garden stake—one of those pointed metal rods you could push into the dirt around the edge of a yard—while my mother dragged me out to the backyard. She threw my pillowcase and lasagna into the bushes. Then he beat me while my mother held my arms. It was like she was hugging me except that I was trying to get away, and soft as her skin was, she was a lot stronger than I realized.

"I'll teach you a lesson," my father kept saying. "I'll teach you a lesson."

I wasn't tough like Reuben. I didn't keep a stone face and say, Fuck you, or You can't hurt me. Instead, I cried and begged. "Stop, Daddy! Stop! I won't do it again! Stop! Stop! I won't do it again!"

But it was not like learning to ride a bike, where all I had to do was ride and I wouldn't get hit. The neighbors couldn't see what was happening because we were behind a fence, and they couldn't hear because of all the traffic, and my mother never told my father he was crazy and should stop. She just held me tighter, as if she was happy that he and she were a team for once and wanted to make sure she did a good job. And sure enough, with her help he beat me so hard that the backs of my legs bled and I couldn't even run when he finally stopped. He threw the stake down with a clang on the patio and went inside because the evening mosquitoes were coming out. Then my mother let go to swat one and went inside, too, leaving me to lie there in the grass by myself. I thought my legs were broken, but they weren't—they were just bleeding and swollen.

Probably I would have lay there forever except I was also getting bitten. So I got myself up and went to rescue my pillowcase and the lasagna, which was still wrapped up and a little warm—not like rubber yet. Then I went inside and cleaned up my cuts with Bactine. They stung so bad, my eyes started crying all over again.

Of course, my father never did say he was sorry. It was just the rules. Just as, back in Yonkers, Reuben was not allowed to play hooky, and Lisa was not allowed on Jennifer Lane, I was not allowed to run away. I got it. There was a reason that every Chinese New Year, my mother held up an orange and said, *Tuántuán yuányuán*—meaning, Whole family together. That was supposed to be a happy thing, that all the sections belonged to the whole. But what if they didn't want to? When I was older, I would think about Tibet and Taiwan, and how their lesson was my lesson. There was no leaving a Chinese family.

Meanwhile, I had another lesson to learn. After my beating, I wanted to run away again, but since I could hardly move, I lay under my bed, on my stomach, on the wooden floor of my room, wondering if anyone would come look for me. In the summer, I liked to sleep on the floor because it was cool, but this was different. My brothers and sister all knew I'd been beaten; I waited and, I guess, hoped.

As I probably should have known, though, I waited for nothing. Just as no one came for my crying mother when Nai-ma was fired, no one came for me. I was happy that back when my brother was getting beaten on his knees, I had at least tried to stop my father. But I was sorry that I didn't knock on Reuben's door afterward to make sure he was okay—none of us did. I guess he seemed so tough, we didn't think he needed us. But also, it just wasn't done in our family. We believed that troublemakers deşerved to be punished; we believed that there was a lesson they needed to be taught.

And besides beating, this was the other instructional method we used: the shutout. It was a method I would come to know well in the coming years. In the meantime, I lay with my cheek against the floorboards, deserted and defeated and alone. Then I got bored, shimmied out, and, as much as it hurt, stood up.

CHAPTER V
A Dance

I knew what this book was going to say even before you wrote it, my mother says now. I knew it was going to say I was a terrible mother, blah blah blah blah. The first part explains how I became so terrible. The second part says how terrible I was.

And you don't feel a little bad, looking back? I say.
A lot of girls help with cleaning. It is normal.
And what about the hitting? Was that normal, too?
In China, of course.
What about here, Mom? I was out of gym for months.
Why don't you ask Dad? I never used a metal stake. He is the crazy one.
He was wrong, too.
I'm glad you realize that.
He was wrong. He had quite an anger problem, and even if it was okay to beat people in China, it wasn't okay here. And I wish I could forget it, I do. But you know, a lot of kids get hit by their parents and still love them—a lot of Asian kids especially, but a lot of non-Asian kids, too. And he hit us all, whereas you scapegoated me, Ma.
It is better to hit everyone?
It isn't always, I'm sure. But in his case, it was at least

clear what he wanted. No more playing hooky! No more going to Jennifer Lane! No more running away! And that was less hurtful than targeting one child the way you did. It was less manipulative than playing favorites.

Favorites are normal. You ask anyone in China. All families have favorites.

But here, Mom.

You think people here don't have favorites? Chinese people are more honest, that's all.

You are right that in China it's not unusual for boys to be treated like princes and their sisters like servants. There's no pretense.

That's right.

But here, Mom. Forget that everyone got a big bedroom, while I got a Harry Potter room. Forget that if we had meatloaf, everyone got a middle piece and I got the burnt end. Forget the shopping sprees you went on with Lisa, pointedly leaving me at home. Reuben threw me down a whole flight of stairs, and you said nothing.

So what do you want? Do you want me to say I'm sorry? I will never say it, she says. How is your life today? Is it okay?

I have to nod.

I don't think I should feel sorry for you. I think you should feel sorry for me.

I do feel sorry for you. How did such a smart, lively girl turn into a person who could rant on the phone for an hour nonstop? You yelled so loud, my kids could hear you across the room without a speakerphone.

So you got the last laugh and the last word, she says. What else do you want?

I want to have had a real mother, Mom. Just like you wanted. A mother who loved me. I want to have had a mother like Nai-ma. I want not to have a mother-shaped hole in my heart.

She laughs. How could Nai-ma be your mother? You do not even speak Chinese. I think I was good enough.

. . .

My parents took Reuben on a college tour, visiting ten schools, while with me, they did not visit one. I drove myself to my college interviews and toured the schools myself as well.

You did not need help, that's why, she says now. Everything you can do by yourself.
Was that why you did not even ask where I was applying? I say. You didn't ask Lisa, either.
It is not important.
Only Reuben's college mattered, you mean.
He is the number one son.

On the way back from New Haven, my VW Bug soared over a bump in the road and began to hydroplane in the pouring rain. I careened back and forth across the highway several times before regaining control, then crept into a rest stop, shaking, only to lock myself out of my car. Happily, I was rescued by a kindly busboy.

"You okay?" he asked.

I explained.

"Hold on," he said.

I tried not to stare at his enormous sideburns—"chops," we called them then—as he came out to the parking lot with me and popped the door open with a butter knife.

"Wow," I said.

He shrugged. "Never leave valuables in the car."

"Thanks." I tried to tip him, but he just laughed and waved his hand.

"What're you doing, out driving around by yourself?"

"Visiting colleges." I was a little embarrassed as I said it, thinking that he might not be going to college. But if he wasn't, he didn't seem to mind that I was.

"Where're your parents?"

I shrugged.

"Got it," he said, heading back into his job. "Hope you get in."

When I got into every college I applied to, my father said, "Very good!" My siblings hung a big multicolored Congratulations! sign out of our den window, over the driveway. Only my mother said nothing, though she did still boast about me to Georgiana:

What a shame you are still stuck in Chicago. Are you not moving to New York after all? Anyway, now that you have three children in New York schools, you have an excuse to come visit. Here our number two got into Harvard, Yale, Princeton, *and everywhere else she applied—so many that deciding was a headache. Finally, though, she picked* Harvard.

My father would not have believed it, she says now. A girl, going to Harvard! And I wish I could have told Mother Greenough. Of course, my daughter's English is excellent, I would say. After all, she was born here.
  If you were so proud, why did you never tell me? I say.
  The Chinese say, A child should be hollow like bamboo.
  You know, it hurt, Mom. It hurt that no one even discussed my choices with me, or helped me think through what to do.
  Why should anyone talk to you? You think you know everything already. You know what I know?
  What?
  Tuition is expensive, that's what I know. First Reuben, and then you, and soon Lisa. Then the boys. Dad and I discuss every day how to solve that problem. We cannot say, You cannot go to Harvard.
  Well, thanks for that much, Mom.
  You were a pain in the neck ever since you were born, she says.

No PhD and, more important, no teaching experience. Still, my mother sent out some twenty letters inquiring about teaching jobs.
  No response.
  Until finally, one day, she received a notification about a position in the Bronx. She'd gotten an interview!
  She prepared her outfit a week in advance. Navy blue dress, girdle, new stockings, brown pumps, and should she wear her kingfisher phoenix pin for good luck? She wore it but was sorry as

soon as she walked in the door. It made her look more Chinese, and as it was, she was too Chinese.

"Are you American?" the chair of the hiring committee asked.

"I am an American citizen," my mother answered.

"But not a real American." The chair instructed my mother to stand in front of the classroom and speak, while a row of women sat in the back, clucking and asking one another, "Can you understand her?"

**"Clucking," my mother says now. That's a good word.
Were they clucking? I say.
They were clucking.**

And there she was, the number one English student in her class in China, the student who had gotten herself into an American PhD program and earned thirty points past her master's, being appraised by people who might well have spoken no foreign language at all but who were what she could never be, native English speakers.

"Louder," they said. "Can you repeat that last line?"

And: "Can you repeat it again? One more time?"

And: "That is the British pronunciation. We are not British."

She was surprised she got the job. But she did! Her offer letter said that, if she accepted, she would be teaching third grade, starting in September. Of course, she agreed right away. She was not going to be a professor like Georgiana and my father, but still: she was going to be a teacher, like Mother Greenough and the nuns she had so admired at her school in Shanghai, and like Marnie Mulligan (who, according to her last Christmas card, was also teaching third grade—"the best grade, hands down!" Marnie wrote). She asked my father to show her how to get to her school. She practiced the route to be sure she knew where to turn and where to park.

Then she started work.

They told us to keep a written record of any misbehavior in the classroom, my mother says now. They said to make sure to say what happened and include the date so that they

would have the facts in case they needed to take disciplinary action.

And so you kept a log, I say.

I did.

Well, guess what? I found it, I say. Your log. After you died. It was in your storage locker, along with your teaching materials.

Really?

Yes, really.

Are you going to use it?

Verbatim, I say. If that's okay?

She hesitates.

You never wrote a book, but you did write this.

Okay, she says then. Sure.

The notebook is labeled "Anecdotes 3–4 Mrs. Jen."

11/26
Mrs. Kaufman reported that Tylania poked a fork at the left eye of a boy in her class. Zarak was a witness. Children said Tylania did it without provocation.

11/29
Alvin poked a pencil into Angela and hurt her ear. Witnessed by Dennis and Shawn. Alvin also punched Alina in her face.

There are notes from the children, too. For example, penciled in beautiful, loopy, Palmer Method script:

Dear Mrs. Jen,

Alvin came over and kicked me in the leg while I was in the lunchroom yesterday. He also hit me in the face. I dropped 50 cents that I had in my hand and haven't gotten it back yet. Today Alvin told me that he is going to "make me pay for it."

Maria Marsh

Appended to this is my mother's note, in red pen:

> Serena Cameroon saw Maria drop the money. Alvin threatened to bust Maria's head in my presence and said a curse. He had no homework today and said he left it at home. He did his homework just once since school opened.

Poor Maria, I say now.
Poor Maria is right, my mother says.
Poor Angela, poor Alina, and poor Serena, too. No wonder these kids don't finish school.
They are the unluckiest members of a lucky country, she says.

Many more entries follow.

> 1/22
> In the stairs at dismissal time, while I was hanging up keys, Alvin hit Zarak and the two were in a fight. Alvin choked and kicked Zarak. Mrs. Aetna broke up the fight. Zarak's mother came in the next day to complain. She went to see Mr. Unterberger.

It isn't only Alvin. It is also James and Richard and Tylania, Alfred, Robbie, Nathaniel, and Dawn. One day, Alfred kicks James in the stomach. Another day, James punches Louis in the face. Another, Alfred jumps and kicks Richard "for no apparent reason." And then another, Nathaniel beats up Stanley Jordan in the other third-grade class. On and on it goes, for page after page after page: Richard and Robbie hit Collette, Robbie continuing to punch her in the stomach even though she is crying. Dawn trips and chokes Angela. Nathaniel pushes Veronica down the stairs. One day at the three o'clock dismissal, Dawn pushes the whole line of kids so hard, nineteen children fall down the staircase. There are endless headlocks and karate kicks and reports of children laughing while others cry. One day, my mother writes, "There was a real fight. The children all ran to the back, chairs were pushed and knocked onto the floor." The kids attack each other with sticks and rulers.

My mother appeals to the parents, and at one point Richard's mother responds to her communications: "Please be advised that he does receive punishment for his misbehavior, but evidently much stronger disciplinary measures must be implemented," she writes. Tylania's and Alfred's parents not only come in but threaten to beat the kids with a belt in front of the class.

> *Just like Dad, my mother says now.*
> *He wouldn't have beaten us in front of the class, I say.*
> *Not in front of the class, she concedes.*

More typically, the parents do not respond. If they do, it's to ask why it is always their child's fault, or to insist that it is the school's job to control the child.

> 1/31
> Alvin and James were late for Reading Lab, arriving at 9:20. Other children in class said they got off the bus at White Plains Rd and roamed around the store; that Alvin frequently went to Grand Union and the florist and took things, stuffed them in his sweater at the collar and walked out; that on Wednesday, the previous day, after school, Alvin and his brother went to 5 & 10 and called to the other children, "Come, be my guest!" Alvin was chased by a man from 5 & 10. He ran across White Plains Rd and was nearly hit by a truck, which came to a screeching halt. The children also said he once snatched a purse from a lady in the subway. All these incidents were related in Alvin's presence who did not refute them nor did he appear to be worried or uncomfortable. In fact, he smiled as if relishing these episodes.

> *Why didn't you tell us how tough it was? I say now. You never told us.*
> *You think everyone can be a professor? she says. I have*

thirty points past my master's, but I am ABD. You know what means ABD?

A lot of your students came back to thank you when you retired. And I found a lot of the projects you had them do. They were great.

I had some good kids. The trouble was the bad kids.

Those kids needed help, I say. They needed more attention and more resources, starting with more adults in the room.

You think the city was going to pay for more teachers? she scoffs. Anyway, some kids are just a pain in the neck like you.

Mom. I'm trying to thank you.

She laughs.

You did your best, and you fulfilled your duty to your children. You helped pay our tuition. Thank you.

To the American way of thinking, to do your duty is—how do you say?— not real. Fake. But to the Chinese way of thinking, I am okay.

Because whether your heart was in it or not, you did do it.

It was my responsibility, she says. I am very Confucian.

And thanks to you, the next generation didn't have to do what you did. We didn't have to even notice, really.

She laughs again. That is what luck is, she says.

Meanwhile, your sister wrote things like, "You mentioned that you are now in the teaching profession. Are you teaching Chinese literature? It would be quite suitable for you."

As if anyone here cares about Chinese literature! she says.

They did not understand life in America.

How could they understand? You do not even understand, she says.

Chaucer, Shakespeare, Milton. Tolstoy, Dostoyevsky, Chekhov. Jane Austen. George Eliot. Virginia Woolf. Oscar Wilde, Edith Wharton, Henry James. William Faulkner, Ernest Hemingway. James Joyce, T. S. Eliot. Saul Bellow, Ralph Ellison, Maxine Hong Kingston, James Baldwin, Malcolm X. My mother knew no more of my doings than I knew of hers. But would she really have wanted to know that thanks to her hard-earned money, her least-favorite child was getting to pick up where she had left off in her reading, long ago? And what about the versification class I took with the great translator Robert Fitzgerald? Would she have wanted to know about that?

I had signed up for this class by accident. Though an English major, I had never understood why poetry had to be written in little lines and thought that if I took this English 283, I would finally understand. And that was true. But when on the first day Professor Fitzgerald said that there would be a weekly exercise, I assumed he meant a paper. It was a shock to discover that he meant a weekly exercise in verse.

The first assignment was to write a poem in Catullan hendecasyllables; I was going to have to drop this class, I could see. Still, I sat myself down in a library and tried to write something with eleven syllables per line. I counted; I changed some words; I counted again. Poetry was about what Carmen, my ballet teacher, used to call a method. It had principles. A "mentality." I wrote some more. And right away, I loved what I was doing. I told my roommate that if I could, I would do this for the rest of my life.

But people like me did not become poets. And so, though Professor Fitzgerald handed that first poem out to the class and encouraged me to speak up, too—"And what do you think, Miss Jen?"—I continued to think of myself as pre-med. Never mind that I had gotten a C+ in chemistry and, in contrast, was doing well on one assignment after another in Fitzgerald's class, or at least thought I was. (It took me most of the semester to glean that his grading scale went from "NAAB," meaning "Not at all bad," to "NB," meaning "Not bad," to—or so rumor had it, no one I knew having actually ever received one of these, thankfully—"PB," "Pretty bad.") One day, he peeked over my shoulder as I was reading in the lounge outside class, and commented, "Impressive." And another day, during office hours, he asked me why I was pre-med.

"I guess because I am supposed to be?"

I did not—could not—explain that it was because *Lì lì jiē xīnkǔ*—Every last grain in one's bowl comes of hardship. I could not explain that I owed my presence at Harvard to the self-sacrifice of others and was not free to pursue frivolous paths, if I could even say what they might be. Professor Fitzgerald looked over a paper I'd written about prose rhythms in Henry James, slowly flipping through the pages. With his black beret pulled down evenly around his square face, he looked like an acorn with eyebrows as he flipped back to the first page. Then he set my paper on his desk, taking his time. He didn't mind being seen thinking.

"You should do something with words," he said at last. "Have you considered becoming a poet?"

"A poet?"

We talked some more. I tried to explain what was clearly inexplicable.

I tried again.

"Well," he said finally, "might you at least entertain a career in publishing?"

I had never met anyone in publishing. I had not realized it was a field one could enter, and could not begin to imagine what a publishing career might look like. Still, I must have eventually nodded because he wrote to his editor at Doubleday about me.

I soon found myself in New York, interviewing for a job. I wore a white pin-striped suit and froze when asked what magazines I read, as I did not read any. Neither did I know anything about TV. Thanks to my father's having disconnected our set, I had never seen Walter Cronkite or Barbara Walters; I had never watched *M*A*S*H, All in the Family,* or *The Mary Tyler Moore Show.* Nonetheless, apparently on the strength of Fitzgerald's recommendation, I was hired, first as a Doubleday trainee, then as an editorial assistant at one of Doubleday's imprints, Anchor Books.

Anchor's current hit was the Foxfire books—a series dedicated to Appalachian folklore. Beekeeping, herbal remedies, moonshine- and fiddle-making, the art of cooking on a woodstove—all of it was more exotic to me than Elizabethan England. My boss was an advocate of writerly nonfiction; his wife worked at Farrar, Straus & Giroux and sounded like Lauren Bacall on the phone. They smoked as if it was in their marital vows to keep the tobacco industry alive. I thought them the height of sophistication, and smoked a little to be like them, although cool people smoked Marlboros and I could never progress past Merit Ultra Light menthols.

**Very bad habit, my mother puts in. My mother smoked.
I know, I say. And: It's embarrassing to remember.**

Doubleday was at 245 Park Avenue, right by Grand Central Station. Every day, I walked straight down Park Avenue to work from my studio apartment on East 60th Street, which my mother never saw. In truth, located as it was on the fifth floor of a five-story walk-up whose every floor had high ceilings, it presented a challenge even for my brothers, who had struggled to help me get a mattress up there. (Luckily, I did not own a couch.) But would my mother have wanted to know in any case that I had a sunny apartment with a big main room, a kitchenette, and a walk-in closet in which I had set up a desk and my Smith Corona?

**No, she says now. I would not have wanted to know.
I didn't think so, I say.**

It could have been the arts tent I'd meant to crochet for my bears Beth and Jo. I even had new teddy bear friends, who did not sing and put on plays but who were interested in writing and undaunted by stairs. My boyfriend ate with his elbow in the air when he was excited, and the day he told me he wanted to write a piece about animal rights, it was level with his ear.

"Animal rights?" I said. "How can animals have rights?"

I was skeptical, but I celebrated with him when he pitched the idea to a women's magazine and the editor, astonishingly, took it. So editors actually read things you wrote and, if they liked them, published them? That was something to ponder.

We finagled cheap tickets to musicals, concerts, plays, performances. One day it was Beckett, the next Baryshnikov—one day a woman buried to her neck in sand, and the next a man flying so high, the stage hardly seemed big enough. (Hmm, I thought.) I read *The New Yorker* the day it came out and discussed the stories with another assistant in the office. I read *The Southern Review, The Kenyon Review,* and *The Paris Review* as well and, in between, enjoyed Central Park—jogging around the reservoir in warmer weather and cross-country skiing all the way up to the top of the park when it snowed. Sometimes I wrote a little. Some poetry but, increasingly, fiction, as seemed to make sense: my poems had always been more narrative than lyric. I showed my stories to my teddy bear friends. They liked them. I wrote some more.

None of the stories was about my family, much less about my mother and how she might have been affected by the death of Mao and the end of the Cultural Revolution. But of course, she was affected.

Wasn't your sister finally released from the labor camp? I say now.

She was very very thin and very very weak, my mother says. But since my youngest sister had become a doctor, she got excellent care, and she lived!

It was a miracle.

She said God looked after her, and it's true.

Didn't she cough up blood for the rest of her life?

She did.

But still. She survived.

She survived.

My mother would not have wanted to know I was writing. We weren't in a labor camp, but she was working so our family could "get out," as she put it—so we kids would not have to live in roach-infested apartments and teach in violence-ridden schools. That was not the same as going to plays and doing nothing. Her daughter should have been working so she could do nothing!

That's right! my mother says now.

Her daughter did not even know what work was!

That's right! she says again.

Her teaching log includes a note from Alvin to an unnamed girl that reads on one side: "I love you. Do you love me?" with boxes for "yes" or "no." On the back there is a drawing of a girl with long hair and a necklace and the words "kissing pussy." There is also a note from Dawn to James, reading, "Fuck your dick and kiss your ass." Then there are notes from my mother to the administration. For example:

> Dear Mr. Unterberger,
>
> Someone just threw something into my room through the broken pane over the wardrobe, disrupting the class. I have asked Mr. Pelles to repair it since September. Kindly look into this matter.
>
> Thank you,
>
> A. Jen

Meanwhile, as soon as she had regained her strength, my mother's labor-camp-survivor sister threw herself into caring for my grandmother, reporting frequently on her condition:

> *Mom's health has been deteriorating. Her right hand and right foot are not quite right, so she cannot go up and down stairs. She also often experiences high fevers.*

And:

> *Mom has an irregular heart rhythm that can lead to blood clots in the heart. It also increases the risk of stroke and heart failure, and, as it is compounded by emphysema, she must be watched very carefully. She has been on traditional Chinese medicine continuously for months now, but recently there has been an increase in the swelling in her legs.*

And:

> Mom had another series of high fevers, and her weakness has increased. Last Friday, she fainted in the bathroom while getting up from the toilet. She hit her head on the door, fell to the floor, and couldn't get up.

Of course, I knew they were going to ask for money again soon, my mother says now.
And sure enough, you were right, I say. Though could you blame them, really?

Wrote her sister:

> Mom's medical expenses are relatively high because we are using the best medicine. The money you sent last time helped pay off some debt, but there's not much left. So I hope, considering the relationship between mother and daughter, that you might send more funds to ease her mind, and so that she might even have a little pocket money?

And:

> I am just worried about our mother's condition and urgently need to raise funds for her medicine and nutrition. As her nutrition is especially important, I hope you will remit some money so we can supply her with delicious food that will bolster her immunity. It will show your filial concern for her.

And:

> You can imagine how upsetting it is to sit by her bedside. I hope you can send more money. It's embarrassing to ask, but I believe that even after so many years, you will remember us.

To your credit, you did eventually set up regular payments, I say.

When my sister wrote, "Remember us," I heard my father's voice. Remember us, he told me. And since I had told him I would, I did.

But you barely wrote to your family, and you didn't write to your mother at all.

No, I didn't.

Her sister wrote:

> We received the US$200 you sent! Mom was thrilled! She took great comfort in it and asked me to convey her thanks to you. She would be overjoyed if you could find the time to write. And if you could send a few family photos, it would bring immense joy to all of us. The Lord will repay your kindness.

And:

> We received the wire transfer of US$500! I immediately told Mom, who was very happy to hear that you were concerned about her, especially as lately, with the weather turning warmer, her heart rate is rising and she is short of breath. I'm sure you will find the time to write at least a short letter as well, despite your busy schedule.

And:

> In my last letter, I mentioned that I hoped you would take the initiative to write a letter to Mom. When the elderly get sick, they worry. She says she feels her days are like a burning candle in the wind. Maybe you will understand her mood and take time out of your busy schedule to write to her.

And:

> After receiving this letter, I hope you will reply, even if it's just a few lines, to comfort her.

And:

> How I wish I could talk to you about everyday things. I want to know how busy you and Chao-pe are at work. And what teaching job you hold. And if you are taking medicine for anything. Older Brother and Younger Sister both have hypertension. As for myself, when my dizziness is severe, I have to take to my bed, and if I have to have an injection, it takes several days to recover. Ever since my time in the labor camp, I also cough up blood. We're all getting to be middle-aged, but you have always had the best health of all of us! And aren't your children growing up? Your days of leisure are not far off, right?

Days of leisure! my mother fumes, mad even now. And what teaching job I hold?
She must not have registered that you still had two children to put through college, and another to put through medical school, I say. And how could she understand how sensitive you were about your job?
Days of leisure!
I'm sure she didn't write that thinking it would get you to respond, but . . .
Days of leisure!

Her sister wrote back:

> I was surprised and disturbed to finally receive a real letter from you, only to learn that I had offended you. Please don't take offense. We are thousands of miles away, but

everyone misses you deeply, especially Mom. As for the memories of the past, why don't you just forget them? Though you endured much hardship and many vicissitudes when you ventured into the world alone, wasn't it worth it? Today we all envy you. Our father always said you were the luckiest of us, and you are.

Regarding the fall you had at school, we are all confident that you have recovered. It is terrible that a student pushed you, but surely it was by accident? You have such good medicine for treating injuries over there besides, and how healthy you have always been! You got all the goodness in Mom's womb.

It was terrible that a kid pushed you down the steps, I say now. It really was.

That child pulled a knife on me, too, my mother says.

I remember. And didn't you lose your kingfisher phoenix pin besides?

I don't know what happened to it. Probably it fell on the ground.

Nai-ma's pin!

She is quiet.

Did you write back to your sister?

No, she says. I did my duty. That's it.

It's too bad. Here Mao was dead and Deng was in charge and China was opening! It was such a hopeful time. So many people were reuniting with their families.

I did not want to see them.

You shut them out.

She is quiet.

Bad bad girl, I say.

I don't care.

Your sister said that in another letter, you know—that you were always frank and didn't care about anything.

I don't care.

On Doubleday's dime, I took a writing course at the New School, for which I wrote an improbable piece yoking Henry James to a dog sniffing a hedge. To my surprise, my teacher pulled me aside to tell me, not that it was precious and contrived, but that it was the best piece he'd seen in many moons. Really? It was, in fact, precious and contrived. But was he trying to tell me what Professor Fitzgerald had tried to tell me? That there was something connecting words and me—a red string?

And why then did I apply to business school? My thinking was that if I stayed in publishing, I would neither be making a living nor doing what I wanted, so I should really choose one direction or the other; and if I couldn't decide which, I might as well try the more practical route first. Besides, I figured, it was just an application. I wasn't going to get in. But then—surprise—I did. Did it make sense to choose Stanford because Stanford had a good writing program? Literary critic Lionel Trilling said that the function of art was "to liberate the individual from the tyranny of his culture . . . and to permit him to stand beyond it in an autonomy of perception and judgment." I was not ready for any such autonomy. But liberation from the tyranny of my culture? Yes, I was interested in that.

As you might have been, too, a little? I say now. Did you not recognize in your heart of hearts that liberation lay in those books you found in your father's library long ago?

You just have to talk something crazy, my mother says.

She was not so much interested in liberation as in revenge, which she got. But it was not sweet. Wrote her sister:

> *I received your most recent remittance, which made me very sad. Mom was so happy when she received your previous remittance. Right through the last days of her life, she was still talking about you to her sisters and others. She still thought you might visit us here and she might be able to see you again and meet Chao-pe and her*

grandchildren. But God did not grant her wish. None of us thought that she would have a heart attack so soon. None of us could have imagined that she was so weak. But she had cerebrovascular sclerosis and an embolism, and there was no way to save her.

I know you will be very sad to hear this bad news about Mom. You cared for her in many ways during her lifetime. I believe her spirit in heaven will bless your family.

Mom's medical expenses and funeral expenses have been settled, and we are trying our best to handle her last big event as well. Her urn can be kept for three years before it needs to be buried. We hope that you will make a trip to China and help us find a good place for her.

Many relatives came today to commemorate Mom. She was so kind and generous her whole life, everyone paid their respects to her portrait with deep feeling. They came afterward to eat at my house. Fortunately, because you sent money, the bank remittance could be used to buy groceries and many kinds of fruit. The fruit was of high quality, which everyone said was thanks to your remittance.

Since Mom died, I have been in a kind of trance. Coincidentally, I was just assigned to a new school to teach college English. There is great interest these days in learning English but few instructors. So suddenly I have a career. I am trying to concentrate on teaching the students well, which is a physical and mental struggle, especially now.

I'll stop here. I know you and Chao-pe are very busy at work. I hope you will take the time to write a letter or two. Communication these days is very different than it was, and quite convenient. Our brother was with our mother when she died, and will write to you separately.

Of course, I felt very bad when I heard, says my mother now.

You must have been pretty angry at your mother, that you did your duty but refused to write to her right up until her death, I say.

I was angry, yes, she says.

Are you sorry you didn't write?

I think she should have been happy I sent money every month.

She didn't do her duty by you, but you did yours by her, you mean.

They think all Americans are rich, and it was easy.

But not all Americans are rich, and it was not easy.

No, it was not.

Still, you did it anyway, as a way of telling her what you thought of her. It was a way of slapping her in the face, really.

She is quiet.

I hope that wasn't the only letter you received about her death.

No, I received one from my brother, too. In it, he claimed they had telegrammed me right after her death, but I did not receive any telegram. Of course, as an engineer, he included many more facts about the death and funeral. How she was admitted to the hospital at 1:30 in the morning on January 26, how her heart stopped at 8:58 p.m. on January 30, and how at 9:05 her breathing stopped completely. He described all the layers of clothes they dressed her in, how two hundred people came to the burial, how they held a banquet with eight tables, and how both relatives and friends thought the family did a good job organizing the funeral. His letter was dated February 18. My sister's was dated February 6.

So it's not clear they let you know right away.

No.

Though maybe they telegrammed you and thought you didn't respond.

Maybe.

I am glad I'm not as angry as you were at your mother.

You are angry enough to write this book, she says.

I headed to California. My father looked serious as he said goodbye to me in the airport. It was a moment for gnomic paternal advice, and sure enough, he had some. I leaned in, listening carefully.

"Don't come home wearing flip-flops," he said.

"Like a peasant, you mean?"

He nodded, his face full of concern.

I laughed and promised I wouldn't.

At Stanford, you could register for one class outside of the business school each quarter. I naturally signed up for writing classes, which were also reading courses, really. We worked through stories from Nicolai Gogol's "The Overcoat" to Delmore Schwartz's "In Dreams Begin Responsibilities" to Katherine Anne Porter's "Pale Horse, Pale Rider," looking at very different things than one does as an English major. One of my teachers, Stephanie Vaughn, showed me, too, her file of outtakes from her classic story "Alpha, Baker, Charlie, Dog." This contained eighty-five pages—my first glimpse of what revision entailed.

I read a hundred novels that year and attended so few business school classes that many of my classmates were not aware I was a fellow student, much less that I was, in some cases, in their section. Neither was I altogether clear what courses I was taking. When I showed up the day of an exam, people would look at me in surprise and ask, "Are you in this class?"—whereupon I had to look at my schedule card before I could answer, "Yes." I only passed thanks to my new boyfriend, David, to whom I'd been introduced by a mutual friend. David was a big-hearted runner with the oldest car in the business school parking lot and unnerving blue eyes he trained on me the moment we met. Later he said it was because I was so entertaining; I think he had simply never met anyone so confused. He patiently taught me how to log on to the campus computer system—I had never logged on to a computer before—and, perhaps because I'd shown so little competence in other arenas, he was greatly impressed that I could stop and start a stick-shift car on even the steepest San Francisco hills without slipping backward. Now he breezily coached me.

"What's the exam?" he would ask the night before a test.

"Cost Accounting," I might answer, or, "Microeconomics."
"Okay," he'd say. "You just have to know these three things."
Stanford, luckily, was pass/fail.

David thought I should drop out, but daughters of immigrants did not drop out of graduate school. The first day of the second year, however, I overslept. The second day, I overslept. The third day, I overslept. Was I using sleep as a form of resistance? Had I learned that from my mother?

Don't blame on me! my mother says.

By the end of the week, it was clear that I was not going to be able to get myself to class even once. When I took a leave of absence, though, my parents, who had hitherto shown no particular interest in my plans, were suddenly beside themselves. First there was yelling—a lot of yelling. Then there was reasoning. "You have to have a meal ticket," my father told me. And, interestingly: "If you don't earn money, your husband will treat you bad." Eventually, my mother stopped speaking to me altogether, and my siblings took her side. "You are upsetting everyone," they said. As for what exactly was the matter with dropping out, it was simply "crazy."

No one asked anything like, How are you going to support yourself now that Mom and Dad have cut you off? Much less, Are you planning to apply to writing school? Or just, Are you okay? In fact, I was crying all day and having terrible dreams at night—dreams in which I was being dismembered by birds or chopped up by helicopter blades. A therapist said I was "dissociated." I had bouts of wishing I were dead.

I could not go on.

But I might as well have been hiding under my bed again. No one cared, only David.

A year later, I was moving to Iowa to attend the Iowa Writers' Workshop. At a family dinner at which he toasted each of the five kids in turn, my father said about me, "She do not care about money, she do not care about dress up nice. She want to be writer! Write books!"

My mother was pursing her lips as if to keep her false teeth in. No one was happy that I was back on my feet or curious about what an MFA might entail. The fact that I had gotten a teaching fellowship and would not need family support mattered naught, either. No one spoke to me.

I was still shut out.

Did they see in themselves the underside of Chinese culture? I say now. Did they see in themselves the self-policing that goes on in China even today? Play by the rules, and you are rewarded. Question the rules, and you are ostracized—and not just by the authorities, but by your peers and neighbors and even your family.

That's because you set a bad example, she says.

For whom? I say. And if you wanted us all to contribute to family stability by staying on paths that were going to do that, why didn't you say so? Or were wild children like me not the kind who were going to be the envy of people like Georgiana?

You are always have to ask why, she says. Why you always have to why why why.

My father met me in Iowa City to help me settle in. For this, my mother was not speaking to him, either.

He laughed it off. "She always has to mad of something," he said.

He had his doubts about writing, which he didn't understand any more than he had understood skiing. But he insisted on taking my bags at the airport. He had come to see what I needed and to help me if I needed help.

When we went out for breakfast, a large ruddy man with white wrinkles in his neck asked, "You ever ate pancakes before?"—a pretty funny question given that, in a further attempt to pay tuition bills, my father had left academia and was now running an International House of Pancakes. My father tried to explain.

"Actually, you be surprise," he said. "I own pancake house."

"You?" the man said. "You own a pancake house?"

"Big one," my father said. "Many different kind of pancake."

"Well, how do you like them apples," the man said.

"Apple pancake very good," my father said.

"Do you have Chinese pancakes?"

"No, no."

"You should have Chinese pancakes," the man said.

"We should have Iowa pancakes," I said. "Cow pancakes."

The man turned away and my father laughed, though I wasn't sure he had gotten the joke.

He asked if I needed money. I answered that my teaching fellowship would be enough. Rent was cheap, and students with fellowships paid in-state tuition rates. I didn't mind bundling up to keep my heating bill down, I did not have a car, and I mostly ate something I called "glop," a mixture of Rice-A-Roni, frozen vegetables, and grated cheese.

My father nodded—proud, I could see, that I was not soft and weak but tough and strong. At the same time, he wanted to make sure I wasn't in over my head.

"You need some money, just tell Daddy," he said.

My eyes filled unexpectedly. Maybe I was strong, but I didn't feel so strong. "Thanks," I said.

Teaching assistants were told to get a writing sample from our students the first day, so that if anyone tried to plagiarize, we'd have something against which to compare the questionable piece. I asked my class to write a few paragraphs about anything they liked; almost all of them wrote about the basketball coach. ("You mean you've never heard of Lute Olson?!" they said.) Only one student wrote about how much she was looking forward to reading "poetry writers" like "Shakesphere and Lear." The next week, one of my students was late getting her paper in because her sorority was making an enormous Hawkeye mural out of corn kernels. (The Hawkeye was the college mascot.) "Do you know how long it takes to glue all those kernels?" she said. I was not sympathetic. But how I would have loved to tell my mother all about it—how I would have loved to compare notes about our teaching experiences. And how I would have loved to tell her about other things, too—about how I was almost as amazed by the Midwest as she had been. About how I had ridden on a combine and attended a pig roast and how because the water was heavily chlorinated, I had learned to let it sit on the counter to give the chlorine time to evaporate before using the water for tea. I had also begun greeting my landlord the way he greeted me—with a "How about them Hawkeyes?"

Yet I did not speak to my mother once, not even after knee surgery saw me hobbling down icy sidewalks on crutches. The snow was deep and the temperatures subzero; I had no car; I lived alone in a second-floor apartment. She did not call to see how I was managing.

Because you were crazy, that's why, she says now.

You shut me out the way you shut your mother out, I say. But had I abandoned you the way she did? What was my crime?

I would have loved to tell her how I was reading everyone from Grace Paley to Bohumil Hrabal. Alice Munro, Milan Kundera, Bernard Malamud! My beloved teacher Jim McPherson. Cynthia Ozick, Flannery O'Connor, Isaac Babel, Isaac Singer, Anton Chekhov, Vladimir Nabokov, Franz Kafka, John Cheever, John Updike, Gustave Flaubert, Toni Morrison, Marilynne Robinson, Hisaye Yamamoto, Junichiro Tanizaki, Lu Xun, Eileen Chang, Philip Roth: I was still a book omnivore. I would have loved to tell her, too, how I had entered a Raymond Carver write-alike contest my first semester, and how the women in the class had all signed our stories "Raymond Carver," figuring that our teacher, Barry Hannah, would never pick a woman. And I would have loved to tell her how it felt when Barry held a story up and asked, "Who wrote this?" and I realized that the answer was me. I would have loved to tell her when that story was accepted by *The Iowa Review*—my first published story.

But maybe she knew all along what would happen next: that I would publish that story under my legal name, only to realize that "Lillian" Jen had not written it—that Lillian Jen was the nice Chinese girl my mother had wanted, a daughter who didn't ask why why why. In fact, almost no one called me Lillian anymore. In my high school creative writing club, I had been dubbed "Gish" after the silent screen actress Lillian Gish—another girl whose last name was Hausman had been dubbed "A.E." after the poet A. E. Housman—and, never mind that I had never seen any of Lillian Gish's movies, I had first accepted "Gish" as a nickname, then started using it myself. Probably my mother would not have wanted to know how I now came to realize that this "Gish" Jen had written the story, much less how "Gish Jen" would go on to publish everything else I wrote—becoming a person who was, above all, not her daughter.

Maybe I knew it, it's true, she says now.
Maybe you knew that your mother was right, I say. Maybe you knew that those books in your father's library were subversive, and that just as reading had given both you and me ideas, writing would give me yet more.
Maybe.

Far more acceptable was the news that I was engaged.
"Mister!" my father said. "That's some surprise!"
"You mean someone is going to marry you?" said my mother.
"Shock of shocks," I said. "Can you imagine?"
"David?" she said.
"Yes, David."
"When is the wedding?" my father asked.
"When I graduate."
"Someone is going to marry you!" my mother said again. "David!"
"We're planning to get pregnant beforehand," I said.
"Bad bad girl!" My mother hit me, but it was a playful, almost wistful hit. Not long before this, we had had a knock-down, drag-out fight in which she slapped my face and pulled my hair until I shoved her out of my room. I had rowed crew in college, as she knew, and I had stayed in shape after graduation, or tried to, as she might have noticed. Still, she was clearly surprised to realize that she could no longer hit me because I was stronger than she—that

from here on out, it would be, as she said, up to my husband to control me.

**Poor David, she says now.
I laugh.**

David was in fact her dream come true—a Harvard summa cum laude, Stanford MBA who could reach all the high shelves in the kitchen. I don't think she realized he was also quite the iconoclast: for example, after we had married and carefully shipped to California dozens of elaborate, fragile gifts given to us by guests we did not actually know, only to find ourselves having to pack them up all over again for a move back east, he reacted to my complaints by opening a window.

"Done," he said, tossing a glass out.

And that weekend we held an enormous yard sale, liberating ourselves of all of it. David shied away from nothing, never waffled, and always spoke truth to power.

Yet with my parents, he was amiable and tolerant. The first time he came to visit, they dug out their one can of beer for him, cleaned the dust off its lid with a sponge, and presented it to him, whereupon he cheerfully drank it, warm as it was. He loved Chinese food and ate everything, endearing himself to them. As for perfecting his chopsticks skills before coming, only to discover that my father and brother were eating with forks—he laughed. Now my mother had just one criticism.

"I don't like that beard," she said.

"Too bad," I said. "He has chest hair, too."

She looked shocked.

"Because, you know, who would marry me but a barbarian?"

"Bad bad girl! Too much to say!" she said. But this, too, seemed a bit for old times' sake.

She insisted on her own first choice for a wedding location, "someplace everyone can find it," the Scarsdale Country Club. David and I thought it conventional and boring. Who knew but that she was right, though, and that the Chinese guests would have a hard time getting to an out-of-the-way place? I could just see them driving around Westchester in their best clothes, lost. Also, this was the first wedding in the family. Could I blame my mother for wanting a proper wedding such as she had not had, a wedding that showed how she and my father had "made it" in America? I could understand how she felt.

If she cared how we felt, she kept her concern well hidden.

She was anxious about the guest list. How to handle my father's second brother's two wives, for example? Like her own half brother, my father's second brother had repeat-married, ignoring the fact that in Taiwan the norms had changed and that men were now expected—can you imagine?—to divorce their old wife first. The old wife now insisted that she was still the real wife, as did her children; my father's third brother's wife and children, moreover, sided with her. So which wives to invite and which children, and where to seat them?

"Why don't we just have open seating?" said David.

My mother shot him a look. I laughed.

She expressed no interest in the many friends we had coming from Iowa and California; nor did she help pick out my wedding dress. I bought an off-the-rack dress on sale for two hundred dollars; she never asked to see it. Two years later, she would spend thousands of dollars on a custom dress for Lisa. But for me, there were no fittings. Neither did she come with me to get my hair done, though she got her own coifed into the sort of bouffant out of which you half expect a small bird to emerge.

Still, it was a perfect October day. My dear friend Lori Kahn sang. David's niece, then age eight, scattered her flower petals admirably. And his nephew, then five, would have been an exemplary ring bearer had he not decided his jacket was uncomfortable and done a striptease at the altar. I cried as I said, "I do"; David gently dabbed at my eyes with a handkerchief. Our hippie priest gave a sermon about the evils of technology, much to the amusement of the many guests from Silicon Valley.

We served our favorite dish, Beef Wellington. It was 1983, after all; we had yet to hear the word "cholesterol." And so—chateaubriand, duxelles, puff pastry. My father and I danced to "Top of the World," his favorite Carpenters song, and really did appear to be on top of the world. My mother did not dance, having her hands full keeping the peace.

That's right! she says now.

George and Georgiana Ping danced and raved. An outgoing guy who immediately took off his jacket, George boasted a slight potbelly, bushy eyebrows, and a Chicago Cubs tie clip. He had a respectable jitterbug, but could not hold a candle to Georgiana. Unlike the other Chinese women, every one of whom wore a *qípáo* like my mother's, Georgiana wore a gold lamé wrap dress with a ruffled V-neck. Her lipstick and nails were fire-engine red, and her hair was as loose and wavy as that of a European nymph just done with her bath in a stream. Both she and George were impressed, not so much that I was a Harvard grad as that I was marrying a Harvard grad.

"Summa cum laude in applied math!" George said. "That's not easy!"

"You made it!" Georgiana told my mother. "You made it!"

Standing stiffly in her silver *qípáo,* my mother accepted their tribute with dignity.

"Too bad the Cubs finished fifth in their league," she said lightly. "The Yankees finished third."

George laughed. Georgiana smiled.

"Your son still play?" he asked.

"No, he retired a long time ago."

"Mine, too," he said. "He did great in high school but got outclassed in college. He's still a fan, though."

"Same here—but come meet him. Reuben? Reuben! Come meet someone. Reuben is on Wall Street," she told George as Reuben headed their way.

"Going to be a millionaire?" said George.

She winked. "He's going to hit it out of the park, you watch and see."

Nobody has anything to criticize, she says now, recalling it all.

And that was what mattered? That people weren't gabbing viciously later?

Chinese people like to criticize, she says.
And how about me, your daughter? Did that matter?
I always said no one would marry you.
But lo and behold, someone did.
The Chinese have a saying, **Cōngmíng yī shì hútú yī shí,** *she says.*
Meaning?
Meaning, Smart his whole life, stupid this once, she says.

My mother having proven a better correspondent after my grandmother's death, her brother wrote on behalf of the family to express their delight:

> Congratulations! We received your letter announcing Lillian and David's wedding. The whole family is very happy, though it's a pity we can't witness the grand ceremony in person and enjoy your house full of congratulatory guests. You must be overflowing with infinite joy. We have sent some small gifts.
>
> And your birthday is coming soon! May you live as long as the South Mountains, with blessings as boundless as the East Sea!
>
> Here our television factory introduced Hitachi technology and equipment and built a new branch factory in the suburbs. The entire project was completed last autumn. With self-design, construction, installation, management, and production all deemed excellent, it won a silver medal, and I was awarded first prize by the factory department. I received a certificate and a hundred yuan. (You may laugh.) What's more, a few months ago, the city government awarded me a senior engineer certificate. After so many decades of difficulty, I have found some comfort in all this.

So my mother and her brother were both, in their different ways, back in the fold. And so, it seemed, was I, thanks to David's footing the bill for trips.

You know what I found after you died? I say now. I found your pocket planners.

What pocket planners? my mother says.

Remember those little notebooks you used to keep? The size of a checkbook? You used to record things in them. For example, on January 30, 1979, you wrote, "Mother passed away 9:00 pm" and circled it in red. There are many medical developments, too. For example, on July 3, 1984, you wrote, "8:00 am by-pass operation Dr. Eric Rose 17th floor intensive care."

Dad's first bypass.

Right—when he was sixty-five. Then there are anniversaries, snowstorms, and hurricanes, as well as, on October 8, 1983, the event you thought you would never see: "Lillian wedding."

Those important things, she says.

Including the trips to Sanibel Island and Bar Harbor we treated you to.

We had fun.

I'm glad you remember. And interestingly, you credited not David but me for them, writing "Claremont Hotel Southwest Harbor 207-244-5036 (L. paid 2 nights $169.80 × 2 = $339.60 do not accept credit cards)."

That is to say you are a good daughter.

The kind of daughter who if need be would make regular payments to support her mother. The kind of daughter who, wild as she was, did get married and could now be counted on to do her duty.

Someday you will be old, too, she says. And that day, tell me—who is going to take care of you? If all your children are useless good-for-nothing, are you going to take care of yourself?

We were getting along so much better that she even took a sudden, strange interest in the trouble David and I were having getting pregnant.

I don't see what is so strange, she says now.

It was just such a narrow slice of my life that you focused on, I say. As if my most important function was to make babies.

I write down what's important, that's all, she says. Other things I leave out, just like you.

The doctors never fully understood why David and I struggled. But after many consultations, exams, blood draws, and shots (which David bravely administered after practicing on an orange), something finally worked. We bought a copy of *What to Expect When You're Expecting,* and though some of its recipes seemed written for four-stomached ruminants, we followed them to a T.

Then, at my four-month ultrasound, the technician grew strangely quiet. We knew something was wrong. Still, we were unprepared to hear that the baby had hydrocephalus—water on her brain. That was, it turned out, a symptom of Turner's syndrome; she was missing one of her X chromosomes, which was not always a fatal anomaly. However, in her case it was.

You wrote: Thursday, June 9, 1989, "Lil at Prenatal Diagnostic Center (Baby no chance to survive)," I say now.

That was important, my mother says.

She came to Boston for the dilation and evacuation, and though she saved very few notes in her planner, she did save one from David reading "10:15 Mom + Dad—gone to church. Back in couple minutes. D.O."

David and I had not been to church since we were married. But we went then, that we might kneel in front of a statue of the Virgin Mary not unlike the one that had graced the end of the St. Theresa's parking lot. There we cried and prayed for our daughter's soul, even though we didn't believe in souls. My mother cooked us dinner—something she had never done before and never did again. It meant a lot to us.

How did we manage to become pregnant again? We worried that we would lose this pregnancy as well, but instead, the baby grew and grew. "Mother-baby disproportion," the doctors noted, and indeed, short as I am, my belly was as dramatically cantilevered as Frank Lloyd Wright's Fallingwater house. I could barely reach the steering wheel of the car. When David tried to have the airbag in its center disabled, the garage mechanic informed him it was illegal until he saw me; then he did it anyway. Even other expectant mothers shook their heads. "Are you sure it's not twins?" they said. "Sometimes they miss one on the ultrasounds."

My mother rented an apartment near us; she wanted to be there when the baby was born. (Noted in her planner: "Lil expects this month. Arrive Watertown 6/30/91, Sunday.") Since the apartment was next door to a health club, my father took this opportunity to take swimming lessons at the pool. It wasn't the first time he had tried to learn to do something he'd seen us kids do: once, at a ski area, he had insisted on trying to learn to ski but refused to let any of us teach him. We found him hugging a tree, with one ski on either side of the trunk; he was wearing his Russian fur hat and an overcoat.

"Do you need help?" we asked.

"No," he said.

Now he wanted to learn to swim, even though of the five kids, only Reuben and I knew how. Reuben, natural athlete that he was, had picked it up the way he picked up all sports, and I—inspired by my weekend at Annie Dreyfus's house on Shelter Island—had taught myself to do the crawl by watching others and cautiously experimenting. As I hadn't thought to teach myself to tread water, I almost drowned during the Harvard freshman swim test, but I could swim. My father could not relax enough even to learn to put his face in the water.

"Like this," I said, and showed him again what the teacher had shown him. "Like this."

It was no use. I wished he were younger. As for my mother, did she really have to mock his trying?

How can he learn to swim? At his age? she says now.
You didn't have to call him crazy, I say.
But what is he? You tell me.

He was full of life. He was full of "Yes" and "I try" and "Let's go." The words "too old" never crossed his mind.
He is crazy, she insists still. He is crazy.

In a kinder vein, she took David and me shopping for a crib, changing table, and rocking chair.

On July 28, 1991, you wrote: "Contractions at dinner," I say. And then on August 2, "4:18 am (Lil c-sect.) Luke Jen O'Connor 9 lb 8 oz 21½ L," followed by his Chinese name—Kāng Rényào—in characters.
A number one son! she says.
Did that really still matter to you?
Chinese people believe that way, she says. And I am Chinese.

She wrote to her family in Shanghai:

Our first grandchild—and it's a boy! Nice and fat, and very alert. In America, they grade the baby right away, using something called an Apgar scale. *And our number one grandson got a perfect score. A+. How do you like that? We are very proud.*

Luke peed on the nurse first thing, then fought his way out of his swaddling; it was easy to spot him in the nursery, as the nurses quickly gave up trying to bundle him and simply draped his receiving blanket over his bassinet. Dave and I called him Houdini. He had a hearty love of lunch, and a shocking shock of black hair. My mother loved to hold and rock him, and made a basket of red eggs to celebrate his one-month birthday. I can still see him in his white wicker bassinet, surrounded by the many stuffed animals he had been given, including a black-and-white dolphin-like creature we would soon be able to identify as an orca whale—sea animals, we were to discover, being just one unit in a parent-child curriculum that also included trains, dinosaurs, construction vehicles, and planets.

He would have been a hugely happy eventuality no matter when he was born. But he was especially so because he was born in August when I was thirty-six, just as I had been born in August when my father was thirty-six. As the Chinese astrological cycle is twelve years, that made his zodiac sign the same as my father's and mine, too. We were a trio—as my father put it, "big sheep, middle sheep, and little sheep." What could be happier? Yet one part of the huge happiness of that time was the sense that his birth had precipitated a sea change in my mother. As terrible a mother as she had been, she now seemed to have become a devoted *ābu*—grandmother—to everyone's delight.

Those were happy years in our relationship, even though after Luke's birth, miscarriage followed miscarriage, each accompanied by a "D&C"—a dilation and curettage to clean my uterus out. Or was it exactly because misfortune followed misfortune that my mother and I were getting along?

Children who needed you were children who stayed, I say now. Is that it?
Too much psychological, she says.

In any case, my mother touchingly wrote "DMC" in her planner a number of times—how she must have misheard "D&C." Why didn't she ask what the letters meant? As for all that I shared with her about this part of my life—so much more than I'd shared about any other part—was that simply my responding to her rare show of interest? Her planner entries include: "Lil had ultrasound—fetus no heartbeat; reschedule tomorrow," followed by "M&D to Cambridge ... repeat ultrasound confirmed bad news," and "Lil—DMC today." There is a similar sequence the next year, starting with "Lil—no heartbeat," followed by "Lil—DMC," and so on—such sad entries and yet signs that my mother and I were communicating. It was the most we'd communicated since she sat me down to explain the birds and the bees and told me, "Don't let anyone touch you down there."

By 1997, David and I had officially given up on having a second child and gotten an Italian greyhound. Luke named her Leesa and ran all through the parks with her; they were just the right size for each other. Of course, as so many women seem to get pregnant after getting a dog—the popular myth being that the dog helps the woman relax—people did say, when I got pregnant, that the dog had done it. (I maintained, though, that David did it.)

But that was later. At the time, David and I were so sure we'd be disappointed yet again that we told no one. Then suddenly I was through my second trimester. We were having another baby! I scrambled to wrap up the book I was working on and called it *Who's Irish?*, the title story coming so quickly and easily that I asked my obstetrician if there wasn't some way to replicate my hormone levels after the birth. And then there she was—born in the year of the tiger but aspirationally named Paloma, meaning "dove." A tiger dove! Conventional wisdom has it that a firstborn will be jealous of a newborn, but in fact, Luke was gaga about her. Even Leesa stood up on her hind legs, stretching her neck, trying to get a peek over the edge of the bassinet.

There was just one discordant note, right when Paloma was born: our Asian American obstetrician—flummoxed, apparently, by Paloma's strawberry-blond hair—failed to congratulate David and me or, indeed, to say anything at all.

"Is something the matter?" David asked.

The doctor shook her head, but still the silence resounded.

We vowed then and there to make sure that mixed children like Paloma were welcomed by the world the way they should be— one of the drivers behind my novel *The Love Wife*. In the meanwhile, the person in Paloma's life most like the obstetrician was my mother. She did make a basket of red eggs for Paloma's one-month party. But she insisted on asking loudly and repeatedly, "What's the matter with her hair?" And now that there were five other grandchildren, she was playing favorites again. Some grandchildren were babysat, but not mine. Some grandchildren got pianos, but not mine. Some grandchildren were included in Chinese New Year, but not mine. Our truce was over.

You are too sensitive, my mother says now.
I know this is skipping ahead, Mom, but what about Dad's

funeral? I say. You were going to have every male in the family serve as a pallbearer except Luke.

Everything, you have to make a fuss.

You only agreed because Reuben said it wasn't right. And then you bought an expensive suit for Sean's son to wear.

Because he is the oldest grandson.

Luke is the oldest grandson, Mom.

Sean's son is the oldest grandson with the Jen name. He carries on the Jen line.

And Luke couldn't be a pallbearer because I am a daughter? Ma, this is America.

Chinese just think that way.

It was bad enough that you scapegoated me, Ma. But my children! To play favorites with the grandchildren! When we went through your storage locker, there was picture after picture of the other grandchildren—all the pictures you had displayed in the living room and dining room—but not one picture of Paloma. What was the matter with you?

No answer.

Do you remember when you were in rehab after that pneumonia you caught, and I brought all our picture albums to show you—all the years and years of photos—of the sand sculptures the kids made, the clams they dug up, the cakes they baked? The Halloween costumes, the prom outfits, the graduation robes? Do you remember?

I remember.

Do you remember when I asked you, Aren't you sorry you missed it all?

I remember.

Well, aren't you sorry?

Why should I be sorry? she says. But then she says, Those children so smart, they don't need anyone.

They were going to leave, you mean. They were going to leave because that's what children did in America if they didn't need you, as Auntie Ping warned you from your very first days in Chicago.

Too much to say.

But it's true, isn't it? And you had no safety net. You had no other family to rely on, and no friends, either. Playing favorites was a way of tying at least some of the kids to you. You thought that if you loved them and helped them, they would love you—especially if they needed the help. Because otherwise, who would not desert you the way Nai-ma did? Who would not cut you off the way your mother did? You were afraid of ending up like the Nationalist general's abandoned mistress Auntie Ping talked about—the one who had to sell her jewelry piece by piece as she grew older, to pay for care. It never occurred to you that children might not need to be tied.

Bad bad girl. You don't know how to talk, she whispers then.

Of course, you have to have faith, I say, more quietly. You have to have more faith than fear.

She is quiet.

Things were at least better with her family in Shanghai. I had started visiting China regularly—sometimes for the State Department, sometimes to teach—which excited them. Wrote her sister:

We met with Bilian when she was here for the Shanghai International Book Fair. We are so proud to know a famous author! She was on the news, and many people came to her reading.

But more important, my visits presented a way for her sisters to show care.

You know they treat you well as a message to me, my mother says now.
If only you could have seen the message! I agree. Such elaborate banquets! And they gave the kids so much money for New Year's—three hundred US dollars each.
That's a lot of money.
It was. At one point, I asked Little Auntie if there had been something wrong between you and your mother.
And what did she say?

She said there must have been some misunderstanding.
It wasn't a misunderstanding.
I believe you. But that's what she said.

My mother, in turn, was now sending so much money to China that her family was writing things like:

You are so generous, but we have plenty of money for the new grave.

And:

We can pay for the airplane ticket, so don't worry. You don't have to send any money.

And:

You are very kind, but now I am teaching, and all the brothers and brothers-in-law get promotions all the time, and our baby sister is a big shot doctor. We have a comfortable life. The Lord has blessed us.

My mother sponsored my cousins to come to the United States to study. She sponsored her sisters to come visit. She did her duty.

Did you ever talk to them about your mother? I ask now.
Of course not, she says.
So no one ever understood what she did or what you went through.
No one.
I wish I had known while you were alive.
I don't care.

> **You don't care that no one ever took your side or saw your point of view?**
> **I wished Nai-ma could come back, but that's all.**
> **I'm sorry, I say.**
> **Who cares?**

She may not have cared whether anyone took her side with my grandmother, but she certainly cared with my father. Auntie Ping in Chicago and my grandmother were not the only people ever to draw a big red X across my mother. More and more, my father did, too, even as he showered approval on me, leaving me notes like:

> On the Chinese New Year eve, a hansom [sic] young man walked into our dan [sic] while I was talking to Reuben. He is tall and confident with a kind of success expression on his face.
> Gish! Can you geuss [sic] who is the person?
> Smart, intelegent [sic], brilliant, creative, beautiful, and beloved writer. It took years to build a Rome, writer also needs time to write. Finally, she will be successful.
> David! Who is the writer?
>
> Dad

A favorite joke involved three men who were asked to identify various parts of their bodies. One, when asked where his shoulder was, pointed to his stomach. One, when asked where his stomach was, pointed to his heart. Only the third man correctly identified where his shoulder, stomach, and heart were. But when asked how he knew, he winked and pointed to his head. "Kidneys," he said. And so it was that my father would greet every sign of neural activity in my children with a nod and a wink. "Kidneys," he would say. He was impressed, too, by how tall and athletic Luke was turning out. "Good shape!" he would say. And about Paloma, he would say, "Very cute! Even the book bigger than she is, she can read the whole thing!"

But about my mother, he would complain. "Everything is no," he would say. "No, no, no, no. Mom is just that kind of person. Always has to no."

Just as he wanted to ski and to swim, my father wanted to visit all the places we kids did. He wanted to go to Colorado. He wanted to go to the Caribbean. He wanted to go to Costa Rica and Egypt. I'm sure that if Reuben, who had over the years graduated from baseball to mountaineering, had invited him along to Nepal, he would have said, "I'm come right now!"

My mother opposed these things. Europe was okay. Other destinations were not.

"But why?" I would ask. "Why?"

You are kind of like encourage him, she says now. Everything he says, you agree.
But Ma . . .
Don't Ma me, she says. He is crazy! That's it.

In her planners, there are frequent notes like "Trip canceled; threw tantrum at midnight," "Tantrum—nasty," and "Big tirade." There are three Thursdays in a row, too, on which she tersely notes, "Called Lil." She was fighting with my father, not me. Still, I was to blame for not taking her side.

My father was in and out of the hospital with heart problems for years. As she noted in her planners, it was one procedure or bypass after another. At one point, he had an experimental stent put in his heart. This involved a kind of Slinky with pigskin wrapped around it, inserted via a catheter through the groin. You had to be at death's door with no medical recourse to qualify for the trial; most of the patients who had undergone a version of this procedure in France had died. It was terrible to say goodbye to him as he was rolled into the operating room, and more terrible yet to spot the surgeons in the cafeteria a few hours later, looking for us. They were still wearing their blue surgical caps; we froze. What were they doing here? But as they came into focus, we saw that they were smiling.

"Good news!" they said. "Everything went great!"

The surgery was a success! Wrote my mother's sister:

That kind of success, only God can make happen. Of course, surgeons who are top-notch by Western standards are beyond anything we have ever seen here in China. It will be a hundred years before China can catch up. But even in America, you are blessed by God. That is the only way. Did you know I prayed for Brother Chao-pe every day while he was in the hospital? And now he has been blessed. I am so happy and will return to the church now to thank the Lord for this miracle.

Through all the crises, my mother manned the hospital room. My father would insist that David and I not drive down from Boston to New York to visit him. "Don't come! Don't come!" he'd tell us, only to be thrilled when we did. "Thank you for coming! Thank you! Thank you!" he'd say. In contrast, my mother was never thanked, though she sat at his bedside for hour upon hour. She was simply playing her role—fulfilling her duty, as they both seemed to accept.

Whether he would fulfill his duty in turn was unclear.

He forgot to put your name on his pension, so after he died, you got nothing, I say now.
That's right! He does not think of me, he only thinks about himself, she says.
And wasn't it his job to protect you as your father had? You had always done your duty. Shouldn't he have done his? He wasn't above leaving you high and dry the way your mother did. Abdicating his responsibility to you.
That's right!

The pancake house my father bought after he left academia was not his last foray into business. At one point, he mortgaged our house so he could buy an apartment complex in New Rochelle and condo it.

"You are crazy!" my mother said.

And in this case, she had a point. Had the project failed, we would have been on the street, and these were the early days of condo conversions. It wasn't clear that people would understand what condominiums were, much less agree to buy them.

But he convinced them and succeeded. Where did he then get the idea he could do development? As an engineer, he understood structures, but he knew nothing about construction or marketing. Still, he convinced my brothers to join him, and they convinced banks to lend them money. They found land, laid roads and pipes, and built houses, succeeding so roundly that, as the embodiment of the immigrant success story, my father was invited to the inauguration of the new governor. We kids found five-thousand-dollar checks in our Christmas stockings; my father started investing in stocks, too; and soon my brothers were building a dream home for him and my mother in Bedford. This was, as had been so much of our Scarsdale décor, French provincial in style—a large white stucco house with a steep, gray hip roof and a long curving driveway lined with cherry trees. It was not a mansion. But it had six bedrooms and seven baths and, like my mother's house in Shanghai, could have accommodated an extra seventy-five people in a pinch.

Georgiana came to see it, my mother says now.
And? I say.
"You made it!" she said. "You made it!"
That must have been satisfying, I say.
I don't know. I never liked her, my mother says. But I can hear that she is smiling.

Then my father lost everything. Truly believing that stocks would always rise and never fall ("That's go up," he insisted when I tried to tell him he needed to diversify), he was caught off guard by the dot-com crash of 2001. Many Chinese have a gambling streak; in him it was crossed with a childlike faith in America. (One of his grad students remembered his telling them: "Money grows on trees in America. That's true. Money grows on trees.") His dream was to leave us a million dollars each when he died, and no one had ever doubted that he would.

But suddenly the immigrant success story was over.

"That's it," he said.

He had wanted us to be the Rockefellers, the Kennedys. A big family, a powerful family. His grandfather had once had a dream that though a tree had mostly died, one branch was still strong and blooming. "One branch come out," was how my father put it—and he wanted more than anything for our family to be that branch. He wanted us to be the return of the Yixing Jens; he wanted his grandfather in heaven to think back to his decision to keep him when he was little and say, *"I made the right choice."* And my father had been on the road to realizing his dream.

But now he was not.

As for my mother, who had fought so hard to "get out" and had thought she'd "made it," she had not succeeded, either.

Maintaining the Bedford house, my father complained, "cost a fortune." The gardening bills. The cleaning bills. The heating bills. The cooling bills.

"Dad wants to sell the house," my mother said.

"Don't you kind of have to?" I said.

"I am not going to move."

They had the house appraised.

"We are not going to sell for a price like that," she said.

"If you rent it for a while, prices might rise," I said.

It was hard to think about renting it, though. It would have been hard to think about strangers living in any house they owned, but the dream house that they had designed and built for themselves—no.

"I am not going to rent it," she said, as if it were her decision to make.

Eventually, though, they had no choice but to rent and then sell.

It must have been pretty awful to find yourself displaced all over again in your seventies, I say now. After all you'd been through—talk about traumatic.

You people do not know what means traumatic, says my mother.

Not the way you do, you're right. We don't know it the way you do.

It was all Dad's fault. He is crazy.

I don't know, Mom. A lot of people got caught in the dot-com crash. And if it weren't for his risk-taking, you wouldn't have had so much money to lose to begin with.

But she just says, Who lost the money? You tell me. Who lost it?

Their new house in Chappaqua was smaller than the very first house they had bought on Spring Road, in Yonkers. Still, now that she had agreed to the move, my mother worked on saving face. She wrote to her family:

> As the saying goes, Shēng háizi bèi lǎo. We have children to prepare for old age. And now it is time to reap the benefits of our preparation. Our new house is just two doors away from our son Sean, very convenient.

And certainly, its location was an advantage. All the same, I remember my father sitting one last time in the octagonal dining nook off the Bedford kitchen. Built to accommodate the round table around which we had eaten countless family meals, the nook was all windows; it looked out onto a tiered garden, where, as part of an anniversary celebration, we had planted a Jen family tree. My father rarely sat still unless he was taking a nap in the sun, but now he just sat, frozen. I went to sit with him.

"I took a lot of pictures," I told him, though I should have known that neither parent would ever want to see them.

And sure enough, he said nothing. His face was lined and gray, and his head hung down. He looked suddenly old.

Did you ever invite Georgiana to Chappaqua? I ask now.

Of course not, my mother says.

Something I bet Dad never understood, I say. What it meant to you to have Auntie Georgiana look up to you again. And then to know how she would look down on you once more if she knew what had happened.

In his thinking, it is not important, she agrees. He always says, Forget about Georgiana.

And why not? Why not forget about Georgiana?

It is not just Georgiana. Everyone look down on you. Everyone talk about you. You are the most Chinese of the children. But even you only, say, half understand.

You mean, I fail to get the full horror of being "looked down on."

You cannot understand because you are not part of that world, she says.

Would Auntie Marnie have looked down on you?

Of course not. All she cared was what God thought. Marnie Mulligan was like Mother Greenough. Even after her mother died and Marnie herself got sick, she still kept her faith. Even after she lost her house paying medical bills, she believed.

Whereas you . . .

I believed, too, she says. But after Marnie got cancer . . . She stops.

Angry with my father, she fought with him about where they would be buried. The Chinese like to say *Luò yè guī gēn*—Fallen leaves return to their roots—believing it the natural way of things. Many of the Chinese who came to America to work on the railroads asked as a last request that their remains be sent back to China—which, movingly, they were, in giant earthen jars. And so, too, my father insisted he wanted to be buried in his beloved Yixing. It was very Chinese to love your hometown, after all, and for him Yixing really had been heaven. I could see why he wanted to be buried with his grandparents and parents and brothers in the town his family had lived in for twenty-eight generations, especially as the Jen family plot very unusually boasted a long stone wall, some seven feet high and twenty-five feet wide, before which there was plenty of room for my father to be buried alongside his four brothers. That their wives would be buried with them went without saying, and probably if my parents had never left China, my mother would have, as wives had done for millennia, simply acquiesced. It was her duty.

But she had had enough of the Jen family project.

"He does not consider me," she said. "Do I want to be buried there? He never even asked that question. I have only visited Yixing once. His relatives never welcomed me. I do not feel like a member of the Jen family. And how can you kids visit the grave there?"

"Maybe you guys shouldn't be buried together," I said.

"You are crazy!" she said.

Now my father was insisting not only that he wanted to be buried in Yixing but that he wanted David and me to videotape his wishes so everyone in the family would know.

"Okay," we said.

As for what I thought?

"I think it's your decision, Dad," I answered. "You shouldn't be buried in America if you really want to be buried in China."

He nodded.

"I mean, it's your life."

To this, he was quiet, neither agreeing nor disagreeing, and in truth, even as I said it, I wondered if that was right.

How could your life be your own! my mother says now. Talk about crazy!

He eventually concluded himself that being buried in Yixing was unrealistic. Like my mother, he wanted us kids to be able to visit him. I promised to at least have some of his clothes buried in Yixing, as the Chinese will—clothes being a traditional proxy for a body.

"Your spirit will be there," I said.

He hesitated. "Okay," he said. Then he said, "You tell Mom you talk to me, and so I say okay. No more bury in Yixing. Bury in United States. You say you talk to me, I agree."

"Dad," I said. "I am not going to say I talked you into it when you decided yourself."

"Just say that way," he insisted.

"Dad. Talk to her yourself. She feels bad, you know, that you don't say anything about wanting to be buried with her, and that her feelings don't matter. So why not tell her you care how she feels."

"Just say that way," he insisted again. "Say that way. Say you talk to me, I agree."

What he was really saying was that he wanted me to handle this the Chinese way. My mother, too, was always wanting me to "kind of like persuade" someone else to do something, and it probably would have helped them both save face had I told my mother that I had "kind of like persuaded" my father to change his mind. It would have helped my father give in without giving in, and it would have pleased my mother that I had taken her side. But the American in me was unwilling to pretend I had done something I hadn't, even if it would smooth things over.

"Talk to her yourself," I said again. "Talk to her yourself, Dad."

He let the subject drop.

Maybe I was wrong, I say now. Maybe it wouldn't have killed me to be a little less American.

Of course you were wrong, says my mother.

That was just one in a string of escalating fights, in all of which, just as my mother was supposed to sit by my father's hospital bed, and my father was supposed to protect her, I was supposed to play the role of intermediary. I did to the extent that when a geriatric psychiatrist friend suggested that they both try Prozac, I passed along his suggestion, emphasizing how lucky we were to receive free advice from an expert.

"You'll both feel better," I said. "Why not try it?"

My father agreed. My mother refused.

"He should take it, he's the crazy one," she said.

Then he refused, too. "I'm not going to take medicine by myself," he said. "No."

She wanted me to stop him from looking at buildings to invest in.

"He has a one-track mind," she said.

And indeed, the drive and determination that had served him so well in his youth had over the years become a mania. Even in hundred-degree heat, he would take a cab to the train, a train into the city, and a subway to a building he wanted to see. By then he was producing so little body heat that the temperature didn't bother him the way it bothered others. But still, a trip like that could kill him. He wasn't going to buy any of these buildings, as he had to know; no bank was going to lend him the money. I couldn't stop him from going, though, any more than I could have stopped him from beating Reuben long ago. Nor would I have had the heart: my father had no hobbies and no interests. The chimera of a comeback was all that kept him going.

"If you want him to stop, you have to talk to him yourself," I said.

But my mother just said that she wanted him to stop investing in stocks, too. "Lost enough money already," she said.

"So tell him."

Once again she wanted me to "kind of like persuade" him and was frustrated when, once again, I demurred. Happily, he had a generous life insurance policy; my mother was not going to be on the street. And happily, too, he had learned from his losses. Having recouped some money from the Bedford house, he was investing again but far more conservatively than before. As a former bond trader, Reuben could confirm that the stocks my father had picked—Starbucks, Macy's, Visa—weren't that bad. My father might not make a fortune on them, but he wasn't going to lose his shirt, either. Still, my mother objected, especially when he bought more stocks without her consent.

He told me nothing! she says now. He just did it by himself.

I guess he knew you would say no, I say.

Of course I would say no. He is crazy!

He should have told you, I say. He was wrong. But just as he wanted to learn to swim, he wanted to rise from defeat and rebuild. And wasn't that worth a smile, at least—that at ninety-three, he wanted to start over? He really was indomitable.

But what about me?

You didn't want to find yourself abandoned and penniless once more.

That's right!

From your point of view, it might as well have been wartime again. Instead of staying home and protecting you the

way your father had, Dad was out hiding under lotus leaves and making stoves out of scrap metal.
   That's right!
   You were afraid.
   Of course I was afraid!

She and my sibs had my father neurologically tested, hoping he would prove non compos mentis. However, Reuben reported in an email:

Dr. Szabo was quite impressed with Dad's mental acuity. Memory recall, math calculations, presence of mind questions, etc. were all fine.

Dr. Szabo asked Dad why he was interested in trading stocks. Dad's reply was that interest rates in bank accts yielded practically zero. Dad also correctly answered Dr. Szabo when he asked what the Dow and S&P 500 levels were. Dr. Szabo asked what stocks Dad was interested in. Dad's reply: AT&T, Philip Morris, Visa, Exxon Mobil, Starbucks. He then asked on what criteria Dad chose stocks. Dad's reply: he liked products that people use every day.

Dr. Szabo privately told me that one may not agree with his answers, and that they may even be wrong, but they are certainly not irrational.

His answers might not have been irrational, but, angered by attempts to control him, my father did irrationally threaten to change his and my mother's will.
   "I am going to talk to the lawyer by myself," he said. "No one come with me. Just by myself."
   "What, you think this house is all yours?" said my mother. "Everything is just yours? You think five children, they raised themselves?"
   "I'm go by myself," my father repeated. "No one come with me."
   Would I "kind of like persuade" him to change his mind? my mother wanted to know.

"No, but don't worry. If you drew up the will together, he cannot now unilaterally cut you out of it," I said. "In America, you're protected by the law."

But she didn't want the law to protect her. She wanted her daughter to protect her.

You are his favorite, that's why you stick up for him, she says now.

I was trying not to get dragged into your fights, I say. I could never understand why you couldn't fight your own fights.

No one in China fights their own fights, she says.

But we weren't in China.

We are Chinese people, she says. We are sort of like Americanized. But that's who we are.

In the end, my father did not change their will; he did not even go to see the lawyer. But he remained as frustrated with my mother as she was with him.

"She is that kind of person, cannot listen, do not want to listen. Cannot talk to her, only way is to take action. So now I am take action. First small action, and then you watch. If no one listen, then big action. And if still no one listen, one day you will find I am gone back to China. I am not say anything to anybody. Just one day, gone."

I left New York only to hear two days later that my father was missing. My siblings, worn out by their years on the front line of my parents' blowups, seemed inured to the drama; this was not the first time my father had disappeared. I alone seemed concerned that what with my father's fragility, this crisis might be different. My mother would say nothing over the phone, so, late as it was, I drove back down to New York—exactly, I suspected, as she wanted me to.

It was midnight when I arrived. "Have you called the police?"

The answer was no. He had been gone all day, and she had not called the police.

"Wait until morning," she said. She was in her posy-sprigged flannel pajamas but not asleep. Instead, she was reading the newspaper, refusing to be concerned. Her false teeth were soaking beside her in a rice bowl.

Wait until morning? I did not think my father had gone to China. But he was in his nineties, liked to drive without his glasses, and had been in any number of accidents. We had all begged him to stop driving and, when we failed, pegged our hopes on his flunking his test when his license came up for renewal. Unfortunately, though, at age ninety, he somehow passed even his vision test, whereupon the great state of New York renewed his license for ten years.

"What if he ran off the road?" I said. "How are you going to feel if it turns out he was in the car, dead, and no one was sent to look for him until the morning?"

"You have nothing to say," she said.

"In America, everyone is entitled to an opinion," I said.

"Forget about America."

Why had she called me? As I did not know his license plate number, and she was adamant about not calling the police anyway, we simply stayed up all night, waiting and worrying. It seemed that in the heat of their fight, my father had called her a Shanghai prostitute.

"A Shanghai prostitute?" It was hard not to laugh.

She glared, furious to be seen the way that country people saw Shanghai people—as mercenary and heartless, and barely Chinese. In fact, in the aftermath of another fight, my father had asked Shane to ask her, Do you love Dad? Or is money more important?

You thought all he cared about was money, and he thought all you cared about was money, I say now. I wonder if you can even imagine a marriage where no one fights about money.

What marriage is that? my mother scoffs.

Dave and I have not fought about money once in forty years, I say.

Chinese people believe that if you don't have money, you don't eat.

Meaning that you fundamentally don't believe that the Lord will provide. Even if you're Christian and it's in the Bible, you don't believe it.

Chinese people are more realistic, she says.

My father finally showed up at dawn.

"Oh my God, are you okay? I'm so glad you're okay!" I said. He looked haggard and exhausted, but his anger was keeping him going. "Where were you?"

He would not say. "If no one listen, then big action," he said ominously. It was as if no time had passed since I was last in town. He was simply continuing his earlier diatribe.

"I'm listening, Dad. What is it you want? I'm listening."

He said nothing.

"Do you want to be able to go look at buildings? Is that it?"

"No more buildings," my mother said.

"Mom, just try to listen," I pleaded.

But even as I said that, he exploded. "No. No. No. No. Everything is no. No. No. No. She is that kind of person, cannot listen, do not want to listen. Everything is no. No. No. No."

"You are crazy, that's why," she said.

"Mom," I said. And then, "Dad." And then, "Mom." And then, "Dad." But it was hopeless.

He had threatened violence with my mother before. When in response to one of his stock purchases, my mother moved money into an account he could not touch, he had waved a knife at her. But this time, it was not just a threat. This time, when she did it again, he hit her on the leg with her cane. Five times, my brother Shane reported. He took her to his apartment for safety.

That was terrible! I say now. I'm so glad Shane took you in.

Dad hit me! she says. With a stick!

Hitting is wrong, I say. He was wrong.

He is crazy!

I'm just glad someone did something this time, I say. I'm glad the family didn't just assume you had it coming and ignore it.

I don't know what you are talking.

Even if a cane is better than a metal garden stake, it's still not okay, I say.

She does not answer.

My father moved to my brother Reuben's place in New York City. There he brooded for a couple of days before blossoming in a most extraordinary way. Why had my parents not moved to the city when they sold the Bedford house? Why had they holed up in Chappaqua, where there was nothing to do but fight with each other? Now my father made friends with the doormen; he struck up conversations with perfect strangers. One day, Reuben found him at Starbucks, chatting with a model. Another day, he found him at Chipotle, dining with someone in dreadlocks. By the end of the week, my father could have run for mayor.

Next he came to Boston. We took him to the Museum of Fine Arts, where he was amazed by the mummies. We took him to the Institute of Contemporary Art, where he was even more amazed by people having coffee in the café. He asked a pair of ladies if they did this often—to which they laughed and said, "Of course! All the time."

"Mister!" he said.

Neither had he ever seen anything like the ICA's glass-walled walkway looking out onto the Boston Harbor. He stared at the view, open-mouthed.

"That's something!" he said.

We took him to the science museum and the aquarium and the arboretum. We took him to eat stinky tofu in Allston. We took him to Vermont, where we had a house on a lake that reminded him of Lake Tai in Yixing. He sat in the sun, looking contentedly at the water. He napped. Our house was not unlike the house on Shelter Island my childhood friend Annie Dreyfus had had; we had a dock and a Sunfish, and all knew how to swim and sail. We did not take my father out for either a swim or a sail, though. Instead, we took him kayaking, which he loved.

And back in Cambridge, we got him out for a riverboat cruise on the Charles River. As we glided by the Harvard river houses, I was able to say, "That's where David lived," and "That's where Lisa and Oliver lived" (Oliver being Lisa's husband), and "That's where I lived." I so wished, as I showed him, that he had been able to go to Harvard—that he could have known Harvard from the inside, not just the outside—and I thanked him with all my being for all he'd done to send us to school. It was hard not to cry.

How about me? my mother says now. Did you wish I could have gone to Harvard, too?

No, I admit. To be honest, I was glad to be having a break from you.

You were glad to forget about me.

Yes, I say. I was.

But now that I am dead, you cannot forget.

You're having your revenge, if that's what you want, I say. No, I cannot forget you. You are right. You've won.

I went on talking to my father.

"You know, a lot of our classmates were saddled with debt for years," I told him, "including David. We were paying off his debt for decades. But you would never have considered not paying for our education. And you worked really hard, and you did it. You sent all five of us to college, and to graduate school, too." (In fact, I'd paid for my own graduate school, and Reuben had paid him back for both his undergraduate and graduate education, but I didn't bring that up.)

He nodded with satisfaction.

"You did it," I said again. "And Mom, too. Mom worked hard to pay for our tuition, too."

He agreed, but I could see I'd made a mistake mentioning her.

You see? He thinks he did everything himself, she says now. And you, you let him think like that.

I brought up how hard you worked, I say. I did.

You let him think like that, she says again anyway.

The next morning, David and I woke to find my father gone. No note, just an open bedroom door and, we realized after a few minutes, an unlocked front door. Where had he gone?

We searched frantically all over town. Had he gone to the Dunkin' Donuts? To the bagel shop? To Starbucks? It was early Sunday morning. How would he even have gotten wherever it was that he went? We looked and looked.

Finally, desperate, we drove to the train station in Boston. I went up to the ticket window and politely asked if anyone had seen a little old Chinese man. I knew they weren't supposed to report on their customers. But had they by any chance seen a little old Chinese man, walking very very slowly?

The answer was immediate: "Yeah, we saw him."

"Did he by any chance buy a ticket to New York?"

"Yes, ma'am. He did."

My father had gotten up, called a cab, boarded the train to New York, and taken another cab to Chappaqua, timing everything so as to be making himself comfortable in the kitchen while my mother was at church. In short, he had retaken Chappaqua. David and I had to laugh; we only wished he knew how to take a selfie.

Now it was my mother who was homeless. She moved in with Sean while, furious at my father for outmaneuvering her and tired of having to pick up the pieces, my siblings shut him out. He had some food in the fridge, but they refused to bring him meals, and no one dropped in. How many times did I say, What kind of a way is that to treat a stranger, much less your own father? But he might as well have been King Lear. He was out on the heath.

By the time David and I could get down to New York, my father was so weak he could barely stand. We took him to the Mt. Kisco Diner; Paloma had to hold both his hands to help him up the handicap ramp. In fact, as it turned out, he wasn't just starving; he had a staph infection that could have killed him. He was soon on a peripherally inserted central catheter—a "PICC line," the nurses called it—in a rehab center. He stayed there for weeks.

At one point during his occupation of Chappaqua, my father had grimly predicted that my mother would have to come back. "She has no choice," he said—and, much as I didn't want to, I heard a Chinese harshness in his voice, a frank acquaintance with coercion. But now he was the one with no choice. He was a fragile ninety-three-year-old man with an untold number of complex medical issues; he needed to return from rehab to his home and his systems, and he did.

. . .

A kind of truce was struck. The family would take care of him, but he was not allowed to trade stocks. His computer was taken away, and his Visa card, too. A week before he died, he asked for scallops. My mother said no.

"Too expensive," she said.

"Ma," I said.

"You can go look at the Chappaqua deli. That place is very expensive. $18.99 a pound."

I did go, and immediately returned with the scallops. He ate them with relish. I also soaked his toenails and trimmed them, kneeling at his feet the way he used to kneel at mine, tightening my ski boots.

I can still feel the clutch of my father's hand on the day he died. It was May 2013. He was ninety-three and in a wheelchair, which he hated. He had long fought not only to stand but to stand up straight. Detesting as he did that he had started to stoop, he had cut out all sorts of back clinic ads and showed them to my brothers. "I want to straight!" he would tell them. "I want to straight!" As for wheelchairs in general, his pronouncement in the past had always been "No fun."

But there he was, finally, wheelchair-bound himself. And perhaps because he hated it, or perhaps because he couldn't stand fighting with my mother anymore, or perhaps because two of his college-aged grandchildren had just dropped by to see him—en route to New York City, where they would be interviewing for summer jobs and generally preparing to enter adult life—he stopped taking his meds. He knew I was coming, and I think he planned it this way, that I would be there when he died. I was there when he could no longer chew and swallow; I was there when he could not even keep an ice chip in his mouth. I was there when he began to raise his head like a newborn and turn it toward my mother's voice—a motion I remembered from Luke's and Paloma's infancy, and a revelation: for all their fighting, he loved her.

I had had a hunch he was going to die. We never stayed in Chappaqua because there was nowhere to sleep—no guest room, no foldout couch, not even an air mattress. But that night we decided not to return to Cambridge as we'd planned but to camp out on the couch and floor of the study instead. He was very thin and very weak. Still, as I was wheeling him to bed, he gripped my hand so hard that it hurt. My hand was twisted around backward, the heel of my palm to the front, but because he was holding on to it as if to life itself, I did not adjust my position. With every ounce of what he had left, he was saying goodbye.

He slept so cold in his last few months that even in May, he had many layers of blankets and quilts on his bed. He did not like the lightness of down quilts; way before weighted blankets came into vogue, he used to say, "I like blanket heavy." And even with all that bedding, he sometimes pulled it over his head, so that he was snuggled into a kind of warren. If you came in to visit him, you might have to excavate a little before you saw his face, peeking out bright-eyed, like a child's from inside a snow fort. But when, having a bad feeling, I went to check on him in the middle of the night, he had kicked his covers off because he couldn't breathe. It was a shock. He couldn't talk, either, but he was awake and could hear. And so it was that I could hold his hand and stroke his bony forehead and talk to him, even as I yelled to David and Luke and Paloma to come, and told them to wake my mother.

How they had fought and fought. Yet I will always remember how as he was dying, she gently washed his face with a washcloth—such a Chinese gesture. I will remember her last words to him, too: "Go easy, go easy." And, very movingly: "You don't have to worry about the children anymore."

For that's what they did. They worried about us kids all their lives; it kept them together. My father did not leave us a million dollars each as he had wanted to, but he left us with much more, and I was glad to be able to tell him, in his last moments, what a good job he had done, and how we all loved him and would always remember him. Then, as he had threatened to do so many times, he left.

I still think about him many, many times a day. I cannot see a sunny spot without seeing him sitting in it, enjoying the sunshine, and I cannot answer a question about my sense of humor without saying, I got it from my father—for as endlessly as he had fought with my mother, my father loved nothing more than to "make some joke," as he put it, and was never short of things to laugh about.

CHAPTER VI
A Sutra and a Toast

It is March 2020. There is talk of a coronavirus lockdown in New York, but the talk seems, from far-off Massachusetts, unhinged. Coronavirus? Lockdown? Having lived through the 2003 SARS outbreak in China, I have a sense of what could be up. Still, it seems a bit like talk of Martian colonies or brain-eating bacteria. Barmy.

David and I visit my mother in Chappaqua. Her siblings in Shanghai having all instantly exclaimed when we met them that she was born in the year of the mouse—"No, no, not the cow, the mouse!"—everyone now knows she was born in 1924. Still, she likes to say that she is "Chinese age ninety-five"—never mind that with her birthday falling in October, her American age is ninety-five and her Chinese age ninety-six. We tell her, "You're Chinese age ninety-six, Mom! Ninety-six!" But it's unclear whether she understands.

The Chappaqua house is what used to be called a starter house—a no-frills white clapboard structure with black shutters and two bedrooms, from which a young couple with a growing family was once supposed to graduate. Dave and I had opposed my parents' buying that house, two doors down though it was from my brother Sean, because it sat atop a small hill, and in the best of times, my mother hadn't been a great driver. One of her weakest points, what's more, had always been backing up. She never looked in her rearview mirror, much less turned her head to look over a shoulder, and accordingly had been known to go clear around the block so she wouldn't have to "back," as she put it. It was hard to see how she was going to back out of this new, narrow driveway even if it wasn't downhill, and it was steeply downhill—roller-coaster downhill. What's more, while not long, it was not short. I felt sorry for the brave little mailbox stationed at its bottom, on a post, as soon as I saw it; its days were numbered.

We time our visit so as to catch my mother awake. She has been waking up later and later for a while now—sleeping sometimes until midafternoon. I check with my brothers. I check with her caretakers. She's been a bit more alert, they say. A lunchtime arrival will work. When David and I arrive at one o'clock, though, she is in bed. We wait in the living room, which is small but seems, disconcertingly, the right size for her. ("Fit," my father might have said, meaning both that it was the right size and that it was *héshì*, suitable or appropriate—and using just that one word as, Chinglish speaker that he was, he often did.) As if through some dismaying cross between *Goldilocks* and *Alice in Wonderland*, that's to say, my mother's life seems to have shrunk to fit this room. Then it will shrink, one feels, to a dot, and then to nothing.

Yet for now a large soft light streams in through the living room's south-facing picture window, pooling on the antique round Chinese table that used to grace the grand foyer of the Bedford house. My mother bought it with the help of Shane's old boyfriend Nolan, who was a decorator and could get discounts (Nolan, yes, having become a member of the family despite the general assumption that my father would never accept Shane's being gay). It was the first antique my mother had ever bought and was typically topped with a large seasonal arrangement, also courtesy of Nolan. Now, though, it sports, not a glorious mass of flowering cherry tree branches but heaps of papers. And next to it sits a slatted green rocking chair I bought for my father—an outdoor chair, really, intended for the front porch of a cottage and topped with the only cushion the mall store had, a tufted, pea-green affair that fought energetically with the chair's forest green. I would never have imagined two greens could clash this way—do the green hats of cartoon elves clash with the forest? But in the showroom my father had sat in the padded chair, and smiled, and rocked; and though he was a small man, his feet had reached the floor. "It fits, doesn't it," I had said, to which he had nodded and answered, "Fit." And so I bought it, ugly cushion and all, and today I'm just glad he had a chance to sit in it for a couple of years. It faces the window—empty but warmed, as if in his memory, by the sun; he did always love to bask in the sun, contented as a turtle.

And, right outside the window, there's a tree with classical Chinese associations—a plum tree. My parents didn't plant it, but they have enjoyed its winter-blooming flowers, a traditional symbol of perseverance through difficulty. As the first flower of the year, the plum also represents hope and renewal; and indeed, even its image is perennial, having appeared and reappeared in countless Chinese paintings and poems. In China, every child would know Tang dynasty poems like "Early Plum" by Zhang Wei, for example—a poem that goes:

> There is a plum tree like white jade in the cold,
> Far from the village road, near a bridge over a stream.
> Not realizing that flowers by the water bloom early,
> I mistake them for unmelted snow.

The poet is about to discover, of course, that he's seeing not snow but blossoms—and then what joy! It's the sort of poem that would have deepened what my parents would have called "the feeling" the tree gave them. ("Just have that feeling" being a favorite phrase of both of theirs, as well as—especially when my father was in a bad mood—"don't have that feeling.") My mother has enjoyed that tree.

It is past its bloom, though. And so it is that I "don't have that feeling" when—after an hour? two?—I enter my mother's bedroom at last. For when is spring not spring but when you enter the bedroom of a tired old woman? Her bedroom is jammed with cardboard wardrobe boxes full of dresses, each still in its dry-cleaning bag and hung on a paper-wrapped hanger—dry cleaners of her era having wrapped their hangers in paper advertisements like "Need It Tonight? You've Got It!" and "You Leave It, We Clean It." Though it has long been unlikely she would wear any of these clothes again, nothing has been given away. She has every dress she's bought in the last thirty years at least, maybe the last fifty or sixty, and every pair of shoes, too, including a pair of brand-new, wing-tipped Ferragamo heels she must have bought at a deep discount. Of course, it's hard at any age to downsize. I am old enough to know that myself.

But even in her prime, my mother was a hoarder. My father loved to throw things out; my mother hated to. Now her piles include catalogs from Harry & David, L.L.Bean, Bloomingdale's, and Lord & Taylor, as well as books I've given her: *Life and Death in Shanghai, Wild Swans,* and *Colors of the Mountain.* There are also art catalogs like *Streams and Mountains Without End: Landscape Traditions of China* and *Out of Character: Decoding Chinese Calligraphy*—souvenirs from the decades of Chinese art shows at the Metropolitan Museum of Art that I've taken her to. She has my books, too, amid piles of statements and bills, and a box full of assorted stationery, including dozens of unused greeting card envelopes, brittle and yellow and piled neatly in size order. The children of many an Asian immigrant will recall how their parents seemed unable to waste even one grain of rice; some saved the Styrofoam containers from fast-food hamburgers, and an astonishing number could not part with their Taster's Choice instant coffee jars, the jars' graceful shape and red lids having held, it seems, an irresistible appeal. As for that generation's influence on the next, I will confess that to this day I save Starbucks cups for reuse, rinse out baggies, and compost religiously. Not that frugality is limited to Asians. Many people who lived through the Great Depression never forgot it, and the poet Donald Hall once found a box left by his Yankee grandmother labeled "Strings Too Short to Save."

My mother is their soul mate. It is no surprise that she sleeps in one of the twin beds she and my father bought as newlyweds some seventy years ago. She no longer takes satisfaction in knowing what a good value it indeed proved to be, though; and, jarringly, my father's bed no longer parallels hers. Instead, it occupies the house's second bedroom across the hall—the bedroom where my father slept in his last years, and where he died. A hermit cell of a room, it was barely big enough for the bed, a small chest of drawers, a modest desk, and a scale—the scale sporting an easy-to-read dial so oversized it seemed, well, out of scale, as if it belonged to a *Magic Mountain* reality in which someone else was weighed every day, to see how much water he was retaining as his heart failed. One might think it to have been quite an adjustment for my father to move in here, but in fact it was no big deal. Having been proudly unfussy his whole life ("Too picky no good," he always said), he just *xíguàn le*—got used to it. Now an aide sleeps in his bed—Grace the minister, or else Melanie.

I will never get used to it.

In the Scarsdale house of my childhood, my parents' twin beds had stood like the flanking guardian beasts of an Assyrian palace gate, ensconcing, like a throne, their night table. In lieu of a monarch, though, the table boasted a fake Tiffany lamp with blue-green plastic panes and, below that, in its drawer, a hidden treasure: my mother's notebook record of her temperature. (Despite the slip that gave rise to Sean, she continued practicing the rhythm method of contraception all her fertile years.) To approach the complex, you crossed a sound-deadening expanse of thick blue carpet with two white-brocade swivel chairs; there was a marble-topped fruitwood table on your right, and a dresser and chest of drawers on your left. The hush was palpable, and it was dim in there, thanks to the iridescent peacock-colored drapes. A semi-sheer panel hung between the drapes near the chairs, but behind the throne setup, drapes completely obscured the windows. Indeed, it was only when my parents moved out that I realized there were windows back there at all.

There is more light in this Chappaqua bedroom. But it is as if someone took my mother's old bedroom, gathered it up into a hobo's cloth, and then spilled it out here—willy-nilly and yet somehow, strangely, with its hush intact. Just one thing moves—my mother's body, her chest rising and falling, rising and falling as she inhales and exhales, struggling to breathe. She is otherwise the picture of somnolence in her faded posy-sprigged ivory flannel pajamas; only her white hair is lively and wild, as if dreaming its own dream.

What is it about hair, that when it loses its color, it loses its shine, too? And why does it become hay-like and wayward? One section splays out in a flat whorl; it looks like a storm system on a weather chart. My mother is lucky in still boasting a full head of hair. She's been spared the beach-dune-studded-with-plugs-oferosion-control-grass look. But even she has lost her eyelashes. I am saddened by the puffiness of her eyes—part goldfish, part James Baldwin, I want to say, although I am too sad to quip. I am saddened by the mottled purpling of her hands, too (the result of bullous pemphigoid, Lisa has said, a rare condition in which your immune system attacks the tissue below your skin). And I am saddened by her sheer age—by the spectacle of time having gone stealthily after her cells, one by one by one.

But I am shocked at her dishevelment. It's one thing for the room to be a mess. It's another for the disorder, like a rising tide, to have reached her very bed. Her bedding is a jumble; her pajama top is twisted under her; and the fitted sheet, having for some reason never been properly pulled over the corner of the mattress, shrinks back like a receding gum. It exposes both the incongruously shiny gold brocade mattress on which she lies as well as another truth: though she has her aides and sons to take care of her, my mother does not have herself. Packer of neat suitcases and arranger of neat drawers that she was—upholder of the proper ways of doing things—she straightened my father's bedding right until the end. People often think of me as having started to become a writer when I took the name Gish, but it was perhaps a greater act of defiance when I began to simply throw my underwear and socks into a drawer—when I stopped folding and stacking them as if for some impending inspection. How my mother would have hated to see her bed in this state.

I pull the corner of the sheet over the mattress corner. Part of me wants to blame the caregivers; I can't help but wonder how well she's really being cared for. But later, when I hear how the aides sit far from the other passengers on the train and how they change and wash their clothes as soon as they enter the house, I am glad I kept my doubts to myself. How much more they seem to know about the mystery disease than David and I. Is there a community of caregivers in the city, where they live? Do they talk and confer? So it seems. We are grateful.

At the same time—how my mother loved control, and how little she now has.

I shake her warm shoulder. She resists waking up—crying, half asleep, in a baby voice, "I don't feel good, I don't feel good."

But when I ask, "What's the matter? What doesn't feel good?" she just answers, "I don't know, I don't know," and falls back asleep.

I try again to wake her.

"I want to sleep," she cries. "I want to sleep."

She sounds half awake—awake enough that finally, leaning over, I say, "Mom! Mom! Guess who's here?"

Her lashless eyelids flutter.

"It's not Reuben, and it's not Lisa, and it's not Sean, and it's not Shane," I say.

"Lil!" she says then, opening her eyes. And looking genuinely surprised and happy, she says, "You little stinker!" and caresses my cheek.

It's a touch that should be so familiar, a gesture she should have made a million times. But in fact I only remember it from what seems a hundred years ago. I want to cry. Why did she wait decades to show that affection again?

"Little stinker." Yes, she called me that, years and years ago. I had forgotten.

I wish she would call me that again.

The moment is lost in the process of getting her washed and dressed. Melanie handles this right through the smoothing on of my mother's knee-high stockings. I help only with the working of her feet into the sneakers David and I bought on our last trip to see her. The sneakers are several sizes too big (size 8 when she's always worn a 5½ or a 6) but even so have to be worn unlaced; her feet are as swollen as if she'd sprained them. She's unclear sometimes about which foot is which, Melanie says, though it's hard to know how confused she actually is, as she hears better out of her right ear than her left but not well in general, and of course will not wear a hearing aid.

I sigh. For years, the family struggled to convince my father to wear a hearing aid, too; when my day comes, I vow to be less self-defeatingly obstinate. In the meanwhile, all my mother's colors seem off. It isn't only that her feet are blue and her hands blue-splotched. In certain lights, her brown eyes, too, are almost blue—a milky blue, like the blue of a fine piece of porcelain held up to the light. And her mauve-painted nails belong to a strange register. Evocative of a ladies' luncheon or a dance hall, they seem to reflect a generic notion of what elderly women like; it's not hard to guess that there are half-moons of natural nail near the cuticle where the polish has grown out because the aides asked my mother if she'd like her nails touched up and she said no. Which, of course, my father always said she loved to do—say no, no, no, no—but how little power that "no" now holds. Though her white hair flares out, as per usual, like a broom, there is an improbable patch of black hair at the top of her forehead, like a photo negative of a witch's forelock—all that remains, it seems, of her oppositional self.

The swelling under her eyes seems worse now that she's up, and her eyelashlessness more disturbing. Though I had learned from the Johns Hopkins website that it is the weakening of the muscles and tissue around the eye that "allows the fat surrounding the eye to bulge out, creating that bubble-like appearance," and that "a drop in certain hormones may slow or even halt the production of eyelashes," explanation only helps so much.

Here we just are.

She gets into her wheelchair—her "Cadillac," she calls it—on her own.

"By myself," she chortles. "I think I'm pretty good." And I readily agree—"You are!"—applauding and encouraging her, even though in truth I thought that she had stopped trying to use her walker well before she really had to. Back when she was in rehab, my siblings and I had had to push her to do her exercises, crying, "You have to try, Mom! You have to try!" Wrote Reuben in an email:

> Her lack of faster progress is, I believe, partially psychological. She lacks confidence, and there's also a laziness factor: if you're flying business class and waited on all day long, there's little incentive to do much for yourself.

But we were up against a master of stasis. It wasn't just that she was "a bit stationary in the flesh," as writer Grace Paley would have put it; she reveled in the power of inertia. The Daoists have a phrase—*wú wéi*—that extols a profound embrace of inaction, an embrace I thought of when I saw the great Kurosawa movie *Kagemusha*. In this, over and over, you hear the phrase "The mountain does not move," and when, at last, the "mountain"—that is, the army—does move, the result is disaster, as my mother might have predicted had she been given to prognostication (which she was not). How steadfastly she had refused to apply herself to so many things over the years—to learning how to use an iPhone or iPad or computer, for example. How many times had I explained how to use a keyboard—didn't she know how to type, after all? How many times had I held her finger to a touchscreen so she could see how gently she should tap it? And when that didn't work, how many times had I tried to teach her to use a rubber-tipped stylus? It is in fact hard to learn to tap rather than press. But her brothers and sisters in Shanghai had all learned. I did not believe she could not do it.

"Wouldn't it be fun to see what all the grandchildren are doing on Facebook?" I'd ask her, only to hear, "I'm too old to learn." Instead, she watches TV. Now that my father has died, she can watch as much as she likes.

Once I tried to arrange for a water service for her.

"We can get you a dispenser," I told her. "The jugs for it will be delivered. You won't have to do anything. They're big and last a long time, and can dispense not just cold water but hot—water hot enough for tea. It's really convenient."

But she resisted and resisted, until finally it dawned on her stupid American daughter that what she wanted was not convenience but company. She wanted my brothers to have to bring her water to her, jug by jug.

And so it is that for all the reasons people fudge in these moments, including a kind of largesse of spirit crossed with a frank desire not to hear the same sentence yet again, when she once more says, "I think I'm pretty good," I answer, "Yes, you are, you're very good." Call-and-response.

David folds up her wheelchair, packing it into the trunk of the Mercedes of which he and I had disapproved many moons ago. We were in my father's camp on this. "Just have to show you are rich," he used to tell my mother, preferring old cars himself—cars you didn't have to worry about. He did eventually come to enjoy a new car. After decades of dismissing such frills as soft, he finally bought a station wagon that wasn't a strip model and drove it home from the dealer with the air-conditioning on high and all its windows open.

But how trivial those struggles seem today. Today we are just glad my mother has enjoyed her car. What an enormous repertoire of pleasures David and I have, after all—from walking with friends to reading in the bathtub to napping in the middle of a lake on paddleboards—whereas there are so few things you could even say my mother wants besides to see the Yankees win, and go out to lunch, and be told she's pretty good for her age. With the wheelchair goes an old, flat gray-green pillow with a white stain of some sort on it. Her tummy is as beachball-round as ever, but the way her chin pours straight down to her breastless chest, she seems to be turning into that Japanese anime character Totoro—Hayao Miyazaki's neckless chinchilla with the pencil-mark breast feathers.

My poor mother.

Most days my brothers take her to the bagel shop in Mount Kisco, where she has a croissant with scrambled eggs and decaf coffee. She picks up her *New York Times* there as well. Happily, the staff all know her, as she will often mention—"They know us there" being an important phrase for her, suggesting as it does that she feels not like the outsider she has been for so much of her life but an insider. Usually she eats half the croissant sandwich and takes the other half home in a doggy bag. If, however, we leave the uneaten half behind, as we did the day we took her to the Katonah Museum (afraid that, with the temperature in the nineties, the sandwich would go bad), the owner will run out after us, bag in hand.

"Your mom has trained me," he will say.

My mother will be delighted.

But today we are headed to a new place in Mount Kisco called Village Social. It is my mother's choice. She wants a change, and anyway, by this time (well past two o'clock) the bagel shop is closed. We arrange her pillow and wheel her up the ramp from the parking lot to the sidewalk. Then it's past the pet grooming store where the groomer, it seems, gets bitten all the time. (I don't remember how I got to talking to him one day, but I do remember how he shrugged off this particular occupational hazard. "You get used to it," he said. *Xíguàn le,* in other words—my father would have approved.) We pass a deli, navigate some concrete pillars, and shoulder open the glass door, propping it ajar. By the time we are situated at a wheelchair-accessible table, my mother is no longer a person who seeks approval but one who grants or withholds it.

"Okay, Mom?" I say.

"Okay," she says diffidently.

Nothing else.

Eldercare, American style. David and I start to wipe the table down with the hand wipes we've brought. A waitress appears and wipes the table down again with an old cloth—meaning well, but hasn't she just spread germs all over the table? When she turns her back, we surreptitiously wipe the table once more.

"Okay, Mom?" I say again.

She says nothing. If she is curious about what we're doing, she doesn't ask.

Dave and I wipe her hands with a clean wipe, then split a wipe for us to share. On the drive down, we had learned from our phones that whatever is going on, there are already shortages of hand wipes. We don't want to use two when one is enough.

It's so early in the Covid crisis that the subject of masks has yet to come up. No one knows how the mystery virus spreads; neither are we sure how concerned to be. On the one hand, a lawyer in nearby New Rochelle has infected the better part of his synagogue. On the other, the total number of cases in the state is under one hundred. To reassure people that it's safe, New York City mayor Bill de Blasio has been filmed riding the subway. So is it paranoid to watch with trepidation as a curly-haired child plays around the legs of his mother's chair, then circles through the dining room, giggling and playing peekaboo and touching everything? We're not sure.

My mother pores over the menu, holding it so close to her face she could eat it. With the most animation she has shown so far, she chooses the dandan noodles. Though America has come a long way since the days when few outside our family seemed to eat things like dandan noodles or tofu (*dôu vu,* as we called it in Shanghainese), it's still exciting to see a quasi-Chinese dish in a mainstream restaurant. Yes, it will be Americanized, but still. My mother orders the noodles, as do I, although as soon as they arrive, I realize that they have too much salt for her. How can I not have anticipated this? I am kicking myself, although luckily, they seem to be ramen from a package—not too appealing. And the pork is tough as jerky—far too tough for someone with false teeth to "bite," as she puts it. She samples the dish more than she eats it per se.

I'm relieved.

The last time I made her dandan noodles myself, she was delighted, maybe because I used lots of what we call *là yu* in Shanghainese—chili oil—to make up for the lack of salt; she has always loved spicy food. "I like that," she told me. "That's taste real good." And, "It's good you can make Chinese food, so anytime I want Chinese food I can have it." That phrase "anytime I want Chinese food" is, like "They know us there," important to her; years after she has had to deal with scarcity in any form, the availability of food still registers. I promise her I will bring her some more noodles the next time we come down. In the meanwhile, what a treat to be out and about and eating with chopsticks.

"Chopsticks! In an American restaurant! Isn't that amazing?" I say.

She nods.

"We never could have imagined such a thing when I was growing up."

"At that time, very few Chinese people," she says.

"We had to go to Chinatown for Chinese food."

She doesn't disagree.

"Or Hartsdale. Remember when that Japanese grocery opened?"

She bows her head a little, a quick down and up, remembering.

"Yes, they were always bowing."

"Japanese people."

She will never forgive the Japanese for their occupation of Shanghai. But her voice is neutral, as if she's forgotten why she hated them.

"Yes, they were Japanese people. But the store had all kinds of things," I say.

"Japanese food."

"They had some Chinese stuff, too. Remember? Red bean paste. Ginger. Big bags of rice."

She doesn't respond. Maybe it's too much to have to concede that the hated Japanese were rice-eaters like us.

"Of course, this isn't really Chinese food," I say.

"Chop suey," she agrees—meaning that it is American food, really.

"Still," I say. *"Hái kěyǐ."* Meaning, It'll do.

"Okay," she says.

The food is good enough for her to ask for a doggy bag. But the salt—we shake our heads. No. Sorry. No doggy bag.

She's disappointed. All the same, she got out of the house; she liked the food; she had fun. Everyone is happy. But if I had the idea that she would ask how we were, or what the children were up to, or even pretend to be interested should I volunteer something about, say, how things were going with Paloma's debating or Luke's research—it is like hoping a rock will blow out to sea.

Still, I try to engage her because this is what the daughter of a withholding mother does: she rejects rejection. It is unhealthy to try and try and try, I know—to refuse to accept reality—although, I will say, it seems to have proven great training for a writer. Indeed, my entire childhood was a master class in perseverance. If I had a patron saint, it would be Saint Jude, the patron saint of lost causes.

"So, Paloma's last debate tournament was canceled," I say. "Because of the virus. It was supposed to be in California."

Silence.

"She had to go to a tournament at Tufts instead."

Silence.

"But guess what? She and her partner won. That puts them in first place in the country."

Silence.

"And they might very well stay there because there probably won't be any more tournaments. Because of the virus. It's a big deal."

Silence.

In the past, my mother has refused to react to the news that we had bought a house, that David had changed jobs, that Paloma was going to Thailand, or that black sesame had become a flavor of ice cream. Now she gives a half-hearted nod to the news that Luke has a paper in *Nature Genetics*—"a single-author paper, Mom!" Neither is she much interested to hear how my new novel is doing.

"It's about baseball, Mom. Remember, I told you? It's called *The Resisters*."

"What do you know about baseball?" she says. "I think I should write a book."

With my siblings, she is more engaged. And if someone were to get out a camera, she would instantly become the adorable grandma everyone hearts on Facebook, holding my book up with a look of pride and delight. I've always felt of two minds about the pictures, which are both her and not her—not so much pictures of the mother I have as of the mother I wish I had and, maddeningly, of the mother she seems to know she should be. It's as if there were some lock to her, to which, if I only knew where to look, there is a key. And if I could find it, there would be the mother in the picture, my real mother, freed from her enchanted prison and come back to call me "little stinker."

There is no lock and key. But even today, I wonder: Had she known how little time she had left, would she have acted differently? How about if she read something in which she saw herself? How about if she read this book? Am I writing this trying to reach her even after her death?

You want me to talk to you, and now I am talk to you, she says.
Thanks, Ma, I say.
Of course, I am dead. I am not really talk to you.
I know, Ma. I know. Believe me, I know.

Luke thought her patterns so ingrained she could no sooner break them than leap up from her wheelchair and go jogging out of the restaurant, stopping for a pickup game of basketball. But sitting with her now, it's hard to accept. If nothing else, to say that her grandchildren do so much of which any normal grandmother would be proud is an understatement. They are the sort of children for whom the word "kvell" was coined. And why not kvell? Why does my mother deny herself the pleasure?

In any case, there she is, withholding, and there I am, as always, trying to milk a rock, as I think of it. There's a ball game on the bar TV in the corner. That kid who was touching everything has finally been picked up, kicking, and taken home. A busboy is wiping down more tables.

In the car, my mother is silent. We give the car some gas to make it up the driveway, then unload the wheelchair from the trunk. The concrete sides of the garage are padded with a kind of carpet wainscotting—my father's doing, back when he was alive. It's a small garage; without the carpet, the car doors were bound to knock against the walls. And this was just the sort of practical improvement he had liked to make: to the garage at our Scarsdale house, for example, he added a kind of half-height concrete nose, into which the hoods of the behemoth station wagons we were then driving could slide. He also hung a tennis ball from the ceiling to aid the driver in parking. When your windshield touched the ball, you were in the right spot and could shut off the engine.

"I think I'm very good for someone my age," my mother says.

And for the umpteenth time I agree, because the one thing I do not want to be is withholding like her. Indeed, it's become one of the principles of my life: just as I do not mother as I was mothered, I try to always give when I can, as much as I can.

"You're doing great," I say. Adding, later, as I leave, "I love you, Mom."

She does not say "I love you" back; she never has. But she smiles in response—suggesting that this was what she wanted all along? Not to have to hear about me and my children but to receive—was it love, approval, face? Obeisance? Perhaps she just wanted me to follow her script. Whatever it is, Totoro-shaped as she is, she can have it. Somehow, after all—thanks to the love of my father, my husband, my children, and my friends, as well as, I am sure, to the power of reading and writing—I have thrived; she has hurt but not destroyed me. Indeed, she has perhaps fueled me. In *The Wound and the Bow,* the critic Edmund Wilson tells the story of the Greek warrior Philoctetes, who was abandoned by his compatriots because of the stink of a festering snakebite on his heel but who, as the only one who could wield the bow of Heracles, was needed to win the Trojan War. Philoctetes is the prototypical artist, Wilson said—wounded and shunned but graced with special powers. I don't know that I have any special powers, but I must credit my mother for biting my heel.

"You're very good for someone your age," I say again, unprompted, and she smiles again, with real brightness. She's won.

Last October, when I posted a birthday photo of her on Facebook, it received hundreds of likes. In the picture, she is looking delightedly at the candles, clapping her hands with a childishness that is all too genuine; she has been regressing in any number of ways. When she isn't insisting, "I'm think I'm very good for someone my age," she is asking questions like, "You know who likes that?" and answering, "Me!" In the grocery store, she'll reach for potato chips or Worcestershire sauce—grabbing a bag or a bottle from her wheelchair, and then hugging it to her body with both arms. "I want it. It tastes good," she'll say. And if I wrest the contraband away, saying, "It has way too much salt, Mom," she'll protest, "But I want it! I like that!" adding, "You bad bad girl! You won't let me have it!"

We still glimpse my mother's adult side sometimes. The day that, as the de facto entertainment committee, David and I took her to the Katonah Museum of Art, she asked that we turn her wheelchair so that she could see the artwork and, as difficult as it was for her, read—or was the word "tackle"?—every word of the signage. She concentrated fiercely, her gazed locked on the text, in part because her early reading was of course in Chinese and you really do have to look hard at the characters, especially when the type is small, to discriminate between them. (My mother grew up, too, not on the new, simplified characters introduced by the Communists but the traditional, complicated characters still used today in Taiwan.) But also, she just liked to read. She didn't have favorite books and, averse as she was to public spaces, never went to the library. If I asked her what she thought of, say, Helen Zia's *Last Boat Out of Shanghai,* she might pronounce it very interesting and even assert that she was going to read it again. But she never explained why or discussed any part of it with me or anyone else. Sometimes I thought it might hurt her to talk about something she had once loved, but I didn't know for sure.

She said almost nothing, either, about anything I'd written.

I did say, when I read Typical American, "Ah! Very good. And it's not about anyone!" she says now.

Meaning that you were glad it wasn't about you, I say.

That's right. I think I should write a book, she says.

You used to say that, I say, and I tried to get you to. Do you remember? I always used to say, It's not too late. But I guess now that you're dead, it is.

Of course it's too late, she says. What do you think?

Aside from the books I gave her—and I do think I was her only source of books besides her labor-camp-survivor sister who sent titles like *Heaven Is for Real*—she mostly read the newspaper. Still, reading was something she did for no reason except that she felt like it, and in the Katonah museum, as my mother trained what was left of her attention on the signage, it was like watching an intense beam of sun flash out from behind a heavy bank of clouds. Between the signs, though, her baby voice returned as she pronounced, "I like this one" or "I don't like that." It was sad.

Or was it? Her favorite birthday present was a mechanical stuffed dog that bobbed up and down, barking, *Ruff, ruff, ruff, ruff!* Did she realize it was a child's toy? And did that matter when it made her laugh and laugh and laugh?

I know from the trunk full of dresses she brought to the United States how slim she once was; her dresses fit Paloma when she was in high school. But the mother of my childhood would eat a whole bag of potato chips at a sitting and never went for so much as a walk. She could not bike; she could not swim; she had never touched her toes and had never broken a sweat. In a way, this made for a certain body positivity. I know so many women whose mothers obsessed about their weight; even in her dementia, one mused from her nursing home wheelchair that she "had to get her sex on." And I know how these attitudes haunted my friends. I know how prone they were to seeing someone else when they looked in the mirror—a ghostly overlay with the figure they could have if only they walked more, ate less, lifted weights, got on that bike, took the stairs instead of the elevator. My mother never had any such thoughts. Her most physically demanding activity was carrying her purse. (She was never without her purse.) Yet unlike my father, she mostly enjoyed preternaturally good health. Until her late eighties, she had been hospitalized just five times, for the births of her five children.

Suddenly, though, there was crisis upon crisis, one of which left her unable to breathe. The doctors plainly felt that at age ninety-two she should not be intubated, but Reuben was firm. "Intubate her," he said.

And then there she was, unconscious. For all of our issues—my poor mother. Tubes and tubes, and that mask taped to her face, and so many machines. And on top of it all, her nails were chipped and broken. I knew how she would hate those ragged nails. So though my brothers said we were not allowed to bring scissors into the hospital, I did anyway. I cut and filed her nails, and then I did another thing. I brought in hand cream and rubbed it everywhere I could, including on her tummy. I did this partly because I knew how dry my own skin got and could see how dry and tight hers had become, but also because I knew how soft that skin was: terrible as our relationship was, I will always miss her tummy, against which she must have held me for many months before, little by little, she disowned me. Did she maybe understand how to mother an infant, if not a growing daughter, from Nai-ma, who had nursed her for so long?

Astonishingly, the doctors did get her breathing tube out, thanks to my doctor sister, Lisa, who held my mother's hand and said, "It's going to hurt, but you have to hold my hand and just lie still." And so she did. Her quality of life wasn't great afterward, and I often wondered if she would have preferred to have died.

But no matter. When she was still in the hospital but awake, I told her that I had put cream on her tummy, and she smiled. "When are you coming back?" she asked. And how I wished then that I had a mother who didn't just love me when I was taking care of her. But I didn't.

As they had done to take care of my father, my brothers teamed up. I can still hear my father's approving voice: *Take turn!* It is a kind of Chinese ideal—all the boys working together. That meant not only that they took my mother out to lunch every day but that Reuben sat with her on most days, working from the TV room of her house. Sean took her to Mass on Sundays and supplied crucial backup; Shane administered her shots, which went in her belly. Around this they had a little routine.

"Time for your shot, Monkey," he would say.

"I'm not a monkey!" she would protest.

"I'm going to murderize you!"

"Ouch!"

"How can you say ouch when I haven't poked the needle in yet?"

At this, my mother would laugh, and Shane would, quick, poke the needle in.

The shots were for an anticoagulant called Lovenox—a lovely name with which a poet could do a lot. *Love knocks / it tiptoes / seeks a back door if barred from the front /...* They left bruises on her belly, but she needed them as she had a blood clot in her leg and a risk of clots in her lungs. And those weren't her only problems. The autoimmune disease that produced that horrible blue-black blotching—that bullous pemphigoid—meant that she was on prednisone, which meant that she was immunosuppressed. In addition, she had sleep apnea and attendant carbon dioxide buildup, as well as asthma. She gasped for air whenever she was moved—from the car to the house, from one room to another, from one chair to another. I can still see her, head back, panting, blowing the air out with her eyes closed. She had to will herself to exhale, exhale, exhale.

She could no longer reliably identify her grandchildren by

name. She did mostly know that a given child was her grandchild, and to which of her children the grandchild belonged, but not always. She no longer necessarily knew everyone's Chinese zodiac sign, either, and was greatly confused about birthdays, engagements, and holidays.

It was extraordinary, therefore, for her to one day suddenly start reciting in Chinese. Shane taped her.

"I have no idea what she was saying," he said, sending the video around to everyone. "But I think it was a poem and that she only remembered part of it. She doesn't remember the rest." If he found it heartbreaking that she was ninety-five and surrounded by people who spoke only English, he didn't say so.

I couldn't understand her any better than anyone else, especially since, though the words were in Mandarin, she recited them with a pronounced Shanghainese accent. Luckily, though, I had a Chinese art curator friend to whom I could send the tape. My mother, this friend said, was reciting lines from a Tang dynasty Zhang Ji poem called *"Night Mooring at Maple Bridge."* The lines were:

> *Yuèluò wūtí shuāng mǎntiān*
> *Jiāngfēng yúhuǒ duì chóumián*

Meaning,

> Falling moon, calling crows, a frost-filled sky,
> River maples, and fishing lights meet my despairing sleep.

My despairing sleep.

Just a few days earlier, over Thanksgiving, my brothers had managed to get my mother up to Boston for the family meal. This had involved her staying in a hotel, and my brother Shane sharing a suite with her. She was up all night, he reported, crying out, "Help me! Help me!" and, even more disturbingly, "I want to die" and "I don't want to live."

A despairing sleep, indeed.

How typically Chinese, to express her distress through poetry. In China, anyone in her family would have understood her. And yet who now understood what she was trying to say?

My poor mother.

I practiced a few times and made a tape of the complete poem. In the video, my Chinese is careful and slow; I read it conscious of every tone mark, as well as of the constant criticism my mother had always directed toward my Chinese. I know that every syllable can be faulted. But because my mother was an old woman surrounded by English-speakers, and because I hoped it would cheer her up, I posted the tape to an electronic picture frame I had gotten her—a device called Skylight to which family members could add pictures remotely, and which she could view easily.

No response.

It wasn't until New Year's, when I had a chance to visit, that I discovered why she had not responded. The volume was so low, she could not hear it. I turned it up. For a moment, she did not seem to register what she was hearing. Then her hands began to move in sync with the old rhythms; it was easy to imagine her tutor moving his hands, and his young pupil imitating him. At the end, she smiled and said, "Very good."

Why had she withheld those words until she was ninety-five and I almost sixty-five?

We played the tape a few more times. Now when she heard it on the Skylight, it seemed plenty loud enough—maybe because she understood what it was.

"Very good," she said. "Very good. Very good. Very good."

She beamed.

Did she remember reciting the poem in the hotel, or the despairing sleep that had brought the words back? It did not seem so. Since she seemed to like the poem, though, I pulled up some others on my computer. Despite my efforts to zoom in on them, the Chinese characters were dauntingly small; anyone would have strained to read them. But my mother uncomplainingly worked at making them out. She did not seem to understand that I just wanted her to enjoy the poems and that I already knew what they said. Instead, she automatically translated them—reminding me that for all the problems in our relationship, we did have this pattern. How many times had I brought her this or that piece of writing and asked what it said? And always she answered—proud of how good a translator she was. Now I brought up a very famous poem by a contemporary of Zhang Ji's, Li Bai.

> *That moonlight in front of my bed*
> *I take to be frost on the ground.*
> *Looking up, I see a bright moon—*
> *Looking down, I just miss home.*

She nodded, as I had expected she would. The poem is as well-known in China as Robert Frost's "The Road Not Taken" is in America, after all. Every Chinese child knows it.

I tried a poem by another contemporary of Zhang Ji's, Li Shen:

> *A single sprig of millet sown in the spring*
> *Becomes ten thousand sprigs come fall.*
> *No land is wasted anywhere.*
> *Yet still the farmers starve!—*
> *Hoeing their crops at noon,*
> *Their sweat drips to the soil.*
> *Who sees that there in the bowl,*
> *Every last grain comes of hardship?*

"*Lì lì jiē xīnkǔ,*" she exclaimed, her face lighting up—reciting in such an enthusiastic, childlike voice, I can instantly see her, a tiny girl on my grandfather's lap. *Lì lì jiē xīnkǔ.* Then she again asked, as she had in the hospital after I put cream on her tummy, "When are you coming back?"

Why had we not spent the years reading poetry together? Why did she reject the daughter who liked to read the way she did—the daughter who had understood what she was saying with the Zhang Ji poem, and who understood, too, how important it was to the Chinese that people appreciate the hardship of others? I had to cry.

"You are the most Chinese of the children," she said—something she'd told me before.

"Nǎli, nǎli," I said—something I'd said before, too, meaning, Where? Where? It's a standard way of declining praise

"Sean, Shane, what is Chinese besides their face?" she went on.

"Ma."

"It's true," she insisted. "There is nothing Chinese about them."

"Ma," I said. "The boys come to see you every single day. Do you think all sons in America do that?"

Still, she went on. "Lisa does not even cook Chinese food."

"That's because of Lena's allergies." (Lisa's daughter, Lena, had numerous allergies, including to soy.) "And, Ma, she has taken unbelievable care of you. You would not be alive today if it weren't for Lisa."

"You think Sean's wife can cook Chinese?" she continued.

"Come on, Ma. Stop it. Stop it."

That was the mother I knew best—the one who had to say of Paloma at what would turn out to be our last Thanksgiving together, "She's too pretty to be your daughter." I am reminded of a comment my brother Sean once made about her: "She's mean."

Still, I next returned to Chappaqua with a book of large-type Chinese poems. Maybe it wasn't too late to have the relationship she and I should have had all along? But this time, when I tried to read the poems with her, she looked bored.

Where was the mother I could have had?

Now it was my turn to ask: When are you coming back? And, after a moment, Are you? Are you coming back? Where are you? Who took you away?

Not long after the March outing to Village Social, I stop in Westchester to see my mother once again. New York State has not yet announced a lockdown, but as Paloma and her college classmates have been sent home for spring break and told not to return, she, David, and I are headed down to Danbury, Connecticut, to adopt a shelter kitty. Poor Paloma, stuck with just her parents for who knows how long, after all. She will be happier with a companion.

The good news is that we are planning to hunker down in Vermont, one of the safest places in the country. Also, though many people have been moved to adopt an animal—so many that the shelters are emptying—we have miraculously managed to be matched with a four-month-old hypoallergenic Russian blue kitten. She has come north from Louisiana via Georgia and is ready for pickup; we rush to go claim her before someone else does. Should we really stop on the way in nearby Westchester, a by-now-established hot spot? Paloma asks.

"Yes," I say.

"Why?"

"Because it could be the last time we see Abu alive," I say.

My mother's breathing, her weakness. It doesn't seem possible that she could be sleeping even more than she was when we saw her two weeks ago, but she is. My brothers say she can sleep until five o'clock in the afternoon.

If my mother is surprised that we have dropped in without notice, she is even more surprised that we are wearing blue paper face masks and green plastic painter's gloves.

"Why are you wearing masks?" she asks.

"Because of the virus!" we shout.

The masks are making it even harder for her to hear us than usual.

"Why are you wearing masks?"

"Because of the virus!"

"Why are you wearing masks?"

There is a sign on the kitchen door reading "Wash Your Hands!" in red marker. Grace and Melanie have told her what is going on. But my mother retains less and less. Now she suddenly asks me what "spam" is. She says she heard the word on TV and knew it couldn't be the stuff in cans.

"It's like junk mail, only on the computer," I say. "You know how on the computer, people get messages? Email?"

She nods.

"Spam is like junk mail in your email."

She nods again. It is touching to see her still working on new vocabulary. Though—does she get it?

"Spam!" she says loudly, as if we are the ones who cannot hear.

I sigh. "I brought you some dandan noodles," I say. "They're in the fridge."

"Dandan noodles! Oh! I like that!" she says in her child's voice, placing the emphasis on "that."

"Gish made them for you," says David. "They're better than the ones at Village Social."

She has no idea what he's talking about.

"Do you remember the noodles at Village Social?" I say. "That new restaurant in Mount Kisco? Do you remember how salty they were?"

She looks blank.

"We had dandan noodles at Village Social just a couple of weeks ago," says David.

"Dandan noodles! Oh! I like that!" she says again.

Melanie uses the walker to guide her to the bathroom. Though the toilet seat has been raised, she still needs help. Then it is back into the wheelchair and over to the dining room table.

"The dandan noodles are in the fridge," I say again. "The ones I made."

"Dandan noodles! Oh! I like that!" she says.

"They're in the fridge! We love you!"

"We love you!" Paloma echoes.

"Why are you wearing masks?" my mother asks again.

"Because of the virus!"

"Why are you wearing masks?"

I give her a kiss even though it is, like the visit, inadvisable, and shout again that I love her as I pass the dining room table with its many medicine bottles and inhalers and alcohol wipes—this being what happens to tabletops in old age, it seems. They let themselves go and become catch-alls.

"Bye, Mom! I love you!"

How easily I can say "I love you" to friends, to David, to the kids. To say it to my mother, though, is hard. Maxine Hong Kingston has said that she, too, had trouble saying "I love you" to her mother. But when her mother was dying, she did manage, with her sisters, to say, "We love you"; her trouble was with the "I." My trouble is different. It's more that it seems somehow artificial to say "I love you"—American, I guess.

Still, I say it. "I love you!"

"Bye, Abu!"

"Bye, Mom!"

"Why are you wearing masks?"

Out on the driveway, there is bright light and spring air, but Paloma and David and I are sad.

The enormity of the pandemic is brought home by the words of Queen Elizabeth II, whose coronation my mother watched on TV so many years ago. Addressing the Brits in a rare broadcast, she likens our times to World War II:

> It reminds me of the very first broadcast I made, in 1940, helped by my sister. We, as children, spoke from here at Windsor to children who had been evacuated from their homes and sent away for their own safety. Today, once again, many will feel a painful sense of separation from their loved ones. But now, as then, we know, deep down, that it is the right thing to do....

She finishes:

> We should take comfort that while we may have more still to endure, better days will return. We will be with our friends again; we will be with our families again; we will meet again.

Her words are a comfort. But of course, not all of us will meet again, and not all of us will be with our families again.

A few days later, there is a family Zoom. Zooming is a new thing many of us have heard about but not yet tried; my niece and her boyfriend, stuck in quarantine in her bedroom, have organized this. Shane isn't sure my mother can join us, but she makes it in the end, sharing a square with Sean. By coincidence, she appears on our screen in the middle square, with all of us surrounding her—her five children, our spouses, every one of her grandchildren, and several of her grandchildren's significant others. She is not so much delighted, though, as shocked and bewildered. To see us all there! On the computer! Talking and waving! How can it be? The whole family! In truth, we are wowed, too. The technology! We shake our heads.

She does not have the energy to stay on long and after a few minutes waves goodbye. And so we do, too. Bye, Mom! Bye, Abu! Bye! Bye! She is waving; everyone is waving. "Quick, take a screenshot," says someone; my niece even has the wits to take a video. And so it is that by pure good luck, we have a record of our whole family, reunited one last time, saying goodbye.

That night, my mother develops a cough. Her aides have been careful. They have washed their hands constantly. None of them is sick.

But though my brothers have been careful, too, all three of them now have a cough, fever, and exhaustion. The good news is that Sean and Shane are getting better already. The bad news: of all people, Reuben the family athlete who has traipsed up and down so many Himalayan peaks is now so weak he can barely cross his apartment. And even more worrying is my mother. My brothers have been around her so much, after all. ("Time for your shot, Monkey." "I'm not a monkey!") Up until now, we had not thought much about the phrase "underlying conditions." But now all we can think is, her underlying conditions.

She has given death the slip before. Once, as last rites were being performed over her nonresponsive body, the priest wound up his "In the name of the Father, and the Son, and the Holy Ghost," only to discover that like everyone else in the room, my mother was making the sign of the cross. Another time, she opened her eyes to see a crowd gathered around her bed and asked, "Am I dead?" Then there was the time that as she lay unresponsive yet once again, Reuben leaned over her and said, "Mom. The Yankees are in a slump. The Red Sox are eating their lunch"—whereupon her eyelids fluttered and she suddenly opened her eyes. "That Aaron Boone should be fired," she said, without missing a beat. (Aaron Boone was the manager of the Yankees.)

This time, though, she cannot be roused. Her oxygen levels are dangerously low; she coughs and sleeps, coughs and sleeps. No apparent fever, but any fever she had would likely be suppressed by her prednisone; the thermometer tells us nothing. We call in hospice, grateful that we can get hospice to come. So many people are sick, after all. We are lucky. My mother's aides, too, mercifully agree to keep working.

I want to have her tested for Covid. Tests are hardly ubiquitous, but thanks to friends in Cambridge, we can perhaps procure one, drive it down to Chappaqua, test her, and drive the kit back up to the lab. I want the test done so that my mother's last moments are not any more confused and upsetting than they need to be; I want us to be able to touch her. I do not want us encased in protective clothing. Lisa, though, points out that the test involves shoving a swab very far up your nasal passage, and that virus is sprayed everywhere in the process. What's more, since the test is only 70 percent accurate, it can establish a definitive positive but not a definitive negative. And, as I email a friend:

> Should she test positive, she will not be put on a ventilator anyway. So no testing. Yes, things could still turn around. But she's immunosuppressed, which is not good, and an O_2 sat level in the low 80s is pretty low. Hospice has brought an oxygen concentrator. And her doctor has put in an order for morphine. That's in case her lungs fill up with fluid and she starts to struggle to breathe. So she doesn't panic. In case she basically begins to drown.

I know what morphine is like. David's mother was given morphine as she was dying, and I well remember not only the chips of ice we placed under her tongue because her mouth got so dry but also how out of it she was, and how distressing it was to see her that way. David and I organize for another trip down to Chappaqua.

The morphine is never administered. On April 3, my mother wakes long enough to ask, "Where's Reuben?" The number one son, home sick with Covid, is still the child who matters most. Sean drives down to the city to pick him up. He drives Reuben north to Chappaqua to see her. Then he drives Reuben back home.

. . .

It is April 4, less than a week after the cough began. Melanie comes in to see my mother at seven or eight in the morning. She gives her a little water and some oxygen. My mother is lethargic but responsive. A little later, Melanie hears over the baby monitor that my mother has stopped snoring. She goes in to investigate and, indeed, my mother has stopped snoring.

I don't hear the news until eleven thirty. Sean sent a text at nine thirty, it seems, but I didn't get it; with no cell service in Vermont, I receive only iPhone-to-iPhone texts. How has Sean missed this? Never mind. I am sitting down to take another look at an op-ed I am coauthoring when Shane texts to ask if I am okay. And should he tell my mother's sisters in China the news?

News? I text back. I know, of course. I know, and yet I can't breathe. Did Mom die? I write.

Yes. You didn't know?

No, I didn't know.

So all the time I was working, she was already dead. It seems impossible that that should be the case—as if while my back was turned, an entire continent slid quietly into the ocean. How could that be? How could she be gone?

And gone where? I have been asking that question often as of late—about my father, about pets, about friends. Now it is time to ask it about my mother. Gone where? Where did she go?

At least she was at home. At least she was in her own bed. At least she did not suffer. At least she was never put on a ventilator. At least the aide who found her was Melanie—Melanie whom my mother used to call "my favorite girl," Melanie who my mother had said really cared and wasn't just doing a job. In truth, all the aides were great—Grace and Mary, too. But my mother played favorites to the end, and Melanie was her favorite.

At least the whole family got to say goodbye on Zoom. At least David and Paloma and I got to say goodbye in person. At least I got to bring her one last container of dandan noodles.

At least I knew hours after her death and not weeks, as she did after my grandmother's death.

At least I told her I loved her.

At least, at least, at least.

Still, I can't help but think of my mother-in-law's death, and how my sister-in-law had climbed into bed with her and held her. I have a Chinese friend who slept with her mean grandmother as she lay dying in a hospital; and Billy Lee, son of my father's old classmate Francis Lee, slept with him all through his long illness before he died. "To keep him from falling out of bed," Billy said. How my mother would have loved for one of us to have done that. In our family, no one even moved in with her. The boys did see her every day. Still, it must have been hard to live by herself.

She certainly would not have wanted to die alone; she certainly would have wanted to die surrounded by family, like my father. I wish I had been there to wash her face as she had washed his; I wish I had been there to say, Go easy, go easy. I wish I'd been there to tell her she didn't have to worry about us kids anymore. My poor mother, that she did not have herself to help her pass away.

I wish I had been there to tell her she did a good job, although I was also glad not to have had to make myself do that. I would have. But I was glad not to have been hurt one last time, as she failed to do the one thing I wanted more than anything in the world for her to do, namely to say, just once, that she was sorry.

Who washed my mother's body? I washed David's mother's body and was glad to do it. It is terrible to think of a stranger touching my mother—of a stranger touching her soft tummy. I hope it was someone kind. I hope that whoever it was paused for a moment and thought, What soft skin. I hope no one used bleach.

The logistics of death, the many logistics. The pronouncing her dead, the removal of her body, the arrangement for some sort of sendoff, some sort of ritual. Because of the pandemic, there can be no church funeral; even a graveside service is a question mark. Some cemeteries have suspended all services. Families are being sent videotapes of the burials.

"Should we wait until we can have a real funeral? We don't have to get her into the ground right away," says Shane, adding, "We're not Jewish."

But the morgues are full, so we do. We do have to get her into the ground.

I dig up my grandfather's name for the death certificate. My grandmother's name, too. My siblings do not know either name. They don't even all know my mother's name in Chinese. Loo Shu-hsin, I tell them. They do not realize that she died on Qingming Festival, the Chinese grave-sweeping holiday.

So many reminders that she came from far, far away.

Some notes I took:

You can't imagine what a comfort Paloma has been, Mom, bringing first mocha, then strawberries and chocolate ganache as I talk to Lisa. My friend Martha calls immediately. Other friends, too: Nancy. Maryann. And, of course, Luke calls. More chocolate. Paloma and David sit with me.

We go for a bike ride, our first of the season. The snow is starting to melt, but the lake is still frozen and our road is all mud and ruts. David loads the bikes on the bike rack so we can start our ride on the paved road near the ballfield. We ride down to Willeys—that's the general store. You and Dad have been there many times. I am so exhausted I can barely sit straight on my bike. Still, I struggle up the hill to Highland Lodge, where we get off our bikes and start the walk to the beach. We do not get far—the snow. Even Paloma, who ventured on a bit farther without us, has to turn back thanks to the slush. She has always been an adventurer. On the little walk we took the other day, she climbed into a ladderless tree house, shimmying up the tree trunk. I don't think you ever knew how she loved to climb trees when she was little, but she did—I'm glad she never fell out of one.

We tromp back the long way, winding our way from house to house, and across the empty field with the big rock Paloma loved to play on as a girl. It's a little like the rock I used to like to play on, back in Yonkers, when I was a child. I don't know if you ever knew about that rock. We called it Elephant Rock. Much mush. But as we get back on our bikes, the sky is as clear as a plate.

We talk. Why you were the way you were. Why people—even if they know they are going to die—don't change. Why you didn't change. It is a mystery—a mystery a little like the rescue kitten we picked up in Danbury after we stopped in to see you. Her name is Natasha—three and half pounds and, it turns out, feral. We did not know what that meant before. But now we know. Shouldn't she be wired for survival? Instead, she hisses at the hand that feeds her, hisses and hisses. It is a mystery.

By day, I write notes. By night, I talk to you.

You were a mystery, Ma.
Why, why, why, were you the way you were?
Why?
If I write about you, if I write to you, will I understand you better?

The *Scarsdale Inquirer* runs pages and pages of obituaries. It's the most they've ever run in the history of the paper. Sean, who volunteers with the Chappaqua ambulance corps, says they usually get one or two calls a night but last night got seven. There are so many bodies that the local funeral home has had to pull the pews out of their chapel to make room for them all. The bodies are in body bags, piled up as if fair Westchester is at war.

How lucky that the cemetery where we buried my father will allow a graveside service. Ten people maximum, but they will allow it. And the funeral home can arrange a viewing for my mother, with an open casket. It's not a funeral, but it's something.

We are grateful.

One happy development: after a solid two weeks of trying to coax our skittish kitten first out of her carrier and then out from under the kitchen island, Paloma has finally gotten Natasha to allow herself to be petted. First on her rump and then on her back, and then between her ears. And then there it is—her first purr! Just when it seemed she only knew how to hiss, she is kneading her paws with pleasure.

David and I are trying to produce a pair of ceremonial white ribbons like the ones my mother made for my father. Shane has pictures of what she did, and now that I am examining them, I am astonished by her care. All those complicated characters, each written and lined up so perfectly—how did she do it? I wish I'd been there to watch her. And how is it that we were at such loggerheads all these years, when she had just one child who would even think to make ribbons for her?

I once again enlist the help of my art curator friend. I shouldn't, of course, reuse the part of the inscription about an inseparable couple or the part in which she says goodbye to a spouse of more than sixty years, with whom she has lived through thick and thin. My friend suggests something beautiful, though: *We will not see you on the road ahead, but in our dreams, we may hear you call.* That with my mother's name and *qiān gǔ*—for all eternity—will go on one ribbon. The other will read *"Painfully lost our mother,"* followed by our surname and the generation name, Qìng, that was given to my three brothers. (This "Qìng" was drawn from a couplet granted to the Jen side of the family by the emperor and used ever since to keep the generations straight. In accordance with *Guó ēn jiā qìng / Rén shòu nián fēng*—meaning, May the emperor grant us favor and the family celebrate / May everyone live long and the years be prosperous—every male in my father's generation had "Ēn" in his name, and every male in mine has "Qìng.") Now below the "Qìng" I will write my brothers' given names on the ribbon, from right to left—the traditional way. And below their names will come my name, Bìlián, to the right—and Lisa's, Lìshā, to the left. (Since girls do not matter to the family lineage, we were not given generational names.) Then will come *"All the family and grandchildren grieving."*

How to transfer the words to ribbons, given that all the stores are closed and I have no ribbon? Happily, an email to some friends instantly yields offers to provide material or even to sew a sash. Though it is Passover, after the seder one of the friends has a bag for David to pick up.

What would your life have been like had you had friends you could call on, Mom? I say. What if Marnie Mulligan hadn't moved away? What if you could have stayed friends for life? Imagine.

The fabric is beautiful—material for a wedding veil, it seems. David holds the fabric taut so I can cut it into strips. We mark out squares for the characters onto graph paper, copy the characters in the squares, then trace the characters from the graph paper onto the ribbons. The result is a poor imitation of my mother's ribbons. My rendering of even simplified characters is graceless and childish, and I accidentally leave out the characters for *"Painfully lost our mother."* I'd love to do the ribbons over.

But it's past midnight, and we have a long day ahead tomorrow. I am touched that Paloma has taken careful note of "how the ribbons should look like," as my mother would say.

"Because otherwise, how will I know how to make ribbons for you?" she says.

Masks, hand sanitizer, wipes, gloves, and a change of clothes for after the ceremony. We figure we can toss the clothes we're wearing in the back of the car; any virus on them should degrade in a couple of days. No time for breakfast. For car snacks, we have sugar-free brownies that Paloma has made for us, wrapped in tinfoil; because of the pandemic, we do not want to have to stop for food. Not wanting to have to stop and go to the bathroom, either, we drink as little as possible. Unfortunately, we do have to stop for gas. David is careful as he fills up the tank; he uses plastic gloves, then throws them out. Then comes hand sanitizer. It's raining.

Lisa calls to discuss in what manner we should enter the funeral home. We should go two by two, she thinks, starting with the healthiest of us and proceeding to least healthy. By this logic,

David and I should go first. But should we go in at all? The funeral home has been scrubbed from top to bottom, and my mother has been dead for four days. She is unlikely to be virus-laden. Still, the viewing is indoors. Who knows who has been in the room? Even if you touch nothing and wear a mask, there is a risk. Your clothes. Your hair. Your shoes. We wouldn't worry so much if we weren't planning to return to Vermont, but we simply cannot be the flatlanders who bring Covid to our virus-free corner of the country. We decide not to go in.

We assemble, though, with everyone else in the funeral home parking lot. At least the rain has let up. Because Sean and Shane are recovering from Covid and Reuben is still sick, we keep, at Lisa's urging, not six feet away from one another but twenty-five. It is hard to call us a gathering; a furthering is more like it. We wave and shout across the asphalt through our masks. Many of us are wearing gloves as well. David takes a panorama pic. Like David and me, Reuben wonders if he should view my mother, though his fear is of leaving virus behind him. He is wearing a fancy N95 mask—much sleeker than the hospital-supplied version that Lisa and her husband, Oliver, wear, but never mind. The hospital masks have been tested for leaks and work better than anything we civilians have, especially since medical workers know how to wear them. Reuben keeps pulling his down below his nose.

He looks terrible. He's the most athletic person any of us has ever known, but he walks hunched over, like an old man. As for what he ought to do: should anyone in the funeral home fall ill, we have heard, the whole home will have to be shut down. In the middle of a pandemic. It cannot be. He does not go in.

At least. At least Lisa carries for me, to place in our mother's coffin, Easter lilies on behalf of our aunts and uncles in Shanghai. At least she carries for me, too, some phalaenopsis orchids on behalf of our cousins. And at least she carries for me the white ribbons I made, clumsy characters and all. She emerges saying that my mother looks beautiful. Sean and his wife go next, bearing yet another addition to the casket: a Yankees cap.

Your father, your mother, Nai-ma, your sisters and brothers, Mother Greenough—they're all so far away, I say. They're like something that never happened.
They are, she agrees.

She's answering! I can hear her!

It's as if they were never there, she says.

Following the hearse to the cemetery in our cars, lights flashing, is the most normal part of the day. We cherish it. At the cemetery, we are supposed to stay in our cars until the workers are gone, and so we watch as if at a drive-in as they wheel my mother's coffin to her grave. The cascade of white flowers is glorious; Shane wanted them to be as beautiful as the flowers we would have had at a real funeral, and they are. The gravesite is close enough to the paved drive that we can see them. We are grateful.

We are grateful, too, that although four of my mother's five children are married, Shane is currently single. That means there are nine of us. The priest makes the allowable ten. Of course, here as in the parking lot, we stand so far apart as to look not so much like mourners at a funeral as soccer players covering an infield. It's hard to hear the priest from behind his mask, but I do hear him say how one of the words he's gleaned from talking to us as important to remember about my mother is the word "doctorate."

As in the doctorate she never received?

You know what means ABD? she says now.

He asks for other words to describe her. I volunteer "Yankees fan." I remember aloud, too, how she kept so many Chinese traditions alive, all by herself. In this profoundly foreign country, she kept Chinese New Year going for seventy years. And in many ways, she kept our family Chinese, too.

Stubborn. I might have volunteered the word "stubborn."

Then Lisa supplies, of all words, "loving"—that my mother was loving.

It's hard to hear.

There has not been much weeping. This isn't like my father's death, when we could only have been described as bereft. I myself was completely undone—my precious dad, whom I had loved so much, flaws and all, and I don't think I've ever seen a human cry as hard as Reuben did, for days. Maybe we are just more acquainted with death now. Maybe we realize, too, that Covid is a tsunami my mother was not equipped to outrun. And maybe after decades of parental health crises, our grief is veined with relief. It should be a word, really—"grelief." Also, there's no music; so often it's the music that blows the heart open.

At least the weather held. Indeed, the moment the priest leaves, the rain starts up again—what timing. We take turns standing by the coffin in the drizzle. When it is my turn, I cannot think of what to say. It is quiet.

Then Reuben says, "Something's not right."

And sure enough, the cemetery workers have dug the hole to the right of my father, instead of to the left. Is it due to exhaustion that they made this mistake? Never mind. At least they apologize. At least they say they'll fix it. At least we agree it wasn't right. We are grateful.

A spring nor'easter. It is a long drive from southern Westchester to northern Vermont. There are high winds, with rain and sleet before it all turns to snow around Hanover. Lit by our headlights, the huge flakes seem to come from every direction; it's a snow attack. The dark has never seemed so dark.

A harrowing drive after a harrowing day.

But when we pull up to the house—there's Paloma! There, too, is a snowman she's made and, beside it, a pile of snowballs she's stockpiled. And then, one more thing to be grateful for: that she realizes we are more interested in the wonton soup she's prepared than in a snowball fight. How good it is to have a lovely warm daughter with a shoulder to cry on! Did my mother miss having a daughter like Paloma when her mother died? Of course, she got along better with Lisa than with me, but I don't know how well, really. It could have just been my sister's mood that day, but Lisa did once call her a black hole.

There is talk about a memorial service, but somehow we never get around to it. I suppose it isn't clear who would come when we receive all of five sympathy cards. One is a warm note from Auntie Georgiana's daughter, recalling how her mother "treasured their friendship of so many years." She goes on:

> When we had dinner at your house as children, I recall
> that no one could have milk until after the food was eaten.
> It dawned on me when I was a mother that my daughter
> would not eat food because she had filled up on milk.
> Thank you, Auntie Agnes, for the parenting tip!

I try to recall, as I read this, any parenting tip my mother ever gave me. As for the milk, I wonder if because we were having company, we had been given precious unadulterated milk, rather than the milk mixed with powdered milk we normally drank. That would have been a treat that, yes, she might have worried we would gulp down, or at least that my lactose-tolerant siblings would. Still, I am surprised to hear how my mother was seen, not just by Auntie Georgiana's daughter, but others, too.

Most surprising, for example, is a note from my cousin Eveline, who wrote to say that my mother had essentially been her "mother in the U.S.":

> I want you to know she is the best person I know. When
> I first get married, I will call her for recipes. Even when I
> was dating, she told me not to order too expensive foods
> in the restaurant. I once asked her how much meat I
> needed for a party. She told me three pounds per person! I
> will really miss her.

And, most movingly, there is a note from my godmother, Auntie Marnie, who, though apparently in chemotherapy for the umpteenth time, managed to write:

I always thought your mother was special to God—that He brought her to America for a reason. Maybe it was originally to teach. She was as smart as the dickens, and I'll go to my grave wishing she'd gotten her degree. Dr. Agnes Jen has such a nice ring to it, don't you think? And she promised me she'd finish, you know. She promised! But my mother told me from the get-go that degrees don't do women much good, and I can see today that was not idle talk. Things for your generation are shaping up to be different. Hope they pan out. But I think God saw what my mother saw and changed His plan for yours—that He intended instead for your mother to have plenty of children. Not just three of you but five, and every one a beauty. What a family!

It goes without saying that the raising of you all almost did her in. But now you can call yourselves American, and the day you really grasp what that means, you will thank her, I know. You will thank the Lord, too. But first and foremost, you will see what a beautiful thing she did and honor her with everything you've got. She was an extraordinary woman, your mother, and I'm sure she's happy as a pig in mud up in heaven.

I read this one over and over. Of course, Auntie Marnie, an extraordinary woman herself, is right, and I'll write her back first thing to say so—to thank her, too, and send my heartfelt good wishes for her health. I so hope she'll be okay. But for now I consider my mother: so kind to my cousin Eveline, so helpful to Auntie Georgiana's daughter, and so impressive to Auntie Marnie, but so hostile toward her own daughter. This must be how she had felt to hear, way back when, that everyone judged my grandmother to be consummately kind and generous. It's heartening but hard.

I dream one night that I am in a cab with my mother. She is well, but I hug her whole body the way my sister-in-law hugged my mother-in-law when she was dying. My mother is wearing lipstick.

Elizabeth Arden? I say.
That's right, she says.
Those gold fluted tubes were so 1930s Shanghai, I say. So Shanghai Deco.
I liked them, she says.

I dream another night that I am at an outdoor fast-food sushi restaurant with my family. It has all the ambience of a McDonald's, but the open-air hallway alongside it isn't bad. There is a kind of ivy trellis that makes up for the Formica tables, and at the end of the arcade there is a garden. I bring my sibs to see the garden and am trying to get them to see that they could leave. But the garden has barbed wire atop its fence, and the door that leads out is locked.

I dream that people are getting all these encomia, including me, and then there is my father! I can hear him saying, "Hi, Lillian! It's Daddy!" And then I hear my own voice asking, "But how did you get that recording? He's dead."

And in another dream, there is my father at a table in a library. In real life, he didn't read English very well, but in my dream he has a Harry Potter book open in front of him. "Dad!" I say. He is young and healthy—maybe forty-five or fifty—and smiling. "Gish!" he says.

Before she died, my mother told me that she talked to my father in her dreams all the time. Mostly, she told him about the children. Once, she saw him on the subway; that must have been a memory from their New York City days. But in other dreams, my father was reaching for her from the grave, asking her to join him.

My mother left her imprint on my psyche. It is embedded in my most primitive responses, in my very limbic system; I can infer a lot from my reaction to things. For example, I know that she was narcissistic because narcissistic people bother me so much: I recognize them and avoid them. I think, too, that she was a little crazy because crazy people bother me. Many people find Jackie Onassis's eccentric cousin and aunt in the documentary *Grey Gardens*, for example, funny. But I found them so upsetting I could not finish watching the movie; I had to stand up and leave.

And I know that my mother played fast and loose with reality because of things I have found myself writing. I can't help but notice, looking back, how Marge, the mother in a story called "Lulu in Exile," says at one point, "I am the mother. I am the one who says what is true, do you hear me?" And I can't help but notice, too, how her son Duncan replies, "Faintly"—a line that makes me laugh to this day.

As to whether any part of my surviving my mother can be ascribed to producing versions of her and, having written them, laughing: I am sure it can.

Though from whom did I get my ability to write to begin with but from my mother? Did she finally, ironically, equip me to survive herself?

> **Goose, goose, goose!**
> **You lift your neck to the sky and sing—**
> **White down bobbing on the green water,**
> **Red feet pedaling the clear waves.**
>
> **Do you remember that poem? I say to her.**
> **Of course, she says. I recited that poem on my father's lap.**

So many memories:

I remember my father yelling at my mother because she couldn't read a map. I remember, too, how I once asked her if something was on the left or the right, only to have her yell, "Don't talk to me about left or right!"—and later explain, "No one ever talked to me about that when I was growing up."

"You mean, no one ever told you, Go up to the corner and take a left?" I said.

"First of all, we did not go out," she said. "And second, if we went out, the driver knew where to go."

"Ah," I said.

I remember how much it meant to her that when she was learning to drive, my father taught her how to avoid a tough left turn by taking three right turns instead. "He was sort of like protect me," she said. When he bought her a VW Bug, he bought her a semi-automatic, knowing she'd never manage a stick shift—and how she loved her yellow Bug!

I remember how she used to hunch over a book to read it, and how I always thought this must have been what Chinese scholars did.

I remember the giant walking doll she got for me one Christmas. I was terrified of it and never played with it, and only now that I have her account book realize how expensive it was—"Lillian 40-inch walking doll $8.88," she wrote. How much a part of her picture of what Christmas should be it must have been, and how disappointed she must have been that I did not like it.

I remember the Dr. Nim marble logic game she got for me another Christmas—a proto-computer and an attempt, I see, to get something I might actually like. It touches me to this day.

I remember how delighted she was when she learned the word "crap." "You're going to have crap for dinner!" she'd say if someone was misbehaving. "Watch out, or you're going to get crap!"

I remember how she would check the stove every night before she went to sleep, to make sure it was off.

I remember the raspberry-pink ersatz Chinese mug she got from Pier 1—a mug she never would have thought to replace, even after it got chipped, because it had a lid, and it was hard to find lidded mugs back then. She put tea leaves in its bottom and added water to it all day.

I remember the quilted turquoise robe with rhinestone buttons we bought her one Mother's Day, and how she wore it until its stuffing showed and half its buttons were gone.

I remember the speed with which she ordered at Chinese restaurants—the telepathic relationship she seemed to have with waiters, and her easy command of the menu.

I remember how she loved a good lobster and began beaming as soon as her lobster bib was on. And I remember how she sucked every possible bit out of every single shell, as she did when she ate crab, too, and shrimp.

I remember how she loved a nice cold piece of watermelon, which she would eat with a spoon.

And I remember how she loved the skin of her own tummy. I remember how proud she was of it and how, when I was little, she would every now and then let me touch it. And, indeed, it was astonishingly soft—impossibly soft, even—so like a baby's skin that, touching it, I felt as if I were the mother and she the baby.

How would she react if she could read this account? Such is my faith in words that if I could send this off to her in the afterlife, I would, believing that this, this, would get through to her. Yet a part of me is glad to be spared the pain of my mother's reading it, only to refuse to respond.

> *I am reading it, she says now. I am reading it.*
> *Only in my imagination are you reading it, Ma.*
> *Then I'm not reading it, she says. I'm not reading it.*

More than one friend who had had a difficult relationship with her mother has confessed to being relieved that her mother was dead.

"Honestly, I loved my mother much more after she died," said one.

"Now she can't hurt me," said another. "Now I can get on with my life."

And another, "Now I can remember her fondly."

Is that why I am writing this, so I can remember my mother fondly? Is that the same as forgiving her? Or is it more like forgetting her? Am I inventing as much as remembering her? Erasing as much as preserving her?

> *It is a writer's right to imagine whatever she likes, she says. And if it gives your heart solace, so be it.*
> *So should I thank you, then, or writing? I say. Because, well, "a writer's right" and "if it gives your heart solace"— that is not your voice.*
> *You should thank writing, of course, she says. Writing, your other mother. Writing.*

. . .

BAD BAD GIRL

Some notes I took:

> Do you remember my grade-school friend Lori Kahn? Lori remembers how you treated me like a servant. A scary yeller, she said you were, too.
>
> And says Paloma, wise youth that she is: "The effects of trauma can't be washed away in a generation. It takes many generations, with every echo growing fainter." Adding, "I learned that from a book."
> "Oh yeah? What book?" I say.
> "*The Harafish* by Naguib Mahfouz."
> I smile.
>
> And then, as if that's not enough, Paloma says one more thing: "You couldn't get rid of it all, but you did a good job," she tells me.

I did a good job. What greater relief could there be than to receive a passing grade from the person most likely to find my mother's trauma passed on, despite my best efforts, to her? From Luke, too, I receive a pass when he becomes a parent himself. In a birthday card, he writes:

> To love and care for a child is an extraordinary gift to the child. You weren't given that gift. But you gave it to me, and now I can pay it forward, and maybe my daughter will, too, and so on, like one of those kidney donation chains sparked by one humanitarian donor.

I'll hold on to his words forever. And, indeed, to see him prove an extraordinarily loving parent is the happiest experience possible.

More notes:

> Yesterday I had lunch with Lisa. We do not get together often. But yesterday we did and, as we sat at a courtyard

table by a raised planter full of flowers, we talked about the way that you treated me. And then Lisa said, for the first time, I saw it. It was terrible for her, too, she went on—and I understand, of course, how it must have been. But she did see it. The favoritism. The scapegoating. The hitting. She saw it.

Even writing this now, I can hardly express what it means to me that there was a witness. And when I said I could not mourn you as she did, and that part of me was glad you were gone because I was so angry at having been mistreated, Lisa said that my feelings were warranted.

I cannot express how it felt to hear that word, "warranted," either. To hear that my feelings were warranted. So it was all real. It is a funny thing to be a fiction writer who just wants to know that something was real. But there it is. It was, and I am glad to know that it was.

I wrote later, about the book I am writing this very minute:

This is my tenth book, and every book has been hard. But this is the hardest. My sibs are going to be upset. And I can already hear the disappointment of some readers: It's not funny. They always want you to do what you've done before. Plus, I'm going to have to fill in a lot. Invent a lot. And what is it then? A novel? An autofiction? A memoir? Do I care? It's what I need to do—as if I am finally burying you, or trying to. All that matters is, Can I do it, can I do it, can I do it? Can I do it?

And now you have, says my mother.
You sound like Mrs. Cunningham, I say.
Bad bad girl! she says then. Who says you can write a book like that?
I laugh. That's more like it.

. . .

There is a Chinese saying: Every family has a sutra that's hard to read. My family is no exception. There is an especially hard sutra in my relationship to my mother.

But there is a time to stop chanting, and a way to stop yourself from chanting, and this is that story, too—a victory story.

And now?

Now there are so many moments when I just miss my mother. Why did I not ask her for a list of Chinese names for the grandchildren and great-grandchildren before she died? How I wish she were here to name them. And there's so much else I wish I could ask her. Who is this person in the picture? How about this one? And this one? What do these characters say?

Sometimes Skylight prompts me for more pictures, and I miss her then, too, even though she'd probably ignore the pictures I sent. Then there are the many moments when the children do David and me proud. Though she would deny us any show of her own pride, knowing as I do now that she might still make a private note in her planner, I wish she could be there to see Paloma graduate from law school one day, or Luke take up his first job. Or to see her great-grandchildren. She would spoil it all! And yet at least she'd be there—and, of course, if she were there, my father would be there, too, exclaiming, Very good! Very good! Great! Great!

How I miss them both whenever I hear the Chinese toast *Bǎi suì*—One hundred years! I wish they'd lived a hundred years at least. And while it's true that all stories must end so that others can begin, I still think of them every day. The Chinese say, *Yǐn shuǐ sī yuán*—When you drink the water, remember the spring.

And so I do. RIP, Mom. I remember.

A Note About the Romanization

As my parents spoke Shanghainese at home, I have tried to give a sense of this. Pinyin—the romanization system devised by the Communists in 1958 for the representation of Mandarin—was imperfect for this purpose. However, I had no workable alternative.

Because it is the most widely used system today, I have also used pinyin more generally throughout this book, with a few exceptions. There are, for example, some names whose pre-1958 romanizations have survived all attempts to change them: Hong Kong remains far better known as "Hong Kong" than as "Xianggang," and the Nationalist leader forced to retreat to Taiwan in 1949 remains "Chiang Kai-shek" to most Westerners.

In addition, I have retained the way my parents romanized their names. While they are unlikely, of course, to check on this from heaven, I did not want to represent their names in a way that they themselves would not recognize. And so in this book their names are spelled "Jen Chao-pe" and "Loo Shu-hsin"—their last names appearing first, as is standard for all Chinese names, however romanized. In my mother's case, the choice to retain "Loo" has engendered some awkwardness: since her relatives in Shanghai were forced to adopt pinyin, they came to spell their surname "Lu." Similarly, they switched to the simplified characters introduced by the Communists, while my mother continued to use the traditional characters she had grown up with. I never actually heard her object to the new spelling, "Lu," but it was easy to guess her opinion of the Communist reforms—indeed, her whole family's opinion—by the fact that both she in New York and they in Shanghai chose to have their gravestones engraved in traditional characters. My mother taught me to write my name in traditional characters as well.

Meanwhile, in English, Jen Chao-pe and Loo Shu-hsin were known as Norman Jen and Agnes Loo until they married. Then they became Norman and Agnes Jen.

Acknowledgments

It is not every day that I must credit three editors for believing in a book. But like runners handing off a baton in a relay, my longtime editor, Ann Close, handed it off to my acquiring editor, Reagan Arthur, who in turn handed it off to the anchor, Diana Miller, who brought it across the finish line. What a team! I thank you all for your consummate care, judgment, and faith.

Thanks as well to everyone in Knopf copyediting, production, and promotion. I have relied on you all for decades now and will never cease to be astonished by the exquisite attention you bring to every single manuscript.

A thousand thanks, too, to my agent, Melanie Jackson, for your generous re-embrace of this prodigal author, and to indispensable Matt Dissen: you ease life in a myriad of ways.

I am exceptionally blessed in having such responsive, perceptive, and learned readers. Nancy Berliner, Eileen Chow, Martha Fishman, Elizabeth Graver, Lailai Gu, Martha Minow, Eileen Pollack, Louise Radin, and Ellen Winner, I am forever in your debt and would never have finished this book without you.

Huge thanks, too, to Lillian Hsu for access to your family letters; to Paul French for your spectacularly informative emails; and to Charlotte Brooks for your expert help with the arcana of citizen-

ACKNOWLEDGMENTS

ship. For time, support, and inspiration, I am grateful as well to the Rockefeller Foundation's Bellagio Center in Italy, the Maison Dora Maar in France, and NYU Shanghai in the People's Republic of China.

As for my profoundest thanks of all, they must go to my siblings. Each of you, I know, had a different mother from mine and a different father, too. And each of you would tell a very different story from the one I have told here. I cannot express how grateful I am for your forbearance, understanding, and abiding love.

And finally, I thank yet once again, with all my being, my children, Luke and Paloma, who tirelessly read and reread and reread my manuscript, as well as my husband, David, whose love has never wavered in all our years together. You make this goose lift her neck to the sky and sing.

A NOTE ABOUT THE AUTHOR

Gish Jen is the author of five previous novels, two books of stories, and two works of nonfiction. Her honors include fellowships from the Guggenheim Foundation, the Radcliffe Institute for Advanced Study, and the Fulbright Program, as well as the Lannan Literary Award for Fiction and the Mildred and Harold Strauss Living Award from the American Academy of Arts and Letters. Her stories have been chosen for *The Best American Short Stories* five times, including *The Best American Short Stories of the Century*. She is a member of both the American Academy of Arts and Letters and the American Academy of Arts and Sciences, and has delivered the William E. Massey, Sr., Lectures in American Studies at Harvard University. She and her husband split their time between Cambridge, Massachusetts, and Vermont.

A NOTE ON THE TYPE

This book was set in Celeste, a typeface created in 1994 by the designer Chris Burke (b. 1967). He describes it as a modern, humanistic face having less contrast between thick and thin strokes than other modern types such as Bodoni, Didot, and Walbaum. Tempered by some old-style traits and with a contemporary, slightly modular letterspacing, Celeste is highly readable and especially adapted for current digital printing processes, which render an increasingly exacting letterform.

Composed by North Market Street Graphics,
Lancaster, Pennsylvania

Designed by Soonyoung Kwon